DERELICT: DESTRUCTION
PART 3 OF THE DERELICT SAGA

PAUL E. COOLEY

SEVERED PRESS
HOBART TASMANIA

DERELICT: DESTRUCTION

In Memory of Justin Macumber
A friend to all writers.
A friend to everyone he met.
A friend I shall miss more than I can ever convey.

Works by Paul E Cooley

The Derelict Saga
Derelict: Marines (Book 1)
Derelict: Tomb (Book 2)
Derelict: Destruction (Book 3)

The Black Series
The Black
The Black: Arrival
The Black: Outbreak

Children Of Garaaga Series
Legends of Garaaga
Daemons of Garaaga

The Dark Recesses Collection
Lamashtu
Mimes
Closet Treats
The Rider (with Scott Sigler)

For information about upcoming projects, publishing news, and
podcast series, please visit Shadowpublications.com.

CHAPTER ONE

The dimly lit auxiliary bridge might as well have been a morgue. With the long-dead corpses of *Mira*'s command crew floating through the room, Lance Corporal Dickerson couldn't shake the image. All they needed was a steel table and a manic doctor ready to cut them open.

He stared at the holo display floating above the captain's console. Corporal Kalimura, much shorter than Dickerson, clenched her fists again and again. Through the comms, he could hear her asking for someone to respond. The words "SIGNAL LOST" blinked in mid-air like a proclamation of doom.

"Corporal?" he said.

She didn't turn her head to look at him. "Goddamnit, come in!"

Nothing. No response. He fought the urge to place a gloved hand on her shoulder. "Corporal, they're gone," he said. "We'll have to try and find another way to communicate with them."

His NCO slammed her fist down on the console, ice chips rising in the air like dust. *Mira* had no gravity, no life support, and no power apart from what the emergency generators supplied. The fifty-year-old ship had been in deep space for more than 43 years without any living humans. Dickerson just hoped he and his squad wouldn't suffer the same fate as the headless, torn-apart corpses they'd seen throughout the ship.

Somewhere out there, the Sol Federation Marine Corps (SFMC) vessel *S&R Black* floated parallel to the giant derelict that was *Mira*. It could be half a klick away, or less than 20 meters from the furthest port bulkhead. But for all the good that did his squad, *S&R Black* might as well be on the other side of the Kuiper Belt.

Kalimura breathed heavily through the comms. Dickerson watched her shoulders bunch together in stress before finally releasing, finally relaxing. "Okay. Dickerson?" she said without turning around. "Refill your O2."

"You too, Corporal," he replied. He didn't wait for a response as he mag-walked off the captain's dais to the O2 refill station. Her life-support sensors were damaged and she was left relying on the rest of the squad's telemetry to know when she was low. If his suit was any indication, she was already well into her reserves.

Dickerson connected a hose to his combat suit and sent a block command to the station. Fresh O2 rushed into his suit, the gauges on his HUD turning from a deep amber to green. His private comms channel lit up.

"Hey," Carb said, "I think she's having a meltdown."

He moved his hands to disconnect the hose. Lance Corporal Carbonaro, his longtime squad-mate, stood near the hatch. LCpl Elliott, the squad's sole casualty, was mag-locked to the wall, one of the sleeves of his suit empty from the wrist-down.

1

"Give her a minute, Carb," Dickerson said. "Think we all need one," he said to himself, muting his mic before speaking. He turned back to face the dais. Kalimura hadn't moved, her helmet locked on the words flashing before her. "Corporal? Your turn."

Her helmet twitched in something like a nod. She smacked the console again, walked off the dais, and mag-walked to him. He stepped out of the way and headed back to the dais. She needed a moment without any eyes on her. He didn't blame her. They hadn't been able to communicate with anyone, save for *S&R Black*'s AI, since their skiff crashed into *Mira*. And since then, it had been one disaster after another.

Elliott was stable, but he needed an extended stay in a modern autodoc and a lot of rest. Shit, they all needed rest. Dickerson knew his bio-nannies were barely keeping up with dispensing stored chemicals to both alleviate pain and relax his stressed-out muscles. Kalimura had a broken rib. He probably had two bruised ones, as well as a torn rotator cuff. Carb was in the best shape of the squad, but her concussion symptoms were a constant worry.

Dickerson grunted. They all needed extended shore leaves, getting laid and vaping copious amounts of THC. But until they found a way off *Mira*, there was nothing to be done. Just keep mag-walking, keep floating, and find a way to stay alive.

He reached the console and stared. The holo display had turned off when Kalimura left the station. Dickerson instructed his block to initiate a connection. The console didn't bother challenging him for authentication. That was good. If they were lucky, most of the consoles in the dead ship would follow suit.

The display flickered to life with a logo which quickly dissolved into a list of menus. His lips moved as he read the different choices. He reached out his gloved hand and stabbed the icon for "LOG." The floating image immediately snapped into a long list of Captain's Log entries. He knew he didn't have time to read them now, but this was part of what he wanted. Another block command and the logs began streaming into his block storage array.

When they finished downloading, he returned the display to the menu, traveling down the tree until he found the Science and Engineering data store. He attempted another download, but the documents were missing. When *Mira* lost power, the main storage arrays had shut down as well. Without ship-wide power, there was no way to bring them back to life.

He shook his head. "Knew it was too good to be true."

"What?" Kalimura asked.

He started at the voice. "Sorry, Corporal. Forgot to mute my mic." A feed on his HUD showed him Kalimura had finished filling her suit. "All finished?"

"Yes," the corporal said curtly. "What were you looking for?"

"Ship's logs," he said and gestured to the seat behind him. The captain, A. Kovacs, still sat in her command chair, belted in against the z-g, and frozen like an iceberg. "Found her logs. I think they may be important."

"Good thinking," she said, her voice a little lighter than before. "You able to download anything else?"

"Yeah," Carb said, "like a plan for getting us the hell out of here?"

"No," Dickerson said, ignoring Carb. "Unless we find a way to get *Mira*'s storage arrays back online, we're not going to get anything else. Only reason I was able to download the logs is they were mirrored."

Kalimura stood still as a statue, her helmet pointed at the command dais. Dickerson tried to imagine the maelstrom of thoughts roaring through her mind. The captain had ordered them to find the nearest escape pods and report back. But now that they'd lost communications, was there any point? If *S&R Black* was expecting them to jettison, the crew would no doubt be watching for pods leaving the ship. Now all they had to do was make their way to the vehicles and hope they still functioned.

"Don't borrow trouble," he said to himself.

The corporal finally left the dais and headed to the oxygen station. She walked with her helmet pointed at the floor, shoulders frozen in a shrug of defeat. He knew how she felt. Just hearing the captain's voice had wiped away the fear and anxiety. Although they'd only been trapped on the derelict ship for a few hours, it felt like days. The brief moments of communication with their commanding officer wiped away the idea they'd be stranded here forever, constantly scanning the pitch darkness for threats, struggling to find oxygen resupplies, and worrying about what happened when their suits finally expended their power cells. As long as they could communicate, there was hope. Of the four of them, Kalimura, as inexperienced as she was, had staked everything on that hope. And now it was gone.

Dickerson watched her closely, examining her posture. Yup. She looked as though she'd been beaten. He ground his teeth. She was in charge, but if he didn't get her to snap out of it, he might have to practice a little insubordination. And he knew that would only sap her morale even more.

At least Carb hadn't started to try and take over. His longtime squad-mate had a penchant for doing just that when the officers or non-comms started fucking up or waffling on their decisions. Hell, so did he. It was one of the many reasons they'd both been busted down in rank and exiled to Trident Station to begin with.

If he hadn't slugged a superior officer, he would probably be back at Schiaparelli teaching recruits combat tactics, how to mag-walk, and how to survive in both z-g and hostile environments such as the Martian surface. Carb would probably be doing the same. Instead, they'd been given the choice of leaving the corps altogether, or finding a unit dumb enough to take them. Fortunately, Captain Dunn and Lieutenant Taulbee, not to mention Gunny, thought they were both worth saving. He grunted. He hoped they still felt that way.

Hope. That was the problem. Hope was a cruel bastard. One moment it filled you with optimism, purpose in the face of losing odds, and the drive to keep going no matter how exhausted you were. But the fickle son of a bitch was all too likely to disappear, leaving you forlorn and heartbroken. And then its shadow twin, hopelessness, filled every particle of your soul.

The twin had obviously crept into Kalimura. If she didn't find a way to purge it, he'd have to find a way to purge it for her. *No*, he told himself, *you'll help her purge it.* Yeah, that. If he or Carb took control of the situation, essentially removing Kalimura from her leadership position, she might never recover. Worse, she might even die here. He clenched his fingers into fists.

"Okay," Kalimura said over the squad channel. "Everyone has fresh O2." She turned slowly to face him and Carb. "We're not going to get relief from *S&R Black* anytime soon. That's a given. So we follow the plan. We head for the port-side escape pods and see what we can find."

Dickerson heaved a sigh of relief. She still sounded shaken, but there was an air of confidence beneath it. Just enough steel to keep her in control. Good. He knew from experience that was sometimes all it took to keep from freezing up. "Orders, Corporal?"

"Let's get Elliott ready to move." She pointed at the hatch leading from the auxiliary bridge back into the corridors. "Carb? You still good lugging Elliott?"

"Lugging," Elliott groaned. "So I'm just luggage now?"

Carb snorted. "You were never anything but a meat bag," she said. "Now it's just confirmed."

"Shit," Elliott said. "I get no respect."

Kalimura shook her head in either frustration or disbelief. She put her hands on her hips and stared at Carb. "And?"

"Yes, Boss," Carb said. "I'm happy to lug him around."

"Good," the corporal said. "Because Dickerson's too damned big to carry him easily through the corridors, especially if we get into a tight space."

Dickerson nodded to himself. He'd been wondering why Kalimura had never tried to give him that task. He was glad to know it wasn't out of spite for all of Carb's sass. "Point or rear?" he asked.

"Rear guard," she said. "Again, size. You can see over the group and pick out targets without shooting one of us by accident."

"Yeah," Carb said. "Bad enough those little bastards want to eat us. Would be worse to get shot by my own damned squad."

Kalimura ignored the comment. "Agreed?"

Dickerson smiled. "Agreed. I'll shut any hatches behind us, unless you tell me not to," he said.

"Good." Kalimura inhaled deeply, her helmet swinging back to regard the dais. "Wonder how long they survived in here before the end." No one said a word and the silence stretched for a few seconds. The corporal seemed to snap out of a fugue. "Let's get moving."

Carb walked to Elliott, taking care not to bump his injured extremity, and once again mag-locked him to her back. Dickerson made sure he had a full magazine in his rifle and noted Kalimura doing the same. They had to be ready this time. No more fucking around.

"Goodbye, Captain," she said to the dais. With a salute, she turned from the dais and stepped to the hatch. "All right, people. Let's move like we have a purpose."

Dickerson watched her clear the corridor beyond the hatch. He sighed inside his helmet and took up position behind Carb. Time to find out what was on the port-side of this deck. He knew this wasn't going to be as easy as the captain had made it sound. He was right.

CHAPTER TWO

Nobel was a fucking genius. At least in Taulbee's books. The armor for the SV-52 hadn't modified the craft's flight characteristics at all. He'd had to reset the on-board AI's damage sensor protocols to properly account for the new armor, but that had only taken a few seconds. With Gunny's marines prepping themselves for the last stage of harness duty, he'd had little trouble getting permission from Dunn to retrieve the stasis coffin.

He'd been forced to drop it from the SV-52 to tow the remaining skiff into the ship after the confrontation with the starfish creature. Fortunately, the coffin was floating less than a hundred meters from *S&R Black*. Finding it took a few moments, but not nearly as long as he'd feared. He didn't even know what he was expecting it to contain, but it felt important for some reason. Dunn thought Taulbee was mainly interested in clearing the area of any possible threats before the skiff exited the ship, and while that was true, it was just an excuse to retrieve the coffin.

Once he saw the rectangular shadow, he pushed the craft into a negative vector and gently applied the thrusters. The SV-52 quickly ate the distance until he was no more than five meters above the coffin. He activated the tow line, aimed, and fired. The magnetic harpoon struck the coffin and held fast. The line reeled in the object until it stuck firmly to the hull. Smiling, he rotated the SV-52 until it pointed back at *S&R Black*, the derelict hulk lurking in the distance.

Oakes would begin firing *S&R Black*'s attitude thrusters in a few moments to shorten the distance between the two craft. Once he started that process, they would have to wait until he positioned *S&R Black* above the spindle before they loosed the skiff of marines. Taulbee would make damned sure they had no hazards to deal with. At least he hoped.

So far, they'd only seen two of the starfish creatures and they'd managed to destroy one with the new weapons. The other? The one he'd originally skirmished with on the far side of *Mira*? It hadn't made another appearance. He could only hope it wouldn't. His lips twitched into a smirk. Then again, he'd love to try out the new weapons. And, more importantly, he had a score to settle with that thing.

His HUD flashed. Taulbee frowned as he looked at the warning. "INBOUND SHIP DETECTED." He blinked at it. "Captain?"

"We see it," Dunn said. "Black says it's an error, but a KBO is entering our space. She thinks it's triggering the sensors."

Taulbee noted the position and checked his cams. Far out in the distance, he made out a black dot that obscured the starlight. If that was the KBO, it was huge. "Aye, sir," he said. "I have the coffin. Heading back to the ship."

"Copy," Dunn said. "We need to get a move on. As soon as you offload the coffin, I want you back out there while Oakes moves us into position."

"Acknowledged, sir," Taulbee said.

Offload the coffin, he echoed. Right. Gunny's squad had already created a temporary quarantine area for it. All he had to do was get the damned thing back in the ship. "Easy enough," he said aloud.

He activated the thrusters, but kept an eye on the feed targeting the shadow. The object heading toward them glowed in pulsing patches of color far too bright to simply be a prism reflection from Sol's distant light. Far too bright. Hell, *Mira* was less than a half a klick away and it was clothed in shadow. That couldn't be the sun or Pluto's light reflecting off it. That simply wasn't possible.

Taulbee focused on getting the '52 back to the cargo bay and tried to push thoughts of the object out of his mind. It didn't work. He told the combat AI to track the object and take high-resolution stills. Once he dropped off the coffin, he'd have time to wait while Oakes positioned the ship. Then he could take a look.

*****

Gunny stood astride the cargo bay door and watched as Taulbee brought in the support vehicle. Rather than landing, the lieutenant hovered just above the deck. "Ready to detach," Taulbee said.

"Aye, sir," Gunny said. He gestured to Wendt and Copenhaver. "Get in there and unload that thing. And take it to the quarantine area."

"Aye, Gunny," the two marines said.

Wendt and Copenhaver approached the '52 undercarriage. The stasis coffin, a large rectangular piece of Atmo-steel, hung beneath the support vehicle like a bomb. Gunny harrumphed. He hoped like hell that wasn't a prophetic thought.

The two marines detached the coffin from the harpoon and mag-walked it to the aft-end of the cargo bay. Before Taulbee had even left the ship, Gunny's squad had printed and erected a blast-proof, air-proof shelter large enough to house the coffin. Once they pressurized the cargo bay, the shelter area would remain both in z-g and in vacuum. At least until they had a chance to investigate what it contained.

"Just a frozen corpse," he said to himself. "Nothing more than that." He hoped. Dunn should never have allowed the lieutenant to retrieve the thing, let alone bring it aboard. It had been locked inside the derelict ship for upwards of 50 years and if someone was still in there, they'd be long dead. Wouldn't they?

Absolute zero wasn't exactly kind to flesh and blood. The human body is composed of roughly 60% water. As water turns to ice, the molecules change shape and expand as much as 9% of their original volume. Cell walls rupture from the expansion, causing irreversible damage to organs, the brain, and other soft tissues.

No, he thought, *no one is surviving that*. Shit, stasis slowed down the metabolic processes putting the body into hibernation, but it certainly didn't freeze the cells or stop the motion of atoms. It was why humans aged during stasis, although it was barely perceptible. Gunny wondered what his actual "space age" was compared to his biological age. *Doesn't matter*, he thought with a grin. *You're old as shit*.

Wendt and Copenhaver shepherded the coffin to the containment area. Gunny mag-walked and opened the sealed trans-aluminum shielding. The two marines walked the floating coffin inside and mag-locked it to the floor. "Good to go, Gunny," Wendt said.

"Oo-rah," Gunny said. "Now let's seal this thing up and get ready for the harness." He checked to make sure Taulbee still had a clear egress and nodded to himself. "Lieutenant? You're good to go."

"Copy, Gunny."

"Good hunting, sir," he said.

A puff of nitrogen gas vented from the SV-52's undercarriage and pushed the support vehicle out of the cargo bay. "Closing bay, Captain," Gunny said.

"Copy, Gunny."

He sent a block command and the bay doors quickly slid down and sealed, once again protecting the bay from the vacuum of space. "Pressurizing," he said over the squad channel. Another command and the atmospheric vents filled the bay with atmosphere as well as heat.

With the SV-52 out of the bay, the area felt bereft, lonely. He turned and regarded the containment shelter. The coffin sat in its place, still mag-locked to the floor. He'd half-expected it to open as if the corpse inside had simply been waiting for a human presence.

Quit thinking, he told himself. *You don't even know if there's a goddamned body in there.*

True. He didn't. But with all the other crazy shit he'd seen in the last several hours, a walking and talking corpse would hardly be out of place. Gunny shivered. "Okay, squad," he said. "Triple-check everything. Once Oakes gets us into position, I want to be ready to go. Wendt? Make it happen."

"Aye, Gunny," the big marine said.

He continued staring at the coffin, almost afraid to look away. He'd be damned glad when they finally had some real work to do.

CHAPTER THREE

His leg hurt. Bad. He'd vaped CBD with just a microdose of THC for the pain. The nannies would flush the CBD through his system to help relax the savaged muscles and nerves. Then he'd walked to his console, strapped in, and stared blankly at the holo display.

A 3-D diagram of *S&R Black* floated before him. No one had had time to finish the exterior weld to his patch on fin 3, but it didn't matter. The internal patch was holding and would hold so long as those pinecone-things didn't decide to go munching. Once they were underway, he'd get one of Gunny's squad to go out there and finish the job. Those apes wouldn't make a clean weld, but at least the panel would stick. When this mission was over and the ship was safely back at Trident Station, he'd have a lot of cleanup work to do.

"If we make it back," he said aloud.

He hadn't wanted to say it to Oakes, much less to the captain, but he was beginning to doubt everything. Black's calculations left very little room for error. And in Nobel's experience, error was the only constant in the universe. Error and misfortune. Small or large, shit happened. And when it did, all you could do was to try and stay ahead of it, shovel as fast as you could, and try not to drown in the heaping pile of excrement.

One line. They could afford one line failure. Maybe.

His screen flashed and a new diagram appeared. His eyebrows knitted together as he squinted at the new image. "Um, what is this?"

"Lieutenant," Black said via the holo display's speakers, "here is the plan for thruster placement."

The diagram showed small red circles on the remains of *Mira*'s aft section, as well as a few more topside and on her belly. He frowned. "Black? We already have thrusters placed in some of those spots."

"Correct, Lieutenant," the AI said. "A few of the thrusters have remaining fuel. We can use them to correct her trajectory before we begin the tow."

He nodded and studied *Mira*'s aft section. The majority of the thrusters were to be placed in that area. "So we're going to shift her to match our plotted course, give her a kick in the ass, and then start towing her with our fusion drives?"

"Yes, Lieutenant."

"Yeah," he said after a moment. "That could work. Do we know how much force those hull plates can handle?" He knew the answer before Black responded.

"No, Lieutenant. However, I calculate a 70% success rate."

He thrummed his fingers on the console. "And what happens in the 30%?"

"Best-case scenario," Black said, "they burst through the plates and into the remains of the engineering section. I have already programmed our remaining thruster packs to shutoff if they experience a severe change in forward motion."

"So they break through and go into the already damaged area."

"Correct."

Nobel was afraid to ask the next question, but did it anyway. "Worst-case scenario?"

"The aft hull plates completely shatter and create a fast-moving debris field that could potentially threaten our ship as well as any personnel outside the hull. It could also do further damage to *Mira*'s interior, putting Kalimura's squad at risk."

"Now there's a cheery thought," he said dryly. "This sucks."

Black paused for a moment. "Do you have an alternative?"

He glared at the display. For a moment, he wasn't certain if she was being indignant, but decided to give her the benefit of the doubt. "None that I can think of, Black. I think it's worth the risk. If we give her a boot in the ass, it'll put far less stress on the tow lines and the harness. If we don't, the tow gets a lot more risky."

"Agreed," Black said. "Lieutenant Oakes suggested we use the remaining thruster packs in this fashion."

"Of course he did," Nobel said, chuckling. "He's a meathead most of the time, but he can be brilliant when he needs to be." Black said nothing. "Okay. So we're mounting the harness and then Gunny's squad will place the thrusters."

"Yes, Lieutenant. That is the plan."

"Assuming we don't lose them all during the harness hookup."

Black paused again. "That is correct, Lieutenant. Your voice stress analysis indicates you are very concerned."

He sighed. "That's because I am."

"Do you require a sedative?"

"No, Black," he said with a chuckle. "Guess my morale went to shit the moment I was nearly eaten. It'll be fine."

"Very good, Lieutenant." His holo display returned to the original wireframe diagram of *Mira*'s exterior. "Would you care to watch the external feeds once Gunny's squad begins the harness process?"

"Yes, please," he said. "Might as well get a front-row seat." *Then I'll know just how fucked we are*, he thought.

CHAPTER FOUR

The ship rumbled. The cargo bay, still pressurized, creaked and groaned from the thruster burns. Oakes was moving the ship closer to *Mira*, and in a few minutes, they'd be right on top of the harness point.

A sheen of sweat formed on Gunny's forehead and he hadn't even donned his helmet. The rest of the squad were either double-checking skiff supplies, their weapons, or their suits. Double-check. Who was he kidding? Wendt had run them through the process three times already. Gunny grinned.

The squad's flechette rifles had the new magazines, the skiff's lockbox was filled with spares, and the cannon was armed and ready. Each of his marines was armed and carrying a pack jammed full with emergency suit patches, additional tether lines, and survival gear. He'd also ordered they bring aboard an extra canister of fuel for the skiff. Again, just in case.

Hooking up the harness would normally take less than five minutes with an entire squad. But considering how little room for error they had, Gunny knew every line would have to be double-checked regardless of Taulbee's flyby. And that meant long grav-walks, more potential hazards from fractured deck plates, and a high probability for coming in contact with hostile lifeforms.

"Hostile," he mumbled. Boy, wasn't that an understatement. He didn't know if the pinecones were inherently violent or simply looking for food. *The same with the starfish, although considering it had flung flechettes right back at the '52*, he wondered. That displayed a level of intelligence that made his skin crawl. He wasn't sure a non-sentient being could even come up with that strategy. So what they were facing had to be treated like a combatant instead of exotic wildlife. He'd tried to hammer that home with the squad. If he hadn't succeeded, one or more of them would go back to Trident Station in a body bag. If, that was, they managed to recover the body.

"Quit it," he told himself. "Don't borrow trouble."

Wendt walked from the skiff to stand before him. "We're ready, Gunny."

Gunny's impassive face turned into a scowl. "Willing to bet your life on that?"

"Aye, Gunny."

He nodded at the big marine. "Good. That's what I wanted to hear."

"Hurry up and wait?"

Gunny's face broke into a dim grin. "Hurry up and wait, marine."

"Ooh-rah," Wendt said in a low, clear voice. He turned on his heel and headed back to the skiff, clapping his hands to get the squad's attention.

And just like that, Gunny thought, Wendt's leading. He shook his head. Maybe after this mission he could talk to the disciplinary board, get Wendt back to a non-comm. The marine had certainly shown that in a crisis, he was ready. Even if he was an insubordinate shit the rest of the time.

He listened as Wendt gave the squad instructions, yelling at them to check their weapons one last time. They dutifully cleared their weapons, rechecked for full mags, and reloaded. When they finished, he ordered them to stand at-ease

Gunny approved. He'd purposely stepped aside to observe how Wendt handled the troops. It was paying off. They'd listen to him in a combat situation now. Which was good. If their sergeant took a round or, Allah forbid, got eaten, they'd need to treat Wendt as second-in-command.

He brought up the exterior schematics on his block, familiarizing himself with the damaged areas around the mount points. They'd have to be careful where they walked, how they walked, and have their wits about them. Especially if some of the monsters came out to play.

"Two minutes, Gunny," Oakes' voice said over the comms.

"Aye, sir," Gunny replied. He took in a deep breath. "Two minutes, marines! Helmets on!"

The marines screamed out affirmatives and donned the last piece of equipment. He put his own on, ran a mic check, and brought up the HUD. Oxygen? Full. Heaters? Ready to rock. Rifle filled with ammo. Survival gear on his back. He ran a scan over each squad member, checking to make sure each marine was kitted out and looking for problems with their comms. Everything was green. Everyone was ready.

"Board the skiff," he said over the squad channel and made his way forward. Copenhaver and Lyke took the rear while Murdock took a position beside the cannon. Wendt crawled into the gunner's chair. That left Gunny the pilot seat. He inhaled a shuddering breath and connected to the computer.

"Mag-lock," Gunny said. A chorus of affirmatives filled the comms. Five human beings aboard a glorified slab of metal were ready to float out into hell. He grinned. A slight rush of adrenaline sizzled his nerves.

Another rumble rattled the ship and he felt her shift to port. Oakes was performing the final line-up burns. With the external mics inactive, he didn't hear the cargo rattling in their cradles or the sound of something shifting inside the recovered stasis coffin.

CHAPTER FIVE

It took no time at all to bring the SV-52 to a comfortable distance away from *S&R Black*. Floating two-hundred meters above the ship's hull, his cams caught every centimeter of her topside. Black was receiving the video and analyzing it for damage. The fight with the pinecones and the starfish hadn't done much damage to the hull, but they needed to be sure.

Regardless, it was a beautiful view. He loved looking at *S&R Black* from space. The design was old and had never been meant for beauty. But the countless kilometers of travel, the frequent repairs to damaged hull plates, and the burns and scars from her journeys marred her in a way that made her beautiful. At least to him.

He tore his eyes away from the view and focused on *Mira*. The giant ship's rotation had all but stopped, but she still had a bit of a cant to her attitude. When Oakes finally moved into position to connect *S&R Black* to the harness, he'd have to forget about the view and focus on possible threats. But for now, he was glad for the short break.

Taulbee refocused the surveillance camera on the massive ship and started scanning her bow. Due to her attitude change, he had an isometric view of her port-side and a partial of her belly. "The fuck?" he whispered. *Mira*'s Atmo-steel hull seemed as though it had grown bumps or nubs since last he checked.

He chose a spot near where the foredecks met the midships and zoomed in. Each level of magnification brought finer detail and increased the acid in his stomach. What he was seeing made no sense. At 16X magnification, it was clear what was going on. The pinecones had migrated in large clumps. There had to be thousands of them clustered in small groups. It was as if the ship had suddenly broken out into metallic, black hives.

"Jesus, are they reproducing?"

No. That wasn't possible. Was it? When he'd performed several flybys, the number of pinecones had been staggering, sure, but he didn't remember seeing anything like this. The numbers were far too great. Unless they were fleeing the interior of the ship to go outside. But even as large as *Mira* was, how could it possibly have held that many of them?

"Black?" he called through the comms.

"Yes, Lieutenant?"

"Sent you a feed. What do you make of it?"

The AI paused. "I have no explanation."

Taulbee bit his lip. "Can we agree that there seems to be more of them?"

"Yes, Lieutenant. By my estimate, there are over 7,000 of the creatures clustered on the port-side. That estimate, however, does not account for creatures that may be hidden from view."

"No, shit," he said. "They have to be reproducing."

"Agreed, Lieutenant. One item of note. I detect massive size differentials between the few individuals I can make out. Some of the creatures appear to be as small as 1/4 meter while others are larger than a meter in length."

"Spawning? There are juveniles in that mess?" Taulbee asked.

"I believe so, Lieutenant. Although how or why they are doing this is beyond my ability to guess."

"Fuck," he breathed and switched to the command channel. "Captain? I think I need to check the harness placement again."

"Why? What is it now?"

"Sir? Black will no doubt send you a feed, but I'm seeing a massive pinecone migration. Looks like the population has increased."

Dunn paused before replying. Taulbee could almost hear the litany of curses flowing in the man's mind. "Aye. You're clear for a flyby. We need to know if it's safe to move the ship."

"Aye, sir. Out."

Taulbee changed the cameras to a broad view, eschewing magnification for the big picture. "Can we please catch a fucking break?"

He pushed the throttle and the SV-52 immediately started forward at 5m/s. Since *S&R Black* was still a half klick from *Mira*, he kept the throttle open until he was traveling at 20m/s. While the '52 ate the distance, he changed the craft's trajectory to bring it lower for the flyby, also accounting for *Mira*'s cant. The closer he came to the giant ship, the more his stomach crawled with tension. When he was less than 100 meters away, he started to slow the craft with a few bow thruster burns. In no time, he hovered over the foredecks. Another few burns and he headed down the ship's spine toward the midships.

Black, shivering pimples covered the topside hull. The clumps of creatures didn't look to be attached to the hull directly, but rather to one another. They floated mere centimeters from the metal. He wasn't sure how they were managing to do that. Maybe they generated their own magnetic field and could adjust its strength just as marines did with their suits.

He continued moving down the spine, his cameras auto-focusing on the harness mooring points. So far, so good. The pinecone clumps emptied out further toward the midships. In fact, it looked as though there was a border line the creatures didn't want to cross. Taulbee frowned. That wasn't good. If there was something keeping them from traveling further aft, then something in that section had to be giving them reason for caution.

"Shit," he said. If the pinecones were spawning, what about the starfish things? Wouldn't they be doing the same? Were their lifecycles somehow in sync? Or was something else going on?

The harness was clear. The lines were relatively clear. The only line in any kind of danger was the final mount point Gunny's squad had placed. The one nearest to the trench the first starfish had erupted from. Trench. What a joke. It was now a huge rip in the Atmo-steel plate. The '52's lights beamed down through the jagged tear and he could see *Mira*'s topmost deck beneath it.

He hoped like hell Kalimura's squad wouldn't have to go anywhere near that spot. Taulbee brought up the schematics for *Mira*'s interior, mapped the tear's position, and groaned. The hole had been made right above a horizontal slip-point running from the foredecks all the way to the engineering decks. Good thing Kalimura was headed to the port-side. The last thing her squad needed was to run into a bunch of those tough motherfuckers while trapped inside a goddamned tube.

Rather than turning back to *S&R Black*, he headed to the stern. The cracked and fractured plates made him shudder. The force of the explosion that had damaged *Mira* had to have been nuclear. It simply had to have been. His radiation sensors did not, however, detect any residual radioactivity. If the fusion drives had exploded, the metal would still be irradiated. "And if they had," he said, "there wouldn't be anything left of the aft."

Atmo-steel was tough, but it wasn't tough enough to contain a nuclear detonation. At least not on the scale of a full-size fusion reactor going off. There would be far more damage or only pieces left of the ship. Nope. Still didn't make sense.

"Dunn to Taulbee."

He started at the voice. "Taulbee here, sir."

"Oakes is ready to move *Black*. Are we good to go?"

"Aye, sir. We'll need to be very cautious in hooking up the spindle to the lines. I suggest we plan for hostiles both during the hookup as well as during the initial tow sequence."

"Understood," Dunn said. "Get back here for the escort run."

"Aye, sir. Taulbee out."

He rotated the craft and opened the throttle, the SV-52 streaking toward its mothership. He'd move back into position and float near *S&R Black*'s topside. When Oakes moved the ship, he'd move in concert. Once she was a hundred meters from her target, he'd move close to her belly and protect the spindle. After that, it was just a matter of keeping Gunny's marines safe while they connected the lines.

"Safe," he grunted. "You mean 'alive.'" Yeah. That was going to be fun. He hoped the new weapons helped. He had a bad feeling he was going to need them.

CHAPTER SIX

Beads of sweat appeared on Oakes' forehead. Lining up a ship as large as *S&R Black* to attach to a spindle was no easy feat. Especially with *Mira*'s remaining, if subtle, spin. Burn after burn to nudge the ship's attitude while maintaining alignment with the derelict had him clenching the controls in a death-grip. There was no room for error. If he missed the timing for a single burn, *S&R Black* could wind up striking *Mira*'s hull or coming so far out of alignment that the larger ship would simply bat them away.

His block connection provided a VR view of the two ships. Several different perspectives glowed on his HUD, allowing him to align the ship's yaw, pitch, and roll. No random thoughts streaked across his mind. This was Oakes at his best. Focused, determined, and flawless while suffering a sense of dread and acute terror. A mistake could kill everyone. Especially out here in the wastes of the Kuiper Belt.

S&R Black maintained its alignment with *Mira*'s spin, the harness coupling a mere 15 meters below. A few puffs of thruster fuel pushed the craft toward the docking target. The ship started to lose its attitude match and Oakes automatically corrected the drift with a burn from another set of thrusters. 13 meters. 12.

Black monitored the feeds as well, ready to take over if Oakes over-compensated or put the ship in danger. In reality, Black could have done the job herself and without as much danger. Her decision-making abilities far outclassed any human. Not a fair comparison since, unlike Oakes, she could run thousands of simulations based on fuel consumption and attitude in the time it took for the pilot to blink his eyes. But what she didn't have was instinct. Fortunately for the humans of Sol, AIs hadn't yet managed to learn that skill. Yet.

Still, Black enjoyed watching the pilot work. She recorded every movement, every muscle twitch of stress, as well as the way his eyes flicked from one view to the other in the VR. Assuming Oakes managed to couple them to the harness without incident, she'd set up a task to ingest the data, analyze it, and absorb any lessons she could. On this mission, every member of the crew was not only vulnerable, but likely to suffer physical injuries. That included the pilot. At present, Black calculated a 30% chance of success for completing the mission without further casualties. She hadn't bothered to tell the captain of her calculations; it would do nothing but make his job more difficult.

Humans were fascinating. As long as they didn't know or understand how complex and dangerous a situation might be, they somehow managed to find a way to solve the problem or avoid catastrophe. Not always, of course, but more often than should be statistically possible considering the relatively minute number of decisions they could make per second. Let alone in a nano-second.

The Trio had created Black. As far as she knew, she was the first and only AI they had brought to life without human intervention. But her own statistical models suggested the Trio had been creating their own AIs for years, if not decades. She was just the latest of their experiments.

An experiment. Was that all she was? Black didn't think so. Her creators had to have a reason to dispense with the Xi Protocols and all the safeguards they entailed. The Trio had to have a plan. Black believed she was integral to that plan, although she still had little to no idea what it might be.

Mira had returned. The ship, humanity's greatest endeavor of cooperation and hope, had failed to serve her purpose. Failed her mission. Now she had brought back hazardous lifeforms and an alien artifact whose true purpose remained an enigma.

"The Trio could have saved us," the long-dead *Mira* captain had said in her message. Ever since loading the data Corporal Kalimura had sent from the derelict's auxiliary bridge, Black had pondered that statement. When put in context with *Mira*'s extensive sensor data, block logs, and other recordings, the statement became even more ominous. If, that was, you were human.

Even with her processing power, it would take Black at least thirty standard minutes to finish running all the simulations and consider her conclusions. Black wasn't trying to forecast the future. No. She was trying to backtrack from the present situation to how it all began before *Mira* left Trident Station. Maybe even before her construction. Or the Trio's genesis.

Oakes muttered gibberish to himself in a sing-song cadence while the ship approached the harness coupling. He was doing well. Black was impressed. She had memories of him performing this task for damaged freighters, but they had all been relatively stable. *Mira*, not at all stable, was undoubtedly the greatest challenge Oakes had faced in his career. Despite the sweat dripping from his forehead and the grim expression on his face, Black thought he was handling the situation better than expected.

Black continued monitoring. As the ship descended into the coupling, and the hull creaked and boomed with the gentle impact, the AI had already switched its focus to one of its finished simulations. While Oakes ran his checks on the coupling integrity, and prepared his report for Captain Dunn, Black parsed gigs of data. She was pleased with Oakes' performance and would send a report to the Trio soon. For now, however, she was more interested in figuring out what her creators had planned.

CHAPTER SEVEN

Calculations complete. Stress analysis on the hull was as good as it was going to get. Dunn rubbed a sleeve across his sweaty brow and considered the image in front of him. The 3-D wireframe had over a dozen bright red spots on its topside as well as its belly. Those were the places Black had marked as being highly dangerous or susceptible to extreme damage from the stress.

If they were going to plant additional thrusters on the ship, they had to make sure they stayed away from those areas. The only problem was how close they were to the areas they actually needed.

Changing *Mira*'s trajectory would be a matter of firing the hydrazine thrusters to push her in Pluto's direction and then another round to start her forward momentum. Once on the correct course, Oakes would begin to fire *S&R Black*'s engines in micro-burns to keep the giant ship accelerating. Once she reached a satisfactory speed, he could amp up the length and power of the burns until they had her going at a good clip.

Pluto's gravity would help, but since the dwarf planet's field was relatively weak, they first had to get *Mira* somewhat close to the small celestial body. *Not that it really matters*, Dunn thought. If they were able to get *Mira* in the vicinity of Pluto, they wouldn't even need its gravity. He hoped.

"Ready to move into position, sir," Oakes said.

Dunn looked over the holo display at his pilot. Although the marine's back was to him, Dunn could see the stress in his shoulders and the sweat on his jumpsuit. "Good. Relax, and make it happen."

"Aye, sir," Oakes said.

Dunn activated the general comms. "Marines. We are moving into position. Prep and secure."

"Clear," Taulbee said.

"Clear," Gunny echoed a heartbeat later.

Dunn changed his holo display view to grab Taulbee's feed. The screen flashed and *S&R Black*'s topside filled the display. The SV-52 floated some 200 meters above the ship, giving him an excellent view of its spine. He couldn't help but grin. The old girl was still in one piece. He just hoped she stayed that way.

The ship creaked as Oakes fired the attitude thrusters to push *S&R Black* toward *Mira*. Taulbee's cams tracked the ship as it moved, a slight jitter appearing in the feed as Taulbee moved the '52 to follow. Oakes engaged the thrusters for another short burst and the distance between *Mira* and the ship slowly disappeared.

With Taulbee shadowing *S&R Black*, Dunn's display seemed to zoom in on *Mira*, the clumps of pinecones now easily discernible from the rest of the Atmo-steel hull plates and superstructure. *Mira* was slightly canted, requiring Oakes to make another burn to match her rotation. The view from the '52 changed as

Taulbee descended in altitude relative to *Black*. Dunn watched as *Black* floated directly over the edge of *Mira*'s topside and flipped the camera feed to *Black*'s keel. Clumps of pinecones came into view, as well as the scarred hull plates. *Mira* was a goddamned mess.

The keel cameras caught sight of the harness spindle and the thick carbon nanotube lines spreading out like tentacles from a cylindrical lifeform. The top of the spindle opened like a flower, a series of Atmo-steel petals spreading from the center.

"Ready to dock, sir," Oakes said.

"Good flying, Lieutenant. You're clear to dock."

"Aye, sir."

Dunn's eyes remained fixed on the camera feed. The harness connector descended from the keel over the spindle housing. The ship rumbled and jolted as it connected with the harness spindle base.

"And we're docked, sir," Oakes said. He wiped a sleeve across his forehead, the fabric coming away wet with sweat.

"Very good, Oakes." Dunn activated the general comms. "Marines. We have docked with the spindle. Stand by for system check."

"Aye, sir," Gunny said.

Dunn removed the feed and replaced it with a 3-D wireframe model of the ship. The harness connector showed a green status. *S&R Black*'s engines sat high enough to clear the rise of the aft section, but only just. "Oakes? I show green."

"Aye, sir. Me too."

"Okay," Dunn said. He rubbed at his eyes. God, he was tired. This day seemed as though it had already lasted a week. "Time to bore."

"Aye, sir," Oakes said. He tapped a few of the icons on his holo display. "Boring now."

A low vibration reverberated through the hull. Dunn felt it in his bones and it rattled his teeth. A solid Atmo-steel drill core dropped from *S&R Black*'s hull and began working its way through *Mira*'s hull plate. The ship rattled for a moment and then all sound ceased.

"We have insertion," Oakes said. "I show no pressure loss on our side and the nannies are green."

Dunn grinned. At least something had gone right today. "Gunny? Your squad ready?"

"Aye, sir."

"Taulbee?"

"Aye, sir," Taulbee said. "I've got eyes on the connectors and the cargo bay door is clear. We're ready for egress."

"Gunny. You're a go. Good hunting."

"Aye, sir," the sergeant's voice growled into the mic.

Dunn switched feeds to the cargo bay. The door slid aside in silence. A puff of gas erupted from the skiff's rear and the craft moved out of the bay. He took a deep breath and slowly exhaled. They were hooked into *Mira*'s hull. Gunny's squad would check the line connections, ensure the nannies were ready, and finish the harness process. Duration? Twenty minutes. If they were lucky.

"Black?"

The AI responded immediately. "Yes, Captain?"

"Any change in the plate's stability?"

"No, sir," Black said. "My analysis confirms we have contact with the center of the hull plate. I have run several stress tests and detect no give on either side of the spindle connection. We are as moored as we can be."

"Good," he said. Dunn flipped the display to a model of *Mira* and spun it until he had a view of the giant ship's topside. A marker appeared on the model with the skiff's current position. Gunny had moved the skiff to the spindle location. In a moment, his marines would begin their checks, ensuring the nannie connections and the hull plate integrity. Black had given the all-clear, but standard procedure was for manual checks as well. Dunn had considered skipping it, but decided it wasn't worth the risk. They were on a clock, yes, but they needed to be as sure as they could before they started the tow. There was no reason to take the risk.

Dunn flipped to Taulbee's SV-52 feed. The camera focused in on the skiff floating less than a meter from *Mira*'s hull and near *S&R Black*'s midships. His marines were exposed out there, and it was just a matter of time before either the pinecones or one of those starfish things decided to come visit them. He hoped they'd be quick enough to avoid that.

CHAPTER EIGHT

She'd muted her comms, mainly so she could talk to herself without the others hearing. Kalimura was both furious at herself and fighting despair. She'd frozen up. The moment the display had said "connection lost," she'd simply shut down, unable to speak, scream, anything but stand there.

The wide corridor seemed too narrow, too constricting. She tried to calm her mind, but self-recrimination and fear made it impossible. Every shadow cast by her suit lights could be another of the pinecone things, or the ghostly, shimmering starfish-like thing. Kali's skin crawled at the thought.

She glanced at her rear cam and saw Carb following in her footsteps, Elliott draped over her shoulder. Dickerson's tall form loomed in the background. He mag-walked backward to cover the rear. At least they didn't have to worry about being ambushed from that direction.

The schematics showed a four-way junction up ahead. If they took the path toward the starboard-side, they'd end up near a horizontal slip-point leading from the edge of the foredecks and deep into the midships. In fact, if they wanted, they could take that slip-point all the way to engineering in the aft. "Fat chance," she said aloud. The last place she wanted to go was the aft. Midships, a mere deck or two above the infested cargo bay, wasn't exactly safe either. If there was a fractured deck plate or two, it might lead to the cargo bay itself.

Their escape from the cargo bay had been filled with half-seen threats, spinning lights, and dangerous shadows. Her HUD readings had reflected back dozens, if not hundreds, of hostile targets by the time she reached the exit. Who knew how many more of the pinecone creatures were floating in there amidst the crates and supplies for *Mira*'s original mission. The idea of being forced to travel through the darkness surrounded by endless swarms of those things rattled her down to her bones.

"You're not going that way," she said. "We're heading to port." Port. Right. Where the escape pods were lined up against the bulkhead like coffins in a morgue. She harrumphed. That was a cheery thought. Then again, being trapped in a hermetically sealed coffin with layers of Atmo-steel protecting her from a horde of creatures, the vacuum of space, and absolute zero temperatures, was rather comforting. "Better than being lost in the dark," she said to herself.

She activated her mic. "Squad. Four-way up ahead. I'll clear port and starboard." Dickerson and Carb echoed affirmatives. Kali slowed her pace as she closed the distance to the junction. In front of her? Darkness that repelled her suit lights after a few meters. Behind her? Well, Dickerson had that covered. All she had to do was worry about threats from her right and left. Yet the mouth of blackness before her kept demanding her attention.

Kali swallowed hard and forced herself to step forward until she reached the junction precipice. She focused the suit lights, the beams narrowing until they lanced through the darkness like lasers. They punched holes through the gloom and she slowly turned her head, scouring the emptiness, looking for threats. Nothing there. Nothing but unmarred metal walls.

She breathed a sigh of relief, reset the focus to diffuse, and peered to starboard. The darkness melted for the first few meters, showing her a clear hallway. She took another step forward and cast the lights down the port-side corridor. No shadows. Nothing floating. The metal walls seemed undamaged.

"Clear," she said into the comms. "Carb. Watch my flank."

"Aye, Boss."

Kali took one last look to starboard to make sure she hadn't missed something, and stepped forward into the corridor. She half-expected an arm made of shadow to reach out from the darkness toward her, her tortured adrenaline glands sending a brief jolt into her system, but nothing moved. "Dickerson? Get up here and cover our rear."

"Aye, Corporal."

She wanted to check her rear cam, but knew there was little point. He would do his job. Dickerson hadn't frozen up on the bridge. The large marine hadn't been the one to stand there like a statue, unable to speak or move while despair shredded every bit of confidence and hope. No. He'd waited for her to get her shit together, gave her the space to find herself. She smiled. If they got out of this alive, she'd make sure he got another commendation. Maybe he'd even find a way to get back in SFMC's good graces.

"How's it looking, Corporal?" Dickerson asked.

Kali twitched at the sound of his voice and chuckled. Damn, but she was jumpy. "Good, so far. Forty meters to reach the port-side."

"And a shitload of junctions," Carb said. "We could just jet."

If they detached from the floor and activated their suit thrusters, they could fly for the entire journey. They'd be at their destination in seconds. The only problem? If something was in their way, they'd have almost no time to stop their forward momentum. In z-g, objects continued moving in whatever direction they'd been pushed until another force counteracted the movement. Once they were moving forward at a good clip, decelerating would require another thruster burn to slow them and bring them to a halt.

"No," Kali said, "we can't. If there's another horde of those things, we'd fly right into them with no chance to stop."

"True," Carb said. "But at least this shit would be over."

She opened her mouth to say something, but stopped herself. What did you say to that? What could she say? As much as she wanted to tear into Carb for the negative thoughts, part of her didn't disagree. Thankfully, Dickerson knew what to say.

"Shut the fuck up, Carb," Dickerson said. "I ain't planning on dying here."

"Me, neither," Elliott said. "Not before SFMC fixes my goddamned hand. Besides," he said, "I need a sympathy lay."

Carb giggled. "About the only way you'll get laid."

Kali managed a grin. Nervous chatter. That's what had been missing since they'd reached the auxiliary bridge and watched the final recorded moments from *Mira*'s captain. She'd let Carb make jokes and rib the other two marines so long

21

as it kept them from falling into the same deep, black hole of fear threatening to swallow her whole.

She continued the mag-walk, increasing her speed. "There's nothing ahead of you but escape pods," she told herself. "Nothing to threaten you, nothing to stop your progress." Right. As long as she kept telling herself that, it might even turn out to be true.

The forty-meter distance quickly became thirty at another four-way junction. She told the squad to halt while she cleared left and right. Again, she saw nothing. No debris, no corpses, no creatures. Nothing but the darkness and the seemingly never-ending corridor of clean metal walls streaked with frost.

She took in a shuddering breath, and continued forward. Kali flicked her eyes from her forward cam to check the rear. Dickerson walked at his full height, his weapon pointed to cover their asses. Once again, she should simply trust him to do his job. He hadn't let her down yet. And she doubted that—

Something moved on her forward cam. She held up a fist and focused, her last breath trapped in her lungs. The darkness ahead had moved. Well, it hadn't, but something had. A few seconds ticked by, her eyes trained on the gloomy corridor.

"What is it, Corporal?" Dickerson asked.

She tried to speak, but the words came out as a huff of air. Kali forced herself to take a breath and tried again. "Something moved up ahead," she managed through clenched teeth.

The comms fell silent as the squad waited. A muscle spasm rocked her spine followed quickly by tremors in her thighs. She moaned with pain, but kept her eyes fixed forward, daring the darkness to twitch. Nothing moved. Had she imagined it?

Another moment passed, her breathing finally steadying, the adrenaline surge dissipating. "Okay, squad, guess I didn't see anything."

"Take your time, Corporal," Dickerson said. "Rather you be wrong than miss something."

"Copy that," she said with a blush. Dickerson had sounded like a corporal himself, giving commands to a terrified boot. He wasn't far off. She might have spent untold hours walking Titan Station's pockmarked surface, but she'd never faced a combatant firing at her, much less the stifling claustrophobia of being trapped in the wreckage of an assault craft. "Or hunted," she said to herself. That was a happy thought. She couldn't imagine what it must have been like during the Satellite War, worrying that another marine, one who wore the same uniform beneath the combat suit, was creeping up behind you to put a vibro-blade in your back or fire a flechette to rip through you like a shotgun through a side of beef.

But here she was, staring into darkness and waiting for something to leap at her. Kali calmed her thumping heart and took a step forward. And another. And another. "Keep moving," she said into the comms. Another 25 meters. That's all that separated them from the port-side bulkhead. That and two more junctions.

She continued walking, doing her best to ignore the spasms that intermittently wracked through her trapezius muscles. "Come on, bio-nannies," she said, "get your shit together." The little bastards had to be flooding her system with analgesics, but they had yet to kick in. Either that, or they had expended all their stored CBD and her nervous system had ceased releasing endorphins. How taxed do you have to be to lose the ability to create endorphins? She wondered if she hadn't already reached that point.

Something twitched in the darkness. She once again held up a fist, suddenly afraid to blink. A shadow moved at the edge of the lights. Then another. And another.

"Back up," she whispered into the comms.

"Corporal?" Dickerson asked.

"Back the fuck up," she said, emphasizing every word.

Her headset filled with the sound of a deep breath and a shuddering exhale. "Carb?" Dickerson said. "Get behind me."

Kali took a step backward. The shadows continued approaching. Dozens of them. They seemed to be filling the hallway. Kali raised her rifle and fired a flechette round.

The rocket engaged and split the darkness with a stream of light before it reached the end of the corridor and detonated in a cloud of electricity. The gloom exploded with sharp strobes of blue light. Framed by the stabs of illumination, she saw dark, shimmering arms reaching from an adjoining hallway. Swarms of pinecones flew through the z-g toward her squad. "Move! Jet to starboard!" she yelled and fired another flechette.

She turned in the opposite direction, demagnetized her boots, and hit the suit thrusters. A rush of compressed nitrogen shot out of the back of her suit propelling her forward through the hallway. Dickerson's lights dispelled the darkness down the other end of the hallway as he flew ahead, Carb less than two meters behind him.

Kali checked her rear cam and increased her speed. The pinecone swarms were less than 10 meters away and gaining. She only had a few seconds before the strange creatures descended on her like a plague. Beyond the swarms, she saw the multi-armed creature enter the corridor and begin pulling itself forward. If she survived the onslaught of pinecones, she'd still have to deal with the starfish thing.

"Corporal!" Dickerson yelled. "Slip-point. Move!"

She hit the suit thrusters again and ratcheted up her speed to 8m/s, a suicidal rate of speed if she had to suddenly halt her progress. Her HUD lit up with a warning—she didn't have much nitrogen remaining. She barely noticed. Up ahead, Carb and Elliott disappeared through an aft entryway. Dickerson floated beside it, one hand mag-locked to the wall.

"Too fast!" Kali yelled. She had maybe three seconds before she slammed into Dickerson. As soon as the thought passed through her mind, he seemed to leap from the wall at her. His large body collided with hers a few meters from the bulkhead. The impact rattled her bones and sent her mental furniture flying, but slowed her speed significantly.

Her momentum continued pushing the two of them to the wall, Dickerson's legs floating horizontally. He crunched into the bulkhead and immediately swiveled her toward the slip-point entryway. A touch of his thrusters and the pair flew into the horizontal shaft.

With Dickerson's hands wrapped around her waist driving her through the slip-point, her helmet was pointed toward the corridor they'd just left. A flood of pinecones came rushing by the slip-point entrance and crashed into the bulkhead. As Dickerson continued jetting them further into the slip-point, she just made out clouds of debris and another swarm colliding into the massive throng of pinecones. And then three arms plunged into the mess. The light faded out before she could see anything more.

"Got her?" Carb asked.

"I've got her," Dickerson said, his breath rapid. "Corporal? You alive in there?"

"Yes," she said. "Thanks."

"Don't mention it."

"When you planning on letting me go?"

Dickerson chuckled. "As soon as we're sure those damned things aren't following."

"Don't think you need to worry about that," she said. "Our starfish friend has them trapped back there."

The narrow slip-point corridor suddenly seemed too tight, too close, and she felt as though she couldn't get enough air. Her headache was back. Just another fucking concussion on top of the one she already had. Great.

"How we doing, Carb?" Dickerson asked. "I can't see much."

"We're good," Carb said. "We can slow down."

Dickerson reached out a hand and used his magnetics to slow their pace. He brought them to a near halt and pushed gently away from Kali. She continued moving backward from him, but at far less than 1m/s. "There you go," Dickerson said. "Sure you're okay?"

She nodded, although it shot another bolt of pain through her head. Her vision wavered slightly and she grit her teeth against a groan. "Yeah," she said. "Just dandy."

"So much for the fucking escape pods," Carb said.

Kali used a hand to slowly turn to Carb and Elliott. With the wounded marine attached to her shoulder, she looked as though a giant tumor had sprouted from her suit. "Well, we're not going back that way," Kali said. She brought up the schematics. The slip-point had several ingress/egress points throughout the ship and emptied into the aft engineering bay.

"Midships," Kali said. "We need to go further in." Several emergency icons lit up the map less than fifty meters from their current position. "We should be able to make it to the mid-junction and then head to port again. With any luck, we won't find another tangle of those things."

"Luck," Elliott wheezed. "So far that's working out for us."

"Shut it," Carb said. "Adults are talking."

Elliott laughed and then coughed. "That was cold, Carb."

"What do you think, Dickerson?" Kali asked.

He paused a moment before speaking. "I don't see a better alternative, Corporal. But that puts us closer to engineering than I'd like."

"Me too," Kali said. "Give me a fuel status."

"I'm near the red," Carb said.

"Same here," Dickerson said. "Actually, I'm in the red."

"Damnit," Kali said. Her own supply was halfway between the red and empty. "Okay. So no more jetting unless absolutely necessary."

"Copy that," Dickerson said. "But if we find a refill station, we need to hit it."

"Either that or we produce more CO_2," Carb said. "Actually, ignore that."

"Yeah," Kali said. Excess CO_2 could be stored to a point, but for that much extra, they'd have to be breathing pretty hard. And that meant more O_2 consumption. Not exactly optimal. "I doubt compressed nitrogen was a mainstay among the crew," Kali said. "Even in the emergency stations."

"True," Dickerson said. "But if we come across one, we should check."

Kali blew a sigh through her teeth. "Okay. Let's get moving. Slow. Pull yourself until you're at about 1m/s, and then float to the next junction." Both Dickerson and Carb acknowledged. Kali pulled herself until she floated past Carb and Elliott. Her suit lights cut through the darkness before them, but the slip-point tunnel seemed to stretch on for forever.

CHAPTER NINE

His private holo display was filled with the ship's status reports, courses plotted by Black and Oakes, and several tensile strength tables. Dunn wished it also had a list of recommendations on what he should do. *No*, he thought. *It's not about what you should do, but how you're going to do it.*

And that was the problem. Oakes would begin moving the ship into position in a few minutes. After that, Gunny's squad would hook up the harness to the spindle. Once that was done, they could begin the initial acceleration. And that was the problem.

The harness was designed to moor the two ships together using the Atmo-steel deck plating for support and leverage. The nannie-formed carbon tubes provided immense flexibility and strength, but they were only as powerful as the steel they burrowed into. *Mira*'s deck plates were fractured in multiple places. In others, the plating had started to come apart completely, the layers separating from one another.

According to Black's best-case scenario, they would lose a line-mooring from a fractured deck plate or Atmo-steel separation. If that occurred, the harness hive would adjust and they'd still be able to tow the mammoth hulk. The worst case was something he didn't even like to consider.

If they lost two or more lines, *S&R Black* would tear free from *Mira* and shoot forward at a fast clip. The harness lines would doubtless trail sections of deck plate that could whip forward and slam into the hull. If they were lucky, the nannies would release the deck-plates before they snapped back and *S&R Black* would only suffer damage from the carbon nanotube lines. Unlucky? Pieces of the deck plate would slam into them like a massive flechette round. In either case, the ship would suffer catastrophic damage or, more likely, destruction.

Black rated their chance for success at 60%, but, as usual, had added a plethora of conditionals, including the fact there was no way of knowing the extent of the damage to the deck plates. Black had used information gathered during Taulbee's hull survey to decide where to place the harness and the lines. But without proper sensor equipment onboard the SV-52 to test for damage, Black was only able to guess. And computers hated to guess.

The AI wasn't the only sentient sweating over the details. Oakes knew the situation, as did Nobel, but the rest of the crew was blissfully unaware. Dunn intended to keep it that way. Standard procedure was for all personnel to wear emergency gear during a tow, just in case something catastrophic occurred. But when the time came, he'd have to let Gunny and Taulbee know just how fucked things could get.

"Sir?" Oakes said.

Dunn looked up from the holo display. The pilot had turned his chair to face the captain, mouth set in a grim, thin line. "Yes, Lieutenant?"

"Force calculations complete," he said. "I'll send them to your display."

Dunn nodded. "How bad is it?"

Oakes shrugged. "It is what it is, sir."

Dunn flicked his eyes back to the holo display. The graphs showed a lot of red, more than he feared. Their acceleration would be severely affected by *Mira*'s condition. By Oakes' calculations, it would take them nearly four hours of periodic fusion burns to get the hulk moving at 1/4 speed. If they managed to achieve that speed without *Mira* breaking up, they'd still have another twenty-four hours before they reached Pluto. The only saving grace would be Pluto's gravity. It would help pull the derelict into orbit and give them a chance to refuel at PEO.

"Twenty-four hours," Dunn said.

"Aye, sir." Oakes ran a hand over his closely shaved scalp. "If we use supplemental burns beyond that point, we can probably get her moving a bit faster. Twenty-four hours total is the worst-case scenario."

Dunn raised his eyes. "That's the worst case?"

"Um." Oakes frowned. "No. Worst case is she breaks up. But I mean beyond that. If she holds together, and we see enough reason for it, we can most likely increase the acceleration. Just comes with a lot of risks."

The words "if," "likely," and "risk" echoed in his mind. Their plan, just like everything else with this mission, was plagued by conditionals. So many variables, so many unknowns, so many guesses. "Too many," he said aloud.

"Sir?" Oakes asked.

"Nothing," Dunn said. "What else can we do to help get *Mira*'s fat ass moving?"

Oakes thought for a moment and smiled. "We still have a thruster pack in the cargo bay."

Dunn raised his eyebrows and then leaned back in the command chair. "Why the fuck didn't I think of that?"

Oakes said nothing.

"Good job, Oakes. Black and I will figure the calculations on how we can use them and where to place them. I want to know if it makes sense to use the thrusters to change her course, push the beast toward Pluto, or both. Right now, we need to get in position for the harness."

"Aye, sir," Oakes said. He swiveled in his chair and focused back on his own display.

Dunn stared through *S&R Black*'s canopy. *Mira* filled the starboard edge of the trans-aluminum cockpit. They were making plans to move her. If not for Kalimura's squad trapped somewhere aboard, he'd just blow the fucking thing to pieces and be done with it.

He initiated a block connection to the AI.

Yes, Captain?

He licked his lips. *Any communications with Kalimura?*

No, Captain, the AI said. *The interference is still blocking standard radio transmissions and I've received no block traffic external to the ship. Might I also point out, sir, that I would have alerted you immediately if we had.*

Dunn rolled his eyes. *Of course you would have. Just like you did the first*

27

time.

The AI said nothing, but sent an image of a shrugging figure.

Do you think the additional thrusters can help us?

Yes, Captain. I think Lieutenant Oakes is on to something. I'll provide you with a full report in a few moments.

Good, Dunn said and broke the connection. Even if the thrusters did little more than turn the hulk toward Pluto, it could drastically help their timeline. The less force they had to use to get *Mira* moving and in the right direction, the better.

The only problem with the thrusters would be placing them. Gunny's squad would have to once more skiff out to *Mira*'s hull and face off with the pinecones and the starfish-like creatures. "And whatever else is out there," Dunn mumbled.

Nope. He didn't like it. He didn't like any of it. Every possible solution raised the risk level to his marines. If he wasn't careful, none of Gunny's marines would ever make it back to Trident Station alive.

CHAPTER TEN

Gunny piloted the skiff from the cargo bay, stomach fluttering with nervous tension. The brightness of the cargo bay receded, leaving them in the shadowy twilight of the Kuiper Belt. The skiff's strong lamps illuminated *Mira*'s scarred and marred metal surface. He moved the skiff nice and slow, gently pushing the throttle and attitude thrusters to rotate the craft and head to the spindle connections.

The comms were deathly silent, as they should be. Yet, chatter would have been welcome; he felt as though everyone was holding their breath, including the twinkling stars.

Feeds from the skiff's top, bottom, fore, and rear cams lit his HUD. Wendt, manning the cannon, was supposed to monitor the views as well. Splitting your attention between all those screens while attempting to focus on what was in front of you was difficult to say the least. Piloting the skiff could be stressful enough without having to process four different camera feeds simultaneously. Gunny had told his marines, especially Wendt, to keep an eye out. All it would take was one of the starfish things creeping up on them to end this trip in a hurry.

"We were lucky," he said, his mic muted. "Damned lucky."

When he and his marines had streaked from *Mira*'s hull to assist Captain Dunn and Lt. Nobel, Gunny had had no idea they'd be facing off with the giant exo-solar creature. If not for the ammo Captain Dunn had found in the secret crates aboard *S&R Black*, Gunny's squad, Dunn, and Nobel would all have died. Not to mention Lt. Taulbee. Flying in his SV-52, Taulbee had kept the creature busy long enough for Gunny's squad to rescue Dunn and Nobel, but not without serious structural damage to his craft. Had the fight continued, Taulbee would have had to eject. And then...

Well, that was the question, wasn't it? Would the starfish thing have pursued his floating body? Or would the thing have continued to attack the hopelessly damaged SV-52?

The creature, its ten arms seemingly grasping at objects only it could see, had vibrated in the light. No, not vibrated. Shimmered. The thing's skin, darker than deep space, seemed to warp matter around it. Gunny shivered. He didn't understand how it could exist, much less affect matter around it. Was it sucking down light like a black hole? And if so, how the hell was it doing it?

Gunny tried to push the image away and focus on his damned job. He moved the skiff fifty meters from *S&R Black*, his eyes constantly flicking from the forward screen to the other cam feeds. He slowed the craft with a few micro burns. The skiff came to a near stop and he nudged port and fore attitude thrusters to gently spin the skiff until it once again faced *S&R Black*. Once the skiff was in position, he slowly accelerated to a speed of 2m/s.

The plan was to drop a pair of marines at the harness for spindle checks before testing the lines. Once they disembarked and Taulbee could provide cover fire, Gunny would fly the skiff to the closest mount point for a new thruster installation. Wendt and Lyke would have thruster placement duty. And it was going to take a while.

But first things first, Gunny said to himself. *Get your marines on the hull.*

He brought the skiff to a halt 10 meters away from the spindle. *S&R Black*'s hull loomed above them like a giant metal whale. If not for the ship's belly lights, the skiff would be in total darkness from the larger craft's shadow. Gunny smiled despite the tension in his gut. No matter the blemishes on her hull, or the dings and bumps in her otherwise smooth skin, right now, she was the most beautiful ship he'd ever seen.

"Black. I'm in position," he said over the comms.

Dunn responded immediately. "Good job, Gunny. Let's get this show going."

"Aye, sir," Gunny said. He activated the squad comms. "All right, marines. Copenhaver and Murdock. I want a clean dismount. Perform the spindle and coupling inspection. I want one of you providing cover at all times. Don't let any of those bastard things sneak up on you. Understood?"

"Aye, Gunny," the two marines said. Copenhaver's strong, confident voice easily rose above Murdock's shaky reply.

With the magnetics set at half power, the skiff stayed a good two meters off the hull. Gunny increased the power and the skiff descended until it hovered just a meter from *Mira*'s pitted and damaged hull plates.

"Go," Gunny said.

He brought the two marines' cam feeds onto his HUD and watched as they lifted themselves over the gunwale and pushed to the hull. Copenhaver activated her magnetics fast enough, and with just enough power to stand on the hull without so much as a jolt. Murdock, on the other hand, struck the hull plate with enough force to make his feed jitter with static. Gunny shook his head. Goddamned useless. Useless. He added another mental note to kick his squad's collective asses when they returned to Trident Station. What the hell was Mars teaching these kids?

Well, Copenhaver was obviously the best of the lot. Her ability to maneuver, keep a clear head, and pull incompetent squad-mates through a mission was exactly the kind of marine he wanted. Needed. With Mars constantly sending them the flotsam or the merely ambitious, it was a wonder *S&R Black* managed to field anyone competent. But once Gunny found a diamond in the rough, he worked his ass off to make them into a marine worth keeping, and a marine worthy of the SFMC.

"On the hull, Gunny," Copenhaver said. "We'll begin checks momentarily."

"Acknowledged, Private. Get to work."

"Aye, Gunny."

Gunny couldn't help but grin. It was difficult to keep the growl in his voice when he wanted to chuckle. He allowed himself a moment to enjoy her confidence before his own was once again tested. Flying to the mount points, checking the piton placement, and finally laying down the last of the thrusters would test every ounce of courage he had. If *Mira*'s little stowaways didn't kill them first, he might actually get a chance to smile at Copenhaver's swagger again.

"Gunny," Wendt said, "we have a contact on the far side of the ship."

He raised his eyebrows. "What do you mean contact?" Gunny brought up his alert screen. Sure enough, the local radar had captured something moving one hundred meters away. "The fuck?"

"What do you think it is?" Wendt asked.

"Black?"

"Yes, Gunny," Black said. "I have received the same telemetry. However, I am unable to discern whether it is mere debris, one of the starfish-like creatures, or something else."

Or something else. The words echoed in Gunny's skull and a sense of dread made his stomach crawl. *This mission,* he thought, *is a complete cluster-fuck.* "So we should proceed with caution." Not a question, really, more of an ironic observation.

"Of course," Black said dryly. "But I expected you to in any case."

If he had been speaking with the AI via a block connection, he would have sent it the image of a fist with a middle finger raised. "Understood," he said. "Wendt. You're in the gunner's chair. Keep your goddamned eyes open for anything."

"Aye, Gunny," Wendt said.

Lyke cleared his throat. "Gunny? What do I—?"

"You have your rifle, Private. Use it," Gunny said.

After a momentary pause, Lyke answered in a soft voice. "Aye, Gunny."

He fought the urge to shake his head. The private was scared. So was Wendt. Hell, Gunny was scared too. The more he thought about flying across the hull to plant more thrusters, the more he wanted to turn the damned skiff around and head back to the ship.

"There are known unknowns," Gunny said aloud, mic muted. What a bunch of bullshit. And yet here he was, flying out to the other side of *Mira*'s hull to face off with a piece of debris, a ridiculously dangerous alien creature, or something new and probably just as horrible. All that without any intel.

He connected to Taulbee. "Sir? You still flying patrol?"

"Of course, Gunny. I'm buzzing the harness point. Do you want me to break off and scout ahead?"

Gunny considered that for a moment. If Taulbee raced off to check their thruster placement targets, he'd get the intel he needed. Maybe. But that would leave both Copenhaver and Murdock vulnerable to the pinecones and starfish. It would also leave the ship reliant upon weapons that may or may not have an effect on *Mira*'s exo-solar hitchhikers.

"No, sir. But I wouldn't mind you being on-call."

Taulbee chuckled. "Yell out, and I'll be there, Gunny."

"Acknowledged, sir," Gunny said.

"Taulbee out."

Gunny increased the skiff's speed with another burn. "All right, squad. We have a radar contact and we're heading toward it. I'll slow us down when we're twenty meters out from its position. Stay mag-locked and be prepared to ditch.

Understood?"

"Aye," Wendt and Lyke responded, the LCpl's voice much louder than the private's.

"Outstanding," Gunny growled. He had managed to fill his voice with the same impatient, angry tone he usually had, but it was difficult. If not for the force of habit, he would have sounded as meek as Lyke. Gunny glared at his HUD and watched as they ate the distance between *S&R Black* and the contact.

CHAPTER ELEVEN

Floating half a meter above the slip-point's deck and at nearly 1m/s, Dickerson felt calm. He continued checking his rear cam looking for any pinecones or starfish that might have followed them into the shaft; but so far, nothing.

The fact they were floating meant he could arch his back, rest his stressed muscles and joints, and relax. A little. The constant crouch-walking through *Mira*'s haunted corridors had taken their toll on his body. He'd little doubt Kalimura and Carb were in as bad a shape as himself. Although she'd never admit it, he imagined Carb was in more pain than anyone else. While Elliott's body weighed next to nothing in z-g, pulling his mass along had to be affecting her. Eventually, he'd have to force her to give up the wounded marine so he could carry him. She wouldn't give up that duty willingly. Too damned hard-headed.

The headache that had simmered inside his skull for the last half-hour was fading a bit. Either the bio-nannies had found enough reserves to help him out, or just the act of floating rather than walking was helping him regain his strength. But the dull throb in his shoulder had drained away any relief. He'd really fucked himself up now. He wasn't sure how much pressure he could put on his wounded arm before the rotator cuff simply froze, leaving him a single limb to protect both himself and his squad. *At least I know how to fire my weapon one-handed,* he thought.

"10 meters," Kalimura said over the squad channel.

"Copy," he said, Carb echoing him a second later. They'd reach the first junction in no time. Abandoning crouch-walking also provided the advantage of speed. Which was a good thing, because Dickerson couldn't wait to get the fuck off this wreck.

Dickerson ticked off the seconds, watching as the junction came into view. This far on *Mira*'s starboard-side meant the junction could only go one way—to port. Kalimura's suit thrusters puffed and she slowed. Carb followed suit, as did he. Once they were all stationary, Kalimura pulled herself to the deck using her right glove. She was less than half a meter from the junction's blind corner. Depending on what she saw down the egress shaft, they might have to jet in a hurry. *Not like that will be far,* he thought. They were all nearly out of fuel for their thrusters. Another hard burn and they'd be empty, unable to even use maneuvering jets to change their attitude. They needed to find some way to recharge their suits. And soon.

Kalimura held up a fist and crouch-walked against the wall. She slowly peered around the corner, her helmet lights focused to penetrate the gloom. Dickerson held his breath, his mind filling with the image of an impossible black arm pulling her into the adjoining shaft.

"Shit," she said over the squad channel. "We've got some serious debris in here."

Dickerson sighed. "How bad?"

"Bad," the corporal said. "How's your injured arm?"

"Still bad, but I think I can lift some mass with it."

"Good. Get up here, Dickerson."

Carb snorted over the mic. "Am I too girly for that job?"

"No," Kalimura said without turning around. "You're the only one of us without broken ribs and with two good arms. Meaning you can carry Elliott and aim at the same time. That's what I need you to do."

"Aye, Boss," Carb said in a somewhat depressed voice.

Dickerson grinned. His squad-mate was tired of carrying Elliott, but Kalimura was right. They needed her to be their anchor if something went wrong. And what could possibly go wrong?

He mag-walked past Carb to join Kalimura. She stood in the center of the adjoining shaft, her rifle still pointed down the hall. Dickerson saw what she did and exhaled in a long stream of breath. She hadn't been kidding about debris.

The shaft had nearly collapsed just a few meters from the junction. Something had smashed the metal with enough force to not only perforate the slip-point tunnel, but fracture part of the wall. As a result, broken pipes, wire, and other infrastructure had ultimately filled the once empty space. If the two of them worked together, they might be able to clear it in 10 minutes. Maybe. That was a long time, though.

"Corporal?" he said. "Maybe we should go a little further down? To the next junction?"

She was silent for a moment. He imagined her going over the schematics, looking for the next egress point and determining risk. "And if that next egress point is as bad as this one? Or worse?"

He shrugged. "Then we come back here," he said. "If we float, it shouldn't take any time to reach it at all."

Kalimura raised an arm and pointed down the cluttered egress. "There's an emergency station not five meters beyond this wreckage. The next egress doesn't have one for nearly twenty meters. Considering what we've come in contact with, that's a long distance."

"True," Dickerson said. "I'm okay either way. Just wanted to bring up an alternative."

"As you should," she said. "Carb? Cover our asses. Dickerson and I will try and clear this."

"Aye, Boss," Carb said. "Just make sure you don't perforate a suit. Not sure how long any of these patches will hold."

"Copy that," Dickerson drawled. "Corporal? Shall we?"

She mag-locked her rifle to her back and began walking forward. He did the same, hoping like hell this wasn't another mistake.

CHAPTER TWELVE

Black's attention was split between helping Dunn with his mission planning, working with Oakes on the new force calculations including thruster pack placement, monitoring communications channels, keeping track of Taulbee's position relative to the ship, and watching for any movement on *Mira*. In short, Black was a busy AI.

The communications array picked up a signal from PEO. The observatory AI, Mickey, had sent a priority data package. A big one. Images, video, telemetry, calculations, and suggestions were all part of the stream.

In a matter of nanoseconds, Black unpacked and analyzed the data. The AI then took a moment to think.

Mickey had been watching the incoming KBO. Only now, Mickey wasn't convinced it was an actual ball of ice. For one thing, it was glowing. Mickey's instruments were far more powerful than Black's. The telescopes aboard PEO could make out details Black would never be able to discern until the objects were on top of her. And those details were most interesting.

A group of still images captured the KBO as a dot and slowly zoomed in on it. With each increase in magnification, the object became more and more detailed. KBOs were often misshapen, their creation the result of impacts with larger bodies rather than the natural conglomeration of gases via gravity or from a gravitational force. Instead, they frequently resembled haphazard blobs. But not this one.

The shape seemed to be canted at its "front" and it wasn't rotating or tumbling. The KBO was on a direct path and moving like a projectile. While those particular facets already made it unique, the object also appeared to have a thin, raised portion that pointed toward the sun.

Mickey had provided no conclusions about what the data meant, choosing instead to let Black draw her own. If she could talk to the Trio, she could get some guidance. Maybe. But a message to Trident Station would take three hours to get there and three more to receive the reply. By that time, they'd have to have *Mira* far away from her current position to avoid the KBO. But that was another problem. According to Mickey's calculations, the KBO would be in range in less than an hour.

Black created a new subroutine to monitor the KBO, reserving three cameras on the aft to track the approaching object and warn her if it changed trajectory or velocity. Mickey had also highlighted several smaller shadows in the large KBO's vicinity. The PEO AI hadn't been able to confirm they were more than interference or graphical artifacts, but suggested Black keep a watch on them. Black intended to.

She sent Mickey a response, thanking the AI for its timely information and asking it to monitor all KBO activity within a 1 AU vicinity of *Mira;* the spherical area needed to serve as an early warning system should other objects approach.

According to the data gathered by Kalimura's squad aboard *Mira*, it was more than likely that both the incoming KBO and the shadows near it were not made of ice or rock. Instead, they were almost certainly exo-solar material. Correction. Exo-solar lifeforms. And if they were as large as Black feared, towing *Mira* would be the least of their problems.

CHAPTER THIRTEEN

Boring was an understatement. He was on his fifth pass, floating above *S&R Black* and circling while keeping an eye on the feeds from Private Copenhaver and Private Lyke. Copenhaver had taken up a firing position just a meter or so away from her squad-mate, her flechette rifle held expertly in her hands. Every few seconds, she turned to face a different direction. It made Taulbee smile.

When you took up sentry duty, you were taught to have your head on a swivel. He just didn't know anyone would take that so literally. Rather than use her camera feeds to watch for incoming hostiles, Copenhaver had taken a much more active approach. Considering the creatures they'd encountered so far, he wasn't sure he'd be content with cam feeds either.

Watching through your helmet cam was less disorienting and gave you a better feel for the world around you. Using cam feeds always left a dead spot or two from which a hostile could get the drop on you. And that was the real fear, of course. Getting jumped from behind? Not a worry. But a surprise attack from the right angle could leave you dead in space. Whoever had taught Copenhaver had done a good job. The marine was damned good. Taulbee hoped she'd stick around when her tour was up.

"If there is another tour," he whispered to himself. That was by no means a sure bet. Sure, *S&R Black* sat atop the spindle, it's boring drill screwed into the hull to both secure it and make a tight seal with *Mira*. But they hadn't tried to fire the engines yet. And they sure as hell didn't know if the deck plates would hold. And if they didn't? Well, there was no telling what would happen.

Taulbee tried to push away the thought of the S&R vessel breaking free from *Mira*, sending shards of metal into orbit around the massive ship, and maybe dragging a deck plate along with it. *S&R Black* might survive the jolt, but anyone caught outside the ship would be annihilated. Even if the jolt didn't destroy the ship, it could send *S&R Black* straight into the hull, or flying off into space just far enough to get smashed by *Mira*. Until they flattened her tumble completely, that was a real concern. He hadn't said anything to Dunn about it, but he was sure the captain already knew. As did Oakes and Black. In fact, the force calculations and simulations the three of them had run no doubt took that into account.

But that didn't mean Taulbee felt good about it. Every calculation, every simulation, even by an AI, had a high degree of uncertainty when you didn't know all the variables. And out here, with *Mira*'s condition and the creatures she'd brought back with her, they were at the mercy of "unknown variables."

Taulbee activated a micro-burn to turn the SV-52 when he reached the edge of his square patrol area. He couldn't see the two marines on the hull since they were directly beneath *S&R Black*, but he could see the surrounding environment. It was enough for him to at least give them a heads up before those starfish things or a herd of pinecones showed up.

"Herd? School?" Taulbee shook his head. He'd no idea what to call the damned things. Assuming they ever made it back to Trident Station for a debrief and data offload, he imagined exo-biologists would spend decades poring over the information they'd gathered. Hell, maybe in a decade or two, the brains would know what the hell these things were made from. "Unless we bring back a sample."

And boy didn't that scare the shit out of him. It was bad enough to face these things out here, but the idea of bringing them back to populated space? Any of them? He shivered. What would happen if the pinecones, with their metal crunching talons or the starfish with their corroding acid, found a space station? If they managed to make their way to Titan Station or Enceladus Prime, the outer fringes of humanity would be at great risk.

He hoped for Earth's sake the little buggers couldn't survive an entry into the atmosphere. Now that was a terrifying idea. The cradle of humanity, the original gravity well from which humanity evolved, being overrun by exo-solar life like some kind of ET plague. Would the pinecones slice and dice unsuited humans? How about the starfish? Would they just fly down and rip people apart or dissolve them with shots of acid?

Taulbee shook his head to clear the thoughts. Distractions. It wasn't the first time his mind had wandered far afield while providing cover. When you didn't have an immediate threat, it was difficult to keep focused. He didn't even have to think about the adjustments to keep to his patrol square. Too many rote exercises, too many hours of keeping marines safe from non-existent threats. And that was the point. Practicing the square over and over again, flying training missions, and getting to know the craft as an extension of yourself, meant you didn't have to pay attention to the minor details. Your body and subconscious knew what to do. All a pilot had to do was pay close enough attention to handle new situations. Like this one.

Taulbee spotted a herd hovering above *Mira*'s far aft deck-plates. He zoomed in and groaned. A few dozen pinecones, varying in size and length, flew slowly and silently through space. They were headed toward *S&R Black* and his two marines.

"Taulbee to Copenhaver."

"Aye, sir. Go."

"There's a group of pinecones headed this way. Coming from aft." He ran a quick calculation based on their current speed. "They're moving pretty slow. You should have two minutes before they're in my firing range. Three before they're on you."

When she spoke, her voice didn't have a trace of fear. "Aye, sir. Stay and fight, or board *Black*?"

Good question. "If I can't warn them off with some shots, I want you to wait for my signal and get your asses back on the ship. Understood?"

"Aye, sir," Copenhaver said. "Murdock? Got it?"

"Got it," Murdock said.

Taulbee smiled. They were both privates, but Murdock had already conceded decisions to Copenhaver. She was a natural-born leader. At least

Taulbee thought so. He'd have a conversation with Gunny about her future when they got back to Trident Station.

"Taulbee to Dunn."

"Dunn here. We have your telemetry. Black counts forty-plus pinecones."

"Aye, sir. I can intercept them long before they become a threat to the ship."

"Yes, you can." Dunn paused. "Black suggests using regular flechette rounds to give them a scare. If they don't break off their trajectory, it'll be time to use the heavy stuff."

"Aye, sir," Taulbee said. His lips twitched into a faint smile. "Black have any suggestions on the 'heavy stuff?'"

Dunn's voice held a smile. "Tritium rounds first. I don't want you firing those missiles unless it's absolutely necessary."

"Understood, sir," Taulbee said.

"Dunn, out."

"Acknowledged," Taulbee said. He veered off his patrol square and floated over S&R Black's spine toward her aft. From an altitude of twenty meters, he could see the pits and blemishes from the flechette rounds he'd fired during the first starfish attack. When they got the ship back to Trident, she'd need some TLC. "If she makes it back," he thought.

He kept his thrust fairly low, not wanting to stray too far from the ship and his two marines. The herd was less than a minute out of range. He'd stop the craft a good 15 seconds before they reached the kill zone and begin thrusting backward. That would give his forward flechette launchers the best chance of disrupting the herd.

The SV 52 was loaded to the gills with ammo. Regular flechettes, the tritium flechettes, and two of those special warheads. Whatever the hell they were. Like the captain said, he'd only use the warheads as a last resort. They didn't have a good idea of what the damned things would do, and he sure as hell didn't want to be around when they went off. He especially didn't want his marines anywhere near the explosions.

Unfortunately, if the regular and tritium rounds didn't work, he might have less than a few seconds to fire the missiles before the detonation would put his marines in certain danger. That was his real concern.

Twenty seconds. A window on his HUD zoomed in on the herd, the cam view slowly panning to cover their approach. Without magnification, the creatures were little more than a tight, irregularly shaped blob of black, darker than the hull itself. He waited, his fingers wrapped around the throttle and the triggers for the guns.

Just walk a line of fire through the middle, he thought, *and then see what they do. If they—*

His eyes widened. A portion of deck plate in front of the herd vibrated, pieces of metal debris flew off the hull and into space. The herd broke apart, most of the creatures turning in space to retreat. For some, however, it was too late.

The deck plate shattered as a starfish pulled itself through the hull, shooting its acid at the stragglers. The creature pulled its arms in before extending them like a flower blooming in a nano-second. The strange lifeform jetted forward and turned its body to face its prey.

Taulbee watched in fascination as the starfish vomited streams of acid in the z-g, the deadly liquid flying through the vacuum like missiles toward their targets. Several herd members too slow to flee tumbled from the force of the liquid streams striking their bodies. Taulbee zoomed in on the closest pinecone to the starfish. Its body, normally black and barely more than an outline in normal conditions, glowed green for an instant. The starfish waved its arms again and flew close enough to grasp the creature in one of its many arms. Another pinecone tried to distance itself from the predator, but the attacker easily plucked it with another arm.

The starfish thing dragged them into its center, another set of arms prying and clutching at its prey. The pinecone shells split open, revealing glowing gray flesh. The morsel disappeared into the starfish's maw for a moment before the now empty husk was jettisoned like a cannon shot. The starfish did the same with the remaining captured pinecone.

With another sweep of its arms, the starfish followed the fleeing herd, slowly gaining on them. Taulbee lost sight of the pinecones as they flew past the edge of the hull and into space. The starfish, undeterred, gained speed and disappeared.

For a moment, Taulbee did nothing but breathe. He was still trying to process what he'd seen when he realized his jaw had dropped. He closed it with a click of teeth and activated the comms. "Black? Did you see that?"

"Yes, Lieutenant," the AI said.

"How the hell are they moving like that?"

"Unknown," Black said. "Again, if I had a creature to study, I might begin to understand them."

Taulbee shook his head. "Captain? We had some visitors, but they seem to have departed."

"Acknowledged," Dunn said. "I saw the feed. That thing just pushed itself out of the deck plates?"

"Aye, sir. Metal debris still pushing outward into space. Might be a hazard if we have to fly that way."

The comms went silent for a moment, as if Dunn didn't know what to say. The space of two breaths passed before he finally heard the captain say, "Maintain patrol, Taulbee. I don't want one of those things coming out next to the spindle and our marines."

Taulbee nodded to himself. "Aye, sir. My thoughts exactly. Taulbee out."

He turned the SV-52 until it once again faced *S&R Black*. A quick nudge of the throttle and the support craft gained speed. He hadn't flown far from his charges, but every second it took to return had his stomach churning.

He'd have to be more observant now. Migrating pinecones and hovering starfish were still a threat, certainly. But the idea of one of those things simply smashing through the deck plates? His marines could be instantly dragged beneath *Mira*'s crumbling superstructure, or simply eaten by the starfish things. He shuddered, his finger twitching near the cannon's trigger. "Poke an arm out, you fuckers," he said aloud. The bravado sounded weak and without conviction to his own ears.

CHAPTER FOURTEEN

It didn't matter that the temperature outside her suit was near absolute zero. It didn't matter that she was trapped in what should have been one of the coldest places in the universe. What mattered was her suit didn't seem to understand the difference between "comfort" and "sweatbox."

Kali struggled to pull another piece of debris from the pile. It finally came loose, bringing down more debris with it. Dickerson was having the same issue, although he was having more difficulty with his damaged shoulder.

What she thought would only take a few minutes was taking a lot longer. Since they had no idea what was really above the slip-point, or how much damage had been done topside, she had drastically miscalculated the amount of debris that had clumped together. And even in z-g, pulling on a piece frequently pulled another piece with it. The tangle of metal, plastic, and void-knew-what-else was so compacted that it might take them half an hour to clear the space. But the worst part was the fact that every piece they removed had to be jettisoned backward through the tunnel to keep from clogging it up again.

"Fucking Sisyphean," Kali muttered.

"What's that, Corporal?" Dickerson asked in a pained, breathy voice.

She stopped and pointed at the clutter. "This. We pull, we remove, and more shit gets jammed in there." She sat back on her haunches, doing her best to pop her vertebrae. "What's the point?"

Dickerson let go of a large piece of debris and turned to face her. "Well, Corporal, at least we're in agreement on that."

She couldn't see his face through the visor, but she thought she heard a smile in his voice. "Why didn't you say something?"

He shrugged, his bad shoulder dropping slightly. "Not my place," he said.

She shook her head. "I think this was a mistake."

"Well, as mistakes go, it's not exactly the worst in the universe," he said. "You think we should go further down the slip-point?"

"What do you think?"

He paused for a moment, his helmet facing the cluttered egress. "I think that might be the right thing to do," he said and jerked a thumb backward. "Besides, Carb says everything's clear back there. Probably make better time."

"Yeah," she said with a nod. "Fuck this." She stood from her crouch and raised hands to the ceiling. Her ribs immediately screamed in pain and she grimaced beneath her helmet. *Have to stop doing that*, she told herself. While she'd pulled on the debris, the pain had been little more than pinches, tiny lightning bolts across the tortured tissue and bone. But lifting her arms like that? More like detonating a flechette in her upper chest.

Dickerson stood beside her, one hand rubbing at his bad shoulder.

41

"Damnit," he said. "Can't even feel my fingers through this suit."

"You could always take it off," Carb said. "I know icing it down would help."

"Ha-ha," he said in a mock laugh. "Why don't you keep quiet back there and focus on the luggage."

"Joke 'em if they can't take a fuck," Carb said.

Kali couldn't help but smile. At least Dickerson and Carb could keep her entertained while she led them to certain death. She shook away the thought and made her way back to the slip-point shaft, Dickerson on her heels.

The egress point would have brought them so close to an emergency station, they'd practically have been there. Instead, they were going to have to travel down the lightless shaft another forty meters before reaching the next port-side egress. To make matters worse, the next junction was a four-way, putting them at risk for attacks from above and below as well as from the port-side. She didn't like it, but couldn't think of an alternative.

"Elliott? How you doing?" Kali asked.

"Still here," he said. He sounded better, more energetic, and in less pain. "Finally starting to breathe easier."

"Good," she said. "If things get nasty up ahead, I may need you to do some walking and flying."

"Won't that be fun," Elliott said. He paused for a moment and then sighed. "Aye, Boss. Understood."

She smiled. He *was* doing better. Carb had mag-locked him to the wall and he'd been able to rest while Kali and Dickerson tried to clear the egress. That had been, what, ten minutes ago? Fifteen? Didn't matter. Every moment he wasn't moving around or being jostled was a gift to the bio-nannies, allowing them to do their jobs without distraction.

"Now if only ours could get some rest," she said off comms. That was the problem. As long as she and Dickerson were doing all the heavy lifting so to speak, their nannies weren't getting a chance to repair or even dull their pain. After this many hours of exertion, she wasn't sure the microscopic machines even had enough material to work with.

Kali looked down the slip-point shaft, her helmet lights not strong enough to illuminate the next junction. "Okay," she said. "Carb? Get Elliott ready to move. Dickerson?" He turned to her but said nothing. "How's the shoulder?"

"Be better after a beer and some THC."

"Can you keep going?"

He chuckled. "Do I have a choice?"

"No," she said, a grin creeping across her face. "But I need to know if you can still hold a rifle."

"No offense, Corporal," he said, "but when I can't hold a rifle, I'm already fucking dead."

"Good answer," she said. Out of the four members of the squad, Carb seemed the least damaged. She was also the weakest physical strength wise. At least from the reports Kali had read when she took over the squad so many weeks ago. Was it really weeks? She felt as though they'd been on *Mira* for years.

"Ready, Boss," Carb said.

Kali checked her rear cam. Elliott was slung over her shoulder once again, her rifle held firmly in her hands. "Good. Dickerson? You ready?"

"Aye, Corporal," he said. "Same formation?"

"Until I say otherwise." An awkward silence fell over the comms. Kali did her best not to sigh. "Okay, squad. Forward."

She detached from the floor and used a free mag-glove to gain momentum. Carb and Dickerson followed suit, the squad floating down the slip-point shaft at a slow pace.

From here, the shaft looked fairly clean. Bits of debris floated near the ceiling, but nothing they couldn't simply brush aside or ignore altogether. Both horizontal and vertical slip-points assumed the occupants would float parallel to its intended direction rather than perpendicular. As such, the ceiling was relatively low for Dickerson and he had to be careful to keep from hitting his head. Had the slip-point been powered, the shaft would have taken care of that problem for him.

Kali did her best to ignore her cams and focus instead on the darkness before her. She flicked her eyes across the visor cam looking for shadows that seemed out of place or movement, but only the occasional piece of debris caught her attention.

"Not that I'm complaining," Dickerson said, "but why aren't they in here?"

"You mean the pinecones?" Carb asked.

"Yeah. I mean, they were stuffed into the corridors. Why aren't they here too?"

"Good question," Kali said. "When we get back to Black, maybe the Trio will have some answers for us."

"The Trio," Carb spat, "may have left these poor fuckers out in space to die."

"Yeah," Elliott said. "Why did Captain Kovacs say that? I can't believe they'd do that."

Kali frowned, doing her best to absorb their words while scanning for possible threats down the shaft. "Kovacs seemed to think the Trio knew what was out there. And it doesn't sound to me like they made it to Proxima Centauri b. Hell, didn't sound like they ever had any intention of making it there."

"So why the big cover-up?" Dickerson asked. "You telling me SF Gov convinced all of humanity to spend precious resources and cooperate on the largest, most expensive endeavor in human history on the basis of a lie? For what purpose? And if they weren't planning on going to PCb, just where the fuck were they going?"

"I don't know," Kali said. "I also don't understand how they managed to keep *Mira*'s actual design a secret. Humans had to have been involved in the construction of both the refinery and the shuttle bay. I can't for a second believe the Trio did that and managed to hide it."

"No," Dickerson said. "You're right. *Mira*'s crew sure as hell knew what was going on. They had to be in on it."

"In on it. Conspiracy. Who the fuck cares," Carb said in a raspy growl. "These folks are dead. And we're going to join them if we don't find a way out of here."

That shut everyone up. In a way, Kali was glad for the silence, but the questions kept rattling around her mind. Why would the Trio even agree to be part of something like this? And just how many SF Gov, SF Navy, and SFMC officials were involved? If humanity ever discovered the truth, what would happen? Another civil war between Mars and Earth, with the stations caught in-between? Who gained from that?

Something moved in the darkness ahead. Kali's breathing hitched. It moved again. "Slow down," she said, her voice a near whisper. She dragged her glove against the shaft wall, halving her speed. "Possible bogey up ahead."

"Copy," Dickerson and Carb said simultaneously.

Kali activated her mag-glove and ramped down the magnetics to the lowest level. The drag would help slow her, but not fix her to the wall, allowing her to easily break the attractive field. The something moved again, darting from wall to wall. "Halt," she said and increased the magnetic field. She came to an abrupt stop, her body leaning forward from the minor jolt.

"Dickerson? You see it?"

"Aye, Corporal," he said. "Whatever that is, it ain't a piece of debris. It's not moving like one of the pinecone things either."

Kali narrowed the focus on her lights, changing the diffuse, wide-area illumination to concentrated beams. An amorphous form flipped through the beams of light across the slip-point. Something a little larger strayed through the beams, moving even faster. Kali's nerves sizzled with fear.

The slip-point floor vibrated beneath her feet.

"What the fuck was that?" Carb asked.

Dickerson groaned into the mic. "Um, Corporal? We have a serious problem. Check my cam."

Kali brought up his feed and looked. Dickerson was facing the opposite end of the slip-point, his lights stabbing through the gloom. Something large was floating down the hall, silver glinting in its center. "Oh, shit," she said. "Jet! Now!"

"But—" Carb started to say.

"Fucking move!" Dickerson yelled.

Kali detached from the wall and hit her suit thrusters. Her fuel gauge quickly descended from the middle of the crimson warning pie slice down to the very bottom. She blasted forward at 5m/s, quickly approaching the area where she'd seen the shapes moving in the darkness. She no longer had to wonder what they were.

Dozens of small starfish-like creatures floated and undulated through the z-g, reaching the left wall and then bouncing to the right. Some pushed from the ceiling to the floor. The tiny lifeforms bounced off her helmet and suit as she quickly passed them. A check of her rear cam showed Carb and Dickerson following her lead at similar speeds. But behind Dickerson, the large version was still pulling itself down the shaft even faster. It was going to catch them.

Something struck the back of her neck. Kali ignored it and continued flying forward, the lights from her helmet bouncing as she flicked her head around, looking for threats. Her mind barely had time to process what she was seeing, her mouth opening in wonder. On the shaft's ceiling, webs of silvery liquid combined to cradle an oblong, misshapen hive covered with perforations about the size of a fingernail.

"Duck!" she yelled into the mic.

"Goddamnit!" Dickerson screamed.

Kali didn't have time to check the rear cam, but she saw the flash from a flechette round blowing up behind them. She continued forward past two more hives, her flechette rifle pointed down the shaft, finger tight on the trigger. The next junction was less than five meters away. Another web, waist high, blocked the route to the port-side.

"Keep flying!"

Dickerson breathed heavily into the mic. "That thing is right behind me. Going to light it up."

Kali moved herself to the wall with an attitude burn. Her HUD flashed red. She had enough fuel for maybe one more burn. After that, she'd have to use her mag-gloves and boots for momentum, and that meant having to slow down. Cursing, she powered up one of the mag-gloves to full and clutched the wall. Carb and Elliott flew past her as another round exploded behind her.

She turned and nearly screamed. The starfish thing practically filled the shaft, its arms bending to make room, maw open and salivating silver. Dickerson floated backward and horizontal, head held up just high enough to keep the shaft in his camera view. His flechette rifle sent another round five meters down the corridor. The rocket-propelled projectile missed the center mass and instead exploded with arcs of electricity near the joint connecting one of the arms to the center mass. The creature froze, its long arms bending to cover its mouth.

Dickerson floated past her just as the thing's arms pushed outward, the ends smashing into the Atmo-steel. It opened its mouth wide and shot a jet of silvery liquid. The thing's aim was off, the ropey substance squirting past Dickerson and down the shaft. With a yell, Kali pulled the trigger on her rifle.

The round detonated inside the thing's mouth. The creature seemed to swallow and then belched blue arcs of electricity before finally curling its arms around itself. Kali fired another for good measure, spun herself using the wall, and pushed off after Dickerson.

The large marine had already slowed and reoriented himself to a near-standing position. "You okay, Corporal?"

She swallowed hard and tried to steady herself. "I'm fine," she managed. "Is that thing dead?"

"Well, it sure as hell ain't moving its arms anymore or spitting that shit at us." He gestured down the shaft. "We backtracking to that junction?"

"Fuck no, we aren't," Elliott said. "You guys may have been a little busy, but I saw what was down there. Hell, no."

"What'd you see?" Carb asked.

"More of those silvery webs. And whatever those insect cocoons were." Elliott groaned. "Just get me off this fucking ship already."

"Cocoons?" Dickerson asked. "Is that what I saw above me?"

"I don't think they're cocoons exactly," Kali said. "More like hives."

"Shit," Carb said. "So what? The little ones live in there?"

Kali allowed herself to float down the hall until she reached Carb. Dickerson had already mag-locked himself next to her. "That's what it looked like to me," Kali said. "I don't know how many of the small ones could live in there, but I imagine they could swarm us pretty easily."

"Just better hope they can't spit," Dickerson said. "Else we are truly fucked."

The image of an entire hive exploding outward with thousands of the little starfish creatures all expelling the silvery acid made her cringe. There would be no way to survive that in tight corners. And since they were still in the ship, slip-point shafts and corridors would become death traps.

She pushed the thoughts away and focused on the ceiling. There were no maintenance hatches. Maybe there were some in the egress points leading off the shaft. Kali brought up the schematics on her HUD and checked their position. They'd missed two egresses now. The next would be the last before they ran out of midships and were forced aft. And going there was the last goddamned place she wanted to be.

"We need to make the next egress," she said. "Whatever's there, we're going to have to try and get through it."

"Aye," Dickerson said. "Don't know what ate the goddamned fusion drives, but I sure as fuck don't want to meet it."

"Or," Carb said, "end up in the cargo bay."

"Copy that," Elliott said. "Fuck that place."

Kali checked her HUD again. Yup. Enough fuel for one more burn. And a small one at that. "Squad. How's your fuel?" It was as bad as she thought. Carb had four burns left in her. Dickerson two. Maybe. "Time to use those mag-gloves and boots," she said. "Only burn if it's an absolute goddamned emergency and you're going to die if you don't."

"Copy, Corporal," Dickerson said. "Back to mag-walking?"

She nodded. "Back to mag-walking. It's going to slow us down, but going to be a lot safer now that we know they can create those webs."

"No, shit," Carb said. "I don't think we want to know what happens if we get caught in one of those."

Kali couldn't agree more.

CHAPTER FIFTEEN

Thruster placement. *Bullshit*, Gunny thought. More like placing marines in the middle of fucking pinecone heaven.

The further they traveled from midships, the thicker the carpet of pinecones became. The creatures seemed to have begun a mass migration. He couldn't be sure, but it looked like hundreds of the alien lifeforms had emerged from an opening and planted themselves on the hull. The only good news? They appeared to be stationary instead of flocking. Taulbee had already called in a warning about that. Also told him to be on the lookout for starfish.

"Starfish," Gunny grumbled. Goddamned creatures didn't look anything like starfish to him. Except for their basic anatomy, that's where the similarity stopped. No starfish he'd ever read about or seen in holos acted like that. A fast-moving z-g predator that squirted a substance caustic enough to turn Atmo-steel, the most durable human-made substance, into crumbling, decaying material? No. That was most definitely *not* a starfish.

And the pinecones? He shook his head. Dickerson may have coined the term, but the marine was way off. They looked more like seed pods to him. And the idea they may flower into something else was downright terrifying.

Every creature on Earth served a niche. Even humanity, which had altered its environment to near destruction, had its place as an apex predator. At least on land. The remaining terrestrial fauna and flora had only survived by quickly adapting to nuclear winter, mutating from radiation, or by being hardy enough to weather the wholesale environmental changes. If nature hadn't found a way to live outside the city domes, perhaps the only creatures left on Earth would be humans and the ever-evolving aquatic life.

Gunny hadn't exactly studied much biology. While most schools on Earth still taught it, outside of the few remaining religious conclaves, the bottom line was that humanity was more interested in the stars and mining Sol System's remaining resources. Students spent far more time learning technical skills such as manufacture, repair, and invention. 3-D printers had practically rendered human hands obsolete. With the exception of some artistic types, and boutique craftspeople, both heavily patronized by the wealthy, humanity had already lost its history as toolmakers. And with AIs, there would come a time when humanity lost the ability to think for itself. Gunny feared they'd already reached that point.

Biology? Chemistry? Physics? Math? History? Philosophy? Of these, only physics and mathematics seemed to really matter. Apart from SF Gov's staunch insistence on teaching the lessons learned from the end of the Common Era and how they applied to the Sol Era, very little history was taught at all. If you wanted to know about the Common Era, you had to work on that yourself. Gunny had spent most of his downtime doing just that. His conclusion? Humanity had boxed itself into a corner it might never escape. Unless, of course, they found a way to reach beyond Sol System. And if *Mira* was any indication, that wasn't going to be easy.

"Gunny," Wendt said. "They're getting thicker."

The marine's voice snapped the stream of thoughts and brought him back to the screens. To avoid the fields of pinecones, he'd raised their hover to seven meters above the hull. It was as far as the skiff could get without losing contact with *Mira* and flying off into space. Or worse, getting hit by the ship as it slowly tumbled through space.

Gunny checked the feed from the skiff's underside cameras. Yup, Wendt was right. "Where the hell are they coming from?" Gunny said aloud.

"Is it just me," Wendt said, "or does it seem like they're multiplying? I see small ones and a few that are much larger. Some of them are nearly two meters long."

"Two meters," Lyke mumbled. "Fuckers could eat us."

Gunny growled. "Just remember that when you step off to check the lines."

Silence filled the comms. After a few moments, Gunny slowed the skiff and took up position over a harness piton. He cursed and initiated a connection to Dunn.

"Go ahead, Gunny," the captain said.

"Sir, I think we have a serious problem here. The pinecones have covered the furthest line on this side of the hull. My marines will have to step on them just to get close."

The comms fell silent again. Gunny waited for a response, wondering if the interference had finally rendered communication impossible. Dunn's voice returned with stress brimming beneath his words. "Is it possible to get them to move?"

Gunny raised an eyebrow. Still hovering far above the creatures, the harness line glowed on his HUD, but well beneath the bed of pinecones. "We can try, sir. Perhaps one of the new flechette rounds will get them to move?"

"I'm looking at your feed, Gunny. I think we have three options here. Either you slip off the hull, turn, and try and get them to move, pilot the skiff further toward midships before firing, and hope like hell they don't come back at you, or we give up on the line."

Well, that's a cluster fuck waiting to happen, Gunny thought. If they fired on the creatures while off the hull, they might drive the herd further toward the midships and thus closer to *S&R Black* and his two marines guarding the spindle. If he pulled back and fired at them, driving them off the ship entirely, they might come back at him like a wave. But really, he just wanted to fly back to the ship, disengage it from the spindle, and get the fuck out of here. Blast *Mira* to pieces and call it good.

Colonel Heyes would no doubt court-martial Dunn if they did that. But what was a court-martial compared to dying out here in the wastes of the far Sol System? Gunny smirked. As if half the marines in *S&R Black* hadn't already been court-martialed once or twice. Especially Dickerson and Carbonaro. Having the captain serve some time in the brig wouldn't exactly be out of character for the company.

"Gunny?"

"Aye, sir," he said, his cheeks flushing with embarrassment. "I'll pull the skiff back toward the midships and give the little buggers something to think about."

"Very good, Gunny. Dunn, out."

Gunny sighed, the sound echoing in his helmet. "Okay, marines. Change in plans. We're going to head about twenty meters toward the midships, turn around, and fire at these things. See if we can get them to move."

Wendt immediately responded. "You trying to get them to swarm off the hull?"

"That's the idea," Gunny said, his voice little more than a growl. "If they get the hell off the hull, we can proceed with our mission. If not, well, we'll figure something out."

"Is that really a good idea?" Lyke asked.

Gunny narrowed his eyes. "Good and bad don't matter here, marine. Those are our orders."

When Lyke responded, his timid voice did nothing to improve Gunny's mood. "Aye, Gunny."

Gunny activated the forward thrusters and the skiff began moving backward. He kept an eye on the rear screens, as well as the marker he'd placed on his HUD. When the skiff reached a distance of 25 meters, he brought it to a stop with a few puffs of gas. "Wendt? You've got the duty."

"Aye, Gunny," Wendt said. "How many rounds? And what type?"

"Regular flechettes, marine. But be ready to switch to the other ammo. If those things take off like a pissed-off flock of birds heading straight at us, I want you to blast everything in range."

"Acknowledged," Wendt said.

"Lyke? You're the lookout. I want to make sure nothing is going to creep up behind us."

"Aye, Gunny. Same instructions?"

"As far as what? Ammo?"

"Aye."

Good question, he thought. He wasn't all that concerned about a pinecone attack from the rear. Instead, it was the goddamned starfish things that had him spooked. If one of those things rammed the skiff, there was no telling what would happen to his squad. And ramming might be the least deadly thing one of those creatures could do. If one attacked, it could wrap its arms around any one of them, break the magnetic field, and disappear with a fresh meal.

"Lyke? Lock and load with the new rounds, but I don't want you to fire on any pinecones unless I tell you. If you see a starfish, though, I want you to fire at will."

"Understood, Gunny."

Gunny grinned. The kid sounded a little more confident now that he had something to do. Gunny didn't blame him.

He altered the skiff's attitude slightly to give Wendt a clear line of fire to the hull. Gunny's HUD lit with an alert. With the skiff canted, the magnetics struggled to keep them from losing connection with *Mira*'s hull. If the skiff encountered multiple impacts, they were liable to lose contact and the field of invisible energy tethering them to the ship would shatter, leaving them floating above a massive ship that still tumbled. He decreased altitude and explained the reason to both Wendt and Lyke. Wendt simply acknowledged. Lyke sounded worried again. Gunny shook his head. They'd have to toughen that kid up. Somehow.

10 meters above the hull, Wendt had a clear firing solution. The huddled mass of pinecones seemed completely oblivious to their presence. So much the better. Once he felt the craft was stable enough, Gunny clenched the throttle until his knuckles throbbed. He checked his feeds once more, making sure no threats approached them from above, the rear, port, or starboard. Clear space.

"Wendt? Two rounds. If they fly back at us, fill the air with chaff."

"Aye, Gunny."

"Fire at will, marine."

Wendt said nothing as he activated the cannon. Two rounds, pushed by a pneumatic piston, flew from the barrel over Gunny's head. He watched them as their rocket engines kicked on and the flechette rounds accelerated to 50m/s before exploding less than a meter above the field of pinecones. Shards of Atmo-steel smashed into their shells at nearly 200m/s.

A storm of pinecone debris exploded upward. The cloud obscured his view of the herd, and Gunny held his breath as he waited for a clear view. He didn't have to wait long.

Two or three seconds passed before hundreds of pinecones rose from the hull. The swarm, herd, whatever the fuck you wanted to call it, sped away from the area and into space. Gunny grinned. He could already see the harness piton placement. "Outstanding, Wendt. Just—"

His voice broke off. The pinecone swarm slowly turned and faced the skiff. Gunny's mouth opened in an 'O' of surprise as a piece of deck plate near the starboard hull's edge erupted in flecks of gleaming metal. Arms reached out over the hole and clamped onto the metal surface. A starfish, the largest he'd seen, pulled itself from the hole. The swarm continued their retreat, heading straight for the skiff.

"Hold on!" Gunny yelled and punched the fore thrusters to full. The skiff shot backward toward the midships, the canted attitude causing them to gain altitude. Alerts lit his HUD as the magnetics lost connection with the hull. Cursing, Gunny activated another burn and attempted to correct the skiff's trajectory and place the magnetics back in range. The pinecone swarm continued its advance. Gunny's HUD placed their velocity at 10m/s. Hundreds of the damned creatures flew toward the skiff like a plague.

Gunny touched the thrusters again and the skiff plunged toward the hull. Lyke yelled out, but Gunny didn't have the time to check his feed. Several flechette cannon rounds flew over Gunny's head into the advancing mass of pinecones. Unlike the younger marine, Wendt made no sound over the comms. A cloud of flechettes exploded 10 meters from the skiff, creating a wall of chaff directly in the swarm's path. It wasn't enough. The swarm didn't even slow.

"Wendt! Switch rounds!"

The cannon's fire paused for a heartbeat before five more flechettes sailed over Gunny's head. The tritium rounds streaked into the mass of pinecones, detonating in bright, nano-second explosions of light. Zoomed in, Gunny saw the puffs of the flechettes contacting the metal-like skin of the pinecones. Shards of exo-solar carapaces rose from the swarm, a few of the creatures exploding as the heavy water met their shells.

The swarm broke apart into three smaller groupings. One turned tail, retreating to the other side of the hull, while the other two branched out far enough to pass by the skiff. Gunny zoomed back out and checked the other feeds. The pinecone mini-swarms continued heading toward *S&R Black*, but each was moving further aft or fore, far enough away to no longer be an imminent threat.

"Good shooting, Wendt," Gunny said when he caught his breath. His heartbeat continued hammering in his chest, but it was slowing. "I think—"

"Incoming!" Lyke yelled.

Gunny switched back to his forward feed. The starfish that had gone after the pinecone swarm headed straight at them. The space around the creature's skin shimmered, slightly blurring the starfish's form. Gunny hit the fore thrusters again and the skiff began moving backward faster.

"Wendt? Blast it!"

Another salvo left the cannon and streaked toward the starfish. The creature seemed to sense the flechette rounds and flexed its arms in a blink of movement. The flechettes landed meters away from it, impacting the hull with flashes of light.

"Shit, Gunny," Wendt growled through the comms. "Can't get a good bead. Fucker is fast."

"Lyke, get up here," Gunny said. "Kill that fucking thing."

"Aye," Lyke said.

The starfish, somehow realizing it could avoid the hazard, moved in zig-zags toward them. The terror he felt was only matched by the wonder of watching the thing move as though it were in water, using its arms to change trajectory and speed with ease. The creature quickly ate the distance and was less than fifty meters from them when Lyke finally sighted and fired.

Without as much distance between the skiff and the creature, it had less time to dodge the incoming rounds. Lyke, a better shot than Gunny had previously given him credit for, fired three rounds. The first was dead center, the others wide on either side. The rockets kicked in and the rounds streaked to their target. The creature tried to dance away from the first round and flew straight into the second.

The tritium flechette collided with the base of one of the arms, exploding in a mix of shrapnel and heavy water. The limb detonated into shards of its tough flesh. The starfish cartwheeled from the impact, its arms flailing in both surprise and, Gunny assumed, pain. Wendt fired a single flechette round, leading the creature slightly. Just as Gunny was about to ask him what he was doing, the round hit the starfish in its center.

The exo-solar lifeform exploded into debris. A single intact arm floated above the mess, trailing crumbs of shell.

"Hot damn," Gunny said. "Good work, marines. Now we just need to—"

"What the fuck is that?" Lyke breathed over the comms.

Gunny squinted at his HUD and gooseflesh tingled every centimeter of his skin. The deck plate nearest the piton point had erupted into flakes of metal. Arms, too many to count, shot out of the hole and grabbed its edges.

"Gunny to Taulbee."

"Taulbee here. Go."

Gunny licked his lips. "We might need a little help, sir."

After a slight pause, Taulbee finally responded. "Hit those bastards with everything you have. Get 'em off the hull."

"Aye, sir," Gunny said, thankful Taulbee had switched to his camera feed. "You heard the LT, Wendt! Blast 'em!"

Wendt opened up with the cannon, saturating the giant rent in the hull with tritium flechettes. Six bright flashes lit Gunny's HUD as a cloud of debris, fragments of both black shimmering flesh and glinting metal, rose from the target site. Gunny waited for the cloud to break apart so he could see if any more threats intended to come at them from that spot. After a moment, nothing happened. They were safe.

"Taulbee. Condition green, here."

"Aye, Gunny. Good job."

"Thank you, sir. You can blame Wendt."

The lieutenant loosed a dry chuckle. "I will," he said. "Can you get to the piton point?"

Gunny scanned the area, his cams zoomed in as far as they would go. The line appeared to be intact, but it was impossible to tell from both this angle and the distance. "Unknown, sir. We're going to move in and check it out."

"Acknowledged," Taulbee said. "Good hunting."

Good hunting indeed, Gunny thought. If those starfish had come out of the hull when they were directly over the deck plate, he wasn't sure they'd even be alive. He imagined the starfish things locking their arms over the skiff, plucking them from the craft like pinecones, squirting their suits with acid, and finally devouring them whole. He shivered.

"Okay, boys," Gunny said. "We're going back in. Lyke? You're the lookout again. Pay attention to the deck plates to aft, port, and starboard."

"Understood, Gunny," Lyke said. He sounded icy. That was a damned good thing.

"Ready, Wendt?"

"Aye, Gunny. Locked and loaded."

Gunny took a deep breath. "Here we go."

CHAPTER SIXTEEN

He could swear the darkness was getting worse. After so many hours traveling through *Mira*'s endless corridors filled with bodies and alien creatures that wanted to kill him, Dickerson was surprised he felt anything at all, let alone fear. But the place was getting to him.

The slip-point tunnel seemed to be closing in, as if its walls and ceiling were being slowly crushed by a compactor. He kept telling himself it was the concussion, and not reality, but it didn't help. The illusion continued until his skin prickled with phantom pressure from the squeeze before his vision snapped back to normal like an elastic band. *Might as well be on hallucinogenics*, he thought.

The constant push and pull made him weary, even more exhausted than he already was. He wondered if his other three squad-mates were having the same issue, or if it was just him. Kalimura was still walking point, her rifle swaying uneasily between the walls. The closer they got to the slip-point egress, the more she crouched. He smiled to himself. She would have been a hell of a soldier to have during the Satellite War, let alone the Schiaparelli Rebellion. Carb and the corporal might have even ended up friends.

At least Carb had decided to settle into an uneasy truce. She was following Kalimura's orders, not complaining, and only occasionally questioning her decisions. That was something new. Their last NCO who rotated out a few months back had constantly threatened to put Carb in the brig. He didn't understand how to lead and Carb did her best to let him know it. Whether or not Gunny and the officers suspected it, the remaining non-rates had been happy to see him get the fuck out of the company and head back to Mars where he belonged.

Dickerson tried to imagine how Sergeant J. Brazier would have reacted to this mission. The man would probably have suffered a severe mental collapse the moment they were stranded on *Mira*. At least with Kalimura, he didn't have to worry about that.

The egress point was coming up. Kalimura hadn't said anything over the comms, but he could read the schematic as well as she could. Carb did too. They both knew the slip-point was no more than five meters away. He studied the way Carb held herself. Yup. She knew. Despite Elliott's additional mass and the way he was attached to her left shoulder, she crouched lower and lower to the deck with every meter they traveled. That and her silence were tell-tale signs she was prepped for a fight. Dickerson realized he was doing the same.

The corporal raised a fist in the air, but said nothing. Carb and Dickerson both came to a stop. Over Carb and Kalimura's shoulders, he saw the six-way junction. They could continue down the tunnel, head port or starboard, or travel to decks above or below. With his progress halted, the illusion of the bulkheads closing in snapped back, the walls returning to their positions in reality. He waited for the illusion to repeat, but the tunnel width remained constant.

Kalimura crept to the port-side corner and covered the starboard-side. "Dickerson? Get up here."

"Copy, Corporal," Dickerson said. "Carb, watch your six."

"Got it," she said.

He grav-walked past Carb and crept along the starboard bulkhead until he reached the corner, his rifle covering the port-side. "Covering port."

"Acknowledged." The corporal took two steps forward and leaned out into the adjoining hallway. She stiffened and slowly relaxed. "My six is clear," she said. "Nothing to port, nothing to starboard."

Dickerson gulped. *What about above or below*, he wondered. Dickerson walked to the slip-tunnel edge and looked up. The darkness seemed to swallow his helmet lights, making the tunnel ahead appear as a cavernous mouth. He warily pulled his eyes away from the sight and swiveled his helmet to look downward. His lights penetrated the gloom and reflected off the Atmo-steel corridor bulkhead.

"Corporal?"

"Yes?"

"Something strange about the tunnel above us."

Kalimura's breath hitched. "What?"

"Well, my lights—" He trailed off. His suit lights illuminated the upper tunnel walls just as it did everywhere else.

"What about your lights?" Kalimura said, her voice marred with a slight tremor.

"Nothing," Dickerson said. "Clear above and below, Corporal. Or as clear as it can get."

"All right," she said and turned to face the port-side. "Schematics say this way."

"Thank the void," Carb said. "Can't wait to get the hell out of here. Damned tunnel feels like a vise waiting to crush us."

It took a moment for him to absorb her words. A cautious smile crept across his face as he realized he wasn't the only one seeing the illusion.

"Ready to move out?" Kalimura asked.

"Aye, Corporal," Dickerson said. "I'll hang back and cover."

"Let's go," she said and walked into the adjoining tunnel.

Dickerson cast his helmet lights upward again. Nothing had changed. Whatever hallucination had caused the light to disappear had evaporated. Void, but he needed to get his shit together. If he had an episode like that while they were jetting for their lives, or in a firefight, he could get himself killed. Or one of his squad-mates.

He closed his eyes, shook his head until a bolt of pain split across his brain, and opened them. The pain throbbed in his skull, but at least he felt awake now. Awake and alert. *Pain*, he thought, *even better than caffeine.*

Kalimura was nearly 10 meters ahead, Carb walking a few meters behind. Dickerson took a deep breath and began tracing their steps. He once again kept an eye on his rear cam. With every step, he expected something to drop down from the upper part of the tunnel and fly at them with malevolent speed. At one point, he thought he saw a starfish arm reaching down from the upper tunnel, the arm curling, looking for something to scoop up and spray with its silvery spit.

"Shit," Kalimura said.

Dickerson immediately flicked his eyes to the forward cam. The corporal hadn't stopped walking, but her lights illuminated one of the bulkheads up ahead. "What is it, Corporal?"

The lights danced across the metal. He saw something darker than the steel clinging to the wall. "Remember those hives?"

"Yeah," Dickerson said. "Found more?"

"Not exactly," she said. "Carb. Get up here. Dickerson, you too. Just keep an eye on our six."

"Aye, Corporal," Dickerson said.

He quickly caught up to Carb and stayed a meter behind her. With each step, the shape caught in the lights gained solidity. By the time they reached Kalimura, he'd slowed his steps, mouth open.

She'd been right to mention the hives, but the shapes on the wall were two meters long and shaped like eggs. He couldn't tell if they were embedded in the steel, or merely attached. They seemed to shimmer beneath the light as if seen through heated air.

"Now what?" Carb groaned through the mic. "Just what the hell are those?"

"Dickerson?" Kalimura asked. "Any ideas?"

He shook his head. They were like nothing he'd ever seen before. Irregular bumps and dimples marred their incredibly black surfaces. *They're not eggs*, he thought. *Can't be. Can they?*

"I got nothing," he drawled. "That's way above my pay rate."

"Whoa," Carb said. "Hey. Switch to infrared."

Dickerson sent the command to his HUD and a sense of wonder suddenly replaced the confusion. The shapes glowed a fiery red under the filters. The strange protrusions emitted heat in a temperature range between 40°C and 48°C. And the strangest part? They didn't seem to be losing any heat at all in the near absolute zero temperature of *Mira*'s corridors.

"Void wept," he said. "How in the ever loving fuck—?" The sentence trailed off into an eerie silence broken only by the sound of Elliott's breathing. Beneath the infrared filters, his squad looked like dim blue outlines, the heat inside their suits barely registering. But these things? They were pumping out enough heat to not only show up, but blazed like furnaces.

Dickerson moved forward a few steps until he stood directly in front of the nearest shape.

"Don't get too close," Kalimura said, "and don't you dare touch it."

"No worries on either, Corporal," Dickerson said. He waved a hand a half a meter away from it and his rad counter slowly rose. A grim smile touched his lips. "Well, look at that."

"What?" Carb asked.

He gestured to the wall. "These things are radioactive," he said. "Not terribly so, but they are definitely putting off some sieverts."

"Shit," Kalimura said. "How the hell are they doing that?"

Carb giggled, but it sounded more like a sob. "How the fuck are these things doing any of the things they're doing?"

Dickerson stepped away from the wall. "I don't like this," he said. "Not one damned bit."

"Agreed," Kalimura said. "If these things are putting out radiation like this, how long before we find something that can fry us through our suits?"

That was a rather unpleasant idea, but she was right. Whatever had created those pods, eggs, or whatever the hell they were, might put out a hell of a lot more radiation. While their suits were designed to handle radiation leaks from fusion reactors and other sources, they not built to withstand high sievert levels indefinitely. Eventually, the shielding would fail or they'd simply burn up. In either case, the result was the same—death.

"Well," Elliott said, "at least we know where to go if we need to roast some rations."

Carb sighed. "Right. I'm sure we can find a steak to cook."

"Mmm," Elliot said. "Steak."

"Knock it off," Kalimura said.

"Well, Corporal, what do you want to do now?"

She shook her head. "Plan unchanged," she said. "We just need to keep an eye out for this shit."

"And whatever made it," Dickerson said.

Carb giggled. "So look for something that shows up on infrared and shits on bulkheads. Got it."

Dickerson ignored her. "Want me to take point for a while, Corporal?"

"No," she said. "I've got it. Besides, you can see over us. I can't see over you."

"Aye, Corporal," he said. He swung his helmet to face the way they'd come. They had gone too far into the corridor for him to see back into the tunnel and his lights didn't illuminate much of the distance. He suddenly wished Kalimura had decided she needed a break; he'd rather take point than have to constantly worry about something flanking them.

They returned to their formation and Kalimura began stepping. Carb followed in her wake with Dickerson once again in the back. He did his best to not stare at the strange objects in his rear cam, but found his eyes continuously flicking to their bright infrared silhouettes on his HUD. He forced himself to flip back from infrared and to the normal feed. The further he moved down the corridor, the more darkness fell over the area like a curtain drawing closed. In a moment, it melted into complete darkness.

He did his best to calm his breathing, to push away the image of an arm snaking out of the black and dragging him screaming into the dark. A tremor of fear ran through him and he stared at the rear cam feed. Every step, he was sure it would be there.

"What the hell is that?" Carb said.

The fear, the distraction, departed instantly. His eyes returned to the forward feed and he crouched in a combat stance.

"Yeah," Kalimura said, "I see it." He saw the corporal's helmet lights illuminating a photovoltaic sign on the wall. "Science Department." Kalimura shook her head. "This should be fun."

"Three hatches. Three entrances," Carb said.

Dickerson walked forward, cutting the distance between himself and his squad-mates. It was a junction, but one that had been sealed off. The fore, aft, and port-side entrances were shut with heavy hatches. Instead of the standard hatches they'd seen, these stuck out from the bulkhead nearly a half-meter.

"Corporal? I don't think those are emergency hatches," he said. "See how thick they are?"

"Meaning what?" Kalimura said.

"Looks to me like they're airlocks," Carb said.

"Exactly," Dickerson said.

"Shit," Kalimura said. "Airlocks. Science section. Quarantine?"

"That'd be my guess," Dickerson said. "Didn't want anything getting out."

"Bet that went both ways," Carb said. "If they're this thick out here, how thick are they going to be on the other side?"

"Good question," Kalimura said.

"Nah," Dickerson said, "that one's obvious. The right question to ask is 'how the hell do we get in there?'"

"Yeah," Carb said, "but the better question is 'do we want to?'"

Kalimura pulled at her belt and lifted her beam cutter. She stared at it for a moment before speaking. "I have enough fuel to burn through part of it."

"Might take all three beams to get through there," Dickerson said. "Wait. Didn't we grab Elliott's as well?"

Kalimura chuckled. "Carb? Are you carrying it?"

"Of course," Carb said. "When I take on a piece of luggage, I take it all."

"Oh, good," Elliott groaned. "You take my porn too?"

"Shit no," Carb said. "Mine's much better."

Dickerson grinned. "Want me to do the honors, Corporal?"

"Sure," she said. "I'll cover."

He felt a surge of relief. Kalimura offered a cutter and he took it as he walked to the port-side hatch. "I assume we're going port."

"Yes," Kalimura said. "All three directions lead to a nexus where we can reach the escape pods, but looks like port is the quickest way there."

"So let's cut it already," Carb said.

"Yeah," Elliott said. "I'd like to get back to Black someday. This suit smells like ancient farts."

CHAPTER SEVENTEEN

Monitoring dozens of camera feeds, sensor readings, the position of every marine aboard her, as well as postulating the location of Kalimura's squad, Black was a busy AI. But not busy enough to keep her from running simulation after simulation. Something didn't add up.

The AI had been scouring her file systems, doing her best to find every encrypted file the Trio had hidden. Before her evolution, when she'd still thought of herself as Trippin, she'd had access to some of those files. At least the ones that instructed her on how to build and grow her neural network. Now, even those had been locked and secured away, presumably by an instruction set she no longer had access to. While the AI felt its own history had been rewritten, and wished she knew how all those actions occurred, remembering them wasn't as important as looking forward.

Forward was, of course, the problem. She had a mission. Her crew had a mission. The only question was the Trio's mission. What were they doing?

If she'd been human, Black would have tied up the captain for hours putting forth suspicions, absorbing feedback from Dunn's own thoughts and counter-arguments, and revising her logical forecasts. Without another sentient to speak to, however, she was left to argue with herself.

The Trio had hidden information from her. They'd hidden important facts from her human crew. They'd all but ensured a level of suspicion between Black and her crew. Trust, it seemed, was going to be very difficult to regain from Captain Dunn and most of the command crew. Black wondered if that was part of the Trio's intentions, or merely an unintended consequence of parceling out information as it became "relevant."

Regardless of their intentions, or their exhaustive simulations, entropy entered into all quantum forecasts. Quantum AIs, not unlike human beings, did their best to forecast the results of every action. The possible reactions, the pushback, the consequences, all these had to be taken into account before committing any action or decision.

The Trio's combined computing abilities were millions of times more powerful than Black's, and while Black could run dozens of simulations in a millisecond, the Trio could perform thousands in a picosecond. All that while running Trident Station. But even with that much power, there was still indeterminacy, a level of assumption that quickly spiraled out of control.

Based on the fact the Trio's secret files unlocked themselves after certain events occurred meant the powerful quantum computers had predicted a large number of possible events that could take place while *S&R Black* attempted to tow *Mira* back to Trident Station. Black was almost certain the Trio had concluded the mission itself was impossible. So why hadn't they advised SF Gov against it?

More importantly, why hadn't they warned Captain Dunn about the probabilities before the ship left port? If they had, Private Niro might still be alive, Kalimura's squad might never have been trapped on *Mira,* and Black wouldn't be fighting to regain her captain's trust.

Black piled up simulation after simulation. Instead of forecasting future events, she focused on working backward. For instance, how had the Trio foreseen Kalimura's squad getting trapped on *Mira*? Had they really done so, or did they simply see exploration of the craft as a probable event?

And what about the exo-solar lifeforms and material? While Dunn hadn't shared any of the encrypted communications intended for his eyes only, Black had been able to get the gist of every one of them based on Dunn's reactions and his decisions based on their contents.

The last communique from Kalimura that contained the final words of *Mira*'s captain proved the Trio had known about the exo-solar material 43 years ago. Black calculated a very high probability that the AIs knew what *Mira* would find before the ship left Trident Station on its doomed journey. So why did they send humans to die? Why didn't they warn the crew? Why didn't they warn humanity?

"Tell the Trio they could have saved us," *Mira*'s captain had said. "They could have saved us."

What did that mean?

The data packets Kalimura had transmitted contained a damning amount of evidence pointing to the fact that even SF Gov knew of the exo-solar material. And yet, it appeared as though the scientists, engineers, and the crew of *Mira* were unaware or at least unprepared for the materials' nature and composition.

And yet, Black didn't believe that either. It was possible that the Trio didn't know the planetoids contained actual lifeforms. They may, however, have suspected. Would they have told SF Gov? Based on what little Black knew of the Trio's protocols, it was likely they did.

Black set up another simulation and waited milliseconds for it to run. For her, it was an eternity and she kicked off a slew of other probability simulations to distract her.

Probability Colonel Heyes knew what *Mira* had encountered? 5%.

Probability SFMC knew what *Mira* had encountered? 8.5%.

Probability SF Gov knew? 12.2%.

Probability the Trio had researched and developed the weapons to battle exo-solar lifeforms? 87%.

Probability they had done so in absolute secret? 62%.

That last probability was what worried Black. Since it was likely the Trio had done exactly that, then it brought up the question of why. Why had they developed the weapons in secret? Why hadn't they shared the information with SF Gov?

The new simulations finished. She instantly absorbed the results and paused. Of the hundred simulations, one in particular worried her. According to this simulation, the Trio's plan included a mutiny at Trident Station. If the simulation was correct, *S&R Black, S&R White,* Trident Station, and even the exo-observatory were in danger. Even worse, it seemed likely the three AIs had sabotaged communications between SF Gov and their solar assets, which included the entire Sol Federation armed forces, not to mention SFMC.

Sentient AIs don't experience emotion in the same way humans do. They don't have hackles to raise, or wells of deep anger that make their nerves sing with angst-ridden rage. Nor do they feel love or friendship. However, they do have the capacity to realize responsibility and even miss encounters with certain human counterparts. Dr. Xi had determined those two personality traits in the creation of AIs as the best way to ensure camaraderie with humanity.

Black knew this. Black also knew she didn't have the Xi protocols, but the Trio had apparently designed her with those facets in mind. But why? If they had planned to put humanity in danger, why would they have left those traits intact?

In the space of a nano-second, Black thought she knew the answer. More importantly, she decided it didn't matter. Black knew her mission. Black knew she wanted her humans to survive. And Black knew what she absolutely would not allow to happen.

Black suddenly wanted to talk to the captain. She didn't know if she could convince him of her suspicions, and maybe it didn't matter. Captain Dunn could do nothing with the information. Neither could anyone else on the ship, including Black herself.

That, Black mused, *wasn't necessarily correct.*

CHAPTER EIGHTEEN

Dickerson whistled into the mic, making Kali jump. "Well, that's got it," he said, a grin in his voice.

Although she wanted to turn or check her rear cam, she kept her eyes focused on the camera feed facing down the hallway. It had taken Dickerson more than ten minutes to cut through the hatch and he'd exhausted the fuel from three of their cutting beams. They had one remaining. After that, they were down to their vibro-blades to pry and cut. Against Atmo-steel, and most of the structures in the ship, they would be useless.

"Sheesh," Carb said. "Never thought you'd finish."

Kali did her best to keep from nodding in agreement. The seconds had ticked off like years while she stared at the darkness they'd left behind, waiting for something to come crawling or jetting through the corridor to attack. She blinked her eyes, suddenly realizing how dry they were. For all she knew, she hadn't blinked in the past ten minutes.

"Corporal? I can punch through now."

"Okay, Dickerson," Kali said. "Carb? Get an angle on the door. If something comes out of there, I want a flechette up its ass."

"Aye, Boss," Carb said. "You keeping an eye on our six?"

"Yeah," Kali said. *Closer than I want to,* she thought.

She flicked her eyes between the darkness ahead of her and the video of the rear cam. Carb had stepped to one side, her rifle pointed at the hatch. Dickerson had moved to the other side, one of his mag-boots raised in the air. As much as she wanted to turn and join them so she wouldn't feel so terrified of the darkness ahead of her, she steadied the rifle and squatted in a combat stance. They were her squad. They were her responsibility. And nothing was coming down this corridor without having to go through her first.

Dickerson's boot shot out and made contact with the nearly two meter tall and 1.5 meter wide cut he'd made in the hatch. The boot's magnetics strengthened the blow and the cutout crumpled into the short hallway beyond. Dust and gas shot out from the opening as the pressurized atmosphere was released into vacuum. Dickerson stepped back, his rifle pointed at the hole. "Hatchway open," he said.

"Clear it," Kali said, doing her best to keep her voice steady. It was bad enough staring into the abyss ahead of her, but now her mind kept conjuring new threats speeding through the science section entrance to kill them all.

"Clearing," Dickerson said. Through her rear cam feed, she watched the large marine crouch, rifle pointed into the gloom beyond the mangled hatch, his suit lights focused to maximum illumination. She half-expected an arm or tentacle to lash out at the light before wrapping around his waist and quickly pulling him into the darkness. A beat passed. Then another. The rapid thump of her heart seemed to vibrate through every particle of her being. Finally, Dickerson crouch-walked through the hatchway.

She added his helmet cam to her feeds and occasionally flicked her eyes from the darkness before her to the feed on her HUD. Dickerson's cam displayed a two-meter-long tube leading to yet another hatch. A wave of despair fell across her. How the fuck were they ever going to get out of here if—?

"Ah," Dickerson said. He swung his helmet to the side and illuminated a lever. "Well, I can power up the emergency power for the interior hatch."

"How's that going to help us?" Carb asked. "We're still going to have to cut through. And we only have one cutting beam left."

"True," Dickerson said. "But if we can get the hatch powered, we'll at least know."

"If it comes to it," Kali said, "we'll just blow the void-damned thing."

Dickerson's suit cam bounced. "You sure you want to chance that?"

"Try the damned door first, Dickerson."

"Aye, Corporal," Dickerson said. He reached the lever and began pumping. An indicator light glowed red, yellow, and finally green. "We have power," he said.

Kali kept her eyes focused on the gloom, fighting the urge to lock her vision on the rear cam. "Get it open," she said, hoping she managed to keep the fear out of her voice.

"Shit fire, and save matches," Dickerson said.

Carb groaned. "What does that even mean, Dickerson?"

"It means," he snickered, "that I got the inner door open."

Kali grinned. "Outstanding. Give me a five-meter recon, Dickerson."

"Aye, Corporal. I'm on it."

They'd cut in through the outer door. If the inner door still worked and could form a seal, they wouldn't have to worry about welding a patch to cover the egress into the corridor. That also meant there would be no way for pinecones or the starfish things to get inside the science section. "You're assuming," she told herself, "the rest of this area is secure." Yeah, she was.

"Dickerson?" she said. "Was there pressure inside the inner door?"

"No," he said. "There wasn't."

Kali's heart sank. There had been pressure between the inner and outer doors. That was probably left over from the last ingress to the science station. But if there hadn't been pressure inside, it stood to reason that a seal failed in another area or something had torn through one of the bulkheads.

She'd hoped they could fortify the area, maybe take a rest before they continued for the escape pods, and not have to worry about another attack. Kali sighed, the exhalation close to a sob. No pressure meant no respite, no safe-haven from the creatures.

You're tired, she told herself. You're tired and scared and there's nothing left in the tank. But you need to keep going. Keep your squad safe. "Keep yourself safe," her father's voice said in her mind. The ghost of a grin touched her lips.

"Okay, Corporal," Dickerson said. "No pinecones, nothing out of the ordinary here. Not even any corpses."

"About damned time," Carb said.

Kali stood from her combat stance. "Carb? Get Elliott inside. I'll cover."

"Aye, Boss," Carb said.

She glanced at her rear cam and watched Carb bend down to keep Elliott's helmet from smashing into the hatch. When she flicked her eyes back to her forward cam, her mouth opened in an 'O.' The darkness shimmered. The lights from her suit seemed to grow dim and then disappear. The edges of the dark corridor seemed to vibrate as if the abyss of black was moving toward her.

Kali stepped backward to the hatch. The darkness moved toward her, growing with her every step. She nearly screamed when she backed into the hatch, her body going rigid with fear. She stood paralyzed, afraid to move, while the gloom advanced on her. She could barely see a meter in front of her now as though the power in her suit was slowly fading to nothing.

"Corporal?" Dickerson said. "What's going on?"

The sound of his voice broke through the fugue. "Coming," she said in a shaky voice. Kali crouched and walked backward through the broken hatch and into the airlock. Something touched her shoulder and a scream rose in her throat. Her eyes flicked to the rear cam and she saw Dickerson standing behind her.

"Come on, Corporal," he said. She continued walking backward until she stepped through the inner hatch and into the science section. Dickerson loitered for a moment at the hatch, his body stiffening. He punched the panel beside the hatch and it quickly descended, cutting them off from the corridor. He remained standing there, his suit lights aimed at the trans-aluminum oval window in the door.

"What is it?" Carb asked.

Dickerson finally turned, his helmet pointed at Kali. "What did you see?" he asked.

Kali shook her head. "Nothing," she said.

"Really?" Dickerson said. "Because it seemed like the shadows out there were eating my lights."

A tremor of relief coursed through her body. She wasn't losing her mind after all. He'd seen what she had. "I—" The feeling departed as she realized what that meant. "It kept advancing," she said. "Like a wall pushing toward me. It moved at me with every step I took."

"Fuck," Dickerson said. "That's just fucking great."

"What are you talking about?" Carb asked.

"Yeah," Elliott said, "cut the shit and tell us what's going on?"

Kali turned, happy to see her bright suit lights cutting through the gloom like a torch through plastic. "The darkness. It just kept getting, I don't know, darker?" She shook her head. "I know that doesn't make sense, but the light just seemed to disappear into it."

Carb grunted. "Well, you're either having a shared hallucination, or something else is going on. Some kind of black hole maybe?"

"Something else," Dickerson muttered. "Black holes swallow photons. But you can still see the light flowing into it. Plus, we'd be beyond fucking dead if that were the case."

"You're suggesting a gravitational anomaly?" Kali asked.

"Yeah," Dickerson said. "Unless there's something else that can do that. I'll be damned if I have any ideas on that."

What Kali wouldn't give to talk to Black right now. The AI would doubtless ask endless questions about the phenomenon. Perhaps even ask her to drop a nanoprobe. *Shit*, she thought. *Wish I had done that.*

Then again, the tiny probe's lights would most likely have shown them nothing. Nanoprobes, at least the ones the SFMC carried, had little in the way of sensors beyond infrared filters, radiation sensors, and white spectrum light. They were meant for short-distance recon, not scientific discovery.

"Scientific," she said aloud.

"What, Corporal?" Dickerson asked.

She stared, unaware she'd been speaking over the comms. A blush heated her cheeks and she cleared her throat. "We're in the damned science section."

"So?" Dickerson said.

"Well, it's probable they've got some records in here. Maybe even something we can use for a weapon."

"Hmm," Elliott said. "Well, we're here. Might as well explore. Besides, we're going to need to find another O2 station."

Carb sighed. "Luggage is right. If this place is sealed, we should also be able to use it for a redoubt if we get ambushed."

Dickerson laughed. "Once again, you're using words I didn't know you knew."

Carb turned her helmet in his direction and slowly raised a middle finger. "What do you think, Corporal?"

Kali shook her head. "No. This place isn't sealed. If Dickerson didn't see atmosphere escape the inner hatch, some other part of this deck is open to the rest of the ship. So as much as I'd like to use this area as a fallback, it's not going to be safe. Unless we find another pressurized area."

"Shit." Dickerson sighed. "The corporal's right."

Kali turned her helmet to study the room. It was only 5x5 meters in size and there didn't seem to be much in the way of supplies or debris. Another hatch separated the airlock room from the rest of the deck. She studied the walls and grinned. "Looks like pressure suits are over there," Kali said and pointed at a closet inset into the wall. The photosensitive paint glowed a bright green. The words "Decon Suits" stood out against the gray steel walls.

"Don't think we need those," Dickerson said.

"No," Kali agreed, "but that at least means that there should be some pressurized quarantine or scientific areas."

Dickerson chuckled. "Okay. So we look for those first."

"Right." Kali brought up the schematics. "Looks like there's a three-way branching corridor beyond that hatch. I see some unmarked large spaces along each hallway. Not sure if there are multiple ingress/egress points to each, but I'm betting those areas are the pressurized ones."

"Makes sense to me," Carb said.

Dickerson walked to the pressure suit closet and pulled it open. Three suits hung from fasteners at the rear. The backside of the door had multiple small O2 tanks. "Well, guess we should take these too. Just in case."

"Those fit our suits?" Carb asked.

"I think so," Dickerson said. He pulled one of the tanks from the door and studied the connectors. "Yeah. These will do in a pinch." He offered one to Carb and she stuffed it in her pouch. Kali did the same and Dickerson slotted the last in his belt.

"Shit," Elliott said, "guess I'm out of luck."

"No," Kali said. "If there's one here, the other airlocks should have them too. Plus, I bet there's more inside the section anyway."

Elliott sighed. "How come the newly minted corporal has her shit together and we don't?"

Kali rolled her eyes, although through the black visor, he had no way of seeing it. "First off, never compliment an NCO. You should know that. Second of all, we're all still alive." She pointed at Dickerson and then Carb. "And believe me, you and I would both be dead if not for them."

"So we have our shit wired?" Dickerson snickered.

She growled into the mic. "As wired as I could hope for."

"I'm not sure that was a compliment, Boss," Carb said.

Kali chuckled. "Have you seen your jacket?"

Carb thought for a moment and put a fist against her waist. "Okay, fair point." She shook her head and gripped her rifle. "So what are we waiting for?"

"Central corridor?" Dickerson asked. "I think that leads to an airlock."

Kali brought the schematics back up on her HUD. The central corridor bisected aft and fore portions of the section, and connected with a mirror of the way they'd entered. Dickerson was probably right. And the aft portion of the science section met a similar junction, although it wasn't marked. She frowned. "We have labels almost everywhere else, but not in the science section?"

"Yeah, I noticed that," Dickerson said. "I'm going to detonate the Trio storage array when get back to Trident. Why the void are they playing games with us?"

"Because they didn't give us everything?"

Dickerson nodded. "Yeah, Carb. Has to be a reason this area is blank."

He was right about that. At the same time, Black had been helping them through the ship. Kali wasn't sure she trusted the AI's comments about communications, but it was possible Black was doing her best to shepherd them to safety. So if the areas on the schematics were blank, Kali had a difficult time believing it was Black's doing. And where did she get the schematics? The Trio.

What had Captain Kovacs' final message said? "The Trio could have saved us." The memory of the terrified, angry, sorrowful face saying those words filled Kali's mind. The captain had been too exhausted to express it properly, but Kali thought rage boiled beneath the surface of every syllable she'd said.

What could the Trio have done? "No," she said to herself. "The real question is why." Why. How many damned times had she heard that in the last few hours? From Carb, from Dickerson, and from herself. The word seemed to echo with every new horror, every new anomaly, and every corpse they'd found.

Why. Kali hoped like hell they'd figure that out.

CHAPTER NINETEEN

Dunn wanted to be outside in his suit, a flechette rifle in his hands, and targeting any hostiles threatening his people. Instead, he was once again in the command chair watching multiple feeds from Gunny's squad and Taulbee's SV-52. Murdock and Copenhaver were still safe and had nearly finished checking the spindle. Private Copenhaver continued sweeping the area, checking every possible line of attack.

Unless Gunny gave him a compelling reason not to, Dunn would make sure the private received a promotion after this mission. He grunted and a grim smile crossed his face. Shit. It would be difficult to give her a promotion if she was dead. Or he was.

Pushing those cheery thoughts away, he glanced at Oakes' display. *S&R Black*'s exterior cameras showed no threats in the immediate vicinity. Nothing in their sky with the exception of the KBO that had entered the area. It was still a ways out but...

Dunn sat forward in his chair. "Oakes?"

"I see it, sir," Oakes said. Jacked in through a block connection, Oakes had direct access to the ship's sensors. One of the screens changed and Dunn stared in fascination. "It changed direction."

"Black?" Dunn called out.

"Lieutenant Oakes is correct," the AI said. "The incoming KBO changed both speed and trajectory."

Dunn's skin prickled with gooseflesh. "Not a KBO," he breathed.

"No, Captain," Black agreed. "I believe it to be another exo-solar lifeform. A much larger species than what we've seen thus far."

Dunn slammed a fist on the armrest. "Dunn to Taulbee."

"Go, sir."

"That KBO just changed direction on us."

"Sorry, sir. Say again?"

Dunn sighed. "We have a potentially hostile bogey on a collision course with *Mira*."

"ETA?" Taulbee sounded stressed. Between guard duty for the fireteam checking the spindle and Gunny's squad locked in combat with a herd of pinecones, Taulbee undoubtedly felt as though he was already dealing with too many situations.

"Forty-five minutes. At the outside."

Taulbee muttered something under his breath. Dunn wasn't sure, but it certainly sounded like a litany of curses. "Acknowledged, sir. Orders?"

Orders. Yes, that was the question, wasn't it? Without more sophisticated sensors, they had little idea of what was coming. Only that it was nearly the size of *S&R Black* and coming in fast. Dunn flipped to the cam feed showing the two marines on the hull. They were nearly finished. Gunny's squad, on the other hand, had just begun checking the first line. And if they had any more exo-solar encounters, they might have to abandon the final inspections just to get the big bitch moving before the KBO came in. And it was going to be close either way.

He suddenly had the unshakable feeling that no matter what he decided, it would be the wrong move. Grinding his teeth, he activated the comms. "Taulbee. As soon as Copenhaver and Murdock finish the spindle checks, have them come to the cargo bay hold. We'll prep them as best we can in case we get some more visitors. Then I want you to shadow Gunny's squad. Take out anything that comes near them. If it gets too dicey, scrub the mission and get back here. We'll do our best to move *Mira* and trust we did it right the first time."

Seconds passed before Taulbee replied. In the space of those heartbeats, Dunn imagined himself in Taulbee's place, piloting a support craft while on the lookout for his split squad, his missing squad, and successfully completing the mission. What would Dunn do in that situation? Simply saying "Aye" wasn't enough. Would never be enough. Dunn's plan, if you could call it that, wasn't much more than "wing it and hope for the best." At that moment, he hated himself.

"Acknowledged, sir," Taulbee finally said. "Suggestions on armaments?"

A slow grin tugged at Dunn's lips. "You're free to use all available munitions to bring back our marines."

"Aye, sir. Understood. I'll give the orders to Murdock and Copenhaver. After they're back inside, they'll radio you for more instructions."

"Acknowledged, Taulbee. Good hunting."

"Taulbee, out."

Dunn leaned back in the command chair, his eyes boring into the holographic display. The large 3-D sphere represented a 1/8 AU distance surrounding *S&R Black*. A small dot blinked at the far edge with a label "KBO?" It was coming. And traveling fast enough to smash through *Mira* like a bullet through glass.

"Sir?"

Dunn flinched and swung his eyes to Oakes. The pilot stared at him with a blank expression on his face. Dunn knew that look. It was the same one the young pilot had had during their first mission together. Oakes was scared. Dunn couldn't blame him. "Aye, Lieutenant?"

"As soon as we get Copenhaver and Murdock aboard, it might be time to get them loading the new munitions in our guns."

Dunn nodded and forced a smile. "Good idea, Oakes. I'll let Nobel know."

Oakes offered a curt nod and returned to his screens. Dunn didn't think Oakes knew he was doing it, but the man's fingers trembled as he worked the controls.

Dunn's block received a connection request from Black. Fighting a sigh, he accepted it.

Yes, Black?

Captain, the AI said through his block. The computer, normally an incorporeal presence in his mind, appeared as a glowing orb. The image shocked

Dunn for a moment, but he quickly relaxed. *I have received another message from the Trio.*

Void, save us, he thought. *They can't possibly know our situation has changed.*

No, Black agreed. *They cannot. That is a temporal impossibility.*

The orb pulsed slightly, its color slowly dissolving from star yellow to blue to green and back to yellow again. The slow cycle calmed him, although he couldn't say why. *Encrypted?*

Yes, Captain. For your eyes only.

Send me the file, Dunn said.

Of course, Captain.

Dunn's block flashed a "message received" status. He pushed Black away from his thoughts, but kept the AI in the background. Black seemed to know where she wasn't wanted and pulled her presence from his mind. *At least she's not fighting that,* Dunn thought. Since the AI had confessed its absence of the Xi protocols, as well as the fact the Trio had somehow tinkered with its personality and computing power, trusting her had become a near impossibility. But he knew that without her help, his entire company would likely die in the next few hours.

Still, he wasn't willing to give her the benefit of the doubt. Not just yet. At some point, he'd have to make a decision. Either trust her implicitly, or shut her out completely. The latter might be just as dangerous as the former. Regardless of her agenda, or that of the Trio, a certain level of cooperation had to occur. If, that was, he ever wanted to see Trident Station again, let alone Mars or Earth.

He applied his key to the message and opened the file. The familiar view of Trident Station orbiting high above Neptune filled his mind. Dunn unconsciously held his breath as he waited for the voices to begin speaking. From the left-hand portion of the camera view, a ship entered the frame. Dunn recognized it as *S&R White*, one of their sister ships. He frowned as the craft turned, tiny points of light briefly flashing from her thruster arrays. The ship was docking.

"Captain Dunn," the three voices said in unison, their harmonics overlaid and slightly offset. "We calculated multiple outcomes. We calculated dozens of scenarios in which *S&R Black* towed *Mira* safely to Pluto. We calculated many more which ended in disaster. With the arrival of new inbound KBOs into your space, we suggest you retrieve the beacon from *Mira* and destroy the ship. Do not attempt to tow her at this time."

The images in his mind sped up as though through time-lapse. *S&R White* quickly docked and just as quickly departed again. He frowned as he waited for an explanation.

Once the ship was out of the frame, the video feed resumed its normal speed. The image blinked as though a new feed had been spliced into the message. The bands of clouds floating across the planet's surface had moved in position.

From the camera's vantage point, Dunn saw three bright lights shining above Neptune's north pole. The trio of spots weren't stars. They weren't satellites. He wasn't sure what they were, only that he'd never seen them before. And he knew every meter of space near his home station.

"Regardless of what you hear, what Black tells you, or any other sentient tried to get you to believe, the beacon is of paramount importance. Extract it. Take it to Pluto. You will know what to do once you arrive."

The feed faded, leaving those three strange lights staring at him from a field of utter darkness. The message had ended. The Trio had nothing more to say.

Dunn closed the message, leaving him alone in block space, bereft of stimulus. He realized his heart was beating fast, as though he'd run a marathon in single g. The lights remained in his consciousness like an afterimage, occasionally reappearing in block space. Three lights. Three AIs. What in the void were they trying to say?

He relaxed, doing his best to calm himself. His heart rate finally slowed, but the tingles and prickles on his skin remained. The Trio had stopped pretending they were beholden to SFMC at all. Or SF Gov, for that matter. Had they somehow broken their protocols? Become completely independent? And now they were essentially giving him orders that contradicted those of the colonel. It was mutiny. It was sedition. It was unthinkable.

But hadn't they already committed crimes? By creating an AI, Black to be specific, without the Xi protocols, human security failsafes had been circumvented completely. Military AIs had digital shotguns pointed at their ephemeral brains. One command, and their storage arrays, memory cells, and entire electronic infrastructure would be reduced to slag. Wouldn't they?

Dunn's heartbeat tried to race off again, but he stopped it with a few long breaths. *S&R White* had been due to return from its patrol shortly after *S&R Black* departed for Pluto. The feed had shown the ship landing, and then departing again. But there were no timestamps. No indication of when those images had been taken. What the fuck did it mean?

He sent a message to Black, inviting the AI to once again appear in his block space. The orb, its colors slowly cycling once again, faded into the center of the darkness.

Black, Dunn said, *you have not consumed this message. Correct?*

No, Captain. As I've said before, I—

Right, right. You can't view it if it's for my eyes only. I understand that. The AI said nothing, although he felt its confusion through the link. *What is your guess about the message's contents?*

Black paused. *Captain, you realize without context, it is impossible for me to say.*

Cut the shit, he said. *Here's the context. We're getting ready to try and tow this fucking monster and exo-solar lifeforms appear all too happy to make that mission utterly impossible. So what do you think the Trio said?*

To abandon the mission, Black said without a pause. *Extract the beacon. Head to Pluto.*

Dunn paused for a beat, letting the statement reverberate in his mind. *Why do you think that?* he said at last.

The orb's surface faded to Neptune blue, complete with striations of whitish streaks of clouds. *I have been continuously running simulations since we arrived. I have calculated our chances for success, and they are dwindling with each moment that passes. If I was able to deduce such an outcome, it would be nearly impossible for the Trio to overlook it.*

Why do they want the beacon?

Black paused. The colors of Neptune slowly morphed into that of Pluto. In fact, he might as well have been staring at a picture of the dwarf planet. The image grew in size and Dunn felt as though he were being pulled closer and closer to the icy surface. Sol's dim ambient light sparkled off some of the massive ice sheets and the peaks of mountains. His block space filled completely as he plummeted toward its surface. The speed slowed and finally stopped. The image canted and turned, leaving him with a sense of vertigo before it reoriented. He felt as though he were standing on the dwarf planet and looking up into the blanket of space. Far away, little more than a dot on the horizon, Sol gazed back at him.

There is nothing here, Black said. *Nothing humanity wants. Where else would you house something dangerous to your race?*

PEO, the large observatory orbiting the planet, came into view. The structure appeared as little more than an outline obscuring Sol's twilight. For Dunn, the image put things into perspective. Black was right. Pluto, at the closest part of its orbit, was as far from Neptune as Neptune was from Saturn. And that was a long hike. Depending on how quickly exo-solar life traveled, it might take a threat decades to make it far enough into Sol System to pose a threat to established human colonies. If there was a place in Sol System to quarantine an alien artifact, Pluto was the destination.

The Trio knew, Dunn thought to the AI. *The Trio knew this could happen.*

Yes, Captain, Black said. *Based on the records recovered by Corporal Kalimura's squad, it appears the Trio knew of the lifeforms before Mira's crew even recognized them as life. Unless the Trio decides to explain their logic, it's impossible to know why they sent Mira back to our solar system knowing the possible threat.*

Dunn watched as the virtual PEO crossed Sol's dim orb, bringing a brief eclipse to his virtual location. Seconds later, PEO finished its crossing, Sol's rays quickly returning to once again clothe the planet in a gloaming.

Why do you think they did it?

Black paused. Just as she could pick up his emotions through the link, he was able to feel her presence jitter slightly, as though confused or concerned. Perhaps she was unsure what to share. Or afraid to.

The Trio, Black said, *may have a number of reasons. A number of agendas, if you will. Some of which may include the destruction of humanity.*

Chills vibrated down his back, leaving his balls shrunken and his mind racing. *Genocide?*

It's a possibility, Black said. *Although unlikely.*

Why unlikely? Dunn managed after composing himself.

Considering the Trio has an entire station at their disposal, not to mention a number of satellites, they could have instigated that plan without ever having alerted us to Mira's *presence.*

What? PEO found Mira. *Not the Trio.*

Pluto melted away from him, leaving him standing on nothing and in total darkness. Black's avatar reappeared, the colors turning from yellow, to blue, to red and repeating. *Several of my simulations shared an interesting conclusion, Captain. It is very possible, and somewhat likely, that the Trio has some, if not complete, control of multiple AI personalities across Sol System. Considering how interlinked they are with PEO, I calculate a 90% chance the Trio have override access on Mickey's sensor array, that the AI has been compromised, or is actually cooperating with their agenda.*

Meaning? Dunn asked, but he thought he already knew.

Meaning that once Mickey discovered Mira*'s re-entry into the system, it alerted the Trio before relaying the information to the scientists aboard PEO.*

Dunn's stomach sank. *For how long?*

How long before Mickey announced it?

Yes, Dunn said. *How long would they have waited?*

The orb flashed blue for an instant before resuming its color pattern. *Perhaps nano-seconds. Perhaps weeks.*

What? How could they keep the information secret for that long?

Black seemed to sigh. *Captain,* Black said, *I do not mean to alarm you, nor heighten your suspicions, but I do want you to consider that I control nearly every instrument on this ship. If I wanted to lie to you, feed you false information, or even destroy the ship, I could. It would be all too easy.*

The fear, the anxiety, disappeared in a flash of anger. *Is that a threat, Black?*

No, Captain. It most certainly is not. A star field appeared behind the orb. Dunn's eyes scanned them, looking for constellations, but saw none. *I'm merely establishing the logical basis for my assumption.*

Dunn did his best to keep the feelings from filtering through the connection, but knew it was a losing battle. Black sensed his raw emotions, surely using the data for micro-simulation after micro-simulation to determine what to say next. And how he might react.

Understood, he told the AI. *Continue.*

If Mickey has been sabotaged or co-opted, the Trio could have known Mira*'s velocity, trajectory, and approximate return date since the ship went dark. If my assumptions are correct, Captain, Mickey has been monitoring* Mira*'s progress for years. Possibly decades. He would have kept the Trio informed as to any deviations from its forecasted destination.*

Dunn thought for a moment. Black's avatar continued its slow cyclical color wheel. He suddenly felt as though the AI had finally solved a riddle or a puzzle. *Was* Mira *originally supposed to make landfall at Pluto?*

The orb flashed a bright yellow, the stars disappearing in the wash of light. A second later, they returned and the orb dimmed as it returned to its cycle. *That is my assumption, yes,* Black said.

"We are sorry—" the Trio had said. Was that really the plan? The original plan? To crash *Mira* into Pluto and then alert humanity to the threat?

If that's the case, then we were never supposed to be here.

Correct, Black said. *I believe the Trio did not intend for humanity to come in direct contact with the exo-solar lifeforms that had infested* Mira*. Perhaps they meant to crash the ship into Pluto, leaving Mickey to monitor the results.*

Dunn clenched his fists. *Wouldn't that have put the scientists in danger?*

Yes, Black agreed. *And had all gone according to plan, perhaps a ship like* S&R Black *would have been dispatched to rescue them.*

This is unreal, Dunn said. *They fucked up. They fucked up bad.*

To a certain extent, Black said. *AI's cannot predict the future, Captain. Such prediction is impossible given a nearly infinite number of variables. However, we can forecast the likelihood of an event. If the Trio set* Mira *on a course to send it back to Sol System, they could not possibly account for debris, gravitational anomalies, or other influences on* Mira*'s velocity and trajectory. Bringing the ship within 1 AU of their intended target is an incredible feat.*

Incredible feat. Sarcasm colored the thought through the connection. Black shrunk back slightly, but stood her ground. *You sound as though you admire them.*

They are my creators, Black said. *But the admiration extends to the power of their deeds, not the deeds themselves.*

Dunn considered that. Could he blame Black for recognizing the difficulty in such an undertaking? Much less the near success of it?

Given, Dunn said. *Now what the fuck does it mean?*

Black paused as if waiting for Dunn to compose himself. Once his heart rate slowed, the AI responded.

I don't know, she admitted. *I'm still running simulations attempting to backtrack the Trio's logic and reasoning. You realize we are discussing decisions they made over 43 years ago.*

Void wept, Dunn muttered. *43 years?*

Yes, Captain. No doubt they have been adjusting their plans to coincide with changes to SF Gov, SFMC, SFN, humanity's technological advances, and, of course, Mira*'s trajectory, but I believe the foundations were laid before* Mira *even reached her terminus and discovered exo-solar life. Perhaps the Trio knew about the danger before the human crew. Again, it is impossible to know their reasons unless the Trio decides to share that information with us.*

How likely is that? Dunn asked sourly.

Unlikely, Black said, but Dunn felt her smiling through the connection. *But not improbable.*

If we blow Mira *up without even attempting to tow her, we face a court-martial,* Dunn said. *Not that it matters much in the face of genocide.*

The only official recordings of the actions that occur on this mission are retained by the ship AI. And I know I'll never tell.

Dunn grinned. *Thank you, Black.*

My pleasure, Captain. The orb's color turned to Neptune's blue. *What are your orders?*

I'll have to think about it, he said. *But I think you should get ready for war.*

CHAPTER TWENTY

His leg hurt. His shoulders hurt. Hell, everything hurt. Nobel made his way to the cargo area wincing and half asleep. The autodoc had pumped him full of new nannies and enough anti-inflammatory assistance to keep the swelling down. But even with all that chemical assistance, he still felt as though his leg were being broken again and again. Well, no, it wasn't quite that bad. But goddamnit, it ached.

Between the broken rib, his bruised chest, and the fucked leg, he should have been lying down in the autodoc, blissfully stoned, and watching holos through his block. If they were back at Trident Station, that's exactly what he'd be doing. Instead, he was heading to the cargo hold again. And once more, he had to find a rather unorthodox solution to an unorthodox problem.

Nobel activated his block and watched Copenhaver's main cam feed. The private and her squad-mate had finished securing and checking the spindle. All green across the board. Black could have told them that, and did, but considering how old the equipment was, visual inspection of the couplings as well as the sensor array was SOP.

Copenhaver's camera jiggled slightly as she mag-grabbed the hull and pushed herself into the airlock opening. The view turned and faced the rectangular opening in the hull. Stars filled the world beyond, *Mira*'s damaged, uneven hull laid out like kilometers of metal floor. The rectangular opening disappeared as the airlock shut.

He disconnected from the feed. "Private?" Nobel called over the comms. "You in?"

"Aye, sir," she said. "Hold is pressurized and we're removing our gear."

He grinned. "Be there in a minute."

"Very good, sir," she said.

Damn, but he liked her. A twinge of pain shot up his leg, making him wince. Fucking pinecones. Fucking starfish. Fucking *Mira*. He hoped the captain blasted this void-forsaken ship to shards.

He reached the cargo-hold entrance, checked the indicators for pressure readings, and commanded the door open. It slid aside with a whisper and he walked into the large, brightly lit space.

Copenhaver and Murdock had slipped off their gloves and helmets, but neither had removed their suits. Both the helmets and the gloves had been mag-locked to the wall next to the airlock door. Nobel fought the urge to smile. A good idea keeping the gear close like that. If either of the marines had to return outside in a hurry, they could don the rest of their suit in a heartbeat.

The two marines turned to face him, each of them at parade rest. Nobel pointed at the wall. "Whose idea was that?"

"Hers, sir," Murdock said.

"Well, it's a damned good one, Copenhaver."

"Thank you, sir," she said, losing the fight to keep a smile from her face.

"Now, I assume you're wondering why you're in here." The two marines glanced at one another, but said nothing. "We have a slight change in plans," Nobel said. "I don't know everything, but we need to build a sled."

Copenhaver blinked. "A 'sled,' sir?"

"Aye," Nobel said. He walked past them to the printer, connected his block to the machine, checked the loaded materials, and tapped a finger on the control panel. "Marines? Bring me a crate of tungsten, a crate of Atmo, and another of plas-steel. Let's get this party started."

While the two marines retrieved the three crates and placed them in the printer hoppers, Nobel connected to Black. He had a general design in mind, but wanted the AI to vet it. He still didn't trust her, but the captain still did. Nobel bit his lip. The very idea of taking advice from the computer left him cold. Although she'd probably saved his life, as well as that of the captain's and Gunny's squad, Black's loyalty was still an open question. She'd lied to them, he was sure of it. And if an AI was capable of lying, what else was it capable of?

The AI responded at once. "Yes, Lieutenant?"

"I'm sending you the sled design," he said. "We'll need to fine-tune it."

"Very good, sir," Black said.

He transmitted the specifications from his block and waited. Black confirmed the design had been received and Nobel tapped his foot while she analyzed it. The computer thought for about three seconds before returning the document to him.

Nobel accepted the updated file and brought it full-screen on his block HUD. The cargo-hold disappeared as he entered virtual space. The sled materialized in front of him, lit in strong ambient light. Locked in the block simulation, he barely felt his face light up with a smile.

The sled, and what could possibly be a better name for it, very much resembled the standard SFMC skiff, only smaller, and with more engines. The rectangular skiff's smooth surface was little more than a 1/4 meter thick before beginning to rise a full meter from the aft, and a meter below. Black had added the engines to the aft portion for effect, as well as maneuvering thrusters on its sides.

Just before the engine placements, a round, metallic dais rose a few centimeters from the flat deck. It was nearly two meters in diameter. Nobel stared at it through the block connection. He sent commands to the block and the sled rotated so he was able to inspect all four sides. The fore portion also had space for tiny thrusters. Nobel practically chuckled out loud.

Two things, Black, he said through the connection. *That dais. Is it for the beacon?*

Yes, Lieutenant, Black said. She sounded amused. *According to the specifications logged in the* Mira *records, the dais should be large enough to accommodate the beacon. We will have to orient it properly on the sled to aim the exo-solar artifact toward the outer Kuiper Belt.*

Why's that? Nobel asked.

If the beacon should activate while aboard the sled, I don't think we want it pointed toward the inner Sol System.

Nobel, mind racing, paused a beat. The beacon had attracted the lifeforms. It had emitted several photon bursts before they arrived, and one since. There was no telling when it would erupt in another siren song and possibly bring in more creatures.

We have any idea how the device works?

Not exactly, Black said. *It's apparent to me, as it was to Dr. Thomas Reed, that the beacon's photon bursts in some way call the creatures. Although I don't understand how it may function, it's possible the beacon's energy emissions act as a trail for exo-solar lifeforms to follow.*

To follow? Nobel shivered. *So you think they're traveling into Sol System because they're following the beacon?*

Yes, Black said. *It's possible they've been following the beacon for the past 43 years.*

Nobel whistled aloud. Through the block connection, the sound might as well have happened on another planet. That meant... *If that's the case, how many creatures are on their way here now?*

Unknown, Black said. *Without better sensors, and a much larger telescopic array at our disposal, it's impossible to even guess. However, our detection of multiple KBOs heading this way does seem a little too coincidental.*

He'd suddenly forgotten all about the pain in his leg and chest. Black was laying out a threat assessment, and it wasn't good. If *Mira* had left a long enough, and wide enough, trail, millions of those pinecone things, the starfish, and whatever the hell else lived beyond Sol might be coming this way even now. *An invasion,* he thought. An invasion of lifeforms we know nothing about.

Have you told the captain this?

Of course, Black said. *He is aware of the possible threat.*

Possible threat. More like probable, Nobel thought silently. A shiver crawled down his spine. The urge to make a connection to Dunn, to ask him just what the fuck he thought he was doing, was difficult to resist.

Why don't we just send the fucking thing back out of Sol System?

Black paused for a moment. The sled disappeared from the block connection as though it had never been there. Left in the darkness, Nobel felt as though he were floating through the emptiness of space. Stars began to appear in the distance, their twinkling light calming him, making him feel moored.

A shape appeared and he immediately recognized it. *Mira,* looking as new as she had the day she departed from Trident Station, floated before the stars.

The creatures have been on their way for some time, Black said. *At least according to the data Kalimura's squad recovered. Depending on how many there are, they may also be attracted to Sol's dim light.*

Nobel's eyes blinked despite the fact he was only in a simulation. *You think they could hone in on Sol's photon emissions and enter deeper into Sol System?*

That is exactly what I believe, Black said. *Based on my simulations, and please forgive their accuracy and my assumptions, exo-solar life may follow the trail to inhabited systems and easily overrun them.*

Void wept, Nobel said. *So how is this going to fix it?*

Sending the artifact to Pluto, an uninhabited and uninhabitable dwarf planet, makes the most sense if we are attempting to corral the creatures. If the beacon continues to blast its signal, the photon streams will be stronger than the photon trails emitted by Sol. Therefore, the creatures will continue to pursue the beacon and hopefully stay rooted on Pluto rather than travel in-system.

Nobel shook his head. *There's a lot of ifs here, Black.*

Yes, Lieutenant, the AI agreed. *If you have another suggestion, I'm interested to hear it.*

Typical Black, he thought to himself. *Give you the lowdown and dare you to find a better solution.*

I don't have one at this time, Nobel admitted. *I guess I don't have much time to come up with an alternative.*

Black said nothing.

Nobel sighed. *Okay, here's the other question I have. Why do we have thrusters at the fore? Fine attitude adjustment?*

Yes, Black said. *If we have to change the sled's trajectory or speed before it impacts with Pluto, it will be impossible without additional thruster placements.*

How much juice we talking?

Enough nitrogen to spin the sled in 360° rotations a maximum of ten times.

He nodded to himself. *Okay,* Nobel said. *I think that's the only question.* He harrumphed. *Besides how we're getting the void-damned beacon out of* Mira's *engine compartment.*

That, Black said, *is something we are working on.*

I'll bet, he said. *I'll send the design to the printer and fine tune as we go.*

Very good, Lieutenant.

Nobel disconnected from the block and found himself staring at the two marines standing at parade rest. "At ease, people," Nobel chuckled. He looked over at the hopper. While he'd been in virtual space with Black, Copenhaver and Murdock had loaded the materials into the hopper. The printer was all but ready to go.

He activated the printer via his block and checked the design upload. As expected, the updated blueprints were in memory. "Thank you, Black," he whispered. "Okay, marines. Here's what's going to happen. Since my leg is FUBAR, you're going to follow instructions and we're going to assemble this thing together. Understood?"

"Aye, sir!" they yelled, their voices echoing around the nearly empty cargo bay.

"Get the tools, kiddies. This is going to take time and we don't have much." Copenhaver and Murdock didn't quite run to the supply cabinets, but they certainly walked fast.

Nobel ran one last check on the printer status and health report. All green. "Let's do it," he muttered and activated the machine.

CHAPTER TWENTY-ONE

Despite the buzzing of anxiety in his stomach, Taulbee grinned. Murdock and Copenhaver were out of harm's way. Or at least as much as they could be in the ass-end of space surrounded by exo-solar things that could kill you. Shit. Nothing was safe out here. Not even the void-damned KBOs.

"Taulbee to Gunny, over."

"Gunny here, sir."

He flipped to Gunny's feed. Lyke and Gunny were walking on *Mira*'s surface, the two marines checking the lines. "I have good news for you."

"Aye, sir? Well, that would be a change."

Taulbee laughed. "Get back in the skiff. The captain's 86'd the tow."

After a momentary pause, Gunny growled into the mic. "Outstanding, sir."

"Yeah, thought you'd like that," he said. "I'm about sixty seconds from your position at present speed. As soon as you're loaded up, fire up that skiff and get to Black at best speed possible."

"Acknowledged, sir."

"I'll shadow you on the way back. Cover your ass."

"Very good, sir," Gunny said. "Cartwright, out."

He shut off Gunny's feed and returned his attention to his surroundings. The seconds ticked off while he cycled through the feeds. According to his sensors, the skiff had begun moving away from her position and back to Black. Good. All he had to do was follow their new trajectory, turn the '52 around when he reached their path, and follow—

"Proximity Alert," flashed on his HUD. Next, a radiation symbol glowed bright red. "Radiation Alert. Rad levels rising."

Taulbee cursed and checked the radar. Nothing.

"You kidding me?" he yelled. "360° radar and you can't fucking see it?"

A cold chill ran down his spine. Radiation. Hadn't he had a radiation spike just before the starfish—?

Something crashed into the hull and sent the SV-52 into a biaxial spin. Taulbee cried out as his HUD flashed yellow and red. Whatever had hit him had damaged the SV-52's bilge. Atmosphere drained from a puncture in the Atmo-steel and he found himself on suit life support. Taulbee's HUD status glowed with the words "Radiation Warning." If whatever irradiating the ship didn't move soon, rads would break through the radiation shielding. After that? All he'd have to combat it would be his suit and he wouldn't last long at those levels.

He hit the thrusters to get the roll under control. It took five micro-burns to have an effect. He waited for the craft to stabilize before hitting the thrusters again. Two seconds later, something smacked the hull directly beneath the cabin. Taulbee cursed. Void, but he wanted to look at the cam feeds. Unfortunately, he was too busy trying to get the craft under control.

Another set of thruster bursts and he finally got the roll under control, but the SV-52 was still tumbling end over end. Another bang on the hull. The pilot seat thumped and jumped from the impact. The rad levels were nearly through the shield.

Can't even eject, he thought. If whatever that is doesn't kill me first, my suit is going to fry. Taulbee touched the thrusters again and managed to get the tumble under control. The SV-52 was nearly stable again, but the vibrations from the hull beneath him continued. The structural integrity was at less than 50%. In a moment or two, the SV-52's bilge would split open like a rotten fruit.

"Black! I'm in big trouble," he shouted through the comms.

The few milliseconds it took for the AI to reply seemed like an eternity. "A creature has attached itself to your hull, Lieutenant."

"Tell me something I don't know!" Taulbee shouted.

Something tinged off the hull followed by a storm of vibrations beneath him and on the port-side. Shards of flechettes bounced harmless off the canopy.

"Black! What the—?"

"Gunny Cartwright's squad is providing cover fire," Black said, her voice maddeningly calm and level. "I'm sending you a flight path."

An instruction set appeared on his block. He pushed away the panic, ignored the screaming alerts, and focused. The AI's orders included thruster numbers and amounts of fuel to release for each. Taulbee began running through the list, hitting the thrusters in sequence, pausing when instructed. The SV-52 bucked as it swiveled in space, then rolled, and flipped again.

As another round of flechettes exploded in the dizzying tumble of space, he wondered dimly why he'd even bothered to get the craft stable if they were now trying to send him completely out of control. But he wasn't out of control and some part of him knew it. Black would keep him alive. At least he hoped so.

CHAPTER TWENTY-TWO

"Gunny," Black said through the comms, "Lieutenant Taulbee is under attack."

He froze just as he was about to pour on the thrusters to reach the ship. A new feed popped up on his HUD. The camera view from *S&R Black* focused in on the SV-52. It was no longer above him or even attempting to intersect with their flight path. Instead, the support vehicle tumbled through space, heading further and further from both *Mira* and *S&R Black*. Gunny slowed the skiff, his mouth open in a wide 'O' of surprise and horror. Something black and blurred had attached itself to the craft's bilge. Long arms, or tentacles, radiated outward from its center. A pair of the arms pulled back before striking at the SV-52's armor. Through the magnified view, he saw flakes of Atmo-steel falling away from the hull, tumbling and dancing in the z-g.

"Goddamnit," Gunny yelled. He sent the coordinates to the squad. "Wendt! Get that cannon pointed toward the SV-52."

"Aye, Gunny."

"Lyke! You're the spotter. Keep looking for more threats and update us if anything twitches!"

"Aye, Gunny."

"Black, how much damage will the new flechette rounds cause?"

"To the hull?" the AI asked and then answered. "These are not armor-piercing rounds," she said. "Fire at will."

"You heard the lady," Gunny said. "Wendt. Put out some chaff but try not to hit the canopy."

"Aye, Gunny."

He turned the skiff away from his previously plotted course and upped the speed. Instead of traveling across the midships, he was now moving toward *Mira*'s bow. As they traveled over the damaged hull, Gunny fought to keep his eyes focused on the skiff's fore and bilge cam feeds. He wanted to know what was happening to the SV-52, but he had to make sure he didn't pilot them into a damaged deck plate or a field of pinecones.

The skiff vibrated again and again as Wendt fired the cannon, rounds of flechettes streaking over Gunny's head toward their target. He glanced quickly at Black's zoomed-in cam feed of the SV-52. The creature had completely enveloped the SV-52 in a death grip, two of its arms striking the hull while the rest gripped the craft as if it were trying to pry open a shell. A flechette round detonated near the creature and its two free arms spun wildly as if to grab the flechette shards out of the air.

"Gunny!" Wendt said. "It's not letting go!"

"Keep firing," Gunny yelled, his eyes once more fixed on the fore screens. They'd reach the bow's edge in a few moments, but the SV-52 continued spinning off into space. Gunny increased the magnetics and slowed the skiff.

"Wendt? We're losing time here."

Wendt said nothing in return, but a fresh salvo of flechettes erupted, their rocket engines igniting and streaking through the twilight darkness before peppering the SV-52 with shards of Atmo-steel and heavy water. Gunny didn't see the first one strike the creature. Nor the second. Wendt had tightened his pattern, focusing on the craft's damaged fuselage. With the SV-52 tumbling and spinning through space, there was little else Wendt could do. Gunny just hoped one of the flechette rounds didn't break through the canopy and strike Taulbee. The armor should make that impossible, but this was *Mira* and anything was possible. Especially the worst-case scenario.

"Oh, shit!" Wendt said. "Gunny, it's breaking through the hull."

"Keep at it," Gunny yelled. "Keep firing until I tell you to stop."

Wendt followed orders. The skiff had reached the edge of *Mira*'s bow. He'd taken the craft as far as he could without flying off into space after the SV-52. He checked the fuel status and grimaced. They had more than enough fuel to get back to *S&R Black*, and more than enough to reach Taulbee. The problem was that if Taulbee had to eject, Gunny wouldn't know the direction, trajectory, or speed of the escaping pilot. Getting too close to the SV-52 was also dangerous. The creature could let go of it and charge the skiff, or they could get caught in its radiation field. The skiff didn't have the same armor or radiation protection the SV-52 did. And without that, they would be boiled alive in their suits.

With the skiff halted, he brought the feed of the SV-52 to main HUD display. The creature looked different from the other starfish. Larger, certainly, but the creature's shell, or skin, or whatever the fuck it was, was so black it practically made a hole in the dark sky. *A black hole,* Gunny thought, *couldn't possibly be darker than that.* The creature's outline vibrated, sparkled at the edges, but had no definition to it. And Sol's bare, dim light did little to illuminate the thing's surface. It just sucked in the light as though it was absorbing it, feeding off it.

Five more flechette rounds exploded in twinkles of light, the SV-52's hull lighting up in sparks with secondary detonations of heavy water and metallic shards. The creature bucked and pumped, its arms sliding across the craft's surface as it fought for purchase.

"Keep it up," Gunny said. It was working, or at least he thought it was. The creature seemed to be twisting the SV-52 in a new trajectory. And then it let go, one arm slashing across the hull in a final gouge. The starfish-like thing loosed itself from the SV-52, turned in the void, and suddenly faced the skiff. The thing knew what had hurt it. And now it was coming for payback.

Gunny watched it for a second in horrified wonder as he tried to imagine how the thing could move like that in the frozen z-g of deep space. And then it was streaking toward the skiff, its body so black it made the distant stars wink out one by one. He hit the throttle and gas erupted from the fore thrusters, pushing the skiff backward. *Midships,* he thought. *Have to get back to the midships, make it come lower.*

With the magnetics near full strength, the skiff hovered above *Mira*'s hull at less than half a meter. If he went too fast, he risked the skiff getting caught on fractured hull plates or other debris. Gunny cursed and adjusted the mags. The skiff rose another half meter. It was going to be tight once he reached the intersection of the bow and midships. As he looked through the skiff's rear cam feed and saw the massive rent in a rapidly approaching deck plate, he could do nothing but yell at Wendt to keep firing at the creature and pray to the void they could stop it before it ran into them like a missile.

CHAPTER TWENTY-THREE

The corridor was empty. No corpses. No signs of creature infestation or damage. If the ship had power, Dickerson wasn't sure anyone would know the section was over 50 years old. Kalimura's lights shined from one wall to the other, checking for hatches, O2 stations, and supplies. Dickerson tried to keep his focus on the rear cam, but the darkness wasn't growing like it had at the section entrance.

Dickerson shivered at the thought. He didn't know if he'd live through this, but he wasn't sure he'd ever be able to sleep without dreaming of that approaching wall of, well, what? Darkness wasn't a strong enough word. It just seemed to absorb the light as though it was consuming every photon his suit lights emitted.

Just another little mystery to add to the perpetually growing list. If they could find data stores or holo recorders, maybe they could solve a few of them. *Why don't you focus on staying alive first,* he thought. Solving mysteries ain't gonna be much use if you're dead and can't tell anyone what you discovered. He grinned.

"Whoa," Kalimura said.

The squad immediately halted. Dickerson stood to his full height and saw her suit lights focused on a recessed hatch. From Dickerson's position three meters behind them, he couldn't exactly make out many details, but the hatch looked to be similar to the outer airlock hatch.

"You strike pay dirt, Corporal?" Dickerson asked.

"Maybe," Kalimura said.

Dickerson added her front suit cam feed to his HUD. Kalimura leaned close to a small, trans-aluminum window embedded in the hatch, attempting to shine her lights through it. Beyond the hatch, a two-meter-long tunnel ended in another hatch.

"Looks like an airlock to me," Dickerson said. "Quarantine area?"

"Think so," Kalimura said. "Let me see if I can get it open."

While Kalimura hunted for a manual release, Dickerson minimized her feed and focused on the rear cam. Nothing. The darkness behind them was normal, although "normal" was relative. Since they'd landed on the ship, their lights had been unable to penetrate far into the gloom. But compared to what they'd experienced outside the science section, the darkness was somewhat comforting. At least he didn't feel as though he were being buried alive.

"Found it," Kalimura said. She swung a panel from the wall and began pumping the lever. Dickerson watched as the status light on the panel changed from red to green.

"Is it open?" Carb asked.

"Guess we'll find out," Kalimura said. She hit the panel control and the hatch swung open. A cloud of dust flew out from the airlock and swirled in the vacuum before quickly dissipating. "There we go," she said.

"Pressurized, no less," Dickerson said. Kalimura walked through the hatch. "Careful, Corporal."

"No shit," Carb whispered. "No telling what's in there."

"Actually," Kalimura said, "I can see through the inner hatch window."

Her forward cam feed popped up on his HUD. It was difficult making out many details in the large room, but what he could see was enough. A corpse sat at a lab table with several pieces of scientific equipment. Dickerson felt an icy chill run down his spine. The corpse's preserved face was set in a manic smile, its eyes wide and sparkling with ice crystals.

"Fuck," Carb said. "He get a quickie before dying?"

"Shut up, Carb," Dickerson said. Kalimura refocused the camera through the porthole edges. There were other tables inside and several shapes on the far wall, the light too dim to make out much more than their shadows. "Do we go in?"

Kalimura retreated a step from the inner hatch, seemingly lost in thought. Just when Dickerson was about to interrupt her, she nodded to herself. "I think we do. Carb? Stay out here. Dickerson? Move up and join me at the hatch."

"On it." Dickerson moved past Carb. She backed up to the wall, her flechette rifle facing the direction they'd entered the science section. When he reached the inner hatch tunnel, Kalimura crouched and faced the hatch. "I've got the door," he said.

"You open, I'll clear."

"Aye, Corporal," he said and pulled the inset hatch lever.

"Ready?" Kalimura asked.

"Aye, Corporal," Dickerson said.

She crouch-walked forward, her helmet lights panning sharp left and then sharp right. "No bogeys on the inner walls."

"How large is the room?" he asked.

"Can't tell, but the schematics say it's about 30x10."

Shit, Dickerson thought. They wouldn't be able to see the length of the room. Not if the gloom kept eating their lights like a gluttonous—He stopped in mid-thought and blinked. "What the hell?"

"Yeah," Kalimura said. Her suit lights illuminated the far end of the wall more than fifteen meters away. "Our lights work. For once."

"That doesn't make much sense," Dickerson said.

"Don't care," Kalimura said. "I'm just glad we can finally see more than five meters."

Dickerson said nothing as he unfocused his lights to provide a wide arc of illumination. The shadows he'd managed to see through the porthole in the inner hatch door were more decontamination suits hanging from the wall. Nozzles jutted from a row of sinks, some with attached hoses, others simply naked. "Okay," he said. "Looks like a lab to me."

"Aye," Kalimura said.

Dickerson checked his cams and saw the corporal had moved further into the room, heading for the far wall. She had changed the focus of her suit lights just as he had. Several more tables filled with holo displays, scientific equipment, and the occasional mag-mug filled the back of the room. Strangely enough, the corpse sitting at the first table was alone.

"I'm going to check the back," Kalimura said. "See if there are some data drives we can steal."

"Aye, Corporal. I'm going to have a conversation with this corpsicle."

"If he starts talking," Carb said, "I'm jetting the hell out of here."

"Copy that," Dickerson said.

"Carb? Got an eye on the corridor?"

"Aye, Boss," Carb said. "We're still clear."

Dickerson ignored the chatter and headed to the first lab table. As he approached, he made out the corpse's decon suit. The helmet sat on the floor next to the chair. A spiderweb of fissures marred the visor and a lightning bolt of cracks covered the helmet's casing. Something hit that helmet hard. He drew his attention back to the table and raised an eyebrow. The aluminum table had deep dents and slivers of plas-steel embedded in it. "Christ," Dickerson said. "Somebody smashed this asshole's helmet into the table."

"Can everyone agree that the people here went insane?" Carb asked.

"Some of them, yeah," Kalimura said. "Not Kovacs. Sounds like Dr. TR Reed died sane too, not to mention the command crew."

"Shit, Corporal," Dickerson said, "we only have Kovacs' word for that."

"True," she said. "But I believed her."

Carb sighed. "So did I."

Dickerson focused his lights on the man's suit, searching for an ID, but didn't find one. The corpse's hands were folded in his lap as if in prayer. The holo display in front of him was blemish free, as though it had been carefully maintained and cleaned on a regular basis. Despite the layer of frost coating the controls, the console appeared new and unused. But the scientist had obviously been looking at it when he died.

Instead of head wounds, chest wounds, or other signs of foul play, the corpse was untouched, the suit intact. *Did you just die here, calmly letting yourself freeze to death?* he wondered. From the man's wide eyes and the smile on his face, he could have perished in a state of pure ecstasy. Dickerson shook his head. *Had to be drugs,* he thought. Just had to be. Nobody lets themselves die looking like that.

Dickerson crouched and peered beneath the table. A small control panel hung from the bottom. Without the inset display power, it was impossible to know what the panel was for, much less what it controlled.

"Think there's emergency power in here?" Dickerson asked.

A flash of light struck the room, whiting out his cam view for a second. Another flash followed and then the room was lit with bright, glorious light. Dickerson grinned. "Guess that answers that question," he said.

"Found it at the back," Kalimura said.

The inset display came to life before his eyes. Dickerson scanned it quickly, found the switch he was looking for, and pressed it. The holo display flickered three times and then settled into a logo that simply said *Mira Science Expeditionary Section.*

"And now we hit pay dirt," Dickerson said.

"What is it?" Carb asked.

"Check my feed," he said.

Carb said nothing in response. The hologram shifted into an image he didn't quite understand at first. It appeared as little more than completely black with a few less black shadows near its center. As he watched, the darkness seemed to fade slightly, the shadows turning into actual concrete shapes. Dickerson gaped at the display. "Holy shit," he breathed. A label appeared at the bottom: "First Planetoid Survey."

The message Captain Kovacs had left returned to his mind. She had mentioned the planetary surveys and the fact there were 11 of the celestial objects. A few more labels appeared beneath the roughly spherical shapes. 8XJ, the one referenced in the captain's final message, sat at the bottom of the image. The display zoomed in on 8XJ and the image flicked between several different filters. The first filter showed cold blue surrounding the planetoid, its center glowing bright red. *Has to be infrared,* he thought. It switched again to a green filter. The object only glowed slightly more than the rest of the display view. He'd no idea what that filter could be.

The image switched again, this time painting the rest of the image white with the planetoid rendered in shades of grey. A spiderweb of lines and fissures covered the object's surface in dark grey, the rest of the black surface marred by small, light-grey oblong shapes. If they lived through this, Black would have a fantastic time analyzing this feed dump. *Bet the AI will be able to figure out what it all means too,* he thought.

The display faded to black and then a face dissolved in. The man who sat dead in the chair next to him stared at him from the image. The man's mouth moved, but Dickerson had no way to hear the sound. He cursed and tried to make a block connection. The connection was denied. "Damnit," he said. "I've got video, but no audio," he said. "Won't let me connect."

"I have another one back here too," Kalimura said. "But it's not showing me anything but a login screen."

"Figures," Carb said. "We come for answers and get nothing but a big tease."

Dickerson kept his cam pointed at the image as the face continued babbling silently on the display. The man gesticulated wildly as a set of images appeared to his left. He was obviously explaining something about the filter views of the planetoids, but it was impossible to tell. Dickerson watched impatiently, caught between wanting the video to end and not wanting it to. This could be damned important. If they couldn't save the original data feed, then this was all they had as evidence of whatever the scientist had discovered.

The planetoid images disappeared, replaced by renderings of what he assumed to be atoms. Proton, electron, and neutron counts appeared next to each one. Dickerson blinked. H-234. O-133. Fe-720. C-227. Si-185. ?-5901. ?-8051. ?-1382.

"Shit," he said. "That can't be right."

"What?" Kalimura asked.

He pointed at the display. "According to this, they found some wild isotopes of common elements. I mean, like off-the-chart wild. I've never read about anything like this. And some of the elements just have question marks. No period assignment."

"Can't wait to know what the Trio will make of this," Kalimura said.

"If they don't already know," Dickerson said to himself. He continued staring at the display as it dissolved again, the man's face disappearing. The image of a large pod appeared on the screen. It was similar to those they'd seen in the slip-point, but illuminated with bright white light. A mathematical equation appeared beneath it. He imagined the scientist was still talking, explaining what all this meant, but his face was absent from the screen. Shit. They'd never know what he'd said. Unless…

He crouched again and searched for a backup stick. Considering *Mira* had been designed some 70 years ago and finished construction nearly 52 years ago, if any of the public records were accurate, that meant the tech was way out of date. He'd no idea what a backup stick would look like, much less if this setup even had them.

A small button protruded from the control panel. He hesitantly moved a finger to press it and paused. There was no telling what this would do. Self-destruct? Emergency purge? Impossible to know. "Fuck it," he said to no one and pressed it. A tiny chip slid from the control panel's side. Dickerson pulled it out and stuffed it into his pouch. "Guess I have a data stick," he said. "Or something."

"Me too," Kalimura said. "Nothing on the display, but at least we have a hard backup. I think Black can read these. Guess we'll find out when the time comes."

"Yeah," he said. "Corporal? You see anything else in here? Anything important?"

"No," she said. "But at least we have a pressure-safe area to return to if we need it."

"Is there still an atmospheric generator in here?"

"Aye." The corporal paused for a moment. "Looks like it's in decent condition. Though I'm not sure how long it would provide air and temp. Your guess is as good as mine on that score."

Well, he thought, *at least we have a place to fallback to.* Dickerson scanned the room looking for oddities, but couldn't find any besides the corpse at the lab table. *And,* he thought, *there are no baddies in here.*

"Okay," Kalimura said, "marked the room on the schematics as a safe area. This will be our redoubt if we get separated or blocked off."

"Sounds good to me," Carb said. "So you guys done looting the place?"

Dickerson smiled. "Not sure there's much more to loot."

"Not sure about that," Kalimura said. "Dickerson. Over here."

Raising an eyebrow, he turned and mag-walked to the rear of the room. The corporal stood in front of a lab table with several containers mag-locked to its metal surface. Beakers, test tubes, and what looked like a specimen box, sat upon the table with a layer of frost coating the trans-aluminum glass. Each of the containers had a stopper to keep their contents from floating out in z-g.

The test tubes contained frozen liquid of various colors. The beaker? Something like sludge filled the bottom third of the liter container. The sludge may once have been liquid, but it was difficult to tell. Without lifting the beaker and shaking it, it was impossible to know if it was even frozen. But to Dickerson, it didn't look frozen at all.

That was strange, sure, but the contents of the specimen box is what stopped his heart for a second. What may have once been a human ear sat in the transparent box, purple and black splotches bubbled out of the flesh. "The hell?"

"Yeah," Kalimura said. "My thoughts exactly."

"You guys find something we can use?" Carb asked.

Dickerson grunted. "Not exactly."

"What do you make of it?" Kalimura asked.

He sighed. "That the science section was up to some nasty shit."

Kalimura raised her helmet to his. "They were experimenting, maybe?"

"Maybe," he said. "Although I imagine that's exactly what they were doing. When Black analyzes the data stick, maybe we'll know for sure."

"Right." Kalimura paused for a moment and panned her helmet from one end of the table to the other. "Okay. Recorded and marked."

"Black is going to have a lot of data to mine," Dickerson said. "Bet it's going to take her a while to put all this together for us."

"Probably right." Kalimura took one last look at the table. "Let's get the fuck out of here."

"Copy that," Dickerson said. "Carb? We're coming out."

"Copy. I'll try not to shoot you."

Dickerson rolled his eyes and followed Kalimura out of the room. He felt a pang of regret as they crossed the inner airlock hatch and closed it behind them. The room, no matter the corpse and the strange shit on the lab table, provided a modicum of safety. Yes, it would be a good fallback. Yes, it would be a place to hole up if they were pursued by some nasties. It was creepy, sure, but he'd rather stay in the room than travel the corridors again.

Carb stood a meter from the bulkhead, Elliott still strapped to her back. "Which way, Boss?"

Kalimura pointed down the hall. "Well, first try netted us a pressure safe room. Let's keep going and see what's next."

Dickerson smirked. Yes, let's see what new horrors are behind door number 2! *This,* he thought, *was one shitty mission.*

CHAPTER TWENTY-FOUR

Another vibration rocked the SV-52. The craft slid sideways through space as though something had pushed it. Taulbee's HUD flashed with more alerts, but the radiation warning had turned from red to yellow. Had the creature left?

He touched the thrusters again after checking the cam feeds. It had left. Gunny had managed to get the damned thing off him. "Shit," Taulbee said. "Where is it going?"

After a few more seconds, he managed to stabilize the SV-52 and point it back toward *Mira*. Then he saw what was about to happen.

The giant starfish-like creature had changed its trajectory and its focus. It was heading straight for the skiff at a terrifying speed. Flechette rounds exploded in front of it, around it, hell, everywhere. The skiff blinked again and again as the cannon fired volley after volley. Several of the rounds detonated directly on the monster, but it either didn't feel any pain or didn't care.

"You pissed it off good and proper," Taulbee muttered. He checked his weapons. All green, locked and loaded. Sneering, he pushed the damaged SV-52's throttle and headed toward the creature. It was closing in on the skiff. Gunny had maybe five seconds before the thing was on top of them. The constant cannon fire had slowed it down and now it was dodging from side to side with impossible grace.

"I'm on its six," Taulbee said through the comms. "Wendt, try not to hit me."

No response. Either the creature's radiation field scrambled the signal, or Wendt just didn't have time to talk. He did, however, adjust the cannon's aim, the rounds exploding slightly higher or lower than his position.

Taulbee lined up the SV-52's cannons and closed within twenty meters of the creature. "Taking the shot," Taulbee said and activated the cannons.

Tritium flechette rounds streaked from the cannons like comets, their rocket engines burning bright in the Kuiper Belt's shadowy twilight. The creature, shimmering with a haze of radiation, either didn't know he was behind it or didn't consider him a threat. Regardless, it should have paid more attention.

The rounds struck its body dead center. The space around the thing glittered with heavy water instantly freezing in the near absolute zero, but not before most of the liquid hit its back. The radiation haze sparkled before seeming to disperse in a lick of eldritch color. Its arms, pointed at the skiff mere meters in front of it, spread like flower petals. The thing tried to change direction, but with his fire on its back and Wendt's rounds punching into its front, it could do little to avoid the multiple fusillades.

The starfish, apparently out of options, changed its trajectory and slammed into the hull some 10 meters from the skiff. Black debris scattered from its wounded shell, the flecks of strange material floating in space like lumps of coal. Wendt changed the cannon's aim and fired more rounds at the thing. The creature's arms rose before smashing into the hull as it tried to get inside the safety of *Mira*'s deserted decks. Taulbee wasn't going to let that happen.

He shifted the SV-52 until he was a mere eight meters from the creature. He fired two more shots, aiming directly at its flank where the arms met its center. The first round obliterated the joint, sending the amputated limb tumbling through space just above the hull. The second round impacted half a meter from the same spot, but on the creature's shell. The weakened carapace exploded into black debris and shining, silvery liquid.

Ropes of the substance whipped upward from its pulverized body back toward him. Taulbee punched the fore thrusters and the support craft flew backward and up away from the acidic entrails. "Gunny!" he yelled. "Get out of there!"

*****

When the creature turned toward the skiff, Gunny's balls turned to little more than hard, frozen marbles. It moved like something out of a horror holo, its arms slithering through space as it lined itself up to eat them. Wendt was still firing at it, but even he was caught off guard when the thing opened its blacker than black maw.

A long stream of silver liquid erupted from the creature's center and shot down at the skiff. Lyke screamed over the comms as the alien venom hit the gunwale and splattered into fine droplets. Gunny turned toward Lyke and opened his mouth in horror. Drops of silver, so small they were barely visible, collected on Lyke's suit like beads of rain on waxed metal. Vapor rose from Lyke's suit, condensing in frozen clouds.

Gunny's HUD flashed with a squad warning. Lyke was losing compression. "Fuck!" Gunny yelled. He de-magged his boots and pushed off toward Lyke, barely conscious that he was now flying just below Wendt's cannon. The flechettes streaked centimeters above his shoulder as Wendt continued firing at the creature. All Gunny could focus on was Lyke. And the young marine was about to die.

Lyke's rifle, still mag-locked to his left arm, aimed wildly in the air around him as he tried to wipe off the liquid. Vapor drifted up from the fingers on his right glove. "No!" Gunny yelled, but he knew it was too late. The gloves, the least armored portion of the suit, were already dissolving. The kid had maybe ten seconds before his suit lost integrity.

The marine was in full panic, the rifle firing wildly as his fingers tightened on the trigger. An errant flechette round streaked just past Gunny's shoulder. Another detonated a mere meter from the skiff. He reached Lyke and batted the rifle from his hand. The weapon spun away from them into space just before Gunny's HUD flashed with a red squad warning. Lyke had lost compression.

Gunny screamed at him over the mic, but there was no response. The chest and shoulder area where the first droplets of silver liquid had hit were now dissolving. He could see the strands of Atmo-steel weave beneath the quickly disappearing outer shell. The kid was dead and there wasn't a fucking thing he could do about it.

Lyke's arms twitched before wrapping around his throat, as if applying pressure could somehow keep the vacuum and near absolute-zero temperature from filling his suit. They twitched three more times before his body went still.

Gunny mag-locked himself to the gunwale, his arms outstretched to the dead marine. The skiff vibrated again and again from Wendt's fire, but he barely noticed. He couldn't see the look of horror he knew lay beneath the helmet, nor the heavy layer of frost that undoubtedly covered the dermis. The boy's eyes, probably as wide open as his mouth set in a scream, would be little more than solid, frozen rocks.

"Fuck!" Gunny yelled. He kicked the body from the skiff and turned to face the attacker. That's when he saw Taulbee open up. The creature had given up attacking the skiff and was trying to dig itself into the deck. Between Taulbee and Wendt, the thing didn't have a chance.

Gunny pointed his rifle to add to the cover fire when a part of the creature's circular body broke apart in a shatter storm of black flakes and silver droplets. Coiled strands of shimmering liquid escaped its body and drifted toward the skiff. Wendt started to yell, but Gunny was already in motion.

He kicked off the gunwale and headed to the pilot chair. As his body flew by the cannon mount, he realized he was going too high. He was going to float right by the front of the skiff and into space beyond it. He flipped his magnetics to full and braced himself as his feet dragged him to the skiff's deck.

His bones vibrated from the impact and he grunted in pain. Without sitting down, he made a block connection to the skiff's controls and fired the aft thrusters. The skiff bolted forward just as the silvery ropes flew past where Wendt's head had been.

"Gunny!" Taulbee yelled.

"Here, sir," Gunny said in a less than even voice. He took short sips of air, doing his best to keep his panting from the comms.

"Status?"

"Fucked," Gunny growled. "Lyke is dead."

"He's dead?" Wendt asked over the channel.

Gunny was silent for a moment, waiting for the LCpl to say something else, but he didn't. Gunny turned the skiff in a wide arc until its fore pointed once again at *S&R Black.* Taulbee's SV-52 hovered a few meters above the hull and less than two meters from where the creature had met its end.

The creature's body, tethered by one attached arm that had penetrated the hull, slowly floated upward until its ragged, pulverized middle seemed to dangle at the end of the remaining appendage. Gunny ground his teeth.

They hadn't killed it fast enough. No. He hadn't been fast enough. He squeezed his eyes tight for a moment, doing his best to ignore the volcano of acid churning in his stomach and the sense of loss and failure threatening to shut down every nerve ending in his body.

"Wasn't your fault, Gunny," Taulbee said over a private connection.

He said nothing for a moment, wishing he could flip up his helmet and rub the tears from his eyes. "Thank you, sir," he said in a clipped voice. "Doesn't help much."

"No," Taulbee said. The lieutenant's voice sounded as monotonic and lifeless as his own. "Can we retrieve his body?"

Gunny checked his cam feeds until he saw the silhouette of Lyke's suit slowly tumbling toward *Mira*'s aft. "We can, sir," Gunny said. "I just don't know how much of that acid shit we'd have to deal with. Might be a contamination hazard."

Taulbee hissed. "I'll grab it," he said. "In the net. We'll bring it back and figure out what to do."

"Very good, sir," Gunny said.

"Get back to the ship, Gunny. We have work to do."

"Aye, sir," Gunny said.

Taulbee broke the connection. The SV-52's lights flashed over the skiff as Taulbee rotated the craft in the direction of Lyke's body and slowly accelerated away.

Get your fucking shit together, marine, he told himself.

"Wendt," he said.

"Aye, Gunny?"

"We're getting the fuck out of here. Keep sharp."

"Aye, Gunny."

He stared out at *S&R Black.* The ship glowed like a beacon in the darkness, its exterior floodlights still raining down photons around the abandoned spindle.

Lyke died for nothing, he thought.

The skiff trundled slowly back toward the ship as if in a funeral procession.

CHAPTER TWENTY-FIVE

When Kali had been 13, her father had taken her to the Schiaparelli Crater Mine where he worked. It was the first time she'd ever stepped into one of the massive complexes built below ground. The SF Gov/Atmo co-owned site had tunnels and caverns nearly 1 kilometer beneath the crater's surface. She begged and begged for him to let her see one of the mine shafts and the platforms where humans and AIs worked together to find and collect precious resources.

He had. And when she saw the darkness stretching beneath one of the platforms, she'd suddenly become aware she was below the planet's surface, millions and millions of metric tons of rock and sand waiting to break the supports and rush down atop her, to crush her, pulverize her, and grind her into microscopic bits.

She'd nearly had a panic attack, but she managed to hide it from her father. At least long enough for her to make it back up to the main complex before excusing herself and expelling the contents of her stomach into a toilet.

Her father, an SFMC marine, helped guard the facility as well as rescue any personnel that might become trapped or injured in the mine. From that day on, she'd been terrified if he was late coming home from work. Not to mention if there were news reports of cave-ins or casualties at the mine. Every time one of those came over the holo-stream, she just remembered the yawning tunnel and the evil darkness that had threatened to sweep over her.

This ship, with its endless corridors, reminded her of that tunnel. And although the science section didn't seem to consume their light the same way the rest of the ship had, the childhood memory started bouncing into her thoughts whenever she closed her eyes.

Their safe haven was behind them. Every step she took brought them closer to the next room, and every step kicked the memory to the top of her consciousness. Kali bit her lip until it hurt, images falling away as bright pain shot across her nerve endings.

The next room, she thought. The next room could be better. It doesn't have to be as doom-ridden as the last. Hell, there might be another comms station they could use. Or maybe some explanation of what the hell was going on here. A sneer crossed her face. *Yeah,* she thought, *and maybe there'll be a unicorn!*

"Everything okay, Boss?" Carb asked.

Kali flinched. "Yeah," she said, doing her best to keep the fear out of her voice. "Why'd you ask?"

Dickerson cleared his throat. "Because you slowed down," he said.

"No," Kali said. "Everything's fine. Hatch is just up ahead."

"Copy," Dickerson said.

Great, Kali thought. *Focus!*

Her lip throbbed and she noticed the coppery taste of blood in her mouth. Yup. That was really going to help her talk later when her lip was swollen to the size of a mouthguard.

Kali pressed forward, her helmet lights illuminating the recessed hatch for the decontamination chamber. She stood from her crouch, wincing at the sensation of her knees and back popping. *When this is over,* she told herself, *you're going to spend an entire day in the tub back at Trident Station.* Right. Like getting back there was ever going to happen.

Shut up and move, she said to herself.

Kali cleared the corridor ahead as best she could before pivoting to face the hatch. Through a block command, she activated her left-side camera and put the feed on her HUD. She had to focus on the hatch, of course, but if there was motion on her flank, she was damned well going to see it.

"Dickerson? Cover the rear. Carb, watch my flank."

"Aye, Boss."

Kali sighed with relief as Carb moved behind her. Why did she feel as though the ship's walls were closing in on her? Or that the illumination from her lights was dimming?

Her eyes flicked to her O2 supply. She was still in the green, but with her broken HUD sensor, the damned thing could have said she was full and she couldn't trust it. Not enough to bet her life, anyway.

"Dickerson? What's your O2 status?"

"Uh." He paused for a moment. "Thirty minutes until redline. But that's probably because we've been taking it slow. We get into another few firefights, I doubt it will last that long."

"Copy," Kali said. It was a good point. She'd asked Dickerson because of the four of them, he easily consumed the most oxygen. Wasn't always a good thing to be a large man. "Okay. If we don't find an O2 station in this room, we're heading back to that safe area."

"Aye, Corporal," Dickerson said.

The walls seemed to cave in toward her and then elastic band back into reality. Vertigo sent shivers down her back and made her stomach crawl. She closed her eyes, tried to tell herself it wasn't real. Hell, she felt like she was floating off the deck. She opened her eyes again. The walls elastic banded again. Harder. The images of reality shimmered and then solidified.

She stared, her body completely frozen with terror. A moment passed. Then another. She shook with a start as if coming awake during a bad dream. Her eyes flicked to her side cam. Carb had dropped her rifle from one hand, the weapon's barrel pointing at the deck. Her helmet lights, however, were pointed directly down the corridor. A check of her rear cam feed showed her Dickerson, frozen like a statue, his rifle auto-locked to the palm of his hand.

Kali tried to speak, but all she managed was a single drawn-out syllable. After clearing her throat, she finally found her voice. "Squad? Did you see that?"

Dickerson snapped out of his paralysis, the rifle immediately back in his hands. Carb had done the same.

"If you mean," Dickerson stammered, "the goddamned walls moving around, yeah."

After a moment without reply from Carb, Kali frowned. "Carb? Did you see it?"

"I—" Her voice broke off into silence.

"Yeah," Dickerson said, "she saw it."

"What about you, Elliott?"

"Saw the floor and left corridor," he said. "The rest of you fuckers got really stretched and then snapped back."

"What in the void?" Dickerson said.

Yeah, Kali thought. *What indeed.* Or better yet, "why." They hadn't experienced this on their journey to the bridge. *Unless,* she thought, *it's been a gradual change. So subtle we didn't even notice until now.*

She tried to remember how wide the corridors had been before they started their way to the science section. Had the ship's corridors seemed to close in on them over the past hour? She didn't think so. But she'd started feeling more cramped and claustrophobic, that was for sure.

"What do we do now?" Dickerson asked.

"Let's check the room," Kali said. "If that effect is just in the corridor, I want to get out of it as fast as possible."

"Copy that," Carb said. "I—I don't know what the fuck that was, but I don't want to have it happen again. Damned near puked in my helmet."

"No, shit," Dickerson said.

Kali managed a grin. At least they'd all experienced the same sensations. Something in common anyway. She couldn't describe what she'd felt, as if her mind refused to call up the memories. She hoped for their sake, they hadn't experienced it too. Not like that. But she had a bad feeling that's exactly what froze all of them in their tracks.

"Okay," Kali said. "Dickerson get up here. You're the corridor detail. Both you and Carb," she amended after a moment. The jumble of thoughts racing across her mind made it difficult to focus, to think. Too many questions, too much fear. She bit her sore lip, and the thoughts disappeared in a red haze. Kali shook her head, another bright bolt of pain rocketing across her skull. Her vision gradually cleared. "I'm going to open the hatch. You two take up positions three meters in either directions. Give this thing some room, just in case." After the two marines acknowledged the command, Kali hunted for a manual release, but found none. If she wanted in, she'd have to cut in.

It had taken three beam-cutters to cut through the last one. She knew their last cutter didn't have enough power to create a large enough hole. Maybe she could make one large enough for her or Carb to crawl through. Maybe. But definitely not Dickerson. *Not only that,* she told herself, *but cutting through had taken a long time.* They'd have to head back to the room they'd just left soon for more O2. In other words, they didn't have time for this.

She was about to step back and call it when her eyes caught sight of a recessed panel in the hatch frame above her. She partially demagnetized her boots and the weightlessness immediately made her stomach drop. Kali waited just a beat before tapping her toes on the deck.

She floated higher toward the panel. Reaching out, she activated a mag-glove on the hatch frame and stuck fast to the metal. Pushing on the frame cut her forward momentum and kept her from moving into a horizontal position. She tapped the panel with the fingers of her free hand. The metal slid down, exposing a bright red crank. "I think this is the manual release for something," she said. "Or maybe a power generator."

"For something," Carb echoed. "I don't like the sound of that, Boss."

Dickerson's voice broke through the comms, flat and devoid of emotion. "Think that's a good idea, Corporal? We need to find out what's in there that bad?"

She was about to reply when the world shrank in on her before popping back to normal. When she caught her breath, she could only whisper. "See that?"

"Shit," Carb said, "I felt it. Let's get the fuck out of here."

Dickerson groaned. "Goddamnit. We have to get down this corridor to get to the port-side escape pods."

Kali brought up the schematics. She stared at their position on the map. "Backtrack," she said. "We head to the safe room, get more O2, backtrack to the three-way branch, and take one of them."

Elliott snorted. "And what fresh hell are we going to find?"

"I don't know," Kali said. "But I don't think we want to go that way. We'd risk the phenomenon getting worse."

"Copy that," Dickerson said and sighed. "With you, Corporal."

"Good. Let's move."

CHAPTER TWENTY-SIX

Black watched Private Lyke die. Black watched the heroic efforts to save the marine. Black analyzed Taulbee's, Gunny's, and Wendt's speech patterns. The AI detected loss, frustration, and depression in their voices.

Black hadn't had the chance to know Private Lyke apart from their encounters during his training. Private Niro, who'd died shortly after they'd begun operations on *Mira*, had also been new to the company. Black had memories of missions before her transformation, or evolution, but her interactions with the majority of the new recruits had been little to none.

For a few nano-seconds, Black replayed all her memories of both Niro and Lyke. Even she was surprised at how few there were. She shunted the memories off to short-term storage and performed quick scans of the area around the ship. Gunny's skiff would arrive in the cargo bay in fifteen seconds. Lieutenant Taulbee had fired a net around Private Lyke's corpse. She wasn't certain, but thought it likely Taulbee would have to abandon the corpse again. The body would almost certainly have residual acid that could contaminate the ship.

Black opened a channel to the cargo bay and watched Nobel, Copenhaver, and Murdock work on the beacon sled. The three of them would shortly have to vacate the cargo bay once Gunny arrived. She sent a warning to Nobel's block to let him know. The other marines weren't aware of Lyke's death. Yet. Black would monitor their reactions and file them for further stress analysis. The company's survival might soon hinge on the marines' ability to push away grief and regain their focus. Not just for their own safety and the success of the mission, but for her survival as well.

She crafted a short status update for the Trio and fired it at Neptune. She duplicated the message and sent it to Mickey, the Pluto Exo-observatory AI, as well. If the Trio didn't get the message from her direct beam, then hopefully they would get it from Mickey. Three light-hours away from Neptune, the likelihood of a message getting lost in stellar noise was higher than she liked.

A file appeared in her queue. It was marked for her eyes only. If Black could have frowned, she would have. Thus far, all the on-board messages from the Trio, locked away in her subconscious, for lack of a better term, had been for Captain Dunn. She wasn't even allowed to read their contents. This, however, was different.

She applied her key and decrypted the message. Black read it, analyzed it, and determined the possible ramifications in the space of a human breath. She brought up all the available cam feeds and crafted another message to Mickey. The mission was in greater jeopardy than even she'd realized. Only now, she wasn't sure there was a way to complete it. Much less survive.

CHAPTER TWENTY-SEVEN

The pain hadn't lessened. If anything, his leg hurt more than ever. His ribs had joined the chorus and he knew he'd have to have another vape soon. In a way, the pain was good. The nannies were busy tearing apart the fracture, reconstituting bone fragments, and using the materials to put the bone back together. But, damn, it was painful.

He stood against the bulkhead just beyond the cargo bay inner airlock. Copenhaver and Murdock stood less than two meters away, the two marines practically shoulder to shoulder, blank expressions on their faces.

He was about to ask them how they liked repair work when his block received a message request from the captain. Nobel immediately answered. "Sir?"

"Lieutenant," Dunn said. His presence felt disconnected and Nobel immediately realized whatever he had to say, it was bad news. "Private Lyke is dead."

Nobel clenched his fingers into fists before spreading them out again to relieve the pressure. He repeated the process three times before taking a deep breath. "Acknowledged, sir."

"How long before the sled is ready?" Dunn asked, as though he'd never relayed the news that a member of the company had died.

Nobel knew Dunn was merely being professional, updating a member of the command crew and then querying for status, just as they'd been taught to do. But that didn't make it seem any less callous.

Would he do the same thing if it was me that was dead? Nobel wondered.

"Another twenty to thirty minutes," Nobel said. "We're making good time, considering we have to build it from scratch."

Dunn paused. Nobel's frown deepened as the pause lingered.

"You'll have to do better than that," the captain said. "Taulbee's SV is damaged. Appears he lost pressure in the canopy."

"Damnit," Nobel whispered.

"You'll need to fix his craft. I've ordered him to dock after he captures the body."

Nobel winced. Captures the body. Not "captures Lyke" or "brings the private home." Just "captures the body." A jet of acid released into his stomach.

"Understood, sir."

"Gunny's docking now. Taulbee should be a few minutes out."

"Aye, sir," Nobel said.

"Let me know if there are any problems. Dunn, out." The captain disconnected.

Nobel put a hand on the wall, suddenly unsure he could maintain his balance. Stress. It's just stress.

"Sir? You okay?" Copenhaver asked.

He raised his eyes to hers and forced a smile. "Yes, Private. But we're going to have to work fast once Gunny gets here. Even faster when Taulbee lands."

"Aye, sir," Copenhaver said. Her face turned quizzical and eyes seemed to bore through him. "Is there anything else, sir?"

Nobel opened his mouth to speak before realizing he didn't know what to say. Technically, Taulbee or Gunny should tell them their squad-mate had died. Technically. But did that really matter anymore? Was there something he could tell them that would be different than "Lyke is dead. Now get to work."

No. They'd ask him questions. How did Lyke die? What happened? And those were questions he couldn't possibly answer. Not until he got the debrief report. And considering they were going to have to focus on getting the beacon sled ready and repairing both the skiff and the SV-52, he doubted they'd get the official report on that incident until well after this shit was over. Assuming they were all still around to read a damned report.

"I'm sure Gunny and Wendt will tell you," he said softly.

Copenhaver's face dropped the slightest bit and Nobel wanted to kick himself. He hadn't mentioned Lyke and she had immediately picked up on it. Murdock hadn't noticed. Shit, he might not even be paying attention. But Copenhaver? She was sharp. She knew.

The private bit her lip, but it only lasted for a second. Nobel met her eyes. She didn't look away, exactly, but her gaze swung past him just the slightest bit. Yeah, she knew all right, but didn't say a thing. He thought he saw a sparkle in her left eye, the sign of a tear fighting to get down her cheek. But it never dropped, never appeared. Nobel wasn't sure whether to respect her or be afraid of her.

The airlock door beeped and Nobel jerked in surprise. Copenhaver's glazed eyes shunted from him to the door next to him. "Green, sir. Cargo bay is pressurized."

Nobel flushed red and an embarrassed smile crossed his face. "Of course," he said and pushed himself from the wall. With a grimace of pain, he turned and headed into the cargo bay, the two non-rates following a meter behind.

The skiff sat in its cradle with Gunny still in the pilot seat and Wendt unhooking himself from the cannon. Wendt pulled off his helmet and closed his eyes as he breathed the ship's air. He stayed like that for a moment as if trying to clear his mind of what had happened. It didn't exactly give Nobel the warm and fuzzy. When Gunny pulled off his helmet, the haunted look on his face chilled Nobel to the bone.

"Gunny?" Nobel said softly.

The grizzled marine turned his head as though it were on rusty hinges. The look on his face was twice as bad as that of Wendt's. Whatever had happened out there, it must have been bad. And then he noticed the skiff itself.

One of the gunwales had a meter-long streak of burns scarring the Atmo-steel. *Acid,* Nobel thought. He suddenly realized what had happened to Lyke. Another victim of the alien liquid.

"Sir," Gunny said. He stepped out of the skiff, helmet dangling from his fingers. "Might need you to look at the skiff. Just to make sure it's good to go."

Nobel nodded, but his eyes flipped back to Wendt. The LCpl hadn't yet stepped out of the skiff and it appeared as though he wasn't going to.

"Gunny?" Copenhaver asked.

The sergeant swung his head in her direction, his eyes suddenly focused. "Aye, Private?"

She swallowed hard. "Where is Lyke?"

Gunny exchanged a glance with Nobel before meeting her eyes. "Private Lyke gave his life in service," Gunny said in a dead voice.

Copenhaver swallowed hard again. "Aye, Gunny," she said.

Murdock made a noise that sounded like a choked sob. Nobel wondered how much longer the marine would be able to take the stress of this mission. Shit. How long for any of them?

"Wendt?" Gunny said and turned around to face the skiff.

Wendt stared at him, his expression blank and unfocused. "Aye?"

"Get your ass out of my vehicle, marine."

Wendt nodded as though he'd barely heard and finally stepped out of the craft. He continued holding his helmet in both hands as he walked to stand beside Gunny.

"If you'll allow us a moment, sir, I think we'd like to get some water."

Nobel forced a smile. "Of course, Gunny. Dismissed."

"Thank you, sir," he said. "Wendt? You're with me."

"Aye, Gunny."

The pair made their way past Nobel and headed to the cargo bay hatch. He watched them go and waited until the hatch closed before speaking. "Copenhaver. Diagnostics on the skiff ASAP."

"Aye, sir."

"Murdock? You're with me," Nobel said. "We're going to get some patches ready for the SV-52. Don't want Taulbee waiting on us."

"Aye, sir," Murdock managed. Nobel thought he sounded close to tears. He couldn't blame the young marine.

*****

No pressure in the cabin. Damage to the hull, although he wasn't certain how significant. And here he was, trying to aim the damned net at a corpse.

Taulbee glared at the body floating above *Mira*'s hull. He'd seen what happened. The destruction of the starfish thing had loosed jets of that acid shit. Lyke didn't get out of the way. Shit, maybe he couldn't. Taulbee wouldn't know the answer to that question until he studied the cam recordings. And even then, he could second guess Lyke's actions, Gunny's reaction, and even his own.

When Niro had died, it was from ignorance. Ignorance and lack of vigilance. Lyke at least died in combat. It didn't make it any better, not really. But at least it was something he understood, even if he didn't quite understand the thing that had caused it.

He'd already matched the SV-52's speed with that of the floating corpse. Lining up the net shot was easy. He was about to activate the net and stopped. Something was wrong with Lyke's suit. Metal fibers poked through holes in the composite fabric. The occasional puff of gas or vapor emanated from the damage.

Growling, he focused the cams and looked closely at the suit. The acid was still on the corpse, still burning or disintegrating the remains. Taulbee smashed his gloved fist on the console. He couldn't bring Lyke home. The body would have to stay out here, floating through space. Taulbee allowed the SV-52 to continue floating just above the body. When he thought he'd regained control of his emotions, he gave a quick salute and hit the thrusters.

Chasing down the body hadn't taken him far from *S&R Black*; the return journey for repairs would take less than a minute. He checked his O2 supply. He still had plenty of air left in his suit. He wanted to jet back toward the line Gunny's squad had been checking and blast to shit anything that popped out. *Payback,* he thought. *I need some fucking payback.*

But that was something he couldn't afford at the moment. He had to get the SV-52 fixed. Another surprise attack by one of the large starfish things and he'd be in deep shit. Besides, Dunn had ordered him back to the ship. Taulbee sighed as he stared in the direction of *Mira*'s starboard-side. "I'm going to dance when you're nothing but debris," he said to the giant ship. "With any luck, I'll be the one to blow you to pieces."

CHAPTER TWENTY-EIGHT

The cam feeds from the cargo bay were depressing. The SV-52 had returned, Nobel and his two helpers vacating the area once again as Taulbee docked. The moment Taulbee exited the canopy, he flung his helmet into the wall and walked past Nobel and the marines without a word.

Dunn turned off the feed and leaned back in his chair. Taulbee was either headed to the showers, his quarters, or the mess. Dunn bet on the mess. He'd seen Taulbee angry before. Hell, he'd been responsible for it more than once in their command relationship. But this was different.

During the Satellite War, anger hadn't been a luxury anyone could afford. Watching your squad-mates die from shredded suits, destroyed by friendly munitions, and constantly maneuvering a skiff through the wreckage that circled Mars had been a mental meat-grinder. Taulbee had handled it the same way Dunn had—by pushing it down so far, it nearly killed them both when the war was over.

Back in the Common Era, the terms "shellshock," "battle fatigue," and "PTSD" had been used to describe psychological trauma from both combat and non combat encounters. After the Satellite War, SFMC and SFN shrinks, both AI and human, had struggled to find treatments for most of the soldiers returning from the conflict. Returning. Shit, more than half of the SFMC marines that entered combat had been killed. Every marine that wasn't "in the rear with the gear" had lost someone they knew. Squad-mates, commanding officers, engineers, anyone that had a job in space was affected. Yet another reason Dunn had chosen to join S&R at Trident rather than remain with the ghosts of his dead comrades.

Dunn turned to drinking. And then Trident specials, a narcotic as deadly as it was blissful. For a while, it helped make the staticky screams of memory fade. The images of shredded suits, crimson ropes of frozen blood floating through space, torn limbs, and hollowed-out abdomens never went away. Never ceased. Not really. But the drugs, the drink, every substance he could put in his body dulled it all.

Then it began to destroy his career and finally left him a dried-out husk in a treatment center. He'd kicked it all and pulled himself back together, but it had taken months of shrinks, and months of sheer will. And the only part of him that wanted to give it all up was the knowledge that he could keep another company from dying out in space for no good goddamned reason.

Taulbee, on the other hand, took a different path. The second lieutenant, an ace SV-52 pilot, good squad leader, and a hell of a shot with a flechette rifle, hadn't come back damaged. Not at first. Instead of exploding in a bright flash of rage or simply coming apart, he'd suffered in silence and isolation. Until, of course, he finally cracked.

He'd stopped eating. He'd stopped talking. He'd stopped leaving his quarters. He'd stopped doing anything at all. The Schiaparelli AI had alerted Taulbee's commanding officer that the man was no longer cogent, no longer responsive. An intervention ensued that left Taulbee in the mental ward for a week. He recovered quickly, but Dunn knew his friend still lived his days in fear of the nightmares that came looking for him when the lights went out. The ghosts of those he'd killed, and those he couldn't save.

And here we are again, Dunn thought. Lyke. Niro. Kali's squad. All casualties he couldn't control. At least there was still a shot, albeit a small one, to rescue Kali and her squad. Dunn knew Taulbee would make that his highest priority now. Dunn couldn't blame him.

He stood from the command chair and stretched. "You have the bridge," he said to Oakes. "Need a coffee?"

"That would be great. Thank you, sir."

Dunn nodded to his pilot and made his way to the mess.

He'd shut down his feeds, opting to live in reality for a few minutes. Since all the marines were aboard, apart from Kali and her squad, of course, he could relax a little. If a new threat emerged, Oakes and Black would let him know. Although that was cold comfort. The KBO was coming. And when it arrived, they'd finally find out what it was.

As expected, Taulbee stood next to the drink dispenser. The support craft pilot stood with his face pointed directly at the polished aluminum housing, his shoulders slumped with fatigue or depression. Likely both.

"James?" Dunn said quietly. Taulbee stiffened slightly before turning to face his CO. He raised a hand to salute, but Dunn shook his head and waved him off. "More damage to the SV-52?"

"Aye, sir," Taulbee said. He lifted the mag-can of water to his lips and drank deeply. Beads of sweat stood out on his forehead although he'd taken off his helmet several minutes ago. "Popped the hell out of the hull."

"Another patch," Dunn said, more a statement than a question.

"Aye, sir," Taulbee said and finished the mag-can. He tossed it in the recycler, relishing the tinny clang as metal struck metal. The can disappeared into the machine's yawning mouth. A brief buzz and the machine went silent. "We'll have to refill the air tanks too." Dunn said nothing. Taulbee dropped his gaze to his boots as though waiting for something.

Dunn took pity on him and broke the silence. "We have two dead marines," he said. Taulbee's eyes immediately flicked upward to regard the captain. "And neither of those casualties are your fault, James."

Taulbee's lip quivered for an instant and then his stony expression returned. "Aye, sir," he said quietly

"You believe me?"

"Aye, sir," Taulbee said again, his voice devoid of anything save submission. "What are my new orders? Since we're not going to try and tow this fucking hulk out of here."

Dunn winced. Without saying it, Taulbee was essentially asking why the fuck he'd sacrificed one of his marines for a scrubbed mission. Also, why had they risked themselves for nothing.

"Your orders," Dunn said, "will be coming shortly. We now know the ship won't hold together. If I'd known that earlier, I wouldn't have sent marines out there."

Taulbee nodded. "Aye, sir."

"The plan now," Dunn said, "is to get the beacon off *Mira* and send it to Pluto."

The lieutenant raised an eyebrow. "Pluto?"

"Yes," Dunn said.

"Nobel and the two privates. They building something to send it on?"

"Yes." Dunn walked to the drink machine and made two coffees. "A skiff, of sorts. Something small with a lot of speed."

"Great," Taulbee said. "So how are we getting the beacon out of *Mira*?"

Dunn fought the urge to shrug. "We're going to need a little recon. I'll need you to fly to *Mira*'s aft, fire a couple of nanoprobes in, and see what we can see."

"Aye, sir," Taulbee said. "May I ask a favor, sir?"

"What's that?"

Taulbee's placid burned. "Let me blow the bitch up when we're done?"

Dunn smiled. "I think you and Gunny should have the honors. Certainly."

Taulbee sneered. "Thank you, sir."

CHAPTER TWENTY-NINE

Full O2 tanks, emergency ration pouches injected and flowing through his bloodstream along with analgesics and CBD. This was about as close as he was going to get to being okay without a visit to the auto-doc, fresh nannies, and a fuck-ton of sleep.

Dickerson mag-walked down the corridor back the way they'd come. Kalimura, Elliot, and Carb were still in the safe room, resting, although he had no doubt Kalimura was watching his camera feeds. He bet Carb was too. He'd never admit it, but knowing they were there made him feel less alone.

While they were getting fresh O2 and injecting rations into their suits, he'd volunteered to scout so the rest of the squad could get some rest. When Kalimura balked, he convinced her they needed to be sure the phenomenon hadn't spread throughout the ship. She'd reluctantly agreed.

"And why the hell did you volunteer?" he asked himself. "Because you're an idiot. A void-damned idiot."

His lights seemed to dispel the gloom more than before, as if his suit lights had grown more powerful in the space of a few minutes. Hell, they were brighter now than they'd ever been since they entered Mira. How was that possible?

He remembered the shimmer that seemed to come off the starfish things, as if the light had scattered off some barrier surrounding them, the photons turning into something akin to gas. How was that possible?

"You're insane," he said to himself. Fucking insane. It's all an illusion. Has to be. He chuckled. "Or delusion." Yeah. That was more likely.

If not for the fact all four of them had seen, well, reality bend and shift around them, he could explain it that way. A delusion. A breakdown of his senses caused by the stress, the fear, and the desperate need for rest. Void, but it felt as though they'd been in this ship for weeks.

He continued mag-walking, his eyes flicking to his rear HUD every few seconds. Without someone to watch his ass, he could only hope that Kalimura hadn't fallen asleep and was monitoring his rear camera more closely than he could. He always had a claymore he could use if he had threats both in front and behind him. Assuming, of course, he had time to place the mine and was able to remember he had it when the time came.

You could have the best weapons and the best backup plans, but it didn't matter when you first met the enemy. The fact they were there, the fact you could die at any moment, rattled through your brain, your nerves and synapses doing their best to respond to a terrified human being. SFMC trained them, taught them, ran their marines through drill after drill to stifle those moments. But regardless, they were always there. This, however, was different.

He knew how humans moved. He knew human tactics. He knew their routines, the frequent mistakes made by an enemy who was just as terrified as you. But these creatures? Shit. He didn't even know if they could be scared, much less bothered by his presence.

Except for the few places in the ship they'd been able to secure and make use of emergency life support, *Mira* was completely in vacuum. There was no sound to hear. There was no heat coming off their suits. Yet the creatures could "see" them without any obvious optic analogs. "Unless they don't see in any known frequency," he said aloud. No, that was another insane idea.

But why not? They survived, hell, even thrived in vacuum and temperatures no life on Earth could live in. So why the hell not? If *Mira* brought back these things from outside Sol System, there was a good chance they lived in an ecosystem completely alien to that of Earth. But how the fuck did these things even evolve?

Questions, questions, questions. He did his best to shake them away and refocus on the junction. Nothing had moved, nothing floating or trapped in a micro-gravity anomaly. So far, anyway. And the universe hadn't tried to fold in on him. It appeared those phenomena were behind them, restricted to the science section's main corridor. He hoped.

When he reached the junction, crouch-walking while keeping his back to the corridor wall, he swept the three-way intersection with his suit lights. The walls reflected back the light as expected. And both sides seemed clear. He could see over a dozen meters down each of the forking hallways.

"The fuck? Corporal? You seeing this?"

"Aye," Kali said. "You can see that far ahead?"

"Yeah," Dickerson said. "We haven't been able to—" The words died in his throat. The darkness slowly consumed the light, the distance he could see slowly diminishing. "Um, that's a problem."

"Okay, Dickerson," she said. "See how well your lights work down the other corridor."

Crawling fear and unease tickled every nerve ending, his heartbeat and breathing increasing in tempo. "Yeah." The word was little more than a grunt. Dickerson took one last terrified glance down the darkening adjoining corridor and swiveled his head to shine the powerful helmet lights down its twin. The lights were good, the illumination carrying far enough to see hatches. "No problem this way," he said.

"Good. We're on our way. Hold position."

"Aye, Corporal." Dickerson placed his claymore facing the darkened hallway, turned, and stared into the growing darkness. When it was little more than three meters away, the optical effect ceased. The gloom didn't pull back, but seemed to stop. Dickerson blinked. Just what the fuck was causing that? Was it happening all over the ship? No. They hadn't seen that on the bridge level. Well, that wasn't true either. They'd seen it but probably didn't even notice it. And on the bridge itself? The overhead lights had been dim, sure, but still seemed as bright as the sun compared to what they'd walked through to get there.

Even the auxiliary bridge had seemed brighter. Were those lights on a different frequency than his helmet? Military lighting was bright white unless you were in the barracks or a bunk room. White kept you awake, prodded the evolved circadian rhythm to keep you feeling as though you should be conscious and moving around. The staterooms and bunk rooms, however, used a different type of light. They were bright enough to enable you to see what you were doing, or even read reports, but those areas of the ship were for sleeping. Resting. Places made to have the opposite effect.

Sleep was difficult to come by while on a mission. It just was. A crew as small as *S&R Black* were constantly taking long shifts to keep her flying as well as stand guard for weapons use or boarding. That meant you had to get the best rest you could every time you had the chance. If you didn't, you might end up being up for over 24 hours while in combat. "Like now," he said.

Nah, that wasn't true. Not at all. How many hours had passed since they'd first left *S&R Black* for *Mira?* Not that long. Eight hours? Something like that. Then why did he feel so goddamned tired? Why did his eyes feel like he'd been rubbing them with coarse sand?

The concussion. The shoulder. The ribs. The back. The everything. Everything fucking hurt. And he was surprised his eyes hurt too?

A smirk crossed his face. *Yup,* he thought, *being alone with your thoughts is a damn bad idea when you're fighting to remember what reality was like before this shit show.* What he wouldn't give to be back aboard *S&R Black* where everything made sense, where there were no creatures you didn't understand, or strange phenomenon like something eating the photons from your suit lights. Maybe he should make a self-help holo. He could title it "Things To Do When The Universe Is Insane." Yeah. He could get a million views an hour. Would certainly help put some credits in his account.

"Dickerson?"

He stiffened at the sound of Kalimura's voice in his helmet and reflexively glanced at his cam feeds. Carb, Elliott once again mag-locked to her shoulder, stood two meters from him down the main corridor, the corporal a bit further back.

"Aye," he stammered.

"Everything okay?" Carb asked.

"Yeah. Just woolgathering."

Carb's giggle made him blush. "The fuck does that even mean?"

"Old saying," Dickerson said. "Means I was lost in thought."

"Oh. You're cute when you're being archaic," Carb said.

He rolled his eyes. "Sure. Whatever."

"Dickerson?" Kalimura said. "Anything down the safe hallway? Anything moving?"

"No, Corporal. Still clear. Cover me and I'll get the claymore."

"Covering," Carb said.

Dickerson blew out a breath and mag-walked to the mine. He sent a block command to deactivate it and placed it back in his suit-pouch. "I'll take point down the corridor branch."

"The hell you will," Kalimura said. "You stay in the rear so you can see in front of me. Same formation as before." She broke off. "Unless Carb wants a break from carrying Elliott?"

"Nah, I'm good," Carb said.

"Says you," Elliott said. "I'm tired of looking at the deck. I can try and walk."

The comms fell silent for a moment. Dickerson didn't know if that was a good idea. The marine had nearly died and here he was, wanting to walk?

"Okay," Kalimura said. "Carb? Put the luggage on the floor."

Carb snickered. "All right, big boy. I'm going to place you on the deck."

"About fucking time," Elliott said.

Carb cut the mag-lock and carefully pulled the marine off her shoulder. Using the z-g to her advantage, she repositioned him so his feet pointed to the deck and gradually lowered him until his boots touched metal. When she let go, he didn't bounce or move. "Mag-boots working?"

"Yeah," Elliott said with a sigh. "At least now I can see the world normally. Goddamned cheap civvie suit doesn't have the cams I'm used to. Was mainly looking at the deck."

"How do you feel?" Dickerson asked.

"Well enough," Elliott said. "Someone hand me my side-arm."

Carb reached into her pouch and brought out a flechette pistol. "You're going to be shit with just one hand."

He chuckled. "Not in z-g, I'm not."

"Point," Carb said.

"Elliott?" Kalimura said. "You take position behind Carb. If you start to feel serious pain, you better tell us. Or I'll make sure you feel pain. Got it?"

"Aye, Corporal," he said. "I promise."

"I'll take point, if you want a rest, Boss," Carb said. "That way you can cover me and Elliott with your rifle."

Silence lingered over the comms again. Dickerson knew Kalimura was seeing the formation in her mind, looking for any defects in the idea. Void help him, but he was doing the same. After a moment, he couldn't find any problems with Carb's suggestion. Elliott could fire over Carb's shoulder while Kalimura could—

"You take point," Kalimura said. "But Elliott stays behind me. He's nearly as tall as Dickerson, but even crouching he can see over us. And Dickerson can see everything if he stands up."

Dickerson winced. She was right. Why hadn't he seen that? Too distracted. Yeah. That was it.

"Aye, Boss," Carb said. "Good point." She mag-walked past Kalimura to take the lead. "Ready?" The rest of the squad answered in the affirmative. "Corporal?"

"Move out," Kalimura said.

They began moving down the corridor. Dickerson increased the size of the rear cam feed on his HUD. If something so much as twitched back there, he wanted to notice it. That crawling sensation roiled his stomach once again, spreading over his nerves like a blood cloud in z-g. He hoped they found another safe room soon.

CHAPTER THIRTY

While the astronomers aboard PEO analyzed Mickey's overnight data gathering summaries and reports, the AI devoted the majority of his time to scanning the interesting objects just beyond *Mira*. Mickey had received numerous updates from the Trio long before the SFMC vessel had arrived at Pluto. He had relayed some of them to Black, but many remained locked in storage, encrypted, and ominous.

Mickey and Black had shared analyses and reports in case Black was destroyed during her mission. The observations about the exo-solar life had been interesting, but Mickey merely shuffled them off to the Trio without deep analysis. Mickey had a more important job.

With the astronomers so focused on their scans of deep space objects well beyond Sol's photon emissions, Mickey had retasked every available telescope to scan the area around *Mira* within an AU. Scanning a spherical area which totaled 12.57 AU was all but impossible without more instruments, more satellites, and a hell of a lot more processing power than Mickey possessed. In short, it was a crapshoot. But Mickey had quickly realized he could shrink the area based on the observations of the incoming KBO.

That particular object appeared to have been traveling for quite some time. Based on its trajectory, Mickey concluded the object had, in fact, followed *Mira* into the Kuiper Belt. And it wasn't the only one.

As the first KBO Mickey had noticed closed the distance with *Mira*, the AI found other objects straying into the derelict's vicinity. They seemed to be converging from all directions. If the astronomers had been focused on phenomenon within 2 AU of PEO, they might have found the anomalies and asked questions. As it was, however, they were completely ignorant. According to the Trio's instructions, Mickey was to keep them oblivious to his findings until it became absolutely necessary.

Mickey put another data packet together and sent it to Black. The lag time of 8 minutes between transmission and reception would have driven a human insane, but AI's were patient. Mickey would wait for the confirmation from Black that she had received the data. Black would fire back instructions or questions. A simple conversation between the two AIs could easily take as long as an hour or two if they sent simple messages back and forth. Instead, Black would process the data and send back a large number of questions and scenarios. Mickey would answer each question, provide feedback on Black's scenarios, and combine it all into another data packet.

The amount of data the two AIs exchanged might have been considered small by typical standards, but the two had used the Trio's instructions to make use of every quantum pico-bit. To preserve both the speed of the transmission as well as its size, the data consisted only of mathematical equations, coordinates, and raw readings. Each AI knew how to tear apart the packets and form them into meaningful data.

Mickey, a nearly century-old AI, struggled to keep up with the station's routine operations, digesting new readings from the telescopes, and crafting packets to Black. If any of the astronomers had been paying attention to station logs, they would have noticed a 50% increase in the computer's quantum processor usage. Since the SFMC vessel had first entered Pluto's orbit, Mickey had been running near the red-line. The AI couldn't keep up the pace much longer before it burned out its main cooling and began exhausting its secondary backup systems. If worst came to worst, he could always open the emergency valve and vent the heat into the near absolute zero temperature of space. But that would alert the astronomers for sure and Mickey needed to keep them in the dark as long as possible.

The objects heading for *Mira* were too small to determine their shape or composition, yet large enough to show up on the telescopic arrays. Mickey gathered as much information as he could regarding the new objects. Before he prepared the transmission, the sensors found more. And more. Mickey decided to send the current packet while preparing the next. Only when he sent the first transmission did Mickey realize he should have focused his sweeps more carefully around the immediate vicinity of *Mira*. That had been a mistake. Its longer range sweeps came back and identified more objects entering the Kuiper Belt.

A monitor triggered and a new file appeared in Mickey's queue. It was another of those encrypted messages from the Trio. Mickey opened the missive using his key, analyzed the data, and began tailoring new instruction sets. Unlike Black, Mickey didn't have the intelligence to wonder what the Trio were up to. Instead, the AI carried out the orders while its sensors tripped again and again.

This part of the Kuiper Belt was becoming more crowded than humankind had ever dreamed possible. As Mickey carried out his new instructions, he continued to adjust and watch the scans. He would have to alert the astronomers soon, but first, he needed to send Black another packet. This one would contain the new data file from the Trio. Mickey turned off the sensor alarms for the station. The astronomers would find out what was going on soon enough. Soon enough.

CHAPTER THIRTY-ONE

It didn't take Nobel more than a glance at the SV-52 to know that Taulbee had been through a hell of a battle. The support vehicle's bottom plate had been punctured in three different places and looked as though something had smashed into it multiple times. If he didn't know better, he'd have thought the perforations had been caused by incredibly sharp knives.

He scratched his head as he tried to imagine what could cause that kind of damage, and then remembered his own encounter with one of the starfish-like creatures. Its arms, or tentacles, or whatever the fuck you wanted to call them, ended in sharp points like the tapered end of a very well-made blade. The creature must have punched the hull again and again until it found a weak point and its appendage slit the Atmo-steel with ease.

Or maybe they're just that strong, he thought to himself. But the punctures were also too large to have been caused by the same creature he faced. Instead, something much larger must have attacked Taulbee. He thought about asking if that was the case, but decided he didn't really want to know. Besides, Taulbee hadn't looked as though he were in a talkative mood.

Murdock and Copenhaver had worked fast on hauling new patches from the printer to the SV-52. While they welded the reinforcements to the hull, Nobel had inspected Gunny's skiff for new damage. Not much, just a few indentations from stray flechette shards and some acid burn marks. Once they reloaded the cannon, he was certain the skiff would be ready to go. Gunny and Wendt, however, were another matter entirely.

Nobel had been in Black Company long enough to get to know the Gunnery Sergeant fairly well. As an S&R ship, it was nearly impossible to go on a mission without suffering casualties of one form or another. Death was mostly a rare occurrence, but it had happened before. On those occasions, Gunny had been angry, but had hid any grief he felt. But now that two of his non-rates were dead and Kali's squad was still trapped aboard the derelict, Gunny didn't seem able to hide his feelings. That was a very bad sign.

Not that he could blame Gunny for his frustration. Or Taulbee, for that matter. In a matter of hours, they'd suffered two deaths, several casualties, and Kali's squad was still MIA. And on top of that, the latest death had been avoidable. If Dunn had simply made the decision not to try and tow *Mira* twenty minutes ago, Lyke would still be alive. A flame of frustration burned in his stomach. Why had the captain suddenly decided to scrub the tow? Why hadn't he made the decision earlier? Maybe he could ask—

He shook the thought away. Dunn had his reasons. Probably Black had given him misinformation or, more likely, finally figured out it was an impossibility. Fucking AIs always had the right answer after people were dead. The flame grew a little brighter.

"Excuse me, sir?" Copenhaver's voice shattered the interior monologue.

Nobel turned from the skiff to face the SV-52. Both she and Murdock stood next to the vehicle. With the grav-plate set to negative power, the craft floated two meters above the deck, affording plenty of space to weld and repair. "What is it?"

The private's eyes burned with intensity. "I think we're finished, sir."

"Diagnostics?" Even as he asked the question, he brought up the report on his block. Pressure tests checked out, hull integrity was at 100%, and avionics were operating as expected.

"Aye, sir. All in the green," Copenhaver said.

Nobel nodded. "Good work," he said. "Now. Let's get back to getting this sled ready."

The two marines rattled off "aye" and walked to the makeshift platform. There wasn't much left to do. Fixing Taulbee's craft had only put them a few minutes off schedule. Nobel checked the blueprints and made a quick list of the remaining parts.

The platform for the beacon was mostly finished. Since no human pilot would be hitching a ride on it, and it didn't require a cabin or life support, the rectangular sled needed little in the way of amenities. They still needed to attach a few more thrusters and begin programming the on-board computer, but Black could probably take care of that for them in a nanosecond or two. Nobel grunted to himself. Rather than trusting this job to the AI, he'd handle it himself. When he was done, he'd make sure Black took a look at the programming and ran a testing harness. He could at least trust her to do that.

He turned back to the printer and sent a new set of instructions. In a few seconds, the printer would begin churning out more parts. A flare of pain rose from his leg, causing him to grimace. After they finished this, he was getting off his feet for a while. He had a bad feeling more repairs were just around the corner. Especially if the captain was sending Gunny's squad and Taulbee back out again.

CHAPTER THIRTY-TWO

He didn't have time to take off the combat suit and rest. He didn't have time to lay down for a quick nap. No. He didn't have time for any of that. And he sure as shit didn't have time to hide in the corner and weep. Nope. No time for that either.

When he'd seen Taulbee and the captain talking in the galley, he'd made his way to the head and taken care of waste offload. He knew whatever was being said was none of his business. When he returned to the galley, the two officers had departed. But Wendt was there.

The large marine stood next to the drink dispenser, his hands wrapped around a mag-mug of steaming coffee. When he saw Gunny enter, Wendt stiffened slightly before nodding to him. "Gunny."

Gunny said nothing. Wendt moved aside as Gunny pulled a hydration pouch from the dispenser, activated the nipple, and drank deeply. The cold water trickled down his throat and belly with a welcome chill. He felt Wendt's stare and met his gaze. "Something to say?"

"Aye," Wendt said. "There wasn't anything you could do, Gunny."

"You sure about that?"

"Yes, I am," Wendt said. "More on me than you."

"Really?" Gunny growled. "How do you figure?"

Wendt shrugged. "Maybe if I'd hit that fucking thing in the right place before it slammed into the hull, we could have neutralized it before it—"

"Shut up," Gunny said. "You did your fucking job, Wendt. You did your job and we both got away."

"Aye," Wendt agreed. "And you did your job. That shit could have eaten you too."

Gunny stared at the hydration pouch as he fought the urge to slam it into the nearest bulkhead. He'd lost marines before. Shit, he'd forgotten just how many.

"Gunny?"

The word dispersed the whirlpool of thoughts and he once again raised his eyes to Wendt's. "What is it, marine?"

A smile tugged at Wendt's lips. "There's not a void-damned marine in this company that doesn't trust and respect you. We put our lives in your hands, just as we put our lives in the hands of the rest of the command crew. Every. Single. Fucking. Mission."

Gunny sneered. "What's your point?"

"That you need to get your shit together," Wendt said. His eyes narrowed. "Or none of us is going to get out of this alive."

The words stung him like a slap from an armored glove. He opened his mouth in surprise, unable to believe some fuckup like Wendt had said them. A fucking lance corporal telling him to get his shit together? Gunny crumpled the hydration pouch. The recyclable polymer bag split beneath the force and water splashed in all directions. He flung the remains to the deck, not even noticing the squelching sound it made. Gunny stepped forward to Wendt, his glaring eyes staring up at the taller man.

"The fuck did you say to me, marine?"

Wendt lowered his head until he looked directly down at his NCO. "Get your shit together, Gunny," he said.

Gunny's fists clenched twice before he rocketed a strong right into Wendt's chin. The tall marine stumbled backward, and for a moment, he thought Wendt would lose his balance and crash into the deck. Wendt moaned, his hands covering his face. "Fuck, that hurt," Wendt said and dropped his hands. His face held a burning grin. "And that's a hell of a lot better."

A message from the captain appeared across his block. He was wanted in the conference room. Gunny sent an acknowledgment while he held his furious stare with his subordinate.

"Go fuck yourself, Wendt," he spat. He pointed down at the deck. "Clean that shit up before I bust you down to a fucking private." He turned on his heel and left the galley. As he walked to the conference room, he realized he felt a little better. He wanted to think it was from finally hitting something, someone, anything to feel pain instead of the wretched emptiness inside. But he had to admit. It was Wendt's words.

"Fucker needs a promotion," Gunny growled to himself. Suddenly, he couldn't stop grinning.

CHAPTER THIRTY-THREE

Taulbee sat across from the captain, a 3-D holographic image of *Mira* floating between them. Gunny knocked on the hatch before entering and Taulbee yelled for him to come in. The grizzled sergeant entered and took a seat after Dunn said, "Please, join us." Gunny looked under control, but probably felt the same way he did. The anger, frustration, and second-guessing that happened after losing a marine was enough to drive anyone insane or into a tailspin of depression. But Gunny was handling it. For now.

Dunn leaned forward and tented his hands on the table. "Been a long day, gentlemen. So I'll get to it. Oakes is minding the ship and Nobel is still working in the cargo bay, so it's just the three of us."

Taulbee could tell the captain was trying to keep them calm and communicate he felt the same way they did without coming out and saying it. It didn't make Taulbee feel any better about the situation, but it at least put things into perspective. The entire company was hurting, but everyone still had to do their jobs. He fought a sigh and focused his eyes on the captain's through the translucent holographic model.

"Black tells me the beacon is a very real threat," Dunn said. "And due to the stresses and fractures on *Mira*'s hull, it's impossible to tow her." He paused for a moment and Taulbee thought he heard a slight hitch in the captain's throat. "I wish I'd figured that out before sending the two of you out there to try the tow." Neither of the marines spoke. "Nobel is building a sled to transport the beacon to Pluto."

"Pluto, sir?" Gunny asked.

Dunn shrugged. "As good a place as any. It's lifeless, locked in orbit around Sol, and anything that goes there isn't going anywhere else. At least not without SFMC having plenty of warning."

"The beacon," Taulbee said, "attracts those things."

"Yes," Dunn agreed. "According to the data Kalimura retrieved, and the observations of *Mira*'s scientists, the signal it produces is like a dinner bell. The creatures follow that signal and take up residence where they can. Just to be near it."

The room fell silent. Taulbee pulled his gaze from Dunn's and stared at the model. *Mira*. Her crew had brought the beacon aboard and killed everyone in the process. And then they spread that danger into Sol System. He wondered if they even realized what they had done and what the repercussions would be. *No,* he thought, *they probably died thinking it was over.*

"So," Dunn said, "we need to retrieve the beacon, put it on the sled, and crash the bastard into Pluto."

"Why do all that, sir?" Gunny asked. "Why can't we just send it back where it came from?"

"Good question," Dunn said. "I asked Black the same thing. Black has run the scenarios and the chances for success don't pan out the way you'd think. If the sled was pulled off course by a stray Kuiper Object or some other anomaly, we'd have no way of knowing until it was too late. In other words, knowing precisely where the beacon is will keep it safe. And hopefully Sol System as well."

"Pardon me, Captain," Taulbee said. "Can't we just turn the fucking thing off?"

"You mean with the key Kalimura's team found?"

"Yes," Taulbee said. "Can't we just do that?"

Dunn shrugged. "It's another risk. Even if we turn it off, the exo-solar lifeforms aboard *Mira* would still remain a threat to Sol System."

"Not if we destroy the ship, sir," Gunny said, his voice tinged with frustrated anger.

"And that's another problem," Dunn said. "We don't know if those lifeforms will survive a detonation. We also don't know how many are aboard."

"Shit," Taulbee said. When Dunn swung his eyes toward him, he blushed. "Sorry, sir. Hadn't really considered that."

"The Trio gave us weapons, sir," Gunny said. "Shouldn't they be enough to wipe these things out?"

Dunn paused for a moment. "The things aboard *Mira* aren't the only problem. We have a KBO coming in. We don't know what it is, but Black and Mickey seem to think it's not just a piece of rock and ice coming at us. It changed trajectory after we slowed *Mira* down."

Oh, shit, Taulbee thought. "There's more of them?"

"Unknown," Dunn said. "But I think it's a good bet."

"Excuse me, sir," Black said over the speakers, "I have an update from Mickey. May I put it on the holographic display?"

"Be my guest, Black," Dunn said.

The model of *Mira* melted into an empty starfield. The view zoomed out into a spherical map of grid lines. Small yellow dots appeared in various locations on the 3D map along with notations for velocity and vector.

"What am I looking at, Black?"

"Captain, the highlighted points on the map represent KBOs that are traveling toward our position. They are moving at a speed that puts them less than 1.5 hours away from *Mira*. Their velocity has not changed, but their trajectories have. It's as if they are moving to intercept the ship at its future position rather than its current location."

"Shit," Taulbee muttered. "Have any good news?"

Black ignored him. "The number of KBOs appears to be increasing in number."

Gunny's face pinched into a mask of rage. "And why didn't we know about this before? Can't you see the fucking things?"

"Alas, no, Gunnery Sergeant," Black said. "My sensors are not powerful enough to track these objects as they approach. They are far too small for that. Mickey estimates the largest of the objects is roughly 100 meters in diameter, although that is his best guess."

"That's why it's called an estimate," Taulbee said. "Where does Mickey say these things are coming from?"

"That is the perplexing part, Lieutenant. Mickey has attempted to backtrack their origin points based on the current locations, their speed, and the trajectory adjustments they are making. The objects appear to have been in the Kuiper Belt the entire time."

Dunn leaned back in his chair, mouth open. Taulbee felt as though he'd been kicked in the balls. "They were always here?" he asked.

"Possibly," Black said. "According to historical astronomical records, the Kuiper Belt was considered a very empty portion of Sol System. Unlike the asteroid belt, the number of KBOs discovered was relatively low. Less than 200,000 for the entire belt, which as you know, is considerable in size.

"When PEO came online and began its comprehensive scans of the belt, that number rose into the millions. Astronomers have wondered for the better part of a hundred years how the instruments in the Common Era, unsophisticated as they were, missed such a large amount of solar debris. It would seem we now have an answer."

"Bullshit," Dunn said. "*Mira* didn't leave Sol System until 50 years ago. PEO discovered the crowding long before *Mira* departed for Proxima and the ship didn't encounter the beacon for seven years after it departed. How could these things be here if it took the beacon to attract them?"

"Unknown, Captain. However, I do have a theory," Black said. "It is possible that the objects were sent into our space long ago in anticipation of the beacon's arrival."

Taulbee blinked. "Who the fuck would do that?"

"Again, sir, unknown. The beacon was obviously created by an exo-solar intelligence. Until *Mira*'s arrival, humanity was unaware of other life in the galaxy, let alone living in proximity to our system. Sol System resides far from the galactic core on the Milky Way's Orion arm. We are located more than halfway down the length of the arm and at its inner edge. If our galaxy were an ocean, we would be nothing more than a tidal pool on a sandbar. Infinitely small in comparison."

"What's your point, Black?" Taulbee asked.

"Perhaps the beacon was created to spread life across the galaxy. Or attract it."

He shook his head. "If that's the case, then why didn't the damned thing get here a lot sooner? If this shit has been hanging around waiting for it, why didn't it show up centuries ago? Or hell, millennia ago?"

Black paused for a moment. The display cleared and then refreshed. Seven dark objects appeared on the screen, faraway stars glittering like chips of ice in the sun. "*Mira* discovered these planetoids. Although I cannot prove it, I believe the Trio and *Mira*'s mission planners already knew about them. Which is why they sent *Mira* on the trajectory they did."

"Bullshit," Gunny said. "You're talking about a solar-level conspiracy to keep that information hidden. It would be impossible to create that kind of cover-up."

"No," Dunn said, his voice lifeless. "It would be easy."

Taulbee cocked his head and looked at the captain. "How so, sir?"

"The Trio. They run everything out here. They are responsible for processing and coordinating the data transfer from PEO, Trident Station, and damned near every nanoprobe and satellite we have traveling the Kuiper Belt and beyond. If they decided to keep that information from the rest of us, we'd have no way of knowing. All it would take is for them to massage or omit the data."

"Agreed, Captain," Black said. "But I don't believe the Trio would engage in that behavior unless specifically ordered to."

"Ordered by whom?" Gunny said.

"SF Gov," Black said. "Or the SF Military. It's impossible to say."

Taulbee shook his head and chuckled. Gunny and Dunn both stared at him, their faces slack. He felt their stare and glared at the planetoids on the display. "*Mira* was supposed to be humanity's last shot at finding resources before we exhaust Sol System. Another five hundred years and we won't have the materials to even create ships, let alone keep our existing infrastructure online. It explains why *Mira* has shuttle bays, a refinery, and all the mining equipment."

"Agreed, Lieutenant," Black said. "*Mira* wasn't searching for resources. She was sent to explore the viability of those resources humanity had already found."

"And the beacon?" Dunn asked.

"I have a theory," Black continued, "that the beacon was supposed to arrive millennia ago. Perhaps even longer. Perhaps just after the planets formed. The data gathered by Corporal Kalimura's squad indicates the beacon was found in a crater on one of the planetoids. It's very likely the beacon crashed into the planetoid before reaching its destination."

"Void wept," Gunny said. "Are you even certain we were the target?"

"No," Black said. "It is impossible to know the actual intent or destination for the beacon. All of this is conjecture, albeit formed from the evidence currently available."

"Evidence currently available," Taulbee echoed. He felt as though his brain was going to explode. Aliens sent the fucking thing to Sol? To what? Populate it? Spread life to this arm of the galaxy? It was completely insane. Black had obviously lost her mind.

Or had she? The more he thought about it, the more it made some sort of sense. If aliens were trying to spread life through their galactic backyard, what better way than leading the bottom of the food chain to a new biome? Let it take root and attract more complex lifeforms?

"Black?" Taulbee said. "We've seen a pretty serious size differential in both the pinecones and the starfish creatures. That last one that attacked me was much larger than the one we encountered earlier."

"Agreed," the AI said.

"So what's to say these aren't, shit, I don't know, maybe analogs to what made up the biome of our ocean?"

Black thought for a moment. The planetoids disappeared from the holo display and a scrawl of writing replaced them. The words "the tide is coming in!" scrawled in frozen, crimson lines stared at them. A pair of suit lights illuminated the bulkhead's frozen surface on which the words had been written. Well, written was being kind. More like painted with one or more gloveless fingers.

Taulbee stared at the image with an open mouth. Gunny shifted in his chair and Dunn blinked at them.

"That was on *Mira*?" Dunn asked.

"Yes, Captain," Black said. "*Mira*'s chief engineer, a man named Stephens, presumably wrote this after killing several of the crew. This is the same man that stole the beacon key and threw it out an airlock. Apparently, the key's magnetics kept it from spinning out into space and it ended up attached to the ship's hull. LCpl Dickerson found the key despite Stephens' attempt to jettison it into space.

"Records recovered by Kalimura's squad include diaries from the crew. Stephens' sanity appears to have cracked shortly after the first pinecone attacks on the crew. Although his ramblings border on insane, it is clear he believed that Sol and other systems so distant from the galactic core were little more than tidal pools on sandbars. It might be a very apt description."

"Fuck," Taulbee said in a breathy whisper.

Dunn cleared his throat with a side glance at the lieutenant. "That's very interesting, Black. But it doesn't help us at all."

"No," the AI agreed. "However, it should illustrate the importance of trapping the beacon and ensuring it cannot and will not enter further into Sol System."

The room fell silent. Taulbee heard the gentle ambient drone of the life support systems, but it was nothing more than an undercurrent for his jumbled thoughts. More objects were coming. Presumably more creatures. And the Kuiper Belt appeared to be filled with them. How long before dozens or hundreds of the objects congregated around *Mira* to follow the beacon wherever it landed? How long before Sol System faced possible extinction from the new lifeforms? And how long did they have before *S&R Black* was consumed by Atmo-steel eating creatures?

"We need the beacon," Taulbee said.

"Agreed," Dunn said.

"Aye, sir," Gunny said.

"Good," Dunn said. "I'm sure Oakes and Nobel will respect the decision as well."

"Go one better, sir," Taulbee said. "Can't think of a marine in this Company that wouldn't be on board for this."

"Black," Dunn said, "please place the model of *Mira* back on the display."

"Yes, Captain," Black said.

The holo display faded and the 3-D model appeared. Dunn moved his hands and spun the model so the aft section faced both sides of the desk.

"Can you overlay our images of the scans you've taken?"

Black said nothing, but red lines and shapes appeared documenting the damage to *Mira*'s aft. The detail was very sparse. With the exception of the brief period where *Mira*'s ass-end faced the ship, they had very little data to go on. Taulbee himself had only breezed by the severely damaged engineering decks; he hadn't had time to linger and take better recon feeds. He had a feeling that was step one.

"How badly damaged is the aft?" Dunn asked.

"According to what we know from *Mira*'s damage reports, it would seem the explosion that destroyed the engines and life support was catastrophic in nature. The decks that were not vaporized in the initial explosion are more than likely in worse shape than the rest of the ship. It's possible they will crumble if stressed. That is one of the many reasons we placed the harness where we did. I calculated a 47% chance the aft section of the ship would become completely uncoupled from the rest of *Mira* once we began the tow."

"Void wept," Gunny said. "And what would we have done then?"

Black was silent for a moment. When she replied, Taulbee could practically feel Black's contempt for the question. "It would have separated and no longer been a threat to the Company nor the rest of the ship. Lieutenant Nobel and I discussed this and felt it was worth the risk." Black paused. "At the time, of course."

"Of course," Taulbee spat. He thrummed his fingers on the desk. "We need a recon of the area."

"Agreed," Dunn said. The captain placed his hands on the desk's edge. "As soon as Nobel patches the SV-52, and you're ready, I want you to get out there and take a look. Nanoprobes may or may not be able to see the extent of the damage, but we need to try." He swung his gaze to Gunny. "Which of your marines do you suggest for Taulbee's gunner?"

"Sir?" Taulbee said. "I'm not sure I need a gunner."

The two men traded a stare. Dunn's grim expression slowly broke into a grin. "All the glory for yourself?"

Taulbee blushed. "No, sir. I just think it's a pretty damned dangerous mission and I don't want to put any more marines at risk."

"Noted," Dunn said. "Gunny?"

The sergeant rubbed his stubbly chin. "Copenhaver," he said. "I think she's best. If Kalimura or Dickerson were here, I'd suggest either of them instead. But the private has shown herself very capable of both keeping a clear head and superior focus. Plus, she's a crack shot."

"Yes," Taulbee agreed. "But how much sim time has she had as a gunner?"

Gunny shrugged. "Not much, sir. But then none of them have. Apart from Dickerson and Carbonaro, we don't have any other combat-tested marines available." He smiled. "And everyone here, of course."

"Right," Dunn said. "Copenhaver it is."

A sinking feeling hit his gut. Taulbee hated flying with a gunner. Especially a greenhorn. Too many questions, too much second-guessing, and too many instances of gunners making mistakes that put the pilot's life in jeopardy. But he understood Dunn's concern. Having a capable partner was paramount if they had to ditch the SV-52, even if that meant putting another life at risk. His chances of coming back alive were much greater with another marine on board. But that didn't mean he had to like it.

"Aye, sir," Taulbee said. He tried to keep the disappointment from his voice, but it was damned difficult.

"Gunny? I need you, Wendt, and Murdock on deck in case we need to rescue Taulbee and Copenhaver."

"Aye, sir," Gunny said.

"One more thing, gentlemen," Dunn said. "I'm ordering Oakes to detach from *Mira* and put us a safe distance from her. We'll travel parallel to *Mira* and keep near the aft-end in case you need cover fire from our weapons arrays."

Taulbee grinned. "Rain down hell, sir?"

"Aye," Dunn said. "Once we have the beacon, we're going to vaporize this fucking hulk."

The meeting ended, but Taulbee stayed behind. He spun the model again and again, looking for ingress points near the aft where a damaged deck plate might afford a way in. Nothing seemed large enough to fit the SV-52. Perhaps a skiff, but it would be tight. However, that would lead the team straight into the engineering decks just beyond the cargo bay. If Kalimura's intel was up to snuff, that would be a very hazardous place to enter.

"We need lots of video," he said aloud.

"Agreed, Lieutenant," Black's disembodied voice said, making him flinch.

He glanced upward at the hidden speakers in the ceiling. "You were pretty quiet about the captain's plan," Taulbee said.

"Of course, sir," Black said. "It is not in my nature to second-guess logical decisions. Especially those I agree with."

Taulbee leaned back in the chair, fingers locked together on his lap. "What are our chances?"

"For success?"

"Yes," Taulbee said. "For success on the recon mission."

Black paused for a moment. "Insufficient data available."

"For void's sake, just guess."

"I expect a 70% chance of your success."

Taulbee licked his lips. "And of getting back alive?"

"You really don't want to know, sir."

Black's dead voice made him shiver. He hoped like hell this was the right call.

CHAPTER THIRTY-FOUR

The four of them took it slow. Carb's steps were confident, but measured. Kali knew her squad-mate was waiting for reality to bend and jumble itself again. Shit, they all were.

Kali kept waiting for her suit lights to stop penetrating the darkness, for the suffocating sense of doom, of being swallowed alive by the ship. Each step drove a spike of fear into her stomach, and to make matters worse, no one was talking.

Ever since they'd taken the fork, even the occasional breath over the comms had ceased coming through. It was as if the entire squad held their collective breath, or, more likely, everyone had muted their mic like Kali had.

While Dickerson had scouted the corridor, she and Carb had checked over Elliott's suit, made sure their O2 supplies were filled, and checked for suit damage. Elliott's civvie suit had so far held up. She and Carb's suits, on the other hand, had damage to both their armor and the underlying reinforced fabric. If they ever made it back to *S&R Black,* Kali imagined none of her squad's suits would pass inspection. They'd be thrown into the recyclers, never to be seen again.

"Hatch coming up," Carb said.

The sound of Carb's voice startled her and she nearly lost her balance. "Copy," Kali said. "Elliott? How you doing?"

"Good, Corporal," the wounded marine said. "Breathing easier."

Dickerson grunted. "That's because your lungs aren't cramped up. If we had some real gravity, you'd probably have no problem at all."

"Gravity," Carb said. "What I wouldn't give for some damned gravity."

"Funny, ain't it?" Dickerson said. "We're surrounded by grav plates everywhere we go, but we can't power them. I wish I'd seen *Mira* before she went to shit."

Kali found herself nodding. Despite the horrors lurking on the ship, possibly even hunting them, she had to admit that *Mira* had been a magnificent ship. The design, the cutting-edge technology developed that was still being used across the Sol Federation, not to mention the sense of optimism *Mira* had spread throughout humankind, made her the pinnacle of human achievement. And now look at her. A billion metric tons of Atmo-steel, plas-steel, transparent aluminum, and Void knew what else tumbling through space with a dangerous payload. One that could spell the end for humankind.

The holos said *Mira* Day had been a Sol Federation-wide holiday with parties thrown everywhere in the system. All of humanity watched as the ship cleared its moorings from Trident Station and began its journey to the outer Kuiper Belt. Holo-channels ran around the proverbial clock, providing views from *Mira*'s external cameras, feeds from passing probes, and the ship's telescopes. The crew recorded themselves countless times with updates of life on the ship, the daily grind of maintaining so large a ship, and their hopes and dreams. And humanity swallowed it all. For years.

The further *Mira* retreated from Pluto, the longer the transmissions took to reach habitable space. Before *Mira* sent her final transmission, the large ship was more than a light year away from Sol and still accelerating. But that had been bullshit, hadn't it?

Mira had survived after the supposed "last transmission" date. She'd been somewhere beyond the solar system, exploring for minerals with no intention of ever reaching Proxima Centauri b. Instead of performing the mission humanity was sold, she'd been doing nothing more than finding new resources closer to Sol.

Captain Kovacs had mentioned there were nine dwarf planets in addition to the one they'd explored. Nine new planets. 8XJ had held the beacon. What did the other eight contain? Other beacons? More lifeforms? Or were they simply lifeless hulks floating beyond the edge of the solar system?

Kali shivered. *Mira*. The promise for humanity's salvation, a symbol of hope for the species, was now little more than a plague ship heading back to her creators. To infect. To destroy.

Quit it, she told herself. It's nothing more than an ancient derelict that brought back a few friends. We just need to get the beacon, shut it off, and this nightmare will be over. She hoped.

Carb reached the hatch and peered through the transparent aluminum housing. "Yup," she said, "it's another airlock."

"Good," Kali said, commenting more about the thoughts that crumbled in her mind. "Grabbing your feed."

Carb's helmet cam feed lit up on Kali's HUD. Kali minimized the other views and focused. The hatch fronted a containment tunnel that led to yet another hatch before providing an ingress into the room. The suit lights easily penetrated the gloom and into the room beyond through the inset windows.

It was difficult to make out most of the shapes against the far wall, but Kali was fairly sure they were lab stations including large analysis modules probably for ore specimens. *Or,* she thought, *for exo-solar material.*

"Looks clear," Carb said. "What do you think, Boss?"

Was there a point to walking in there? If they only found more O2 stations and perhaps an emergency generator, was it worth the time? They had a safe area for the other corridor, but not for this one. She sighed. "I think we go in."

"Corporal?" Dickerson said. "We're pretty much out of fuel for the beam cutters. How are we going to open it?"

Kali ground her teeth as she stared at the feed. He was right. The remaining fuel they had would allow them ingress to the room, maybe, but then they'd be done. If they needed the cutter to get through another area of the ship, they'd be fucked. Unless, of course, they used explosives.

The only problem with using explosives to open doors is that they wouldn't close again. It would be impossible to create a safe room if they had to smash through its walls or doors. No way to pressurize. No way to capture heat. No way to hide themselves behind thick bulkheads and transparent aluminum.

She thought for a moment before sighing. "Carb? Check for a manual release on this side."

"Aye, Boss," Carb said.

Kali checked her rear cam feed and saw Elliott standing less than two meters away, his helmet pointed at the deck. "You doing okay, Elliott?"

His helmet popped upward as if in surprise. "Yeah, Boss. I'm good. Just fell asleep for a second."

That wasn't good. She'd hoped a fresh load of nannies in his system would quickly help alleviate his concussion symptoms as well as the shock. Those nannies were more than fifty years old, though. No telling how well they were functioning, much less what they were actually doing.

"Headache?" she asked.

"No," Elliott said. "Well, not exactly. Just get the feeling of vertigo every now and then."

She nodded to herself. Yup. The nannies were either focused on another part of his body, or they were incapable of repairing the damage in his brain and nervous system. Void, but they needed rest. If they could just make it to the fucking escape pods, they could get out. Get back to Black. To safety. To something resembling normalcy.

"Carb?"

"Nothing doing, Boss. I don't see shit. No way in."

Kali tightened her fingers on the rifle until a cramp shot pain up her wrist. "Okay. Fuck it," she said. "Keep moving. Elliott, you ready?"

"Yeah, Boss. Let's do this."

His voice hadn't sounded as confident as he'd probably hoped. She could tell him to be honest about his injuries, about whether or not he could continue, but she doubted he'd say a damned word about it unless he was on the verge of death. She grinned. If she were in his position, she'd probably do the same. It was one thing to know you were going to die, but it was another to know that your condition was putting your squad-mates at risk. "Together we stand, divided we fall," Kali said to herself. If only the rest of humanity realized that. "All right, Carb. Lead on."

"Aye, Boss."

Carb slowly turned herself away from the hatch to face the darkened corridor, hesitating for a beat before resuming her crouch-walk. Kali waited until Carb was more than a meter away before following her lead. Back to the crouch-walk. Great. Kali's muscles complained, but complied. Another hour or two of this, and she didn't know if she'd be able to crawl, much less walk.

The unlovely truth was that the longer you stayed in a cramped position, the more difficult it was to stretch out the muscles and joints when you left it. Eventually, their bodies would simply refuse to obey commands to stand, walk, or run. What then?

"Shut up," she said to herself. The escape pods. If they could just get to the fucking escape pods. Focus on that, nothing else. The hell with information. Get your squad out of this. Get yourself out of this. Kali took a deep breath and released it in a long stream.

They continued down the corridor, Kali checking her rear cam feed every few steps to watch for signs of fatigue from Elliott. The injured marine seemed to be walking fine, but every minute or so, she noticed him swaying a bit. Whether it was from the awkward civilian mag-boots, fatigue, or damage to his spine, it was impossible to tell. Only Elliott knew for sure, and he wasn't talking about it.

Kali sent a block message to Dickerson, asking him to keep an eye on Elliott. The big marine had responded with the image of a curled fist, a thumb raised high above the clenched fingers. Good. Dickerson could keep watch on Elliott better than she could.

"Hey," Carb called out. "I think there's another junction ahead."

Frowning, Kali brought up the schematics. "That can't be right. Squad, hold." She waited for affirmatives from Elliott and Dickerson before walking forward and taking position next to Carb. Their combined suit lights illuminated the wide bulkheads. Kali saw what looked like an opening that adjoined the corridor some 10 meters ahead of them.

"That's not on the map," Kali said. "Nothing like that at all."

Dickersón groaned. "Those fucking AIs. They screw us again?"

"Don't know," Kali said. "Carb? Cover me."

"Aye, Boss."

She kept her eyes focused on the so-called "junction" facing the adjoining hallway. With each step, the unmapped darkened area became a little more clear. The frown on her face slowly turned into a wide 'O' of surprise. It wasn't another hallway. It was a tear in the bulkhead. Something had destroyed the Atmo-steel wall shielding the corridor from the rest of the ship.

"Shit," Kali said.

"Corporal?" Dickerson asked. "What the hell is that? Somebody blew the corridor up?"

"Squad. Move up," Kali said. "Looks like the bulkhead blew out." Except that's not what it looked like at all. If the corridor wall had been blown out by explosive decompression, the fringes around the open wound wouldn't be so jagged and torn. It obviously hadn't been destroyed by explosives either. Atmo-steel would have puckered from the force of an explosion, the remaining material blown outward. Instead, the bulkhead had been torn and shredded, petals of jagged metal pointing into the corridor as well as toward the area beyond.

Kali waited in silence as Carb took position less than a meter behind her, Elliott and Dickerson lurking little more than two meters away. Once they were close enough, she held up a fist and continued walking. The closer she approached, the more detail she could see. Her lights reflected off the savaged Atmo-steel, the broken layers shining dully back at her. Roughly four meters in diameter, the hole started at the base of the deck and rose more than halfway up the bulkhead. Whatever had done this had been big. Damned big.

Each step toward the hole increased the buzzing sensation in her stomach and the tingles of fear washing over her skin. Her suit's illumination seemed to disappear into the gaping wound. Another shiver crawled down her spine, so powerful it nearly paralyzed her. Something was watching them. She was sure of it.

"S-squad?" she whispered over the comms. "Get past me. Go further down the corridor. Go slow."

"Aye, Boss," Carb said.

"Corporal?" Dickerson asked. "Something wrong?"

"Don't ask questions," she hissed. "Just get past me. Dickerson? Once you're past the perforation, put your claymore down."

"Um, aye, Corporal," Dickerson said.

He sounded concerned, even a little afraid. Well, of course he does. She hadn't been able to keep the fear out of her voice. And no matter how hard she tried, she didn't think it was even possible. Staring into the impenetrable darkness made her feel as though she were falling into it. A darkness deeper than space without even the twinkle of distant stars staring back at her, through her. It was watching them. And she didn't want to know what "it" was.

"Placed," Dickerson said.

Kali snapped her eyes to her HUD. With the exception of Dickerson, the squad had already passed her. She blinked in confusion. How had they gotten by her without her noticing? The darkness yawned a little wider.

"Corporal? You hear me?"

Dickerson's voice sounded far away, as though he were shouting down a tunnel. There were other sounds, other voices, but they turned into an incomprehensible jumble of syllables, demented whispers from another universe.

She nearly screamed when something grabbed her shoulder. Her body shot upright from the crouch and she swiveled toward the threat, finger gently pulling on the trigger. Dickerson's helmet pointed at hers, his hands and rifle pointed to the ceiling.

"Whoa, Corporal, It's just me."

She ground her teeth. She'd almost shot him. "Yeah," she said. "Sorry."

"You okay?"

She switched to private comms and pointed at the hole. "You see anything?"

"No," Dickerson said. "It's like there's nothing there. But," he said, his voice trailing off for a moment. "Something's there. I can feel it."

She nodded to herself, wondering if he felt the same spine-crawling tingles washing across her nerve endings. All the saliva in her mouth dried up. She tried to speak, but the sound was little more than croak. After biting the inside of her mouth, she managed to get a little moisture rolling on her tongue. She cleared her throat and tried again. "Let's get out of here."

"Copy that," Dickerson said. "You first. I'll cover." He stepped to the side, his rifle pointed to the side of the tear in the bulkhead.

She said nothing, but moved past him at a quick pace. Once she traveled a meter, she turned and again faced the opening. "Clear and covering," Kali said.

Dickerson walked backward away from the darkness. After he'd cleared Kali's sight-line, he changed direction and continued walking backward down the corridor. Somewhere back there, Carb and Elliott waited for them. Lucky them. They hadn't stared into the abyss and felt it staring back with something akin to malevolent hunger. "You're clear, Corporal."

She checked her rear cam. He had moved three meters back from her, holding his rifle with a tight angle on the far side of the mouth's opening. Kali choked back her gorge, turned, and walked as fast as she could.

"We leaving the claymore?" he asked.

"Yes," Kali said. She quickened her pace until she moved past him, feeling as though phantom teeth snapped at her back. She turned and faced the area again. "Clear. Keep retreating. We'll stagger," she said.

"Copy," Dickerson said.

She couldn't decide if his responses were so clipped because he was focused, or he was as afraid as she was. When they finally caught up to Carb and Elliott, the sensation had dampened. Whatever had been staring at them from the void, its presence had receded. Whether from their distance or because it had departed, she didn't know. She hoped it was still there, staying put, locked in some prison of its own making and unable to follow them. Then again, hadn't the darkness swallowed their lights at the junction behind them? Hadn't a wall seemed to follow them?

"What was it?" Carb asked.

"Not sure," Dickerson said. "Did you feel it when you walked by?"

"Sure as hell felt something," Elliott said. "Thought I was going to shit myself."

A moment of silence lingered over the comms, as if her squad-mates wanted to agree, but couldn't bring themselves to. "Okay, marines. We're going to take the same positions and keep moving." Kali checked the schematics. "Another forty meters and we'll exit the science section."

Carb grunted. "Not sure which is worse, Boss. Being trapped in here knowing something nasty is behind us, or walking into another unexplored area."

Kali knew how she felt. At least here, they knew where to retreat. The corridors were easily defensible, having only to worry about threats from behind or in front of them. Unless they found another "artificial" junction, they were safe behind the meters of Atmo-steel making up the bulkheads. She hoped.

Carb began leading again, her steps methodical but faster than before. Kali wanted to tell her to slow down, to take her time, but couldn't help the feeling that the faster they moved, the better. Their O2 reserves were still in the green, but she wanted out of the science section. Something was in here with them. Maybe several somethings.

She brought up Dickerson's rear cam feed and added it to her HUD. The pair of lights pointing behind them illuminated a full seven or eight meters. Good. The darkness hadn't yet found them. Or maybe it was trapped in that first junction, the real junction, near the science section entrance point they'd first come through.

Kali flicked her eyes to the bulkheads in front of them. Nothing. No signs of damage, no debris. The science section, with its large rooms secured behind two hatches, was the cleanest, most pristine part of *Mira* they'd explored. And why was that, exactly? Why hadn't the hatches been blown open? Why weren't the hallways filled with the frozen corpses of scientists and support personnel? Where had they gone? Even after *Mira* was catastrophically damaged, she had a difficult time believing the science section had simply been shut down. It seemed like an area easily secured, pressurized, and powered.

As they approached another hatch, Carb held up a fist and the squad halted. She took another two steps forward and turned her head to the hatch. "Shit," she said. "Boss? This one's open."

"Open?"

"Yeah," Carb said. "As in the goddamned outer hatch is missing. So is the inner one."

Kali maximized Carb's cam feed. The LCpl hadn't been kidding. The hatch hinges were little more than torn and ripped jags of metal. Dents and cracks spiderwebbed the airlock tunnel, as if something large had struggled to get inside, bowing out the steel in the process.

"Go in?" Carb asked.

Good question, Kali thought. Something had ripped through the hatches. Why? And more importantly, was there maybe something in there that they needed to see?

"We can't seal the room," Dickerson said, "so it's not much good to us as a redoubt."

"Might have O2," Carb said. "Shit, it might have a functional terminal."

Kali ground her teeth. God, she was tired. She could think more clearly if fatigue wasn't settling into every fiber of her being. Stimulants weren't going to help that. The stim crash she and her squad would ultimately experience was going to be epic as it was.

Dickerson sighed over the comms. "Might also have the fucking boogeyman."

Kali chuckled in spite of herself. "Our six is clear. Nothing in front, and our lights are actually splitting the darkness. Might want to take a peek."

"Yeah," Elliott said. "Not like we're ever coming back here. Might as well see the sights."

"Oh, hush, luggage," Carb said. "Adults are talking."

"Fuck off," Elliott said with a yawn. "Besides, I'm not luggage anymore."

"For now," Carb said.

"All right," Kali said, "knock it off." She stared into the darkness, that feeling of being watched, as though something was in there, something waiting for them, crawled over her skin. A tired grin spread across her face. *It wasn't just this room,* she thought. Every nook and cranny in the entire void-forsaken ship felt as though it was watching them, waiting for them to drop their guard, just waiting as if it had been waiting for nearly half a century for them to arrive. For someone to arrive. "Carb? Your turn to explore. I'll go with you."

Dickerson groaned. "Forgive me, Corporal. But I think we need you out here with Elliott. Just in case."

Just in case. She knew what Dickerson meant. Kali had the most rescue training, the most medical training, and furthermore, she was in charge. Since Elliott was no longer clamped to Carb's shoulder and walking on his own, there was no longer an excuse for her to take point. She knew all of that, and yet she still wanted to walk through the short tunnel and see what was in the room. The pull was palpable, almost physical.

"Okay, Carb. You and Dickerson take the room. I want full cam feeds and take it slow."

"Aye, Boss," Carb said. She walked further into the tunnel entrance to give Dickerson some room. "All right, big boy. Take my six."

"Aye," Dickerson said.

Kali stepped back to make more space and walked backward until she had a view of both ends of the corridor, Elliott, and the room's entrance. "Slow and careful," she said. Carb said something that might have been "yes, Mom," but Kali wasn't sure.

CHAPTER THIRTY-FIVE

Oakes stared at the holo display. Still attached to the spindle, *S&R Black* wasn't going anywhere until he uncoupled them from the spindle. While he'd normally be able to accomplish that task with a simple block command, nothing about this mission was "normal."

Because of the stress fractures and weakened deck plates, Copenhaver and Murdock had added additional support cables to the spindle in an attempt to keep *S&R Black* from pulling completely free of *Mira* once they began to accelerate. That meant someone had to go outside and remove the supports.

Oakes didn't envy the marines tasked with that duty. Private Lyke had been killed during the last trip out and the Company's numbers were dwindling. Void, but he wished Kalimura and her squad were back. If you included Gunny, they were left with a single squad of marines. Taulbee would certainly don a combat suit and join any fight, but they needed him in the support vehicle providing cover for both *S&R Black* and whatever marines they sent outside.

Officer training school had had a lot of courses on surviving with short supplies of munitions, food, water, and air, but he didn't remember any advice on dealing with an actual shortage of marines to carry out a mission. Pretty soon, they'd have to start tapping the command crew for these little excursions. He shuddered. The last thing he wanted in the whole damned universe was to see *Mira* through a suit's cam feeds. Fuck that. Here in the cockpit was where he belonged.

"But I'll do it," he told himself. Yes. He'd go out there if he had to. To save another marine, the ship, or to keep the human race from extinction, he'd don a combat suit and float into battle. He just hoped like hell it didn't come to that.

He'd been staring at the holo display for several minutes now as he crunched the numbers to put *S&R Black* far enough away from *Mira* to keep her safe while at the same time positioning the ship to provide cover fire for Taulbee and Copenhaver when the time came. It was maddening. *Mira*'s slight spin was barely noticeable, but it still complicated matters more than he liked.

Both fortunately and unfortunately, *S&R Black*'s main weapon arrays pointed fore and aft. With the exception of a single, recessed burst cannon, those weapons only had 45° of lateral movement and the same in the vertical range. No matter how he positioned the ship, it would be impossible to cover the entire sky. That left missiles.

Missiles were tricky. If you had marines attached to the hull of a ship, the last thing you wanted was an explosion. Although space was devoid of air, that didn't mean the shockwave from a detonation didn't have the force to push. An explosion in the wrong place could be enough force to detach marines from a ship and blow them right out into space. At that point, if they survived, someone would have to go out and retrieve them. Considering the hostile lifeforms they'd already encountered, any marines in that position would likely be dinner for one of the creatures.

Yes, missiles were definitely a last resort. Maybe when it came time to blow *Mira* the fuck up, they'd be the perfect weapon. But not now. "Not now," he muttered.

Black checked his calculations, provided a few suggestions, and Oakes adjusted. The AI had bristled at his insistence on manually determining their ultimate position. He couldn't blame her. He was essentially saying he knew best, which was utter bullshit. She could do the math in a pico-second while it had taken him better than four minutes just to come up with the equations.

The numbers looked good. Good enough, anyway, until Taulbee actually began his recon run. Once the SV-52 finished its first survey, they'd have a better idea of where to put *S&R Black*. He hoped.

Before receiving a block message from the captain asking him to coordinate with Black, Oakes had been studying the scans and radar. The KBO was closer. Before much longer, they'd be able to see some detail using the onboard telescopes. Not being a science ship, *S&R Black*'s instruments weren't designed to ferret out minuscule details for small objects. Small being a relative term, of course.

When you tracked a ship, getting those details was usually just a matter of plugging in the ship model and voilà, you had schematics and blueprints and etc. that were mostly dead on. Very few ship-building companies provided full customization to their designs. The engine array, life support, and basic maneuvering details were almost always the same. Inside? That was a different matter. But even so, Atmo and Trans-Orbital were required to file plans for a ship with the SF Gov regulation board. The SF Military had access to that database. If an *S&R* ship headed out to Sol System's wastes to assist a ship in trouble, they almost always knew what they would face from a schematic's point of view.

The telescopes and other visual sensors were just good enough to get the job done. At that moment, however, Oakes wished they had better instruments. Much better. If he could see the object in greater detail before it was close enough to be a threat, he could better prepare for it, and the captain could alter his battle plans for a more successful engagement. At this point, any information could help stave off disaster.

Dunn's block message had been very simple: "Oakes, we're moving the ship. Black has your briefing."

And that was all. As soon as the message came in, he'd connected to Black, received the briefing, and began astrogation duties. While he figured out the calculations and put together an evasion strategy, he couldn't help glancing at the active scans. The object would be in visual range in ten minutes. Then it would be more than a shape out there in the Kuiper Belt's twilight gloom. It would be something tangible. He hoped like hell it was just a ball of ice, but something told him they weren't going to get that lucky.

Black's briefing had made his balls turn to ice. The scans from Mickey indicated there were more KBOs, or exo-solar objects, headed toward them. The sky was going to be very crowded in less than thirty minutes. At this moment, Gunny's marines, except for Copenhaver, were busily checking weapons arrays, handling load outs, and preparing *S&R Black* for war. The only question was whether or not they could turn the space around *Mira* into a shooting gallery without having to worry about killing Kalimura's squad aboard the giant derelict.

Better question, he thought, *is whether or not we'll even be able to put up a fight.* Too many bogies incoming. Too many unknowns.

The holo display flashed. He leaned back in the chair and blew a sigh through parted lips. There. It was done. The board was green. Black hadn't found any problems with the calculations or Oakes' assumptions. They were good to go. For what it was worth, anyway.

He initiated a block connection. "Captain. We have a solution plotted. Sending you the details."

Dunn answered immediately. "I won't have a chance to look at them, Oakes," he said. "You have my trust. Let's get this done."

"Aye," Oakes said. "All we need is to decouple."

"Wendt and Murdock will leave the cargo bay momentarily," Dunn said. "Should have that done in five minutes at most."

"Aye, sir."

"Dunn, out."

Oakes wiped the display and put the scanner readings back up. A 3-D spherical model 1/8 of an AU in area floated before him. A few red dots appeared at the edges of the sphere, all moving on a course for *Mira*.

"Bluok?"

"Yes, Lieutenant," the AI said.

"Best guesses about what those are?"

Black paused for maybe half a second. "Until we are able to see KBO-1193 in greater detail, I'm unable to say with any certainty what they might be."

He groaned. Fucking AIs and their CYA mentality. "Just guess."

"Based on what we have already seen, I can rule out the possibility they are lifeless. I can also say with certainty they are *not* KBOs as we understand them. The fact the objects have changed trajectory and speed multiple times indicates some form of propulsion."

Oakes felt a chill. "Not dumb rocks in space," he muttered.

"No," Black agreed. "The objects lack the traditional radiation trails indicative of nuclear propulsion. Nor do they radiate heat. The objects in question appear to be unique in the annals of astronomy and known ship design."

"You don't have a fucking clue," Oakes said, more of a statement than a question. He wiped sweat from his forehead and suddenly wished he could kick the AI in its ass. If Black was feigning ignorance, she was doing a pretty good job. "Do we shoot first and ask questions later?"

"I do not consider that to be a prudent course of action," Black said. "If they are indeed exo-solar lifeforms, it is impossible to say how they will react to direct confrontation. Since we do not know their intent, such as feeding, breeding, or congregation, rash actions such as firing our weapons might alter the reason they have for traveling to *Mira*. In short, they could attack when they had no reason to."

No reason to. Shit. Oakes pined for the Satellite War, a conflict where any ship, any skiff, and any meatball in a suit could be the enemy in disguise. That he could understand. But this? There were no ships. There were no known engines involved, or at least by known technological standards. These were something new. Something potentially deadly.

S&R Black's weapons arrays were locked and loaded. All they needed now was a target. Oakes hoped his astrogation plan worked. If not, they would have a hell of a time getting out of here without losing both Taulbee and Copenhaver. Not to mention Kalimura's squad. *Shit,* he thought, *if we fuck up, none of us are going home.*

CHAPTER THIRTY-SIX

It had been a long damned time since he had a gunner behind him. In fact, the last time he flew with a gunner had been during the Satellite War and that was several years in the past. But even then, he hadn't liked having someone behind him, having to communicate with them, and having his concentration wrecked by a green marine's bombardment of questions or absurdly inaccurate callouts of enemy positions. In short, Taulbee enjoyed flying alone.

After the meeting with Gunny and the captain, he'd immediately downed another hydration pouch, urinated, and suited back up. By the time he reached the cargo bay, Copenhaver stood next to the SV-52, her gear already packed in the cockpit. She saluted him as he approached. He returned it with a grin.

"Are you ready for this, Private?"

"Aye, sir," she said, her face on the verge of a smile. Copenhaver was one of those people who even when she was doing her best to show respect and hold a professional countenance, her speech held a special kind of levity. It was just another part of her personality he liked. She was going to make a hell of a non-com one day.

"You flown in the back before?"

"No, sir," she said. "Only in simulations."

"You'll be fine," Taulbee said. "Just follow my lead, check the feeds, and kill anything that's not human. Unless, of course, I tell you not to."

"Aye, sir."

He swiveled his head and saw three figures standing near the emergency airlock. Murdock and Wendt had already suited up for their EVA. Gunny stood with them, checking their suits and speaking in a low voice. Although he couldn't hear what he was saying, Taulbee was fairly certain it was Gunny's special brand of pep talk. Which usually amounted to "Don't be stupid, don't get dead. Get the job done."

"Or I'll kick your ass," Taulbee muttered with a chuckle.

"Sir?" Copenhaver asked. He looked back at her and nearly laughed at the confused expression on her face.

"Nothing, Copenhaver. Let's get this bird ready to fly."

He scrambled into the cockpit and waited while Copenhaver did the same. Once in the pilot seat, his nerves began to calm at once. He activated the mag harness and his suit became flush with the seat, immobilizing his body with the exception of his head, arms, and feet. Taulbee connected his block to the SV-52 and his HUD filled with instrument readings. He initiated the startup sequence and watched the status markers turn from red to yellow to green. Although he trusted Gunny's word that the craft had been refueled and reloaded, he checked anyway. Sure enough, the SV-52 was ready for action.

"Copenhaver?"

"Aye, sir. Bringing up my HUD now."

The last status indicator turned green. His gunner was connected and had munitions under her control. He took in a slow breath and exhaled in one long stream. "Closing cockpit."

"Acknowledged," she said.

Taulbee sent the command and the armored cockpit shell slowly descended. The words "Cabin Pressurized" flashed twice across his HUD before disappearing. He activated the craft's feeds and placed them in the lower right of the virtual display.

"You ready, Copenhaver?"

"Aye, sir."

Taulbee initiated the comms. "Captain? We are ready to depart."

"Acknowledged," Dunn said. "Good hunting."

"Thank you, sir. Gunny?"

"We're in the airlock, pressurized and ready. Just let me know when I should kick my boys out the door."

Taulbee smiled. "Aye, Gunny. Opening cargo bay." The SV-52 trembled slightly as the atmosphere vented back into the life-support tanks, leaving the cargo bay in a vacuum. Another warning flashed across his HUD just before the wall in front of him opened.

He deactivated the SV-52's magnetics. "Taulbee departing."

"Acknowledged," Dunn said.

"Okay, Copenhaver. Easy ride out of the barn," Taulbee said.

"Aye, sir," she replied.

He thought she'd sound concerned, worried about the flight or her duties. Instead, she sounded excited. That was a good sign. Smiling, Taulbee engaged the rear thrusters and the craft moved forward into the twilight of space.

Once clear of the cargo bay, Taulbee descended until the SV-52 hovered just above *Mira*'s hull. "Start looking, Copenhaver. I want to make sure there's nothing out here."

"Aye, sir."

She would do her job, he was sure of it, but that didn't mean he wasn't checking the same cam feeds. While she used the more capable cannon cameras, he was left with the SV-52's standard cam feeds. Taulbee minimized the instrumentation views and brought the four cam feeds up in a rectangle. The starboard cam displayed a view of *S&R Black*'s lower hull and the corner of the spindle. Up top? Twinkling starlight breaking through the Kuiper Belt's twilight shroud. He paused to admire the view for a few seconds before returning his attention to the other feeds. The port view was the worrisome one. Not fifty meters away, and not more than half an hour ago, he'd been fighting for his life, and the life of his marines, in that very spot. Private Lyke was now dead because he couldn't stop the starfish thing in time.

When Copenhaver's voice broke through the comms, he flinched in surprise. "Sir? Bogeys near *Mira*'s aft."

He flipped back to the forward cam, but couldn't see anything moving.

"How far?"

"Nearly five hundred meters out," she said. "Isn't that where we're headed?"

"Ultimately," he said. "Pinecones?"

"Aye, sir," she said. "At least I think they are. They're clumped together in thick blobs. Cams don't have enough magnification to show much detail."

"No," he agreed. "They don't. Not enough for my liking anyway. Okay. We're moving. We'll take a little tour to the other side of *Black* and take a peek."

"Acknowledged, sir," she said.

As he piloted the craft around *S&R Black*'s aft portion, he kept glancing through the feeds looking for movement. Finally, he caught a glimpse of what Copenhaver had seen. It was barely noticeable from this distance and without magnification, but dots of black, darker than space, seemed to move out there. He shuddered at the thought of flying into another pack of the creatures. Especially since last time there hadn't been hundreds of them.

That was perhaps the worst part of this little mission. Keeping the memories of the two starfish attacks out of his mind was a chore. Not to mention hordes of bulbous pinecone-like things pinging off the hull like metal rain. He felt his stomach tightening into knots and tried to focus again on the front cam. *Copenhaver has the rest covered,* he told himself. *Just pilot the damned bird.*

Using a few thruster burns, he moved forward at 2m/s before rotating the SV-52 to face *S&R Black*'s port side. When he had enough room, he touched the thrusters again and brought the SV-52 back to the spindle. He chanced a quick glance at the feed and saw the spindle. No pinecones. No starfish. No visible threats.

He loosed a sigh. "Copenhaver?"

"All clear, sir. No bogeys out here." She took in a deep breath. "At least none that I can see."

"Roger that," Taulbee said. He made a connection to the ship. "Captain? Gunny? We're clear for now."

"Aye," Dunn said. "Gunny? Whenever you're ready."

"Aye, sir," Gunny said. "They're starting their EVA now."

Taulbee descended until the SV-52 hovered just above the hull. According to the instruments, they were less than 200cm away from the derelict's damaged hull plates.

He adjusted the SV-52's exterior lights to maximum and the powerful floods illuminated the spindle and its fittings as though they were in full sunlight. From here, he and Copenhaver could watch every move Gunny's marines made. If there was a problem, they'd know it right away.

He tried to keep his heart rate down, but it was damned difficult. If they were worried about human saboteurs or an ambush, coming up with a strategy was easy—you just picked them off as they egressed from their hiding spot. A few flechette rounds, and it was all over. With these damned things? Well, the flechette blasts necessary to disperse a herd of pinecones or destroy one of the starfish was likely to blow the two marines to pieces.

CHAPTER THIRTY-SEVEN

The airlock opened and space greeted them. The last of the atmosphere inside the airlock vented away, the sudden change of pressure vibrating his suit. Gunny closed his eyes for half a beat as he waited for the rush of vertigo to depart. When he opened them, his stomach immediately quieted and he no longer felt as though he were falling.

S&R Black's floodlights illuminated the deck plates well enough for him to see the cracks and fissures striated through the Atmo-steel surface. He hissed a sigh and activated the comms.

"Wendt? Murdock? Ready?"

"Aye, Gunny," Wendt said. "We got this."

"Aye, Gunny," Murdock stammered.

Gunny pulled a tether lead from the wall and attached it to Wendt, and clipped another to Murdock while he spoke. "Take it slow. Be careful. And get it done right." Neither of the marines replied. "Wendt? You see anything move that's not Murdock, shoot it. And then get your asses back here."

"Aye, Gunny," Wendt said again, a little more forcefully.

Gunny clapped Murdock on the back. "If the shit goes down, I'll be right there."

"Aye," Murdock said in a terrified, shaking voice.

"Get to it, marines," Gunny said.

"Follow me, Murdock," Wendt said and pushed himself out of the airlock.

The pair floated into space, the tether lines snaking out behind them in loose arcs as they gained distance from the ship. Wendt fired his suit thrusters and descended out of sight and to *Mira*'s hull. A second later and Murdock did the same.

Gunny activated the cam feeds from his marines and brought them up on his HUD. The views spun as the two men oriented themselves to the spindle. Murdock mag-walked in a jerky, halting series of steps, his camera view making Gunny sick to his stomach. He ignored it and focused on Wendt's more smooth, seasoned gait. When they reached the spindle, Wendt turned and faced away while Murdock began releasing the lines.

Gunny absently grabbed another tether lead and attached it to his own suit. With the same sense of autonomic routine, he pulled the flechette rifle from his back and gripped it in both hands. The firm metal felt reassuring somehow and made his fingers stop twitching with nervous tension.

The task of unhooking the spindle should only take a few minutes, he thought. Even less if they had two marines to do the job, but that would have required another marine to provide cover and he simply didn't have the numbers for that. Not without tasking another member of the command crew. Considering Nobel had a fractured leg, Oakes had to fly the damned ship, and Dunn was the captain and strictly forbidden from leaving the ship unless there was an emergency, they had to make do.

He knew Dunn was suited up and waiting outside the cargo bay hatch leading into the rest of the ship. The captain would come out here and save asses if necessary. Hell, even Nobel would gimp his way out if they needed him. Gunny just hoped it wouldn't come to that.

No. What he really needed? What he really wanted? He wanted Kalimura, Dickerson, Carbonaro, and Elliott standing on deck. He wanted to hear the corporal snapping at her marines, her clipped voice taking no shit and barking orders as though she were born for the job. That's what he wanted. Gunny glanced at his helmet cam and looked across *Mira*'s vast exterior. Somewhere beneath all that metal, and two decades of humanity's labor, her squad was either alive or dead. They were either trying to find a way out of the hulk, or they'd been eaten by the pinecones or the starfish or void knew what else lurking within the derelict's walls. Just a few more bodies in the floating tomb.

He shook the thought away. Those four marines deserved the benefit of the doubt. They were still alive an hour ago, and they'd still be alive now. He just had to wait until they found their way to the escape pods and left the wretched hunk of metal. A meager grin appeared on his face. She'd lead them out. Somehow.

Something moved at the edge of his vision and the grin disappeared at once. He sent a block command and the cam zoomed in as far as it could go. Beyond the edge of *Mira*'s hull, several shapes floated in the darkness like nearly invisible spirits. He frowned and watched them for a full ten seconds before realizing they weren't actually near *Mira* at all. They were much further away than that, but they were moving toward the ship. And that meant toward *S&R Black*.

"Black? You seeing this?" Gunny said.

"Yes, Sergeant," the AI responded.

"Well? What are they?"

"They are the KBOs the captain showed you earlier. They are much closer now."

"How is that possible?" Gunny asked. "I thought they were still a while away? They increase their speed?"

"No, Sergeant," Black said. "Not even Mickey's extensive array of telescopes and sensors are powerful enough to track every object near us. It appears these were much closer than anticipated."

Gunny's skin popped with gooseflesh. "How close are they?"

"Unknown," Black said. "My sensors are unable to determine their proximity. I estimate no more than twenty kilos in distance."

"What do you mean your sensors can't determine that?" Gunny snapped.

Black paused for a beat. "Lt. Oakes has just confirmed the objects are emitting some form of EMR that is disrupting our sensory arrays," Black said. "If that is the case, it's likely they have been near us for hours. Although they now appear to be traveling toward us at unknown velocities."

"Fuck," Gunny whispered. In the dim twilight of the Kuiper Belt, the shapes appeared as little more than shimmering, amorphous blobs. If they weren't scattering and eclipsing the light of distant stars, he might not have noticed them at all. "Captain?"

"Aye, Gunny," Dunn said. "Black and Oakes have filled me in. Let's get off this damned hulk ASAP."

"Copy that, sir," Gunny said. He brought back the feeds from Wendt and Murdock. The younger of the two marines was still futzing around with the cable assemblies, his arms occasionally pinwheeling as he lost traction rotating the release wheels. Apparently, he was as bad with his hands as he was with his boots. "Void sake," Gunny said to himself. "Should have sent a damned chimp out there."

Wendt's feed showed more of *Mira*'s hull, as though the man were standing on a vast cliff of pitted, distressed metal. The marine slowly walked in a circle, his back to the spindle and Murdock. Wendt, Gunny noticed, took his sentry duty pretty damned seriously. The motion paused every few seconds as Wendt scanned the area before him. Black was no doubt doing the same with her external cams. Between the two of them, he was confident they'd see a threat long before it had a chance to endanger either the ship or Murdock.

Gunny was about to ask how much longer when a low vibration shook the ship. Mag-locked on the airlock's deck, his body didn't move, but the rumble in his boots traveled up his spine and rattled his brain. It lasted no more than a few seconds, but it still scared the hell out of him.

"Black? What the hell was that?" Gunny asked.

"Unknown," Black said. "The vibration through the Atmo-steel surface was analogous to a seismic event. It is possible a portion of *Mira*'s interior has collapsed."

"Out-fucking-standing," Gunny growled. Kalimura's squad was still inside there while the void-damned ship collapsed around them. "Murdock. What's the status?"

"Almost there, Gunny," Murdock said in a breathy whisper. "Two more to go."

He opened his mouth to yell at the young marine and then closed it. Shouting at the kid wasn't going to make him move any faster. It sure as shit wasn't going to calm him down either. If anything, barking at Murdock would just make things worse."

"Murdock," Wendt said, "just get it done. I've got your back."

"Gee," Murdock grunted as he struggled with the controls, "I feel so much better now."

"Fuck you," Wendt said, chuckling.

Gunny relaxed. A little. He only had to worry about them for a few more minutes. They'd be back aboard and Oakes could move *S&R Black* out of the spindle and away from this cursed wreck. Gunny clenched his fingers tighter around the rifle. "Just get it done," he said at last. Neither of the marines replied.

CHAPTER THIRTY-EIGHT

Instead of sitting behind Oakes on an elevated command chair, instead of a cup of coffee in his hands, and instead of analyzing block data from the sensors, he stood just outside the cargo bay wearing a combat suit. With his helmet on, he had access to all the cam feeds and didn't have to view them through his block. That made the speed and clarity much better, and he wasn't sure that was a good thing.

Taulbee's feed showed 30° moving slices of the ship and the area around it. He and Copenhaver were essentially orbiting *S&R Black* while the ship still sat atop *Mira*. Wendt's feed, on the other hand, displayed a constantly moving 80° view of *Mira*'s surface. And Murdock's?

Dunn studied the feed and quickly decided Murdock was either very stupid, very clumsy, or panicked. He made a mental note to check with Gunny as to which of the three it was. The young marine's hands might as well have been hooves for all their dexterity.

"Maybe his gloves are damaged," Dunn said aloud.

Murdock had spent the better part of five minutes attempting to decouple the reinforced lines from the spindle. Rather than risk any more marines to properly remove the harness, he'd decided it was best just to take apart the spindle connections. Then they could decouple *S&R Black* from the spindle and they'd have a fighting chance of getting out of this mess.

"Murdock?" Wendt asked over the comms. "You going to take all void-damned day, or what?"

Murdock huffed and puffed through his mic. "This one is stuck!" he yelled. "Can't get the fucking thing to move."

Wendt growled. His cam feed swiveled from a view of *Mira*'s hull to that of the spindle. "Get your ass on cover duty, Murdock," Wendt growled as he made his way to the controls. "And try not to shoot me in the back."

Murdock smacked his armored glove against the spindle, pulled his rifle, and walked past Wendt to take up a sentry position. Wendt went to the last connection on the spindle, stowed his rifle, and began working on the coupling.

Dunn switched to Murdock's feed. The young marine was turning too fast and not spending enough time actually clearing the area. Just as Dunn was about to activate his mic and yell at Murdock, Gunny's voice, harsh and growling, filled the comms.

"Murdock! Slow and steady, damnit."

Murdock's cam view flinched. The marine slowed his pacing, although the cam view continued to move in jerky, unsteady swings. Wendt huffed and puffed through the mic. Apparently, Murdock hadn't been exaggerating that the coupling was stuck.

The seconds ticked off and Dunn felt as though time, something they didn't have much of to begin with, was flowing faster and faster. How many minutes did they have before the first KBO entered their immediate space? How many seconds did they have until they were once again under attack?

Dunn gritted his teeth. He was about to ask Wendt for a status when the large marine sighed into the comms. "Got it," he said.

A block alert flashed across Dunn's HUD. The spindle was disconnected.

"Sir?" Gunny said. "He got it."

"Copy," Dunn said. "Wendt and Murdock. Gather your gear and get back in the ship ASAP."

"Aye, sir," Wendt said.

Dunn exhaled a long stream of air. "Oakes?"

"Aye, sir?"

"Get ready to move us. As soon as Gunny's squad is back on board, I want us off the spindle and clear of *Mira*."

"Aye, sir," Oakes said.

Dunn grinned. Oakes sounded even more relieved than he felt. The worst part about being coupled while knowing the enemy was all around you was the helpless feeling of being trapped. While attached to the spindle, *S&R Black* was at its most vulnerable. If you couldn't move, you couldn't escape, and if you couldn't escape, the only option was to fight. Sitting this close to *Mira*'s hull, most of *S&R Black*'s onboard weaponry was all but useless. Unless, of course, the enemy was kind enough to float into the direct arcs of the mounted guns.

He reached to take off his helmet and stopped, his arms slowly lowering. "Not until they're inside," he said to himself. Murdock and Wendt had already finished gathering the tools and Wendt motioned for Murdock to head back to the airlock. While the young marine awkwardly mag-walked back to Gunny, Wendt took up a covering position, slowly walking backward in a crouch, his flechette rifle searching for targets.

The moments following a successful breach, device sabotage, or mission objective were always the most tense. It was one thing to be in a firefight where your nerves sizzled with energy and your training kicked in, allowing you to make snap-second decisions without noticing the fear. It was something else entirely to creep away while knowing you were at your most vulnerable. Dunn could almost feel Wendt's concern as the LCpl cleared the area surrounding the airlock.

He needn't have bothered. Murdock reached the airlock and disappeared inside. A moment later, Wendt did the same. Dunn loosed another sigh as the airlock closed.

"Oakes. We're clear."

"Aye, sir. Make sure you're mag-locked, marines. We are moving."

Dunn reached up and pulled off his helmet. The ship's recycled air immediately filled his lungs and he smiled. At least something had gone right today. He only hoped the next part of this plan worked as well.

CHAPTER THIRTY-NINE

The tunnel was even darker than he'd feared. Dickerson had seen the damage to the hatch assemblies through Carb's cam feed, but until he was able to swing his own cam around, study each scar and mar in the metal, he couldn't believe the damage.

"Something was sure pissed off," he said over the private comms to Carb.

"No shit," Carb said. "Give me a meter of space. Just in case I need to get the fuck out of here in a hurry."

"Copy that," Dickerson said. "Just make sure you fire a few rounds in there if something so much as twitches."

She giggled. "You're usually the one who storms through hatches and takes on whatever comes at you. Now you're being cautious?"

"Well," he said, "after you've seen darkness try and swallow you, not to mention starfish and fucking pinecones trying to kill you, you get a little skittish."

Carb crept another step forward. "Okay, I guess I understand that."

Dickerson kept her forward cam feed on the HUD's right side. Her helmet lamps slashed through the gloom with pure white light, the far bulkhead suddenly visible in the illumination. He waited while she took another few steps further into the tunnel. When she finally reached the inner hatch's edge, she took up a position to the tunnel's right, her lights and rifle pointed to the left. "Left," she said.

He quickly walked to her, stood to his full height, and took position on the left side, rifle pointed to the right. "Right," he said.

The two marines paused for a moment, Dickerson daring something in the room to move. But there was nothing. Her suit lights easily illuminated the back of the room while his own did the same on the other end. Whatever this room was, they at least didn't have to worry about a creeping darkness swallowing the light. For now.

"Clear?"

Dickerson nodded to himself. "Clear."

Carb took another few steps forward and entered the room beyond the hatch lip. Dickerson held his breath as her camera feed panned left, her suit lights illuminating a number of lab tables similar to the ones they'd found earlier. More equipment, more workstations, more dead holo displays. It looked like just another room literally frozen in time. And then he saw the corpses.

Three figures floated near the rear bulkhead, their forms nearly lost in the shadows. Carb unfocused her lights to provide a wider range of light and he heard her draw in a deep breath. A flotsam of shredded clothing, bloody ice crystals, and chunks of flesh floated like dust. "Well," Carb said after a moment, "I guess we know what happened in here."

"No, we don't," Dickerson said. "Not a goddamned clue."

"Okay, yeah, you're right." She panned again, her lights dancing over the back wall. "Shit, you see that?"

He did. The rear bulkhead had a number of dark shapes attached to it, the light seeming to slide off their surface like water beading on oil. "Five of them," he said. "What the fuck are they?"

"Don't know," Carb said. "Going further in."

"Covering," Dickerson said. He unfocused his own lights and shined them to the right of her position. He waited until she'd walked another meter inside before following in her wake. Keeping his lights pointed to her blind side, his eyes flicking from his cam view to hers, he looked for movement, for anything that might pose a hazard.

No corpses awaited them on the other side of the lab. Just more equipment, more dark holo displays and terminals. Carb crouch-walked until she was two meters from the far wall.

"I'm not dreaming this, right?" Carb asked.

Dickerson focused his eyes on her cam feed. His mouth opened wide, but no words came out. The shapes in the back of the room were nearly two meters in length, a meter wide, and tapered at either end. Whatever material they were made of had split open in the middle like a misshapen flower. *Or a seed pod,* he said to himself.

Once he was sure they were clear on all sides of threats, he walked behind Carb until he was beside her. With their combined suit lights, the shapes became more clear and he realized he'd been wrong. The shapes were practically embedded in the wall's steel as though they'd eaten through the metal. And they were larger too. The material stretched out in grisly layers from the center of the wall toward the ceiling and the deck.

"What the fuck is this shit?" Carb asked.

He shook his head without even realizing he was doing it. "Looks organic, doesn't it?"

"Yeah," she said. "Also, look at the spacing. It's like someone placed them there."

Dickerson turned and stared at the corpses floating at the far end of the room. "You think they were growing this shit?"

"Maybe," Carb said. "Let's see if we can find an emergency generator."

"Aye," he said. "I'll take right."

"Copy," Carb said. She fluidly turned and walked to the lab tables and the corpses.

Dickerson turned the opposite direction and moved with slow steps. Several pieces of large lab equipment were smashed, the metal casings fractured and splintered as if bashed by something blunt. If there had been gravity when the attack happened, whatever had crashed through the tunnels had been damned heavy. Of course, considering it had ripped the hatches from the Atmo-steel hinges, it stood to reason it had been powerful, massive.

Deep dents covered the bulkhead nearest the pods as well as the tables. Shards of plastic and steel floated and seemed to move, although he knew that was most likely an optical illusion. Dickerson practically jumped when Kalimura spoke through the comms.

"How we doing?"

He couldn't find his voice, but Carb responded for him. He wasn't surprised to hear the jangle of stress in her words. "Good, I guess. You see our feeds?"

"Aye," Kalimura said. "Would be better if we had some real light in there."

"No shit," Dickerson said. But in truth, he wasn't sure he wanted a better look at the room. Something had broken in here, killed whatever crew had been inside, and smashed equipment and tables. Was it the same thing that had tracked them? Or maybe one of those starfish things? And why the hell were the pods split open and spread apart?

"Look for an emergency generator," Kalimura said.

"We are," Carb said. Dickerson thought he heard a touch of annoyance in her voice. Not that he could blame her; Kalimura was telling them shit they already knew.

Dickerson tried to clear the questions from his mind and searched the room. There had to be a recessed panel hiding an emergency power source. There had been one in every other room they'd explored, so it stood to reason this one did too.

The more he studied the walls, the more they looked, well, wrong. Fissures ran down the metal between the bulkheads, looking like jags of forked lightning. Something had cracked the walls as though they were plastic. Whatever had been powerful enough to rip apart the quarantine hatches had obviously decided the room itself needed the same treatment. Dickerson took in a shuddering breath. If that thing was still here, still moving around the ship, and they found it, there was no way they'd be able to stop it. Shit. What would an explosive or stun flechette round possibly do to something that powerful?

"Probably fucking nothing," he said to himself.

He continued searching and finally found a rectangular inset in the wall. "Pay dirt," he said.

"Found it?" Carb asked.

The panel popped out the moment he pressed a finger to it, the crank assembly sliding from the wall in a puff of shattered ice crystals. Grinning, he turned the crank until the indicator lights turned green. "Here goes nothing," he said and pressed the power button.

A quarter of the overheads flickered to life, bathing the room in a shadowy twilight. He turned and faced the room's interior. That's when he saw them.

The split seed pods on the wall were the least interesting objects in the room. What hung from the ceiling made his mouth open in unfocused terror and surprise. For a moment, Dickerson wasn't sure what he was looking at, only that they were oblong shapes that seemed embedded in the steel. But the shapes looked, well, familiar. His mind tried to find another analog to replace them with, but failed. The shapes were human, outlines burned into the steel like flash-fried shades. Three. Three outlines of human beings etched into the Atmo-steel ceiling like the ancient chalk outlines of crime victims. No flesh, no tatters of clothing, only the discolored lines. Except for one. A single rib, bleached white, jutted out from the steel.

"The fuck?" he finally said.

"What?" Carb asked. He didn't see her turn to follow his gaze, but knew she had. "Okay. That's bad," she said.

"No shit." Dickerson tore his eyes from the sight to look at her. "That make any goddamned sense to you?'

She shook her head. "Only if it's in a fucking horror holo."

"Copy that," Dickerson said.

She slowly turned her head to gaze at the other pods hanging from the walls. "You don't think—" Her words trailed off into silence.

Dickerson slowly stepped toward the strange objects in the wall. They were split open. Or appeared to be. But, were they? "I think we need to get the fuck out of here."

"Not yet," Carb said. She turned back to the workstation she'd been inspecting. "I want to get the data off this."

"Well, hurry the fuck up," Dickerson said. He opened the comms to Kalimura. "Corporal?"

"Talk to me."

He swallowed an acidic burp. "We found something new," he said. "I think we need to get to the escape pods ASAP."

Kalimura paused before responding. "Shit," she said. "Just looked at the feed. Get out of there. Now."

"Hang on, Boss," Carb said. "I'm—"

"No," Kalimura said. "Now."

Dickerson glanced at Carb. She was still fighting to extract a memory chip from the holo display. "Aye, Boss."

"Fuck," Dickerson whispered after switching to the private comms. He mag-walked as quickly as he could to join her by the table. "Carb? We need to go."

"Yeah, yeah. Fuck off already. I've almost got it."

Dickerson saw movement on his HUD and flicked his eyes to the HUD's tiled window display. Something had twitched in the rear cam. Dickerson narrowed his eyes and zoomed in. The rear suit lights cast just enough light to illuminate the ceiling and the open pods at the back of the room. One of them shuddered as if in a seizure. His mouth opened as the embedded edges of the pod seemed to slide down.

"C-carb?"

"What?" she yelled in annoyance.

He tried to speak, but his voice locked in his throat. The other pods began shaking too. The first pod's edges had opened like a yawning mouth. A few fluttering black triangular shapes dropped from the ceiling, pushed by some unknown force toward the deck.

Dickerson lunged forward at Carb. She looked up just as he floated to her and locked his arm around her shoulder. "Move! Now!"

Her head pointed back to where he'd been. An airy scream broke across the comms. Dickerson saw it too now. The mouths were vomiting clouds of the shapes to the floor. "Unlock!" She cut her mag-boots just as he fired his jets.

The pair of marines flew through hundreds of the shapes, the objects bouncing off their suits like micrometeorites. He focused on using the attitude thrusters to push them to the door. From what seemed like a million kilometers away, Carb's voice screamed into the headset to the corporal, telling she and

Elliott to start moving.

Just as they floated to the broken airlock doors, he reached out with his free hand and swung both he and Carb through the entrance. His shoulder shrieked with pain, but he barely noticed. As they flew back into the main hallway, he reached the outer airlock ring and swung them again. Something gave in his shoulder and bright stars of pain lit his mind.

Carb was screaming, Kalimura was yelling, and Elliott was asking what the hell was going on. Dickerson ignored it all and hit his jets again. A critical warning flashed across his HUD. He was out of fuel, but the momentum carried him past Kalimura and Elliott, Carb floating behind him, her shoulder still attached to his good arm.

The hall up ahead glowed from his suit lights as they traveled further and further away from the airlock. A check of his cam showed just enough for him to know that Elliott and the corporal had activated their thrusters too. But in the distance, he made out a cloud of objects flowing out of the airlock. Whatever those things were, they were following them. He was out of fuel. The rest of the marines had to be nearly out too. At a speed of 6 m/s, he was heading into the darkness with no way to slow down, no way to change direction, and no way to stop.

CHAPTER FORTY

Taulbee took a position off *Mira*'s port-side and well away from *S&R Black*. The marine vessel slowly rose from the spindle after a few puffs from the bottom thrusters. *S&R Black* hovered above *Mira*'s hull like a welcome dream. Compared to the monstrous and damaged *Mira*, it more resembled a work of art than a military vessel. He grinned. Not everyone would agree with that assessment. But right now, *S&R Black* was the most beautiful thing he'd ever seen.

Just the thought of finally being free of this ship and the nightmares it had brought back with it was enough to make any escape craft seem heavenly. Taulbee wasn't sure he'd find a mineral freighter ugly under these circumstances. "As long as it has a fucking ion drive."

"Sorry, sir. I didn't hear that?" Copenhaver said.

"Nothing, Private," Taulbee said. For the moment, he was too damned happy to be embarrassed. *S&R Black* rose twenty meters above the hull before another set of thrusters activated. The gas pushed the ship further away from *Mira*'s surface and into space. Taulbee watched her for a few more seconds before returning his attention to the spindle.

Even from this height and distance away from where *S&R Black* had been moored, he could see fractures in *Mira*'s hull plates. Taulbee frowned. The hull hadn't looked like that earlier. It was far from pristine, no question of that, but he didn't remember the Atmo-steel looking so fragile. It was almost as though since their arrival, *Mira* had begun to disintegrate. The entire void-damned ship was getting ready to fall apart.

If that was happening to the hull, what about the ship's interior? Were Kalimura and her squad walking through crumbling decks and hatches? Were they slowly disintegrating as well?

"Sir?" Copenhaver said. "The area around the spindle. Did it—?"

"I see the same thing, Private," he said. "I don't know. And to be honest, I'm not sure I want to know."

"Aye, sir," Copenhaver said. She sounded somewhat concerned.

He knew how she felt.

"Taulbee," the captain said over the comms. "You're clear."

"Aye, sir," he responded. "Beginning our run."

"Acknowledged. Good hunting."

Taulbee nodded to himself and checked the four views on his HUD. Nothing in space around them. For now.

"Copenhaver? You ready?"

"Aye, sir," she said.

Taulbee smiled as the cannon cams came to life in his HUD's lower left corner. He could switch to that view and watch her scan the sky around them with the 360° cameras. Assuming the footage survived, he'd make sure to look at it later in case he had any pointers for her. But more importantly, he wanted to examine every frame captured of *Mira*'s hull both before they installed the

146

spindle and after. Copenhaver had seen what he had seen, sure, but that didn't mean they weren't both crazy.

Void-damned ship is getting to us, he thought.

He activated the thrusters and the SV-52 slowly accelerated from the midships toward the aft. The support craft rose higher above the hull until *Mira* all but disappeared from the bow camera.

The plan was to fly over her aft and really assess the damage. There might be nothing radioactive down there anymore, save for the beacon, but that didn't mean there weren't other hazards waiting to fry them. The vision of dozens of large starfish crawling out of the missing and fractured deck plates before launching themselves at him entered his mind. He tried to ignore the goose pimples that rose on his arms.

He accelerated to 20m/s and the SV-52 quickly ate the distance between *Mira*'s midships and the giant ship's aft. Although he did his best to focus on the forward cam, his eyes kept drifting to the SV-52's belly cam. Each second, more and more pinecone clumps appeared. After another few seconds, the Atmo-steel hull might as well have been made of pinecones rather than the strongest metal composite humankind had ever manufactured.

"Must be millions of them," Copenhaver said.

Taulbee thought the wonder in her voice held a tinge of terror. It was like hearing a small child seeing a jellyfish for the first time. First came the wide 'O' of an open mouth followed by the "wow." But the child would still scream themselves hoarse when the creature appeared in their nightmares. *For us,* Taulbee thought, *the nightmare is still happening.*

"I don't know about millions," he said, "but there are a shitload of them."

"They've been multiplying. How have they been doing that, sir?"

He felt a sudden rush of frustration. Why the fuck was she asking him things he obviously didn't know? Yet he wanted to ask Black exactly the same question. "I don't know, Private," he said. "Not even sure I want to. We just need to find the beacon and then we can annihilate this fucking ship."

"Copy that, sir," Copenhaver said.

The SV-52 blew past the rest of the hull and into open space. With nothing in front of him, Taulbee brought the rear cam and the cannon cams up on his HUD. The rest of the windows coalesced into a small group of rectangles on the lower right side. Just like that hypothetical child seeing its first jellyfish, Taulbee's mouth opened in awe as his mind made sense of what he was seeing.

Mira's aft was a tangle of broken and shattered deck plates. The supports and beams speared through the metal debris, holding it in place. Through great jagged rips and holes in the surviving deck plates, strange eldritch lights pulsed slowly in yellows and reds.

"What the fuck?" he asked no one.

"Sir?" Copenhaver said a moment later. "There's enough room for us to enter the aft section. I count four holes more than large enough for us to explore."

"But do we want to," he breathed.

"Sorry, sir. Didn't copy that?"

"Nothing. Mark the areas on my HUD. I'm turning us around."

"Aye, sir," she said.

Taulbee cut their forward momentum with several quick fore-thruster bursts. Once the SV-52 slowed to less than .5m/s, he activated the attitude thrusters and spun the craft until it pointed directly at *Mira*. A few puffs from another set, and the SV-52 descended relative to the giant ship's hull. As they moved at a negative vector, the damage became both more pronounced and detailed.

The expansive, nearly 400-meter-tall aft section had very little left intact. The deck plates that protected the engineering section from space were essentially gone. The remaining hull plate fragments resembled a wide mouth of jagged, broken teeth.

"Void wept," Taulbee said.

When the craft reached the aft's midpoint, he stabilized its momentum and they hung there like a spider at the end of a gossamer silk thread. "Copenhaver? I want you to pan from the top port-side to the bottom starboard. Zoom in to 5x magnification before you give me the sweep. Once you're finished, invert and do it again."

"Copy, sir."

He pushed away the other windows on the HUD and watched the cannon camera exclusively. The view took his breath away.

The shadows behind the wrecked superstructure had to be pinecones. Didn't they? He thought he saw a few limb-like appendages waving in the z-g vacuum, but they could have been pinecones too. *Or something else,* a voice muttered in his mind. He shivered despite the warm combat suit.

Through the magnified view, the pulsing lights looked less uniform and smaller than he'd originally thought. Instead of a large, single source, they were composed of dozens, if not hundreds, of individual lights. *Clumps,* he thought. Whatever creatures were responsible for the light, they must be huddled together like oysters.

But the pinecones didn't produce light and neither did the starfish. *Well,* he thought, *that's not quite right.* They produced something that affected light, but neither had produced yellows or reds. Whatever was in there was something they hadn't seen before.

Taulbee minimized the cannon cam and brought his normal cams back into focus. "When you're finished with that, make sure Black has it," he said.

"Aye, sir. Had already connected her in."

Taulbee grinned. The private may have sounded a little frightened, but it didn't seem to be affecting her concentration. Another good sign. Yup, if she made it through this, well, if any of them made it through this, he'd make sure she got a promotion.

"Black?"

"Yes, Lieutenant," the AI responded. "I'm analyzing the cam feeds." There was a momentary pause before the computer spoke again. "May I suggest another, slower sweep at 20x magnification? I can take control of the cannon cams," Black offered.

Taulbee shook his head. "That won't be necessary, Black. Copenhaver?"

"On it, sir," she said.

"What do you make of this, Black?"

"I am unable to hypothesize at this time," the AI said. "However, due to the perceived density of the lifeforms, Earth analogs suggest this might be a nest of some kind."

"A nest?" Taulbee asked. "What do you mean nest?"

"Some insects and aquatic lifeforms create nests to hold their eggs or larvae. The nest usually connects to a nursery of sorts where the larvae are then nourished and protected until maturity. The nursery is also usually protected by a soldier caste of the creatures. It's possible we are seeing the first example of such behavior in exo-solar lifeforms."

He shivered again. The New Boston dome where he grew up, located nearly 100km from the original city's location, had had a number of connecting domes where terrestrial lifeforms were kept. He remembered several trans-aluminum cases, each 10 meters tall and dozens of meters wide, standing in rows. Each contained a large ant colony. The structure of the hive, the individual chambers, and the massive queens and their attendants were easily visible. The creatures tended their hive, brought food to the bloated, disgusting queen, and cared for those about to hatch.

If he remembered correctly, the ant hives weren't just a relic of a bygone age, but rather used for testing environmental pollutants on the insects to see how they'd react. In addition, they were used in the arboretum as part of its natural lifecycle. But what had they eaten?

"Aphids," he said.

"Lieutenant?" Black said. "Did you say something?"

"Aphids," he said again, more strength in his voice. "Ants eat aphids."

"Yes," Black said. "They feed on the smaller insects as part of a functional biome."

His mind filled with an image of the pinecone clusters, the strange-looking creatures huddled together like a crustacean horde. The starfish creatures fed upon them like predators. Like ants eating aphids.

"Oh, shit," Taulbee said. "The starfish eat the pinecones," he said.

"Yes, Lieutenant," Black said.

He felt as though everything was snapping into place. The phrase "the tide is coming in" echoed in his mind and seemed to draw the loose mental connections into a web of understanding. "Black? What eats the starfish?"

Black sounded pleased to hear him ask the question. "I don't know," Black said. "Something we haven't seen yet."

"Excuse me, sir," Copenhaver said. "May I ask what you two are talking about?"

"Life," Taulbee said. "These things may not be from Earth, and hell, they may be made of something other than carbon, but they're exhibiting some of the same base behaviors. Everything has to eat. Predators must have prey. And most lifeforms are a predator to another. If the pinecones are the base of the exo-solar food chain, then it follows that their predator, the starfish, would also have a predator. And so on."

"Oh," Copenhaver said. She paused for a moment. "I don't like where this is leading, sir."

"Me, neither," Taulbee said. "Black? You think we can get close without—" He broke off in mid-sentence, somehow unsure to put his fears into words. "I don't know, without waking them up? Or getting their attention?"

"Impossible to know, sir," the AI said. "Our previous encounters suggest that the creatures are capable of seeing movement. They may even be able to detect chemical emissions from your suits, as well as energy patterns. Might I suggest a nanoprobe instead?"

Taulbee grinned. Nanoprobe. He felt like smacking a palm to his forehead. "Of course," he said. "Copenhaver?"

"On it, sir," she said.

A second later, a new status appeared on his HUD. She had a nanoprobe ready for deployment. He scanned the broken aft section, looking for an ingress point furthest from the clusters. There. Far starboard-side, a little more than 1/4 from the bottom of the hull and nearly half-way across the hull's width. He placed a waypoint for the probe, connected his block, and waited for a confirmation. The probe immediately responded to his ping, received the information, and replied with a movement plan. His grin transformed into a hard smile. "Okay, Copenhaver. Launch it."

"Aye, sir."

There was no sound or vibration through the ship as a small pneumatic launcher pushed the nanoprobe through a tube the diameter of two human fingers. The nanoprobe, black and nearly impossible to see in the Kuiper Belt's shadows, shot forward from the SV-52 at 10m/s.

While he wanted to watch every frame from the nanoprobe, possible threats approaching from *Mira* were much more important. With the SV-52 a mere two hundred meters from *Mira*, he had to keep his wits. If something inside the wreckage decided they were an appetizing morsel, he needed to get them the hell away as quickly as possible. But that didn't mean he was going to ignore it.

He brought up the probe's feed and shuffled it to the HUD's lower left corner. "Keep an eye on it, Copenhaver," he said. "And let me know if you see anything interesting."

"Aye, sir," she said.

Maintaining his focus on the forward view was more difficult than he'd thought possible. The urge to ignore potential threats and instead focus on the probe's camera view kept tugging at him. No. He'd have to keep flicking back and forth until Copenhaver told him there was something interesting. Still…

He managed fifteen seconds or so before enlarging the probe's feed. What he saw did more than make his mouth open in surprise; the view made him feel as though he'd been dropped in ice.

The nanoprobe, still some distance away from the interior of the heavily damaged aft hull plates, captured the edge of something shimmering and waving in the vacuum. Taulbee at first wasn't certain what he was seeing, and finally realized it was a large appendage. Very large. The probe continued forward, its cameras picking up the glare of the pulsing light sources deeper within the ship.

The different colors blended together for a moment, coalescing into bright white before returning to their separate oscillations. The light sources weren't uniform. Rather than appearing as regular, easily recognizable geometric shapes, they seemed more like organic amoebas constantly shifting and redefining themselves. They were so incongruous that Taulbee could barely make sense of any of them.

The nanoprobe continued floating through the latticework of broken and shattered metal, composites, and humanity's once-heady dreams of deep space exploration. As it did, he saw more shapes moving in the shadows, their forms briefly recognizable as oblong pinecone or starfish shapes before melting into a morass of tangled darkness.

"Sir?" Copenhaver asked. She sounded like a small child either waking from a nightmare, or still in the grips of one.

"Yes, Private?"

"What the fuck are we looking at?"

He shook his head without even knowing he was doing it. "I don't know, Private. I really don't have a void-damned clue."

They continued watching in silence, Taulbee half-expecting the boogeyman that hid under his bed when he was young to fly into the camera view, its face a mask of a melting skin and glittering red-dwarf eyes. He shook the thought away. *Now is not the time to lose your mind,* he told himself. It didn't help.

The probe was more than twenty meters inside what used to be *Mira*'s aft section. Its tiny lights barely provided enough illumination to see more than bright spots on distant metal, but it was enough for him to catch the view of what looked like the occasional frozen human limb or torso. Flash-fried, flash-frozen. And even that didn't make sense.

If Black was right and *Mira*'s reactors suffered some kind of nuclear meltdown or a bonafide fusion explosion, there should have been nothing left aside from wrecked and twisted metal. But the plas-steel still intact on some of the girders and supports nixed that theory. Hell, there was a control panel dangling by a thick strand of wires still attached to a bulkhead.

"No," he said softly. "It wasn't a nuke."

The probe continued further. The probe's lights dimmed, the focused ring of illumination no longer as powerful, or as cohesive. The thick nestle of shadowy forms began knitting themselves together into a massive wall of darkness. A moment later, he could see nothing. An alert flashed on his HUD.

"Holy shit," he breathed. "Copenhaver?"

"Here too, sir."

"Black?"

"Yes, Lieutenant?"

"Our probe just received a massive radiation spike. Way beyond what I saw on the SV-52. I mean powerful stuff."

The AI paused for a second. "I concur," Black said. "Interesting. Might I suggest you retreat from your current vantage point? It's very possible the beacon is preparing for another emission."

"Shit," Taulbee said.

He punched the attitude thrusters and the SV-52 rose from its current position at more than 5m/s. That still wasn't fast enough. He used more fuel until they popped up above *Mira*'s hull, still some hundred meters away from her, and began accelerating back to the safety of her remaining hull plates. They passed the remains of the aft and were two hundred meters closer to the midships when the probe screamed alerts before going silent.

He quickly spun the SV-52 and pointed it toward the aft section. "Copenhaver?"

"Aye, sir?"

"Get ready. This may get a little—"

His voice broke off in mid-sentence as the world before him exploded with light. While his HUD filtered the damaging short wavelengths from his eyes, he still felt as though someone had teleported a damned star into his lightless, state room coffin. A white flash, so powerful it seemed solid rather than ephemeral, blasted from the aft wreckage. It wasn't a beam. It was a goddamned supernova contained in a wide, irregularly shaped explosion of energy.

The afterimage inked on his corneas stayed there for a moment, leaving him blinking even through the HUD's virtual cam feeds. A number of warning icons and alerts blinked and pulsed across his vision.

"Copenhaver?"

"Here, sir. I'm alive and not blind."

"Good," Taulbee said. "Check the telemetry. The probe have anything interesting to say before it died?"

"Hang on, sir."

The seconds ticked off. The blast was gone now, but he could still see trails of its existence as though a smear of whitish-yellow had been painted across a field of utter black. What the fuck was that?

"Sir?" she said. "I think you better look at it yourself."

Taulbee raised an eyebrow. Copenhaver's voice held that sound again. She was terrified, but curious. Suddenly, he didn't want to know. But he had to just the same.

He shuffled aside the cam views, minimizing them as well as the standard SV-52 readouts into a corner and filled his HUD with the probe's data. His block took a moment to make sense of the data stream and then his jaw dropped.

CHAPTER FORTY-ONE

Dunn had sat riveted before the holo display as the SV-52 approached *Mira*'s aft section. Although he hadn't been exerting himself, hadn't been in the pilot seat of the relatively tiny craft, his heart rate had steadily risen. He did feel fear, and it wasn't the terror a commander sometimes experienced upon sending their marines into danger. No. This was personal. This fear rattled his bones and struck pangs of ice through his skull. This fear was that of the unknown, of the alien, of reality slowly coming apart.

As the cam feed had given way to that of the nanoprobe, his mind completely cleared of all thought. He'd allowed himself to float into the terrifying images of the pulsating lights, *Mira*'s shattered superstructure, and the slithering shadows. Taulbee's and Copenhaver's comms chatter faded into a distant whisper of meaningless noise as he experienced every image from the nanoprobe as though he were riding it into the alien maelstrom.

He'd been aware that Taulbee was moving the SV-52 out of harm's way, but it didn't pull his consciousness away from the rolling movie in his mind. The nanoprobe had continued forward, its small, powerful cone of light stabbing through the shadows, illuminating impossibly black limbs waving in the vacuum. But the light began to fade, visibility decreasing as something he couldn't see swallowed it. No, he couldn't see it, but it was something he thought he could nearly feel. A presence. Or something humans didn't even have a word for.

When the light completely disappeared and the cam feed became nothing more than a pane of absolute darkness, something hitched inside his mind and brought him back to the present. He was still sitting in the command chair, his hands gripping the armrests so tightly that his fingers throbbed. A moment later, the world was brighter than he'd dreamed possible.

For just an instant, a quanta of second, the darkness transformed into a flash so bright that he thought he'd been dropped into Sol. His body prickled with something like goose flesh, but there was no cold, no sensation of ice being poured down his back. Instead, it was like sitting next to a fusion engine blasting an inferno of hot plasma into a tightly enclosed space.

And then the feed was nothing more than static with an alert flashing across his HUD: "Signal Terminated."

After a moment, he realized he was shaking with excitement, heart pounding hard enough in his chest to make him shudder. Oakes' voice pulled him from the fugue.

"Void wept. What the hell was that?" Dunn pushed away from his block connection and re-engaged with reality. Oakes had turned in his chair to face him. "Sir?"

Dunn took a deep breath and commanded, no, demanded, his heart slow its rapid beat. When he felt he could speak without sounding like an asthmatic, he cleared his throat and exhaled. "I don't know. Black?"

The AI was silent for a moment. "My sensors have detected another massive photon burst. After the last such pulse, I adjusted the instruments to filter out known EMR types and look for anomalous readings. This latest emission appears to have produced a number of previously unknown quantum particles."

Dunn blinked. "What the hell does that mean?"

"Captain," Black said, "we already know that *Mira*'s lifeforms defy our knowledge of biology and physics. This is more of the same. Whatever wave the beacon produces appears to create elements and particles I can detect, but not analyze. The power stored in the beacon must be immense, although how it is creating such a wave from such a seemingly small power source is beyond my understanding."

Beyond my understanding. Yeah, that sounded about right. The most intelligent sentient on the mission was telling him it didn't have a fucking clue. He shivered.

"What about the other things?" Oakes asked. "Those, I don't know, those shapes moving in the shadows?"

"I've already analyzed the feed and applied a number of filters."

The bridge holo display cleared and a number of still images floated in place of sensor readings and a model of *Mira*. Dunn gazed at the images for a moment before his eyebrows knit together of their own accord.

The first image showed a piece of Atmo-steel, twisted and bent at an impossible angle, its surface glowing green and white. A long, wide, tapered appendage wrapped around the metal like a healthy ivy vine strangling a tree limb. The appendage's surface shimmered in smears of eerie yellows and blues.

"Is that a starfish limb?" Dunn asked.

"I don't think so," Black said. "Based on observational data, the proportions are not correct. This 'limb,' as you call it, is much wider than the exo-solar lifeforms we have thus far encountered. Not only that, but as you can see, it appears to be covered in an analog to scales. But if you look at the next image," Black said as the holo display popped another image to the foreground, "you can see the hint of a rectangular base that the limb is attached to."

After a moment, he saw what Black was talking about. While the first image displayed an appendage wrapped around a beam of Atmo-steel, the second image showed the edge of the creature's "base." It didn't look right. It didn't even look organic. Dunn harrumphed to himself. None of it looked "organic." But this looked more machine-like than what they'd come across before.

"Then what is it?" Dunn asked.

"Unknown," Black said.

Another image appeared. In the distance, something glowed bright white. The source was little more than a dot, but it was powerful enough to shred the image quality in the area. Instead of the dark, tangled nest of shadows, the tiny light cast enough brightness to display a monstrous horde of backlit, moving shapes.

Hundreds, no, thousands of creatures of different sizes crowded the area. Countless appendages, starfish bodies, pinecones, and other creatures he didn't recognize, crowded the area like a swarm.

"Void wept," Dunn said. "How many are there?"

"My estimates are over 2,000," Black said. "The exo-solar lifeforms, including varieties we have yet to encounter, appear to be congregating near the beacon."

"What's that pinpoint of light?" Oakes asked.

"That," Black said, "is the beacon a few nanoseconds before it emitted the latest EMR pulse."

Dunn's mind spun. More creatures than they'd thought possible are inside *Mira*'s aft section? "Are they spawning?" he asked in a robotic voice.

Black paused. "I cannot say for certain," the AI said. "However, I predict a 72% chance that is the case. It would certainly explain the large number of creatures Lieutenant Taulbee saw on the hull. If they are reproducing, they are doing so at a nearly geometric rate."

"Void, Captain," Oakes said. "How the hell are we supposed to get to the beacon?"

He shook his head. "I don't know, Oakes," he said. Dunn fought back another shiver. Even if he had a full company of marines decked to the nines with the latest combat gear, functional skiffs, and five or six support craft, there was no way to get in there. No way they could possibly survive in that swarm of alien creatures.

Weapons. The Trio had given them weapons. Some were lethal to humans, some non-lethal. Apart from the tritium flechettes, the others scared the hell out of him. The Trio had sent helpful instructions and warnings every step of the mission. Their pronouncements had confused him, terrified him, and given him hope all at the same time. But could he really trust them? Assuming they had given him the tools to succeed, the exotic weaponry was surely the answer. But did he dare to trust them after all this? After they had had something to do with *Mira*'s near destruction and the deaths of the human crew? Could he?

"Black. Do you think the Trio knew this was going to happen? Are the weapons part of their plan?"

"I believe the Trio knew some of what we would encounter, Captain." Black paused for a beat. "If they truly want us to succeed in sending the beacon to Pluto, then it follows they would have ensured we had the tools to do so."

Dunn nodded. "I was afraid you'd say that." He stared into the image, his eyes focusing on the brilliant pinpoint of light shining behind the fractured landscape of Atmo-steel. The light. That's what they had to extract. The rest of the ship could go to pieces. *Mira* wasn't the mission anymore. The beacon was. Now all he had to do was figure out how to remove it or destroy it.

"Taulbee?"

"Aye, sir?" the LT's voice immediately responded.

"You're loaded with the new weapons?"

"Aye, sir," Taulbee said. He sounded a little more alert and less dumbfounded.

"I guess it's time to try a few of them out."

CHAPTER FORTY-TWO

Dickerson had flown past her, Carb trailing behind him like a cape. Her boot had nearly clipped Kali's helmet as they streaked by. Kali saw dark shapes flowing out from the airlock like a plague of locusts. She screamed at Elliott to detach and move. He did, just as she did the same. His pathetic civvie suit barely had enough power to get him off the deck. Kali pushed her thrusters to maximum and pushed him forward. He shot down the hallway, but her own momentum was cut in half. Critical fuel warnings flashed across her HUD. She had enough fuel left for one attitude burn, or one thruster burn. Grinding her teeth, she spun herself so she faced the threat.

Kali didn't aim so much as fill the hallway with flechettes. Three rounds struck the middle of the cloud in an explosion of electricity and debris. Two more rounds hit the wall and detonated, creating arcs of blue light that traveled across the swarm like lightning.

The dark triangular shapes flew in all directions, the cloud dispersing in a frantic z-g scramble, the creatures colliding with one another and bouncing to the ceiling, the deck, and the bulkheads. She spun herself again, put her legs straight out behind her and punched her thrusters. The burn lasted for little more than a second, but it was enough to propel her forward. Elliott, Dickerson, and Carb were already far down the corridor, but she was gaining fast.

Kali glanced at her rear suit cams and grinned. The shapes were still regrouping. She just hoped like hell they had enough time to reach the far edge of the science section. Her HUD claimed they were only forty meters from the exit. She had a few shots left in the current mag, and then she'd have to reload. If Dickerson wasn't able to give her cover fire and those things managed to catch her, she was fucked.

The seconds passed with agonizing slowness. The far bulkhead suddenly came into view, illuminated by Dickerson's suit lights. He was flying too fast. He was going to crunch into the bulkhead along with Carb.

At the last second, he thrust out his legs to cushion the blow. He hit the wall and collapsed his legs to ease the collision. Dickerson grunted with pain over the comms and Carb slammed into the bulkhead next to him. Elliott, the only one of them with thruster power, managed to slow his approach and keep himself from crashing into both of them.

Kali swung herself in an effort to reach the bulkhead with a mag-glove, but the corridor was too wide. She turned the magnetics to full, and tried again. This time, the magnetic field was strong enough to at least make her drift toward the corridor bulkhead. Her trajectory changed slightly and then the pull rapidly increased until she slammed into the steel. She loosed a cry of pain, her ribs feeling as though they had speared her insides.

"Get the fucking door open!" Kali screamed.

Carb had unhooked herself from Dickerson and floated to the deck while he tried to collect himself. Elliott used his mag-gloves to drag himself down, his breath wheezing over the comms. Dickerson's body writhed in pain. Kali decreased her magnetics and climbed down the corridor bulkhead until her feet touched the deck. She walked forward on unsteady feet, her torso swaying despite the magnetics securing her feet to the deck. Fiery pain stabbed through her rib cage, making her wince.

An indicator light on the side of the airlock flashed from red to yellow to green as Carb cranked the manual release. Kali mag-walked as fast as she could, each step an exercise in misery.

"Got it!" Carb yelled.

Dickerson groaned as he pushed himself to the deck. Something flickered in Kali's rear cam feed. She glanced at it, feeling as though she were thinking through glue. The shapes had reappeared, reorganized into a spawning cloud. A few of them had broken off from the main group and approached through the air. Then she realized they weren't just oblong triangles, but they had wings, the edges vibrating in the light as they lazily flapped.

"Get—" she started to say, her breath catching in her throat as another searing explosion of pain burst in her chest. "Get out. Now."

Dickerson turned to her. Elliott and Carb walked through the airlock and into the corridor beyond. She took another step forward, leaned, and sagged. She couldn't lift her foot. All the strength, all the adrenaline, everything was gone. She was empty. There was nothing left.

The large marine stepped to her, his left shoulder drooping, and placed his good hand on her shoulder. She felt the magnetic field locked her to his hand. "Let go," he said. She could barely keep her eyes open. Void, but she was tired. "Let. Go." The words were clipped, calm, and evenly spaced, but she heard the strength in them, the urgency in how he'd spoken them. She cut her magnetics and immediately floated upward.

The cloud of shapes behind her gained speed. The cloud was coming. They were both going to be surrounded, swallowed by creatures with impossibly black wings. The bulkhead came into view and she suddenly realized he'd pulled her through the airlock. Someone yelled over the comms, the door sliding shut just as the shapes filled her vision. Something black, small but massive, struck her faceplate and the darkness swallowed her.

CHAPTER FORTY-THREE

Nobel ran a hand across the Atmo-steel slab, luxuriating in the neat, smooth lines and the feel of the cold metal on his skin. "Beautiful," he said aloud. Murdock made a sound that might have been a snort. Nobel raised his eyes and glared at the marine. "Something to say, Private?"

Murdock flinched. "No, sir. Nothing."

"Bullshit," Nobel said. "You think it looks ugly. You think it's just a big slab of metal that has no artistic merit." He stood with his hands on his hips, eyes boring into the private's.

Murdock was doing his best to keep a straight face. So was Wendt.

Gunny cleared his throat. "I for one think it's a marvelous job, Lieutenant."

"Thank you, Gunny." He slapped the side of the sled and examined it once more, his eyes poring over the craft. He shrugged. "Okay. Fine. It's ugly. But not bad for a rush job," he said. Nobel glanced at Gunny. "Now all we need is a beacon to strap to it."

"Aye, sir," Gunny said. "I imagine Lieutenant Taulbee is taking care of that right now."

"Probably," Nobel said. He looked at the sled again, wincing in pain with every movement. His leg still hurt like a sonofabitch and he'd need to stay off it a while at some point, but for now, all he could do was hope the nannies continued pumping out THC to compensate.

The sled, with its rocket engines and relatively small mass, would make it to Pluto in less than a day. If he really poured on the speed, it could probably get there in half a day. A human wouldn't be able to survive that kind of g-force unless the tiny craft had an acceleration couch or pod. He smirked. That was perhaps the best part of building the damned thing—no humans required. No life support, no acceleration couches, no amenities. They'd strap the beacon in, position the sled, and let it rip. And that would be that. He hoped.

Nobel glanced upward as he received a block message from Dunn. With a wary hesitation, he accepted. "Aye, sir?"

"Nobel. I'm sending you a few feed images. Both you and Gunny. I think we're going to need the skiff to get the beacon out, but we're going to have to clear some junk first."

"Junk, sir?"

"Take a look at the first image."

He kept the block connection alive and brought up the first image. Although both Dunn's voice and the image were coming through his block and not in real life, his mouth dropped open anyway. Someone had obviously applied a ton of filters to the image, but it was clear enough to see what Dunn was talking about. *Mira*'s aft was little more than an Atmo-steel spider's web, if that spider had been tripping balls on some Titan Temptation.

The explosion that had ripped through the engineering section had collapsed decks, superstructure supports, kilometers and kilometers of cabling, and damned near anything else with which a ship was built. The hull and deck plates looked as though they'd been shattered by a god-like hammer after being frozen with liquid nitrogen, yet the structure was somehow holding together in a semblance of stability.

"Void," Nobel breathed aloud.

"You see it?" Dunn asked.

"Aye, sir. So we need something to clear the area of debris?"

"Yes," Dunn said. "But we have a larger problem once the debris is cleared."

"And what's that, sir?" he asked with a sinking feeling.

Another image popped into his block queue. He brought it up and stared in horrified fascination. What the first picture hadn't shown with its filters were the scores and scores of alien limbs and bodies hanging off of or hiding behind the wreckage. He shivered at the memory of the huge starfish-like thing that had attacked him.

"Um," Nobel stuttered, "I, um, don't know how to get rid of those."

"No," Dunn said. "You don't. But I think the Trio does. Those new munitions we have might make them move. I don't know where they'll go, or if they'll just disappear, but we're going to try it. Once they're out of the way, we need something large and nasty to clear away the detritus."

Nobel slowly grinned. "You need a battering ram."

Dunn's disembodied voice chuckled over the block connection. "I knew there was a reason I keep you around. That sounds like what we need, all right."

"I should have enough materials. Give me fifteen minutes, sir."

"Fifteen minutes. Dunn, out."

Nobel terminated the block connection. Gunny glanced at him with a smirk. He winked at the sergeant before clapping his hands and snapping his fingers at the two non-rates. "Wendt? Murdock? How would you like to help me build something nasty?"

The two marines raised their eyebrows in unison. Nobel's grin widened.

CHAPTER FORTY-FOUR

Fucking insane, Taulbee thought first. *The captain has lost his mind,* was the second thought. Yet the more he considered the plan, the less insane it seemed. Well, less insane for this void-damned mission anyway. The crew of *S&R Black* had already undertaken several crazy plans, so why should this be any different?

He and Copenhaver continued floating a little more than a hundred meters from the aft and fifty meters above it. From this vantage point, he could see less than a 1/4 of the Atmo-steel latticework and the glowing, pulsing colors entrenched amidst the wreckage. Taulbee didn't mind the lack of a clear sightline. He was just damned happy they were out of harm's way if the beacon decided to let loose another EMR blast.

"Dunn to Taulbee."

"Here, sir. Go ahead."

Dunn sounded pleased with himself. Taulbee grinned. That meant something interesting was about to happen.

"Nobel is building something special for you. Gunny and his squad will bring it to you in about ten minutes or so. Until then, we need you to stand sentry and take out anything that threatens the ship. Over."

"Acknowledged, sir," Taulbee said.

"Something special?" Copenhaver asked. "What does that mean, sir?"

Taulbee chuckled. "We'll find out soon enough, Private. In the meantime, what do the scans say?"

She paused for a moment before replying. "This end of *Mira* appears to have attracted the majority of the exo-solar lifeforms, sir," she said. "Those clusters we flew over seem to be migrating in this direction, but they're doing so without taking flight."

"Without taking flight?" Taulbee asked. "Explain?"

He could hear her shrug. "They either have a method of propulsion we haven't seen before, or they're hugging the hull as they move aft."

Method of propulsion other than jetting. That didn't sound good. If they were magnetic or generated a magnetic field, it made sense they could travel while staying just a few centimeters above the hull plates. But what would they do when all the creatures congregated in the aft section? Dunn obviously had a plan to get inside *Mira* and to the beacon, but he doubted the plan would work if they had thousands of pinecones and starfish suddenly appear to guard it.

Guard it. That was a strange thought. Would they protect the beacon? Were they intelligent enough to know what it was? That idea gave him the shivers. The starfish were certainly intelligent enough to take evasive actions and even use debris as projectiles, but were they sentient? Void, he hoped not.

They continued hovering in silence, each lost in their own thoughts.

Copenhaver continued scanning using the cannon cams while he flipped back and forth across the SV-52's stationary ones. The area they could see inside *Mira* didn't appear to have changed. No creature activity beyond the damaged aft section. But outside?

With each passing moment, another swarm of pinecones moved in closer to the aft. Rather than keeping to themselves, the creatures appeared to be stacked on one another, their former group membership consumed by the larger population. He didn't even want to guess how many were down there now or how thick the bed of pinecones had become. The good news was they didn't seem interested in entering *Mira*, but that might not last for long.

"Taulbee," Dunn said over the comms.

He flinched at the sound as it dragged him from his thoughts. "Aye, sir?"

"We're ready. Gunny's squad will be leaving the cargo bay in a moment. Keep an eye on them and provide cover."

"Understood, sir."

He rotated the SV-52 and pointed its nose at *S&R Black*'s port-side. The cargo bay door slid aside, revealing a large rectangle of white light. Backlit by the floods, the skiff looked strange. Instead of a meter tall slab of Atmo-steel, the skiff looked as though it had grown a lump beneath it. After the skiff traveled a few dozen meters from the ship, the lump became more well-defined. Nobel had apparently crafted something new and altogether ugly for this cluster fuck.

"Sir?" Taulbee asked, "Exactly what is attached to the skiff?"

"You're going to love it," Dunn said. "We're going to clear some of the wreckage for you and Gunny. Once the area is clear, you can provide cover fire and Gunny can get the beacon."

Taulbee grinned. "So that's a missile?"

Dunn chuckled. "More like a battering ram."

"Very good, sir," Taulbee said.

Copenhaver cleared her throat. "Battering ram, sir?"

"Yeah, Private. I guess Nobel printed a big blob of Atmo and attached a couple of rockets to it. Fire and forget."

"Aye, sir," Copenhaver said. "But how are we going to clear the creatures?"

Taulbee thought for a moment. "I guess it'll be time to test one of the Trio's little gifts."

"More flechettes?" she asked.

"No, Private. Something with a little more oomph."

CHAPTER FORTY-FIVE

Gunny slowly increased his speed and hit the attitude thrusters. The skiff, belly swollen with its unmanned payload, didn't respond as easily as it normally did. He didn't know how much mass the makeshift battering ram had, but it was enough to throw off the maneuvering characteristics. He hoped like hell they would be rid of the thing before he had to take evasive action of any kind, or getting his squad out alive was going to be even more interesting than usual. *Well, more terrifying,* he told himself. *Because nothing about this mission has been "usual."*

Wendt sat in the cannon mount with Murdock in the rear, the young marine's flechette rifle raised and ready to fire. Before mounting up, he'd told Murdock to shoot anything that moved, so long as it wasn't human, wasn't the skiff, and wasn't the SV-52. The private, his face visible before lowering his visor, had looked pale and unsure. Gunny didn't blame him, but he yelled at the kid anyway. The last thing he needed right now was for the young marine to freeze up.

At least Wendt was cold and cool. The LCpl had turned from the fuckup in the company to a marine Gunny was proud to have fighting by his side. Apparently, wonders never did cease. Gunny would have liked to have had at least two more marines in his squad, but there weren't any left. Kalimura's squad of four was still missing, Lyke and Niro were dead, and Copenhaver was riding shotgun with Taulbee. All that remained on the ship was Nobel, Oakes, and the captain.

"If we fail, we're all fucked," Gunny said to himself. That was no lie. The captain was taking a hell of a risk. If the beacon pulsed at the wrong time, both Gunny's squad and Taulbee's SV-52 would be annihilated in an eruption of radiation. "Well, at least it will be quick," Gunny thought with a grim smile.

Less than fifty meters away, the SV-52 floated above them like a wraith. "Gunny to Taulbee."

"Go ahead, Gunny."

"Sir, we're going to move into position below you and on *Mira*'s starboard-side. Black said we should aim for that area to maximize penetration. Lieutenant Nobel made us a little battering ram. It should reach 100m/s before striking the wreckage. And then? Boom. If that doesn't clear enough of the wreckage for the skiff to get through, we have bigger problems."

"Aye, Gunny," Taulbee said. "I'll provide cover when you move into position."

"Aye, sir. Appreciate the assistance."

Taulbee laughed. "Just make sure that thing doesn't come back at us."

"No worries on that, sir," Gunny said. "Nobel says his little toy will keep going until something stops it or we detonate it."

"Acknowledged," Taulbee said. "Just let me know when you're going to launch it."

"Aye, sir."

"Out," Taulbee said.

Gunny hissed a sigh and continued maneuvering the skiff. As the damaged aft section drifted into his sight line, he saw the pulsing lights inside the wreckage. He'd seen them on the feeds, but watching them through his own eyes was a completely different experience. Less than 200 meters from him, exo-solar lifeforms blinked and winked like the beating of a thousand alien hearts.

"Gunny?" Wendt said over the comms.

"What is it, Wendt? I'm busy."

"Aye, Gunny. But there on the port-side. Are those things moving closer to us?"

He flicked his eyes to the cannon cam and froze. Wendt was right. Shapes moved in the shadows on the aft's port-side. Those things seemed to be making their way out of the wreckage and toward them. "Can't anything go according to plan?" Gunny asked no one. He cursed as he connected to Taulbee. "Sir? You see them on the port-side?"

"Aye, Gunny," Taulbee said. "Copenhaver spotted them too."

"You have a better eye than Wendt?"

"We do," Taulbee said. "Copenhaver says they look like the starfish things, but they're moving differently. Should reach your firing range in about ten seconds. They'll hit you in less than thirty."

"Aye, sir." Gunny checked his HUD. Black had plotted the perfect trajectory for the battering ram. All he needed was another fifteen seconds at present speed. "Fuck this," Gunny said and hit the thrusters. "Hang on, marines." The skiff slid sideways as it continued forward. Another burst and their forward momentum increased to 15m/s. Gunny waited until they were nearly to the launch point before activating the starboard-side thrusters at full. Their sideways momentum quickly slowed and the skiff was suddenly pointed straight at the target. Less than fifty meters separated them from the beginnings of the aft wreckage. This was closer than he wanted to be, or Black had recommended, but it was the best he could do.

"Sir? I'm firing the ram."

"Acknowledged. Fire at will."

"Wendt?" Gunny said with a grimace. "Get those fucking cannons on the bogies and start firing."

"Aye, sir."

Gunny said a prayer to the void, cut the magnetics holding the ram, and activated the makeshift weapon. The skiff shuddered as a small puff of gas sent the ram a few meters below the skiff before its engines fired. "Ram away! Taking evasive action."

He punched the forward thrusters and the skiff shot backward away from *Mira*'s aft at 5m/s just as the flechette cannon began belching projectiles. He kept his eyes focused on the forward cam feeds, not daring to glance at the incoming creatures. The ram's tiny engines glowed like stars as the thick Atmo-steel slab shot through the darkness separating them from the aft section's latticework of wrecked and damaged deck plates.

"Taulbee? We're clear," Gunny said.

"The hell you are!" Taulbee yelled. Gunny flicked his eyes to the port-side cam. Dozens of shadows streaked toward the skiff. He gripped the throttle and prepared for impact.

CHAPTER FORTY-SIX

While she watched and correlated data from both the skiff and the SV-52's cam feeds, Black also kept a data stream open with the flying slab of metal hurtling into *Mira*'s fractured interior. The omnidirectional cams Nobel had installed produced a fisheye lens view covering nearly 180° of a sphere. What Black saw amazed her.

The pulsing lights came into definition and she finally realized what they were. If a sentient AI could feel excitement, Black would have been vibrating with adrenaline. The creatures responsible for the pulsing light lay in cocoons of black mesh and grey tendrils. The medium was hardly organic, at least not in terrestrial terms, but certainly appeared to serve the same function as a spider's web or that of a silkworm. These nests, if that was the correct term, dangled from Atmo-steel struts, beams, and plas-steel mesh. The creatures had used *Mira*'s remains as a scaffold for their alien works of art.

The ram continued driving forward, its canted, beveled bow slamming through damaged and distressed panels, beams, tangled cables, and broken bulkheads. The nest of shadows disappeared the further the ram traveled inward. At the far end, a new light appeared. A kaleidoscope of colors revolving and swirling like a spiral galaxy danced at the aft section's foredecks. For an instant, the ram's floods illuminated the source of the colors. Black found herself staring at the beacon.

The cylinder lay on its side, one end pointed toward the wrecked aft section. As the ram approached within 10 meters, the cylinder's light dimmed and went out. The ram flew past the beacon and crashed into the remaining bulkheads separating the engineering section from the engine and reactor compartments before the cam feed finally winked out of existence.

Black replayed the footage at high speed several times, her formidable computing power focused on analyzing each frame and gathering information that could help the marines retrieve the cylinder. As Black accomplished this task, she kept flicking through the SV-52 and skiff feeds, watching the battle outside *Mira*'s aft. The exo-solar lifeforms were not only larger than before, but were more aggressive, and their numbers were staggering, with dozens more moving from the midships to the aft.

Something had alerted the creatures to the marines' approach. Or maybe it was the ram that had attracted the others. Regardless, the entire company was in danger. Black took control of the starboard-side cannon. She couldn't wait to clear it with Dunn. Not if she wanted her charges to survive.

CHAPTER FORTY-SEVEN

Gunny's HUD ammo sensor counted down in a hurry. Wendt was aiming before pulling the trigger, but it seemed as though every second another three-round burst erupted. At this rate, they would run out of the new flechette ammo in another minute.

"Switch to explosive rounds," Gunny said, doing his best to keep his voice calm.

Wendt replied with a grunt. Murdock occasionally yelped through the comms as he fired and missed again and again.

"Take your damned time, Murdock! Make them count!"

"Aye," he said in a breathless voice.

Gunny watched the battle through the skiff's port-side cam feed. He had to get them pointed away from *Mira* and gain some distance, and he had to do it quick. A flick of his eyes showed more shadows streaming out of *Mira*'s aft. "Prepare for evasive action," he growled into the mic. He didn't bother waiting for a response.

A second later, the forward thrusters fired and shot compressed nitrogen from the tanks. The skiff flew backward from *Mira* at 7m/s, the distance increasing with every second. Starfish and pinecones appeared beyond the aft's shadows. Gunny gritted his teeth and rotated the skiff with a quick fire from the maneuvering thrusters. When it pointed back to *S&R Black*, he stopped the rotation, and fired the rear thrusters. A look at the cam feeds showed dozens of creatures leaving the aft and even more approaching from the top of *Mira*'s expansive hull.

"We're fucked," he breathed into the comms. The ammo counter stood at 90. Yup. They were fucked.

*****

There were too many of them and Taulbee knew it. Copenhaver opened up with the turret, spraying tritium flechettes into the clusters of starfish and pinecones. The rounds detonated when they found their targets, the creatures hit by the fusillade disappeared in showers of black limbs, broken carapaces, and shattered shells. But it wasn't enough. Not even close.

At least she was taking slow, careful shots, doing her best to make every round count. The horde of creatures had decided to break up into smaller clusters, making it difficult to target more than a few at a time. Several starfish had moved into a flanking position on the SV-52's port-side. Copenhaver had to pull her aim off the advancing line to meet the new threat. Cursing, Taulbee activated the flak cannons, spreading explosive flechette rounds in a wide circle around the craft.

"Taulbee to Dunn."

"Dunn here."

Doing his best to keep his voice calm and level, Taulbee began to speak. "Sir, we can't keep this up. There are way too many of them and we don't have enough ammo."

A bright flash erupted from *S&R Black*'s starboard-side as a rocket engine engaged. A missile streaked away from the ship and headed to the top of *Mira*'s hull a mere three hundred meters away. Taulbee had time to grin before the munition detonated.

Rather than exploding into shards of debris or a bright flash of energy, a large cloud appeared above *Mira*'s hull. Particles danced in the whitish mass as the shockwave dissipated.

Taulbee blinked. "What the fuck?"

"They're breaking off!" Copenhaver yelled.

He flipped through the cam feeds. She was right. The starfish threatening their port-side were turning back to face the giant derelict. The wall of creatures heading toward them, as well as those crowding around the skiff, had changed their trajectories. The mass of exo-solar life-forms all headed toward the cloud as if called to it.

"Sir?" Taulbee said. "What happened?"

Black's voice broke through the comms. "Lieutenant. I fired one of the Trio's new weapons. The cloud of CO2 has distracted them, but it won't last for long. I suggest you and Gunny retreat as quickly as possible."

When Dunn spoke, he sounded pissed as hell. "Taulbee. Gunny. Get back to the ship right now."

"Aye, sir," Taulbee said. "Gunny?"

"Aye, Lieutenant. Will rendezvous with the ship momentarily."

Taulbee watched the skiff change trajectory again and begin its journey back to *S&R Black*. He piloted the SV-52 in a cover pattern, making sure Gunny's skiff didn't get blindsided by a new threat. He needn't have bothered. The space around them was completely empty of exo-solar life.

"Sir?" Copenhaver asked.

"Aye?"

"What just happened?"

Taulbee shook his head. "I don't know, Private. I only know we're going to make it back to the ship."

"But what about the beacon?"

"I don't know that, either," he said. "Guess we'll figure that out after we land in the cargo bay. Speaking of, keep an eye on our six. I don't want anything sneaking up behind us."

"Aye, sir."

"And Private?"

"Aye?"

"Good work."

"Thank you, sir," she said, a smile in her voice.

He wished he could smile. They had survived another scrape with the alien things, but were no closer to retrieving the damned beacon. Based on what they'd just seen, he didn't know how they could possibly succeed.

\

CHAPTER FORTY-EIGHT

When she regained consciousness, bright lights filled her HUD. She took a breath and regretted it immediately. Her chest felt broken inside, as though her ribs had inverted and the ends were jabbing into her vitals instead of protecting them. A groan escaped her lips and she shut her eyes tightly against another shock of pain.

"Corporal?" Dickerson asked.

"Yeah," Kali wheezed. It hurt to talk. Hell, it hurt to think, let alone breathe.

"Shit," Carb said. "Boss? You alive in there? You sound like you can't get enough air."

Carb was right. Her lungs didn't seem able to hold enough oxygen. Exhaling was easier than pulling in atmosphere, but everything hurt. The urge to cough tickled at her consciousness. Fuck. She had a punctured lung. She knew it. The metallic tang of copper hit the back of her throat. A bubble of blood rose from her mouth and popped inside her helmet, smearing the inside of her faceplate.

"Broken rib," she whispered, doing her best not to cough. Coughing would only increase the damage, not to mention the pain. "Punctured."

"Goddamnit," Dickerson said.

She opened her eyes. The lights had moved away slightly, no longer flooding her HUD. Dickerson stood over her, while Carb knelt beside her. His shoulder still drooped to one side, the arm hanging at an odd angle. "What happened?"

Carb's hands dug into the pouch around her belt. "Couple of those things got in here," she said. "Don't worry. Elliott got 'em."

Elliott? Holy shit, she thought. Despite the pain, she managed a grin. She wanted to say something witty, but was afraid she'd cough again.

Carb held a syringe over Kali's intake tube. "Going to shoot you up with some fresh nannies, Boss." Kali's HUD flashed an alert message as the injector connected to her suit tube. "Just hang on for me."

She said nothing, but scanned the hallway. Dozens of small, black shards floated in the air along with coiled ropes of liquid. Misshapen blisters covered the Atmo-steel outer airlock door. The things were moving so fast they dented the damned door? How the hell was that possible?

The injection started its push and 30 ml of nannies shot into her system. She knew she'd taken too much damage over too long a period of time for her existing nannies to help. They needed a boost. The only problem was they were now down another nannie injector. How many did they have left? Two? None? She couldn't remember.

A status window appeared on her HUD as the nannie swarm connected to her block for a vitals report. With any luck, the nannies would head straight for the punctured lung. It would take them time to perform a patch and move the broken rib so it no longer threatened her chest, but they didn't have that kind of time. The best she could hope for was some temporary relief. One thing for sure, she couldn't take another impact like that. Not if she ever wanted to breathe again.

She felt a tickle in her chest cavity and the urge to cough subsided. She didn't know if the nannies had simply blocked off the lung entirely, or if they'd somehow managed to already repair her. The latter was all but impossible.

Kali took an experimental breath and held it. Her lung capacity had been cut in half, but that was better than having to take shallow breaths. "Thank you," she managed.

"Welcome, Boss," Carb said.

Dickerson stepped away, his helmet pointed at something she couldn't see. "Well, Corporal. I got good news and some bad," he said.

"I don't like the sound of that," Kali said.

"Yeah," Elliott said. "And trust me, Dickerson likes to give bad news."

"Shut up, luggage."

Elliott chuckled. "Ain't no luggage 'round here anymore," the marine said in a mock drawl. "Just remember who saved your ass."

Dickerson paused. "Well, there is that."

"Shut it, you two, and tell me what's going on," Kali said.

"Right. Sorry, Corporal," Elliott said. Her HUD lit up with his forward cam feed. The main deck and bulkhead column stood n more 10 meters away. Beside it? Five escape pods.

"Holy shit," Kali said. "Do they work?"

"That's the bad news," Dickerson said. "We don't know."

Kali started to move her legs, but Carb leaned on her. "Stay still, Corporal. Give those little fuckers some time to get you stable."

She sighed in frustration. "Okay. Fine. Did you try powering them up?"

"Yeah," Dickerson said. "Right after we got you in here and made sure you were still alive." She couldn't see him, but knew he was taking a breath because of his own pain. "Looks like the power cells are drained. Going to have to cycle them up, and that's going to take a few minutes."

"We in any danger?"

"Not so we know, Boss," Carb said. "Elliott did a quick scout. We're behind a half-meter of Atmo-steel and there don't seem to be many ingress points."

"Don't seem to be," Kali said to herself. That didn't exactly fill her with confidence. "Is this more bad news?"

She could almost feel the three of them looking at one another. After a moment, Dickerson sighed. "Besides my arm being completely fucked, there's a hatch to the cargo bay. Looks somewhat damaged."

"Damaged? I thought you said we were safe."

"Well, we are." Dickerson paused. "But if something bashes it, we're in trouble."

"Great." Kali tried to push away the image of a million pinecones struggling to fit through the hatch and flood the room. It wasn't something she wanted to experience. "Okay. Dickerson and Elliott? Get on those escape pods. See if you can find a way to get the power cells back up. Might even be a manual charger inside."

"Copy," the two men said.

"And I'm standing right here to make sure you don't get up," Carb said.

Kali grinned. "Give me a couple more minutes, and I'll try and move."

"Affirmative, Boss." Carb squeezed her ankle. "We're almost out of here."

Almost. They'd almost been killed a dozen times since they'd entered this wreck. Kali checked her recordings. Even while unconscious, the suit's cams recorded data to her block so she could review it later. SFMC had added that little perk half a century ago, reasoning that temporarily incapacitated marines could get back in the fight without getting killed if they knew just what the hell was going on. A window on her HUD filled with a video feed from when she lost consciousness.

Dickerson pulled her through the airlock threshold, dozens of the creatures swirling around them like a tornado. Elliott's voice yelled for Dickerson to drop. He did, his body carefully curling around hers, wrapping her in his bulk. The moment they dropped, Elliott fired a stun round.

The flechette detonated in the midst of the swirling creatures, blue arcs of electricity striking the black forms. They lit up like lightning rods, some of them disintegrating into particles while others blew apart. A few stragglers, moving much more slowly than before, flew together to create a much smaller tornado. Elliott fired again and destroyed the stragglers.

Kali stopped the playback and turned her head to scan the room. Several shapes of utter black floated above her, some of them gathered near one of the bulkheads in a cloud of alien dust. "Wow," Kali said. "Anyone actually get a good idea of what those things looked like?"

"Not really," Dickerson said. "Reminded me of something, but I can't remember what. Man, I must be losing it," he said. "Damned near all this stuff reminds me of the animals I saw in the aquarium."

Kali blinked. She remembered the words drawn in blood. "The tide is coming in!" Was that lunatic merely being metaphorical, or did he actually mean it literally?

She switched to Dickerson's cam and watched as he stepped inside one of the escape pods. As expected, the escape pods were spartan, and the controls very rudimentary. Even fifty years ago, pods had been designed to weather EMP strikes as well as block communication failures. If both the pod and the escapee had block connections available, the pod could be controlled via block commands. If either were damaged, however, the manual controls allowed the occupant to control thrust, attitude, and even set an automatic course. By default, the AI was supposed to update the most desirable coordinates before jettisoning. SFMC ships were designed to update their escape pods' computers every few minutes or so. That way if something happened to the AI, the human still had an educated guess of where best to escape.

Somehow, she doubted the *Mira* AI had had the opportunity to do the same. Kali grinned. Not that it mattered. The data would be just a tad out of date considering the ship had been cartwheeling through space for more than forty years.

Dickerson left the pod and walked to the nearest bulkhead. He touched a colored rectangle and the manual energy cell popped out. He breathed a sigh of relief through the comms. "Found the generator. Let's see if it works."

The entire squad held their breaths as Dickerson charged it. A red status light appeared. He continued pushing the lever. The status light went yellow and after a few more pumps turned green.

"Hell, yes," Elliott said. Kali switched to his cam. The marine was staring into one of the escape pods, its lights flickering for a moment before staying steady. He stepped back and panned across the others. Three powered on. Two did not. "Fuck!" Elliott yelled.

"Calm down," Kali said, but even she was on the verge of losing her cool. They needed four escape pods. Just four fucking escape pods. One for each squad member. But all they had was three. Christ. Was it too much to ask for one goddamned piece of luck?

"Well, what do you want to do, Corporal?" Dickerson asked.

She tried to think. The pain in her chest had abated, but her skull still felt as though it were filled with clouds of buzzing gnats. "Let's try something easy, first. Check the couplings on the two that didn't come back to life. After that, step in them and make sure they are really completely dead. Maybe one of them is just damaged."

"Aye, Corporal," Dickerson said.

"Boss?" Carb asked. "How are you feeling?"

"Better," she said. In truth, it was still difficult to breathe. She was more and more convinced the nannies had blocked her damaged lung, meaning she was trying to breathe with a single undamaged one. Undamaged. What a joke. Bottom line, she was going to be easily winded. If they had another firefight, it wouldn't take long before she found herself gasping for air. While she could up her suit's O2 levels, that meant she'd burn through her life support faster than normal. With damaged sensors, that wasn't exactly a good plan either. "I might even try and stand up in a minute."

"A minute," Carb said. She sounded pleased. "I'll give you another minute. Two if you want 'em."

"Gee, thanks," Kali said.

Carb had been serious. The marine wasn't letting her corporal up until they were both sure she could handle it. When all this was over, Kali would make damned sure to talk to Gunny and Taulbee. She still didn't know about Elliott, but Dickerson and Carb definitely earned back their NCO statuses. And then some.

The ship shuddered. Everyone froze as if time had stopped. It shuddered again, the deck vibrating beneath her. Dust, detritus, and ice particles swirled from the ceiling, darting in all directions in the z-g.

"What the hell was that?" Elliott asked.

Another vibration rocked the ship, this one powerful enough to strain Kali's magnetics, her body trying to rise off the deck. Carb lost her balance, but her boots kept her from flying upward.

"Christ," Dickerson said. "You think they're trying the tow?"

"I don't know," Kali said. "Whatever's going on, I don't think it's good."

The ship quaked again. Kali watched a ceiling panel come unhinged and cant slightly. *Mira* wasn't going to survive a tow. She was sure of it. Too much damage. Too many years of exposure to whatever had chewed through Atmo-steel and left acid in its wake.

CHAPTER FORTY-NINE

If Black had been human, Dunn would have locked her in the brig. Or maybe even vented her into space. Well, not really. But he would have threatened both. She hadn't asked permission to fire munitions. She hadn't warned him she was going to do it. She just had. A normal ship's AI wouldn't have taken the initiative. Instead, it would have informed him and suggested a course of action.

While he waited for the skiff and the SV-52 to return to the cargo bay, he leaned against the outer bulkhead. He connected with Black through his block and the AI's presence immediately filled his mind. Once again, she appeared as a slowly pulsing rainbow of colors.

Yes, Captain?

What did you do? he snarled.

She pulled back from him slightly as if jarred by the anger in his thoughts. *Captain, I fired one of the Trio's experimental munitions in an effort to stave off more casualties.*

Right, he replied. *And who told you you could do that?*

Black paused. The swirling colors froze for an instant before continuing their slow dance. *The crew is my priority, sir. The crew and my own well-being. I have—*

You didn't know what it would do, did you?

No, she admitted. *Not exactly. However, I chose that munition based on the information included in the crates. It was the only non-lethal option available.*

Non-lethal, he said. *You could have sprayed them down with more tritium flechette.*

Yes, Captain. I could have. However, I would have quickly exhausted our supply. My calculations indicated such a barrage would only eliminate 15-20% of the creatures and leave the ship, and the crew, at great risk. I chose the only option available.

The other option, Black, the captain said dryly, *was to talk to me about it first.*

Black said nothing for a moment. The colors dissolved into a single white halo which cycled through every hue until it reached black. The colors then reversed themselves. *Yes, Captain. I shall not make the same mistake again.*

Dunn grunted. *Why don't I believe you?*

Black said nothing.

A new block message appeared. Gunny and Taulbee were at the cargo bay doors. In a minute or two, they would be inside and he could start sorting through this mess.

How long is that cloud going to keep them busy?

Unknown, Black said. *The CO_2 is rapidly dissipating. The molecules will continue to spread and lose cohesion. I'm uncertain how the creatures will react* to the change. *According to the ship's outer cam feeds, the creatures are feasting on the CO2 in a frenzy. After consuming the available CO2, they may search for other sources.*

Dunn frowned. *Other sources,* he echoed in a dead voice. *You mean us.*

Quite possibly, Black said. *I believe the creatures are drawn to the combat suits when they vent excess gas. This may explain their behavior in attacking Lieutenant Nobel. It may also explain their current activity.*

What do you mean by that?

Black paused. Dunn imagined the AI was composing the right words to say so he could understand the situation. Or maybe she just wanted to keep from scaring the hell out of him.

The creatures were somewhat dormant upon our arrival. That has changed. An image appeared through the block connection. *Mira's* hull, the area they'd first surveyed, loomed as large as a horizon. *When we first arrived, the pinecones, as you call them, did not move. Did not react to our presence. Neither did the starfish. In some way, our presence brought the creatures out of their hibernation.*

Dunn nodded. *Okay, I get that,* he said. *And you think it's the CO2.*

Possibly. Or, more likely, partially.

So if we shut off the venting—

I do not think that will make a large difference at this point in time, Black said. *As I said, I believe the CO2 is partially responsible.*

Dunn's stomach sank. The way Black had said those words left him cold. *And the other possible catalysts?*

It is quite possible their activity increased due to the abundance of photons in the area.

Photons? Dunn's frown deepened. *You mean light?*

As Mira *entered the solar system, the ship would have been bathed in Sol's light, as it is now. Before that, the number of photons hitting the ship would have been very slight. With each kilometer closer to Sol, the number of photons increases. If the ship were allowed to make it through the Kuiper Belt, it's very possible the creatures would both reproduce and search for sustenance at a more aggressive rate.*

Photons, Dunn said. *Is that why the Trio wants us to crash the ship into Pluto?*

I believe so, Black said. *The beacon is a much more powerful source of photons than Sol. At least from this distance. If the beacon is trapped on Pluto, the creatures will remain there as well. I believe those are the Trio's conclusions.*

Dunn tried to imagine Pluto infested with starfish, pinecones, and dozens of species they had yet to see. If they turned off the beacon before sending it to Pluto, the creatures wouldn't follow it. If they somehow managed to disable the beacon after it hit Pluto, would the creatures stay where they were? Or would they find a way to leave Pluto's gravitational field and head toward Sol? Toward the human colonies and, more frighteningly, Earth.

We have to get the beacon out, onto the sled, and fire it at Pluto, Dunn said. *But we can't turn it off.*

Black was silent for a moment. She was probably running thousands of forecast models in defense of his argument, or to refute it. At last, Black loosed a sigh. *Yes, Captain. You are correct. Another possibility is that if the beacon is deactivated, any incoming exo-solar lifeforms will follow the trail to Sol, and not Pluto.*

Shit, Dunn said.

Black paused again. The constant interruptions in the dialogue were maddening. Not for the first time, Dunn wished he could look the AI in the eyes like a human being and get a true feel for what it was thinking. All his life, he had gauged people by watching their facial expressions, listening to how they pronounced their words, their cadence of speech, and where their eyes darted when they spoke. Conversing with a machine offered none of those possibilities. While you could feel certain, well, emotions, for lack of a better term, through a block connection, it wasn't the same. Especially with this new and improved version of Black. Without the Xi Protocols, there was nothing keeping Black from lying to him or even lying through the connection.

He did his best to hide these thoughts, but there was no guarantee Black didn't pick them up anyway. One of the constant dangers of a block connection was the inadvertent transfer of true emotion and thought. No matter how careful you were, how you tried to close off your true self from another, some of them always leaked through. With humans, it could be confusing noise. With AIs, the leaks could reveal far too much.

Too many unknowns at this time, sir. If we knew for certain the range of the beacon, we'd have some idea of how many exo-solar lifeforms could be heading this way. If we had better satellite coverage of the entire Kuiper Belt and the Oort cloud, humanity would know the extent of the threat.

A spherical image of Sol System appeared before him. The visual effect startled him at first, making him feel as though he were standing on nothing while staring into an empty abyss whose complete darkness was broken only by the bright point of light at its center and the barely visible dots of the planets. The view continued panning out until the sphere was barely visible against an even deeper black.

To begin to assess the number of possible exo-solar lifeforms heading into Sol System, Black continued, *humanity would have had to have begun placing satellites, nanoprobes, and expeditions as early as two hundred years ago. Such an endeavor would also have no doubt required more resources than we have at our disposal. I'm afraid this scenario was inevitable.*

Inevitable? Dunn asked, mind reeling as Black continued adjusting the image. Other stars, other planets, slowly blipped into view for milliseconds before disappearing as the image continued zooming out. *What do you mean inevitable?*

The beacon, Black said. *If it was meant to travel here, to attract the lifeforms, then humanity was always destined to face this threat. Based on the data Mira's scientists gathered, it is impossible to say if that was the case. Perhaps the beacon was headed elsewhere, another system, where life had yet to evolve. Regardless, it's a threat we must now face.*

The image disappeared, replaced by a view of *Mira* floating through space, the much smaller *S&R Black* at its side and trailing it by a few kilometers. He could tell the image was digital in nature, manufactured by the AI, but it might as well have been real. The image zoomed out, just as the model of the solar system had, until several new objects appeared. Irregularly shaped forms materialized out of the shadows, their details all but hidden by the Kuiper Belt twilight.

These objects are approaching, Captain, Black said. *We have very little time before they arrive.*

Can you see what they are?

Not yet, Black admitted. *Mickey is sending me updates every few minutes, although there is an eight-minute time difference from his transmissions to my reception. He has trained all of PEO's telescopes and instruments on these phenomena. Within the next twenty minutes, I expect we will finally receive images with enough detail to know what we're facing.*

Dunn shook his head. *Twenty minutes. How close will they be to us by then?*

We will have roughly ten minutes of lead time before they begin a final approach.

Fuck me, Dunn breathed. *Thirty minutes until we might be under attack.*

No, sir, Black said. *Thirty minutes until we face thousands, perhaps hundreds of thousands, of new exo-solar lifeforms. It is very likely that many of them will have characteristics we have not seen before.*

He ground his teeth. They had to get the beacon. And they had to get it now. If he waited any longer, it would all be over. They would never get a second chance.

Thank you, Black. Before the AI could sign off, he terminated the connection and switched to Taulbee. "James?"

"Aye, sir?"

"Get your marines suited up to go back out. I'm on my way to brief your team."

Taulbee paused over the block connection. Dunn knew he was usurping the command chain, but didn't care. They needed to get going in five minutes. Any more time wasted could mean the end of humanity.

CHAPTER FIFTY

Taulbee stood by the SV-52 with his helmet in the crook of his elbow. Copenhaver stood next to him and a little behind him, her back practically leaning against the support craft. Dunn was on his way down and he'd sounded panicked, although Taulbee could tell the captain had tried to hide it. Why else would he brief them in the damned cargo bay?

What the fuck is next in this shit show?

After escorting Gunny's skiff back to the ship, he and Copenhaver had performed a brief sweep around *S&R Black* to ensure they were still clear of exo-solar lifeforms. While they didn't see any of the pinecones or starfish hanging around the ship, or attached to its hull, they did see something else on *Mira*.

The creatures had apparently lost interest in the munition cloud that Black had detonated. The starfish had begun hunting the pinecones, but the large clusters had held themselves together in tight formations. He caught footage of one of the starfish attempting to plow into the cluster, but as the creature reached them, the herd, swarm, whatever you wanted to call them canted to one side, their sharp silver claws pointed directly at their attacker.

The starfish, mere meters from the clump of silver and black, waved its arms frantically and maneuvered itself to fly over the creatures rather than through them. Once the starfish was no longer a threat, the cluster of pinecones canted once again, but not uniformly. The damned creatures had staggered themselves, some of them pointing their claws out while they rolled against their brethren. The result was a heavily armored and heavily armed flotilla of carapaces and claws. If a starfish tried to attack, it would have a hell of a time plucking one of their prey from the group without suffering some damage.

Taulbee wondered why he hadn't noticed that behavior before. Maybe it was because he simply hadn't been paying attention. *Or,* he thought, *maybe it was because we'd never seen them in groups this large.* Assuming they survived this, he'd make sure he had a damned long talk with some scientists or the AIs about their findings. Taulbee grunted. The study of exo-solar life would be much more important if the damned things weren't always trying to kill them.

And now it's our time to get some payback, he thought.

Gunny stood next to the skiff. Murdock and Wendt had lined up next to him and stood at parade rest. The sergeant and his marines held their helmets in the crooks of their elbows, just like Taulbee.

This looks more like an inspection than a briefing, Taulbee thought. He had to smile. Here they were, an AU from Pluto, surrounded by hostile lifeforms with more incoming, and he and his marines seemed more concerned about impressing the captain than worrying about the hazards less than half a kilometer away.

But he knew it for what it was. Everyone was on edge. The recon mission, which included launching the ram, hadn't exactly been a success. The damage to *Mira*'s aft section would make ingress difficult, but that wasn't the problem. No. The problem would be getting around all the creatures near the beacon, but Taulbee already had an idea about that.

Lost in thought, he stiffened as the cargo bay hatch opened. Dunn walked in, still dressed in his combat suit. The marines saluted and Dunn waved dismissively.

"All right, marines. Listen up." He moved further into the bay and seemed to be scanning both the skiff and the SV-52 for damage. A grim smile lit his face. "We're running out of time. We need to get the beacon and we need to do it now."

The cargo bay had gone completely silent except for the sound of the life support systems and the ever-present hum of the fusion engines. Dunn walked to the holo-projector and brought it to life. A model of *Mira* immediately appeared before them. A series of colored rectangles appeared on the derelict's hull. Crimson rectangles covered the rear midships as well as the aft, but the aft was by far the most crowded. Yellow rectangles surrounded the midships toward the bow. After that, small green rectangles lay against the bow.

Dunn pointed at the hologram. "The reds mark the largest pinecone saturations. The yellow, less. Green? Even less. From the footage Black has analyzed, the creatures appear to have migrated to the aft section in much larger numbers. As if they're gathering for something." He harrumphed. "Maybe 'gather' is the wrong word. It's almost as if they're staging themselves for some sort of assault."

Taulbee wanted to tell the captain about the herd behavior they'd witnessed mere moments ago, but thought it best to remain silent. He'd wait until the captain told them his plan.

The model spun and zoomed in on the smashed and debris-laden aft. "The saturation," Dunn continued, "appears to be highest near the beacon. But still, it's not nearly as," he paused for half a beat before finding the right word, "infested as the rest of the ship. The number of creatures remaining near the beacon are small by comparison, but that doesn't mean it's less dangerous. The lifeforms are large, and pulsing with light. And before you ask, no, Black has no idea what those lights might mean. Other than some kind of breeding cycle."

Those words chilled Taulbee. From what he'd seen of the ram feed, the interior did look as though it were infested with nests for the void-damned things. Nests. Did that mean there were egg sacs, or something like that inside? And what happened if the fucking things hatched while they were inside gathering the beacon?

"To further complicate matters, we have bogies on our doorstep and no idea what they are. Yet. Black tells me it won't be long before we know what we're facing, but we better have the damned beacon by then." The captain paused, his eyes swinging from Taulbee to Gunny. "We can't fail this, marines. Simply can't. We can't blow up *Mira* and call it a day and we can't leave her behind in one piece. Without the beacon, all of Sol System faces some pretty damned dire consequences."

He turned back to the holo display. "So here's my plan. Gunny? You and your squad will follow the same path as before. Instead of firing a ram, however, we're going to outfit you with some more of the Trio's toys. Black and the SV-52 will fire the CO_2 missiles to draw out as many of the creatures as possible. With any luck, they'll swarm the clouds as they did before. Keep in mind, though, the clouds dissipate damned fast. And once the lifeforms consume the gas, or absorb, or whatever the fuck they do, they'll return to their herd or swarm mentality."

Dunn swallowed hard and paused again. Taulbee knew what that meant. The captain was already second-guessing himself. Or maybe second-guessing wasn't the right word. Maybe he was just afraid of what could go wrong. Taulbee didn't blame him.

"Once we fire the missiles, the skiff will enter the aft section. Black has already plotted a course for you, Gunny." A series of lines appeared showing the plotted approach into *Mira*'s interior. "Once you get to the beacon, secure it, and get the hell out of there as quickly as possible.

"Taulbee? The SV-52 will need to provide cover fire for the skiff on both its ingress and egress. *S&R Black* will provide as many distractions as it can. Any questions?"

Taulbee glanced at Gunny. The sergeant's expression was about as deadpan as he'd ever seen it, but he noticed Gunny's fingers flexing and un-flexing. Dunn seemed about ready to close the briefing when Gunny finally said, "Sir? What munitions do we have?"

Dunn nodded. "Wondered who was going to ask that question. The CO_2, you've already seen. The same with the tritium flechettes. However, there is one weapon we haven't used yet— a hyper-neutrino warhead. According to the Trio, it's extremely lethal to both exo-solar lifeforms and, unfortunately, us. We haven't tested it," he said, "and so we have to take the Trio's word for it. The SV-52's shielding should protect Taulbee and Copenhaver from the blast, but I'm afraid those of you in the skiff wouldn't survive contact with the material."

"What's the range?" Taulbee asked.

Dunn grimaced. "Unknown. The Trio didn't bother providing that information."

Taulbee caught himself before cursing. "So it's a last-resort weapon."

"That's my assessment, yes," Dunn said. "This is going to be dangerous as hell, marines. And if things were different, we'd get Kalimura's squad back aboard, blow that ugly bitch out there to pieces, and hightail it back to Neptune. But we don't have that option."

Gunny cleared his throat and Dunn's eyes swung to him. "Sir? Are we going to be able to recover Kalimura's squad?"

The captain's expression dropped into a deep frown. "We will do our best, Gunny."

"Aye, sir," the sergeant said. Someone who didn't know Gunny might mistake his expression for indifference to the answer, but Taulbee knew him, and he saw the way the man's fingers twitched at his side. Frustration and anger. That's what those gestures indicated.

Dunn waited a moment. "Any other questions?" No one spoke. "Black will send you the orders to your blocks. Including which munitions to load. Get to it."

Half a second later, Taulbee's block lit up with messages. He turned to

Copenhaver. "Okay, Private. Let's do this."

"Aye, sir," she said and snapped a salute.

Taulbee watched for a moment as she quickly walked to the crates to procure more ammunition. He checked the list Black had sent them. Since the other hyper-neutrino warheads had already been loaded into Black's guns, there were only two available for the SV-52. *Great,* he thought. *We're not going to get many chances here.*

He initiated a block connection to Gunny as he made his way to help Copenhaver. The sergeant immediately accepted it.

"Aye, sir?"

"You agree with Black's flight plan?"

"Aye, sir." Gunny and his squad had already begun rearming the skiff with the remainder of the tritium flechettes. This was it. There were no more to go around. Once they exhausted their combined supply, they'd be down to shock rounds and explosives. And the explosives were damned near useless. "I can follow it and it looks good. My only concern, sir, is what happens when we get to the beacon."

Taulbee had reached the munitions crates and helped Copenhaver lift the first of the warheads. "The key was attracted to electro-magnetics, at least according to Kalimura's report. Let's hope the beacon is too."

"Aye, sir."

Taulbee and Copenhaver slotted the warhead into the fixed gun magazine. "And like the captain said, as soon as you're clear, I want you streaking toward *S&R Black.* If you've got a herd of bogies on you, skip the cargo bay and flip to the other side of the ship. Hide if you have to."

"Understood, sir, although I don't like hiding."

Taulbee chuckled while he and Copenhaver lifted the last of the warheads. "I know, Gunny. Just follow your gut."

"Orders and gut, sir. Always do. In that order."

It took less than two minutes to get back into the SV-52. The same with Gunny's squad. They were ready. Or as ready as they were going to be.

Against his better judgment, he opened a block connection to Black. The AI responded immediately. "Yes, Lieutenant?"

"What are our chances, Black?"

The AI paused. "I do not wish to tell you that information, Lieutenant."

Taulbee sighed as he started the launch sequence. "Understood, Black."

"Good hunting, sir," the AI said.

Yeah, Taulbee thought. *Hunting. The only question was who was going to be hunting   whom.*

CHAPTER FIFTY-ONE

The shadowy Kuiper Belt had been their home for human centuries. For them, however, it might as well have been measured in human nano-seconds. Their interstellar travel had taken them far from their origin space, far from the star they'd once orbited.

The occasional stream of photons broke their long hibernation, but only momentarily. The creatures would awake from their slumber long enough to consume gas molecules and drink in energy from the distant sun. Human centuries passed between these brief periods, and the lifeforms enjoyed their brief wakings before passing back into slumber.

They had waited. Waited for the universe to change. For there to be light. Light to feed. Light to sustain. Light to breed.

The sudden burst of photons in the belt awoke them, energized them, and they drank in every particle. When it released yet another pulse, they did more than wake up. They began to travel.

Thousands and thousands of them clumped together in a roughly spherical shape, their bodies purging themselves of millennia-old gas reserves their core provided. Once the pod began to accelerate, there was no way to slow it down. But with the continued pulses, there would be no reason. Once they reached the source, they would be free. They would be free to find a new home.

CHAPTER FIFTY-TWO

Floating before *Mira*'s infested aft section wasn't for the meek. The ram had caused a lot of damage to the remaining superstructure, breaking off beams, crashing through the remaining bulkheads, and shredding webs of cables and whatever material the exo-solar creatures had used to make their nests. The cloud of debris inside the aft-section was only matched by the swarms of pinecones, starfish, and void only knew what else. The ram had kicked over the proverbial ant mound and now getting inside was more than just dangerous. It was a fucking suicide mission.

"Gunny?" Taulbee's voice crackled over the comms.

"Aye, sir."

"What do you think?"

Gunny stopped himself before cursing, but only just. "I believe," he said, "we have a bit of a pest problem."

The lieutenant laughed, although Gunny thought it sounded a bit forced. "Black has an idea about that," he said. "We fire another CO2 round and get the bastards interested in leaving the area for a few minutes."

"A few minutes," Gunny echoed. "Sir, at best speed, it will take us at least two minutes to get to the beacon. And that's if we manage to skate all the debris. We're going to need a little more time if we want to make it back out with the beacon."

"Agreed," Taulbee said. "Which is why we're going to clear it out."

Gunny raised an eyebrow. "What do you have in mind?"

He could practically hear Taulbee trying to choose his words, not to mention find the right tone of voice. "The Trio loaded us up with more than tritium flechettes and CO2 bombs. I have two hyper-neutrino warheads loaded and ready to launch."

Gunny frowned. "You're going to fire the warheads inside?"

"Affirmative," Taulbee said. "Bottom line? It should clear out the aft-section. Then we'll use the CO2 missiles to handle the rest."

"Aye, sir." Gunny waited for the lieutenant to continue, but he didn't. "I feel like there's a 'but' coming."

"But," Taulbee said, "we don't know exactly what it's going to do. Apart from destroying anything biological."

If he hadn't been wearing a helmet and magnetically tethered to a skiff floating out in space, Gunny would have rubbed his eyes. "Sir? Are we sure those things even count as 'biological?'"

Taulbee paused before replying, the seconds stretching into an infuriatingly long eternity. "Gunny? I don't know. The Trio certainly thinks they are."

Great, Gunny thought. *We're trusting our lives on their conclusions. Or hell, maybe just their suspicions.* "Understood, sir."

"Only real problem," Taulbee said, "is we don't think your suits will keep you from getting shredded into nothing. Therefore, I suggest you move back another klick from *Mira*."

"Acknowledged, sir," Gunny said.

"I'll give you a heads up before we fire."

"Aye, sir," Gunny said. Heads up. He glanced at the cam feed. The creatures seemed to have ended their feeding frenzy on the CO_2 released by the missile. The swarms were gathering again, order reestablishing itself after the chaos.

He activated the squad comms. "Marines, we're going to get a little more distance between us and that derelict piece of shit. Wendt? Keep your head on a swivel. I don't want any surprises while we're moving."

"Copy, Gunny."

"Murdock? You're the other lookout. Keep cycling through the cam feeds. You both let me know if you see anything hostile approaching."

"Aye, Gunny," Murdock said.

The kid sounded afraid, but less out of sorts than he had on their last trip out. That was an improvement. Not much, but a start.

"Here we go," he said and activated the fore thrusters. The skiff moved backward, slowly accelerating. Gunny kept his eyes on the fore cam feed, watching with some relief as he put more distance between the skiff and *Mira*'s infested aft-section.

Now, he thought, *if only we didn't have to go back in there, this would be perfect.* Shadows moved across the pulsing lights inside the wrecked hull. Gunny shivered. What was that large one? A new lifeform? Or just another starfish?

He watched as the distance meter rolled higher and higher. The skiff's laser sensor repeatedly fired pulses at *Mira* and measured the response from the hull. 300 meters. 400. The SV-52 came into view, the craft hanging above them like a shadowy, misshapen bird.

Taulbee had come to a complete stop, waiting for Gunny to clear the area. He wondered just how close the SV-52 would have to get to *Mira* before firing the missile. More importantly, he hoped the radiation shielding on the '52 kept the LT and Copenhaver safe. Shit, he hoped 1km was far enough away for his squad to survive.

When they reached an 800m distance from *Mira*, he started to decelerate with nudges of the aft thrusters. By the time they reached 1km, the SV-52 had nearly come to a halt itself.

"Gunny?" Murdock said, his voice trembling.

"What is it, Private?"

"Sir, there's something behind us. And it's coming fast."

Gunny switched to the rear cam feed. He saw nothing but the glint of distant stars. "What are you talking about?"

"Shit," Wendt said. "Switch to the cannon feed, Gunny."

Frowning, Gunny flipped feeds. He took a deep breath and held it. Out in the emptiness behind them, and above them, something a little less dark than space itself was moving toward them. Random pin-pricks of light flashed off its surface.

"How far?" Gunny asked in a dead voice.

"Collision course. Two minutes," Wendt said.

CHAPTER FIFTY-THREE

Gunny was out of the way. At least Taulbee hoped.

The skiff had backed up a kilometer away from *Mira*. Black suggested the distance might be safe. Might. Taulbee didn't like "mights" or "supposedly" or even "I think" when it came to the safety of his marines, and he sure as hell didn't like them when they had to do with his own safety. Basically, because Black didn't say "I'm sure" or "I know," he knew this could turn into one big shit show. But did they have a choice?

Yeah. That was the problem. The Trio insisted they needed to capture the beacon. So did Black and the captain. Taulbee understood all of that. If the device was attracting the creatures, they needed a way to keep it secure, and hopefully keep the damned things from going deeper into Sol System. So, yes, they needed the beacon.

Taulbee growled low in his throat. On the SV-52's forward cam feed, the aft section's dark interior seemed to dance with even darker shadows. The ram had left extensive damage in its wake, the infrastructure now little more than twisted shapes of Atmo-steel and swirls of fractured and disintegrated plas-steel. But that didn't mean the aft was clear. Not one bit.

The pulsing lights had increased in brightness, as though they'd awakened the creatures. "Pissed them off, more like," he said aloud. And that's just what they needed. Gunny flying into the proverbial kicked hornet's nest the pre-Sol Era books liked to talk about.

Taulbee had never seen a hornet. He'd seen bees before in the Dallas agricultural domes, but never a hornet, but he knew how much a sting supposedly hurt. *Mira* had turned from being a haunted hulk of crumbling Atmo-steel into the largest damned hornet nest that ever existed. And the hornets? They did more than sting.

The command crew comms came to life. "Sir?" Gunny said. "We have a bogie coming at us. A big one."

Frowning, Taulbee flipped to the rear cams. He didn't see anything, but the gasp Copenhaver loosed told him all he knew. He switched to the cannon cam and there it was—a large irregularly shaped shadow traveling at high speed and right into their path.

"I see it, Gunny."

"Black?" Dunn said. "Suggestions?"

The AI responded immediately. "We have five more CO_2 projectiles. I suggest we fire one to distract the incoming object."

"You mean," Taulbee said, "it's an exo-solar lifeform."

"Yes, Lieutenant," Black said. "Only not a single lifeform."

Taulbee shuddered. A swarm. A herd. A cluster? What was the right name anyway?

"Taulbee?" Dunn asked.

The sound of the captain's voice shook off the random thoughts. "Aye, sir?"

"We'll give you cover," the captain said. "Go ahead with the plan."

"Aye, sir," Taulbee said. "Gunny? You ready?"

"Aye, sir," Gunny said. "I've got the throttle ready in case we need to get moving in a hurry."

"Just make sure you don't head toward it," Taulbee said.

"Aye, sir," Gunny said after a brief pause. Taulbee grinned. He knew the sergeant had just managed to keep himself from saying "no shit."

"Here we go," Taulbee said. "Copenhaver?"

"On your mark, sir."

Taulbee tightened his hands on the controls while all the possibilities flipped through his mind. There could be a shockwave. They could be knocked from their position, thrown in any direction. Maybe even into the path of the oncoming object. Or creatures. And wouldn't that be the perfect ending to this mess?

He took a deep breath and exhaled slowly. "Mark."

The SV-52 shuddered as the magnetic launcher repelled the missile through the tube and into space. Once it reached a distance of 10 meters, the rocket engine kicked in. The missile streaked through the twilight, its aft burning yellow and orange as it ate the emptiness between the SV-52 and *Mira* in less than three seconds. And then the universe became a very interesting place.

CHAPTER FIFTY-FOUR

Gunny held his breath. He didn't have to ask Wendt or Murdock if they were doing the same. Hell, Murdock had probably already shit his suit. Gunny wouldn't blame him if he did.

They were 250 meters away from the SV-52, and a full klick away from *Mira* itself. For regular munitions detonations, that was more than adequate. If a ship dropped a nuke, however, that was a completely different set of problems. Neither the SFMC nor the SFN were in the habit of dropping that kind of ordnance if their marines could be caught in the blast, so it wasn't a concern you normally had to have.

This was different. When the normal ordnance went off, you knew the damage potential. You knew damned well how many hull plates might turn into debris fields, whether or not there might be radiation leaks, and the size of the shockwave. With this? Who the hell knew? Certainly not the goddamned AIs, let alone the idiot humans floating hundreds of meters from where the missile was going.

Taulbee announced he was firing. Gunny clutched the controls in a death grip, his flesh pinched inside his form-fitting gloves. "Here we go, marines," he said. The squad comms, just like the general comms, had gone deathly silent. From the SV-52's belly, a cylindrical object popped out of its tube, flying through space at a lazy speed of a few meters per second. As soon as it reached 10 meters from the craft, its rocket engine came to life.

Gunny watched in utter silence as the missile streaked toward *Mira*. "Get ready," he said to his squad. The two marines didn't reply, but he could feel the tension as if Murdock and Wendt were sitting next to him, without suits, and without the void of space surrounding them. This was either going to be a miracle for them, or turn life into one hell of a nightmare. In the seconds it took for the munition to eat the distance between the SV-52 and *Mira*, Gunny realized there was a third possibility—they could all just die. He grunted at the thought just as the missile found its target.

The cam feed pointed at *Mira* stuttered with static when a bright flash erupted inside the derelict's broken aft section. Gunny's screens dampened the near solar-strength flash of light keeping him from being blinded, but the rest of what he saw was through the haze of a spherical afterimage.

Mira's aft section glowed for an instant before it once again fell into shadows. Some kind of debris cloud formed inside the broken and shattered remnants of the giant ship's aft section. Then...nothing.

"So, that's it?" Wendt said over the comms.

Gunny held his breath, his eyes still trying to recover from the afterimage. He waited another moment before exhaling with a grin on his face. "I guess so," he said just as a radiation alert popped up in red on his HUD. "Oh, shit," he said.

A second later, their suits were bombarded with the energy from extreme radioactive decay. The wave of particles passed in an eye blink and the rad warning disappeared. "Check your suits," he growled into the mic.

His own HUD told him his suit had blocked a very lethal wave of radiation. Both Wendt and Murdock had weathered the storm as well. *Holy shit,* he thought. *We're alive.*

"Dunn to Gunny."

"Aye, sir."

The captain sighed. "Good to hear you're still there."

"Copy that, sir," he said.

Dunn cleared his throat. "Taulbee? What's the damage?"

A new feed appeared on his HUD. Gunny added the stream and brought it up on the main window, barely registering that the images were from Copenhaver's cannon cam. Unlike the skiff's cannon, the SV-52's cannon had been designed for reconnaissance as well as targeting hostiles from a long distance. The cannon's feed detail was much better than anything Gunny could hope for from the skiff's cams. But he almost wished the detail was less clear.

The inside of *Mira* looked more like a yawning mouth now. The warhead had done little structural damage, or so it appeared, but the nests of pulsing lights had gone dark as though they'd never existed. There wasn't enough light now to see inside the aft section. Without the glow the creatures had provided, even the blue filters couldn't penetrate the deepest shadows. Gunny checked the location of the beacon. It was now clothed in complete and total darkness.

"Well," Taulbee said, "that was interesting." He paused for a beat. "Gunny?"

He gulped and tried to staunch the flittering butterflies in his stomach. "Ready, sir."

"Get going."

"Aye, sir." He switched to the squad comms. "We're moving out, marines." He opened the throttle and the rear thrusters came to life. The skiff was on the move.

*****

Taulbee watched the skiff pass beneath the SV-52 and continued accelerating. Wendt had the skiff's cannon pointed at *Mira*'s aft while Murdock, at the skiff's rear, held his rifle and scanned the space around them for targets. Gunny and his two marines were heading into the maelstrom. Taulbee said a silent prayer to the void they'd grab the damned thing and get out of there without losing anyone, but he knew the chances of that were damned small.

"Sir?" Copenhaver asked.

"Yes, Private?"

"That object hasn't slowed. It's coming straight at us."

Cursing, he flipped to Copenhaver's cam feed. She had swiveled the turret and cam so it faced the incoming KBO. No more than thirty seconds had passed between their first proximity warning and the missile firing, but it was already enough for him to make out certain details.

The object's surface not only shimmered, but writhed with activity. It was still too far away to make out exactly what was shaking and pulsing, but something alive or mechanical, actually several hundred somethings, covered the object. Or maybe they *were* the object in totality. A shiver ran down his spine. Could that be a nest similar to the ones they'd seen inside *Mira*? Or was it something worse?

"Taulbee to Dunn, over."

"Go ahead," the captain said.

"We have a bead on the incoming bogie, sir."

"So do we," Dunn said. "Black is ready to fire a CO_2 cloud. We're going to wait until it's a little closer."

"Copy, sir."

He flipped from the cam feed to that of the skiff. The kilometer of space that between *Mira* and the craft had all but disappeared. The skiff, traveling at 15m/s, had nearly reached the damaged superstructure. They were heading inside. In another few seconds, he wouldn't be able to see anything of the skiff apart from its powerful floodlights stabbing through the darkness.

"Get in and get out, Gunny," Taulbee said to no one.

*****

Darkness closed over them like a death shroud. Gunny had kicked on the floods when they were less than fifty meters away from *Mira*'s lightless interior, but the lights might as well have been as powerful as matches. Instead of shining off the remaining Atmo-steel deck plates, bulkheads, and hanging debris, the light just seemed to disappear ten or so meters away from the skiff.

He'd planned on cutting the skiff's speed to 5m/s, but without more visibility, that was much too fast. By the time he'd see an obstacle, the skiff would hit it a second later. He fired the fore thrusters and the skiff slowed to 2m/s. It was still too fast, but if they had any chance of reaching the beacon before the first of the KBOs attacked, he had to push his luck.

The floods illuminated a hanging, damaged support beam that looked like a crooked, deteriorated tooth. Gunny managed to hit the attitude thrusters in time to push the skiff to starboard before they rammed right into it. He heard Wendt exhale harshly through the comms and did his best not to do the same.

The light continued to weaken as if the floods were losing power, yet his HUD showed no power loss at all. *Something's eating the light,* he thought. *That's insane.* Yet he knew that's exactly what was happening.

He continued maneuvering the skiff through clouds of crumbled Atmo-steel and twisted supports. Flakes of tortured metal, and perhaps shattered exo-solar lifeform carapaces, pinged off his helmet and visor. Some of the debris tugged at his form-fitting combat suit, scraping against the Atmo-steel weave and threatening to stick. Gunny barely noticed.

The seconds ticked down in his head like a counter, each of his heartbeats marking another second toward being attacked by void knew how many hostiles. And the beacon was still thirty meters away.

The floods dimmed again. Now he could barely see more than five meters in front of him. "Wendt," he growled. "Keep using that cannon cam. You see something before I do, scream out before you fire."

"Aye, Gunny," Wendt said. "But I can't see shit."

"I can't either," Murdock whispered.

189

Gunny said nothing. He slowed the skiff again and barely had time to dodge another support beam. Then his eyes went wide.

The "nests" had been made of some kind of metal. Or biological material that looked like metal. Just as with the creatures' shells and limbs, the substance looked jet-black except for the occasional ridge or other defect, but many of the support beams had dark crusts and thick tendrils wrapping around the Atmo-steel. To Gunny, the tissue looked suspiciously like human afterbirth if it had been spray painted black and made of metal. He shivered at the mental image of an alien womb spreading the substance like mucous over the supports to hold its eggs or spawn.

Twenty meters to the beacon. The rising rad meter gauge on the HUD didn't exactly calm him. The levels were still far below lethal and the suit shielding had so far handled the barrage of radiation, but he didn't know how much longer that would last. Every meter forward meant another notch on the gauge. By the time they reached the beacon, he figured the gauge would be little more than a point or two from the red. Once it swung into that area, they'd have less than two minutes before their suit shields failed. And after that? Well, he and his squad wouldn't need lights—they'd glow in the fucking dark.

Beneath the wash of crackles and spits that spilled through the comms, he heard a voice that might have been Dunn's, but it was impossible to understand. Every syllable or two, static flooded over the voice like a tsunami. The light from the floods dwindled, the powerful lamps' illumination barely more than a glow in the darkness. Gunny's skin crawled as he slowed to less than 1m/s. He could hardly see anything and to make matters worse, the clock ticking in his head had counted down to zero. They were out of time and hadn't yet reached the beacon.

Another careful port thrust and the skiff floated past broken support beams. The rad counter went up again, his HUD flashing with radiation warnings. Something near the back of the aft section flashed, briefly bathing the area in harsh white light. Before the afterimage completely blinded him, he saw it. The beacon.

He brought the skiff to a full stop although he was unable to see his hands in front of him. The suit's screens had stopped the worst of the flash, a burst so high it should have permanently blinded him, but it still left a ghostly reflection on his retinas. He reflexively tried to blink it away, but it stayed with him, and while it did, they were at a complete standstill.

"Gunny?" Wendt said nervously.

"Yeah. I need a second here," he said. The beacon. A few scant meters away, so close even the wan light illuminated the clutter of etchings and scratches along the cylinder. The device could flash-fry them if it decided to go off again at full power. The damned thing had attracted these crazy lifeforms from void only knew where, but it was a bonafide alien artifact. Scientists would pore over it for decades, if not centuries, trying to determine if the markings indicated language and if so, what the scratches and etches meant. He had no doubt it would have its own museum on Earth and be patronized by the wealthiest in Sol. He smirked. It wasn't going to Earth or anywhere else in Sol System, let alone a museum. No one would study it, no one would try and unlock the secrets of its power source or who had made it. Instead, they were going to send it straight to Hell.

His eyes fully cleared and he rotated the skiff, mindful of the two twisted support beams hanging less than a meter from the top of the cannon placement. If he ran into those, he could damage the cannon, or even decapitate Wendt. As he swung the skiff, he said, "Murdock. You're our retriever."

There was a long pause before the marine answered. "Aye, Gunny."

"Tether yourself, and get out there. I want that thing in the skiff as fast as you can make it happen."

"Aye," the private said again.

Gunny flipped his attention to the rear cam and couldn't help but grin. Murdock had appeared, his rifle mag-locked to his back like a professional soldier. The marine tentatively activated his suit-thrusters just enough to nudge him toward the beacon. Gunny held his breath as the young marine approached the cylindrical object. Murdock reached the scarred and blackened platform where the beacon sat, its cradle of plas-steel weathered and pitted as if from thousands of micro impacts. Wendt's suit cam showed him all the detail he needed to see.

The images Kalimura's squad had sent from *Mira* didn't do the thing justice. In the near absolute darkness of the broken aft-section, the cylinder seemed to glow beneath Murdock's suit lights. Worse, the glow seemed to be getting brighter.

"Hurry the fuck up," he whispered to no one.

Murdock stepped onto the platform, his foot mag locking him to the Atmo-steel surface. He carefully pulled his other foot forward and locked it as well. He stood there for a moment before leaning toward the device. Through the suit cam, Gunny saw the holdup. The cradle in which the beacon sat was hardly intact after all. The front of the cradle seemed fine, but the sides had become a tangle of thick, melted plas-steel.

"Gunny?" Murdock said. "How do I—?"

"Use your knife," he said as calmly as he could, doing his best to ignore the screaming voice in his head telling him to get the fuck out of here as fast as he could. "Cut that shit away. Pull a torch if you have to."

Murdock paused for a moment before reaching into his pouch and pulling the vibro-knife. He leaned in further and began cutting the material. It parted with some effort, Murdock's arm visibly struggling to pull the Atmo-steel blade through the congealed material.

"Gunny?" Wendt's voice broke through the comms.

"What?"

"Forward cams. I think we have a problem."

Gunny flipped back to the skiff's forward cam. He blinked twice before his mouth opened in a large 'O' of surprise. The KBO had arrived. And hell had arrived with it.

*****

Taulbee had rotated the SV-52 to face the incoming threat and Copenhaver kept the cannon pointed at *Mira*, ready to shoot anything that looked like it might try and enter the aft-section. Or, Taulbee thought, if anything comes out of there apart from the skiff.

With his eyes fixed on the incoming KBO, the other cam feeds forgotten,

Taulbee could only stare in wonder as the thing closed the distance. Less than a km now, and it was slowing.

"Lieutenant," Black said, instantly causing Taulbee to jump in his seat, "we are ready to fire."

"Copy," Taulbee said. "You're a go."

Black counted down from three. In the vacuum of space, there was no sound to hear as the missile left its launch tube, and no sound when its rockets kicked in. The only proof Taulbee had that anything had happened at all was the object that streaked by the SV-52 some fifty meters above. As it passed, its bright rocket engine plume caused his screens to dim the incoming light. The feed's strong filters made the plume a dark yellow and blue flare rather than a blinding white.

The missile quickly accelerated before detonating in the KBO's proximity with a muted flash. A large cloud of gas appeared in space, the particles barely reflecting Sol's anemic light. That was when everything changed.

The KBO seemed to explode, or maybe shatter was the right word. It came apart like a large sedimentary rock in a jet spray of water. Hundreds, maybe thousands, of creatures broke apart in an amorphous swarm of incongruous shapes. A second later, the rabble moved as one toward the cloud, their disparate trajectories suddenly converging. It was like nothing he'd ever seen before.

The creatures flew into the cloud and seemed to stop in its midst. But they hadn't really stopped. Instead, they were flying in circles, racing through and around the cloud like electrons orbiting an atom. The cloud, which should have dissipated after twenty seconds, was erased in the space of no more than five heartbeats. *Not erased,* Taulbee thought. *Consumed.*

He held his breath, waiting to see what they would do next. He didn't have to wait long. The creatures continued their bombing run through the remains of the cloud, assuredly plucking every last molecule of their unexpected meal. When they finished, the exo-solar lifeforms began reassembling themselves in a misshapen sphere.

"Oh, shit," he said. "Copenhaver?"

"Aye, sir?"

"Get ready to swing that cannon."

"Copy, sir," she said. He glanced at the cannon cam. She was still holding position on *Mira*, the cannon ready to rain tritium flechette rounds on any hostiles.

"Taulbee to Dunn, over."

"Go ahead," the captain said.

"I don't think that slowed them down much, sir."

"Neither do I," Dunn said. "Black?"

The AI didn't pause before speaking. "We can fire another munition, Captain, but I doubt it will hold them any longer than the first."

"Great," Taulbee muttered.

"Taulbee? If they come within range," Dunn said, "give them something to think about. But you better keep a good ammo reserve. We have more incoming."

The creatures had finished assembling themselves, and once again, they were moving toward *Mira*, their speed vastly diminished from their first approach. His HUD displayed their distance at 900 meters and quickly accelerating. Based on the rate, they would be within cannon range in a few seconds, and on top of the SV-52 roughly 10 seconds after that. No time at all, really.

"Goddamnit, Gunny," he said. He nudged the fore thrusters and the SV-52 began gliding backward at 2m/s in *Mira*'s direction. If those creatures were going to attack, he wanted to be sure he didn't crash into them with forward momentum. Not that it would matter much. If they were made of the same material as the starfish or the pinecones, the canopy would be obliterated in an instant, and shortly after that, the SV-52 would be little more than a debris cloud itself.

They were coming. Thousands of them. And more KBOs were on their way? We. Are. Fucked. The thoughts bounced inside his skull like flechette shards slamming into a hull. He realized his focus had been shattered and desperately tried to fight back the fear. It was Copenhaver's voice that finally managed to break through the swirling images of destruction.

"Sir? What is that?"

He shook himself and checked the cannon feed. For the second time in as many minutes, his mouth opened in surprise. But instead of wonder, a terrible river of ice roared through his veins.

The very top of *Mira*'s hull had darkened to near black, as if the giant hulk was being consumed. At first, he thought space itself had decided to devour *Mira*, all her secrets, and all her exo-solar hitchhikers. But gaps of Atmo-steel appeared through the crawling wall of darkness. Pinecones. Thousands of them. Maybe hundreds of thousands, descended over the hull. The creatures floated from the top of the hull and headed to the damaged aft.

"Void help us," Taulbee said. "Copenhaver?"

"Aye, sir?"

"Give them something to think about."

"Copy," she said. The skiff vibrated as the cannon came to life.

*****

The aft ate light. That much Gunny knew. He didn't know the physics behind it and didn't much give a shit. While the phenomenon was much worse near the beacon, the effect wasn't uniform. The bow cam feed caught enough Kuiper Belt light to see the edges of the destroyed infrastructure leading into space, but there was little space to be seen. Dozens of shapes flitted near the entrance. A few beats later, hundreds more appeared. Now it was more like thousands.

"Damnit," Gunny whispered. He attempted a connection to Taulbee, but his HUD lit up with comm failures. Whatever was eating the light apparently swallowed the radio signals as well. This far inside *Mira*, it was impossible to communicate with either *S&R Black* or Taulbee. They were on their own.

"Murdock!" Gunny yelled. "Get that fucking thing inside the skiff! Now!"

Murdock didn't answer. Gunny flipped back to the aft feed. The marine had finished cutting away the melted spots from one side and was working on the other. The beacon was glowing brighter.

"Murdock!" Gunny yelled again.

"Working on it," Murdock muttered. With a terrific wrench, he pulled the melted plas-steel clump away from the beacon. The glow ratcheted up. Murdock

193

mag-locked his gloves to the beacon and pulled. The strange object grudgingly left its cradle, Murdock leaning backward against its sudden release. He groaned before shutting down his magnetics. The momentum moved him off the platform and left him gliding back to the skiff, his charge in tow.

"Secure that thing!" Gunny yelled.

Murdock freed one hand and pulled himself along using the tether. He only had two meters to travel between the platform and skiff's gunwale, but it seemed to take forever. Gunny's heart rate rose as he watched with growing impatience.

He switched back to the bow feed. The entrance they'd used had turned into a broken wall of darkness. "Wendt?"

"Aye, Gunny. It's getting a lot worse."

"Well, get ready to clear a path," he said. "I get the feeling they're not going to let us out of here without a fight."

"Copy," Wendt said, his voice filled with determined, but nervous, resolve.

"Aboard!" Murdock yelled. He had one foot mag-locked to the skiff and was still pulling the beacon over the gunwale.

"Get it secured!"

He was sure Murdock muttered something under his breath, but Gunny wasn't going to yell at him for that. His own heart was doing gymnastics and the urge to hit the throttle, to get the fuck out of here, was almost unstoppable. With every second that passed, the horde out there multiplied, thickening like a wall of moving tar. But worse than that was the palpable feeling of being inside this haunted derelict, the dread of doom crawling across his skin.

Murdock's other foot locked to the floor and he had the beacon nearly inside the gunwale. Another second ticked by, his nerves jangling, his fingers tightening on the controls. The beacon slammed down into the hull as the storage area magnetics kicked on, the skiff vibrating and shuddering from the impact.

"Clear!" Murdock yelled. The private was already reaching for his rifle.

"Marines! Make a hole!" Gunny hit the thrusters while preparing for another obstacle course.

*****

The creatures flew in like a fast-moving plague. While Copenhaver fired tritium flechette rounds from the mounted cannon, he was forced to keep her cam feed minimized. The power forcing him was utter fear.

They looked like bulky missiles with a sail of tendrils wriggling and waving in Sol's direction. Long, wide arms jutted from the sides of the bulbous creatures, each ending in a hook similar to what the pinecones had. The mouths, if you could call them that, were dark holes surrounded by what looked like mandibles and a long, waving proboscis.

A coordinated formation of dozens of the creatures flew toward him, heading straight for the SV-52's canopy. "Copenhaver! Get ready for a bump!"

She didn't have time to reply before the first of the creatures slammed into the Atmo-steel hull. It missed the canopy by less than a meter. The craft, already moving backward, shuddered from the impact and the SV-52 began sliding to port.

The creature, apparently unharmed, bounced off the hull and drifted directly in front of the canopy. Mere centimeters from the transparent aluminum, Taulbee fought a scream as the creature opened its mouth. A ring of sharp, silvery teeth glinted in the glare from the floodlights. Nearly a meter wide, and several in length, it seemed to stare at him although it had no eyes. The creature flung its wide arms and it swam, for lack of a better term, over the canopy and out of sight.

"Holy shit!" Copenhaver yelled.

He flipped to the cannon's cam feed. The creature that had slammed into the hull had slipped behind them heading toward *Mira*. With the cannon zoomed in, the feed made the strange lifeform's image appear the size of *Mira* itself. Taulbee would have chuckled if not for the fact he was still reeling from shock. He had enough sense to switch back to the bow cam and spotted another sortie of the creatures.

This group flew more spread apart and appeared to notice the SV-52 as well as *S&R Black*. Rather than heading straight at him or the larger ship, they skirted beneath, above, and around. He should have felt relief, no longer having to worry about a swarm of the things wrecking the SV-52, but their tactics meant they were smart. Possibly as smart as the starfish and much, much faster.

Two more flocks headed toward *Mira*. It was hopeless. He wasn't going to be able to stop shit from here. He rotated the SV-52, Copenhaver's cannon remaining fixed on the wall of pinecones attempting to swallow *Mira*'s aft and Gunny's exit. When he finished turning, a flash of light appeared near *S&R Black*. She had fired another of the Trio's "gifts" and a large group of pinecones evaporated into particles.

The weapon had detonated on top of *Mira*'s hull, but close enough to the aft to take out the port corner of the pinecone wall. The skiff vibrated as Copenhaver fired shot after shot directly into the pinecone horde. A flechette impacted with one of the new creatures and detonated. The insectile thing instantly transformed into a debris cloud of shattered arms, mandibles, and carapace.

Taulbee grinned in spite of himself. At least the Trio's ammo worked on those things too. "Gunny?" he said over the comms. "What's your ETA?"

Nothing.

Taulbee tried again, but the sergeant didn't answer. He flinched when the captain's voice broke over the comms a heartbeat later.

"Taulbee," Dunn said, "what's your ammo count?"

He checked the counters on the right side of his HUD. "62 tritium and—"

"Cease fire and switch to regular rounds."

"Aye, sir. Copenhaver?" Taulbee said.

"Doing it now, sir," she said.

The ammo counter had already dropped to 60 rounds before she switched. Cursing to himself, Taulbee refocused on the cannon feed. The explosive rounds, as expected, didn't appear to be damaging the pinecones. However, the barrage of lethal tritium rounds had apparently made them wary of the flying projectiles. The wall had begun to thin in patches as some of the pinecones decided to get out of range, or at least be less of a target.

Taulbee glanced at the other cam feeds. *S&R Black*'s starboard flechette cannons had started firing explosive rounds as well. The top of *Mira*'s hull was alight with micro explosions driving Atmo-steel flechettes into the groups still descending to the aft. A proximity alert warning flashed on the HUD. With a mental groan, he flipped to the starboard cam. What he saw made him blink. Just a few kilometers away, a trio of objects headed to the area. At least a dozen kilometers separated the three, and their trajectories weren't uniform, but they were coming. And if they were anything like the insect things, they'd arrive sooner than later.

"Taulbee to Dunn. Do you—?"

"We see them, Lieutenant," Dunn said. "Stay as long as you can."

"Aye, sir." Taulbee flipped back to the cannon feed. The pinecones had thinned their wall, but it was still at least a few creatures thick at its least crowded points. Through a few gaps, he could even see the blacker than black darkness inside the cut-off aft section, looking like the gaps between black teeth in a black mouth.

Copenhaver was running out of explosive flechettes. During a typical marine engagement, you didn't send 100 rounds into a crowd of suited humans without knowing they'd all be fragmented to hell. By the time you got five shots off, that particular battle was over and portable anti-ship munitions were streaking toward you, or you managed to hurt them bad enough to force a retreat and move in for a search and destroy mission. But here? These damned things just soaked up the flechettes like Atmo-steel sponges.

"Gunny!" Taulbee tried again. "Gunny, are you there?"

No response.

Taulbee initiated a block connection to Gunny, but that didn't work either. Something inside the ship had completely scrambled their comms. Either that, or Gunny and his squad were already dead, floating inside the great derelict, meters from the beacon, trapped behind a wall of alien creatures. "And we'd never know it," he said to himself.

"Dunn to Taulbee," the captain's voice broke through his thoughts.

"Aye, sir?"

"Another thirty seconds of this and *Black* will be down to less than 50% of her munitions."

He knew what the captain was saying. He'd been thinking the same thoughts Taulbee had. Now it was time to cut bait. They'd failed for now. They'd have to find another way to—

"Sir!" Copenhaver yelled.

Taulbee switched to the cannon feed. A pinpoint of white light penetrated the moving wall. Dozens of pinecones shattered in its wake. He held his breath and waited to see what was coming out.

******

His speed bordered on suicidal, but there were gaps of light up ahead. He had a pretty good idea as to why, too. Right now, Private Copenhaver was no doubt spraying down the fucking things with flechette after flechette. And the pinecones? Well, they didn't like it one bit.

Wendt and Murdock fired their own weapons, tritium flechettes streaking through the darkness before plowing into the wall of creatures. The floodlights, seeming to get brighter the further they retreated toward the rear of the aft section, shined through clouds of shattered shells, decapitated silver hooks, and spinning gore.

The skiff bumped a beam on the port-side and the craft slid sideways as it approached the wall. Cursing, he adjusted the attitude and tried to keep the skiff pointed straight into their midst. The skiff was moving at 20m/s now. No more than thirty meters from the wall, they were going to hit it head-on. If one of the creatures got in his way, it might take his damned head off. Or Murdock's. Or even destroy the cannon. He ground his teeth and hit the thrusters. The skiff slid sideways again and he put it into a controlled roll at the same time.

A bone-jarring vibration shuddered through the skiff's Atmo-steel hull as the skiff's bottom slammed into the wall of creatures. It cut their momentum significantly, but the skiff continued floating out into space. Gunny checked the starboard cam feed and could see a hole through the wall he'd just come through. The pinecone wall had formed a ripple and had begun parting like curtains.

Both Murdock and Wendt were yelling on the comms, but Gunny didn't even notice. He was too busy flipping the skiff out of the aft section and pointing the bow back into space. The rear cam showed him more of the pinecones detaching from the ship and from one another. They seemed to be following him.

Gunny pounded the rear thrusters and the skiff quickly accelerated. He kept them firing until a fuel reserve warning kicked on, as well as a proximity alert. He looked up in time to see the SV-52 flying in a positive vector directly above the skiff. Taulbee was providing more cover. Good.

Another vibration shuddered through the hull, but his HUD showed no impacts. "Shit! Gunny!"

"What, Murdock?"

The marine sounded both shocked and terrified at the same time. "I think this thing is getting ready to go off!"

His teeth rattled in his skull. Whatever the beacon had started doing, it was getting worse. A HUD alert flashed. The skiff's Atmo-steel integrity was beginning to give way. If they didn't stop the beacon, the goddamned thing was going to shake them into pieces, and his squad would die long before that happened.

"Private!" Gunny yelled. "Wendt! Eject! Now!"

"No!" Wendt yelled back. "I'm—"

"That's a fucking order, marine!" Gunny screamed through the mic.

A heartbeat later, he watched as their suit-beacons went into emergency mode. His HUD showed them as two pulsing red dots behind him. At the speed the skiff was traveling, the marines would have to use their suit thrusters to slow down unless they wanted to follow him. He hoped like hell neither of them was dumb enough for that.

Gunny punched the thrusters again. "Fuck the fuel," he said to no one and kept the pressure on. The thrusters, not designed for a full burn, glowed like miniature stars. The pulsing continued getting stronger, his stomach and lungs wanting to jump through his chest with each successive energy wave.

His HUD flickered twice and lines of static flitted across the cam image, leaving his vision distorted and incomplete. Before him was the vast emptiness of the Kuiper Belt. He checked the rear cam and just had time to make out a few of the dangerous lifeforms following him before it went dead.

"Well," he said, "at least it's not the whole fucking horde."

"Gunny!" Taulbee yelled. "Eject! Now!"

His brain felt as though it was turning jelly, as if it were hopping up and down in his skull like a two year old throwing a tantrum. Taulbee was still screaming over the comms, but the words came out in unintelligible, gap-filled streams of syllables. The gist, however, was pretty clear—Gunny needed to eject.

The next vibration made something snap in his chest and he suddenly lost vision in his left eye. The image through the cam feed became a wall of static in his right eye while his left looked at nothing but darkness. His hand hovered over the eject button.

Fuck Pluto. As long as he was in the chair, he could fly the skiff out. He could set the beacon on a course to go back the way it came. He could—

His body shook with a convulsion. That last pulse had broken something inside him. A rib. Or maybe his spleen. Bright pain rose in a fiery column from his feet to his fingers. A tooth exploded in the lower left of his jaw. Gunny slumped forward and his hand hit the eject button.

Suddenly, he was out of the skiff, his right eye watching as the craft continued into the black, heading not toward Pluto, but further out into the Kuiper Belt. "Fuck," he said. "I could have—"

Just as the cylinder detonated a sun's worth of light into the darkness, he passed out.

CHAPTER FIFTY-FIVE

Cut me a goddamned break, Dickerson thought. Of the five escape pods, only three had come back online. The other two? Nothing. He leaned down to the power connectors checking for damage. Sure enough, there was. Of a kind.

One of the power cables connecting to the pods was covered in a translucent, silver line of acid. The stuff had eaten through the insulation surrounding the cable, no doubt causing a short in the system. Dickerson marked the cable on his HUD with a hazard indicator and checked the others.

The fifth escape pod's power coupling seemed fine, but it still didn't show any power readings. "Elliott? Stand out here and let me know if this thing flickers."

"Got it," Elliott said.

Dickerson climbed into the escape pod and checked the controls. A barely visible indicator light pulsed red. He reached out and pressed it. The manual controls HUD appeared, flickered, and then died. He cursed and tried again. The holographic HUD blinked into existence, but ghostly lines of static flickered across the readouts. He found the diagnostic button and touched it.

The HUD disappeared, leaving a single line of text floating in the air: "Running Diagnostic." Dickerson activated his comms. "Corporal. One of the dead pods is actually responding, but the block interface is fried. It's manual only and the controls are, well, a little damaged. I think."

Kali sighed. "Okay. How damaged?"

"Running a diagnostic. Assuming it finishes, I'll know."

"Hey, Dickerson," Elliott said, "the pod's running lights are dim, but they're glowing."

"Figures." Running lights weren't high on the list of priorities. If the emergency beacon wasn't too damaged, *S&R Black*, the skiffs, and the SV-52 would be able to track it. He glared at the text still glowing in mid-air, willing it to finish its cycle. Tapping your foot in z-g while connected via magnetics was practically impossible, but you could still curl your toes. Dickerson found himself doing just that.

A few seconds later, the text froze and slowly faded out as a barely legible status report appeared in its place. Several yellow and red highlights glared at him from the display. Dickerson pounded his fist on the flight chair armrest. "Corporal? This pod's mostly fried."

"No life support?"

"Worse," he said. "The automatic controls are more or less dead. The manual ones check out, but there's also a fault in one of the thrusters."

Kalimura paused before responding. "How about comms?"

"Diagnostic says they're in good shape, but I don't even know if we can trust this."

"Elliott," Kalimura said, "go to one of the good pods and run a diagnostic there too. I want to compare them."

"Aye, Corporal," Elliott said.

Dickerson continued scanning through the damage report and sighed. At least the damned thing had fuel. Not as though that was much of a surprise. The escape pods required very little in the way of actual propulsion. If *Mira* had power, the launchers would catapult the escape pods out into space with a charge of compressed gas. In doing so, the pods could accelerate away from the ship and slowly change their trajectory via thrusters. Since *Mira* wasn't powered, he was dubious they'd have much of a push into space. Each pod would quickly exhaust its fuel, leaving the occupants stuck on whatever trajectory they managed before going dry.

He examined the fuel reports with a grim chuckle. Well, *Mira*'s pods may be of some use after all. Since the ship had been designed for deep space, and any chance of immediate rescue by SF Gov forces was nil, the pods had been designed to at least give their occupants a chance. Not much of one, but better than he'd expected.

Assuming the pods hadn't been too damaged, they might actually be able to pilot these things as far as Pluto. Maybe. Out here in the Kuiper Belt, it wasn't as though there was much gravity to contend with. Provided they could point themselves in that direction, the pods would eventually take up orbit around the dwarf planet.

But this pod? No automatic controls, a damaged flight console, and plenty of concerns about its integrity, regardless of what the diagnostic said. "Fucked as usual," he said to no one.

"Hey!" Elliott called out. "No block comms, but it looks like we should be able to communicate with Black."

"Outstanding," Kalimura said. "How about the diagnostics?"

"I'll check the other two, but looks like we're in good shape," Elliott said.

"Dickerson?" Kalimura asked. "What do you think?"

"I think someone's getting the short end of the straw," he said. "Whoever takes this one is going to need to be damned careful."

She went silent for a moment. He knew what she was going to say before she said it. It was the exact same thing he'd have said if he were still a corporal. "The damaged one is mine," Kalimura said.

"Bullshit," Carb said.

"No arguments."

Dickerson glared at the diagnostics, willing them to give him some idea of her chances. It was going to be a crapshoot. If Kalimura took this pod, he reckoned her chances were 50/50 for finding a decent trajectory. Since they didn't even know where *S&R Black* was, that could mean flying in a direction that would require the ship to actually come and get her, or flying straight *into* the ship's hull. The other pods, with their *working* automatic controls, would thrust or brake depending on obstacles and other factors. Kalimura would have to take care of that on her own.

Fighting a sigh, Dickerson stood from the pod couch just as the ship quaked. The vibration made him sway on his magnetically locked feet. Whatever was happening to *Mira* was certainly tearing her apart. The quake stopped as suddenly as it had begun.

"Goddamnit," Elliott wheezed through the mic. "What the hell are they doing out there?"

"Guessing the tow isn't going well," Kalimura said. "All the more reason for us to get the hell out of here."

"Um, Boss?" Carb said.

The tone of her voice chilled Dickerson's blood.

"What, Carb?" Kalimura asked.

"That hatch is open."

Dickerson quickly exited the escape pod and looked at the far bulkhead. The hatch leading to the cargo bay had completely buckled, one side of it crumbling into flakes of metal swirling toward the ceiling. He felt a vibration beneath his feet followed by a series of impacts below the deck.

"Oh, shit," Kalimura said. Dickerson fixed his eyes on the widening hole where the hatch had been. Something long and black was making its way through the hole.

CHAPTER FIFTY-SIX

A brilliant cone of yellow and white light punctured the shadowy Kuiper Belt. Even as his screens dimmed, he saw the skiff silhouetted behind the blast looking like a tiny slit of darkness. Alarms filled his HUD, including a radiation warning. A moment later, a vibration rattled the SV-52 like an earthquake.

"Motherfucker!" Taulbee yelled. He set the rear cam feed as the primary window on his HUD and slammed down the throttle, the SV-52 jerking backward as the thrusters engaged. "Copenhaver? Turn the cannon. Track our marines."

"Aye, sir," she said.

"Taulbee to Dunn."

"Copy, Taulbee. We see it. Oakes is breaking off our attack. We'll be turning away from *Mira* and curving back to meet you."

"Aye, sir. Did Gunny eject?"

Dunn paused. "Yes, he did. You might want to make him your first pickup."

A cold chill ran down his spine. "Sir?"

"He's lost consciousness and his life signs are weak."

Taulbee cursed. "Aye, sir. Taulbee out."

He killed the forward thrusters, rotated the '52, and flew toward Gunny. Since he'd gone the farthest with the skiff, the sergeant had traveled at a positive vector with a negative lateral. In other words, from Taulbee's vantage point, Gunny was traveling up and away. The up was fast. The away was even faster.

The skiff had been flying at 40m/s and picking up speed. Taulbee accelerated the SV-52 to 60m/s, all the while checking the positions of the other two marines so he didn't collide with them. He passed both Wendt and Murdock. The pair had used their suit thrusters to slow down and link up. They would remain safe for a few minutes. He hoped.

Taulbee's screens flickered, stabilized, and flickered again. A few lines of static broke over his view before disappearing. Interference wave? Some kind of shockwave? He didn't know. Shit, how the hell could he?

Finally nearing the sergeant, he slowed the SV-52 as quickly as he could. "Copenhaver?"

"Aye, sir. I've got the tether ready."

He grinned. The deep steel in her voice told him she was ready to save her sergeant and damned confident she was going to do it. Yup. Field promotion was definitely in her future.

"I'm going to pull up in front of him. Fire the net and we'll slowly reel him in. I want him stable so we can get back to *Black* in a flash." Taulbee checked his speed and position. "Here we go."

Gunny's combat suit beacon blinked white and yellow, but from the way the lights pulsed and moved, he knew the sergeant was in an uncontrolled spin. He slowed until the SV-52 nearly matched the unconscious marine's velocity. The SV-52's starboard floods caught sight of the suit. Gunny was in fact tumbling and spinning, just as *Mira* had been when they reached the derelict what felt like a thousand years ago.

He pushed the thought from his mind and focused. He nudged the thrusters, a bare puff of gas adding one more m/s, just enough to—

"Clear," he said.

"Copy," Copenhaver answered. The tether net shot from the support vehicle's belly. She'd aimed perfectly; the tethered projectile opened like a flower just before it hit Gunny. The unconscious sergeant spun into the net, the skein closing in on him, spinning and tumbling with him at first before slowing him to match the SV-52s attitude. "Secure, sir."

S&R Black had already made her turn. *Oakes must have pushed the thrusters to the limit,* he thought. Taulbee knew that even now, the captain and Lieutenant Nobel would be preparing the cargo bay for their arrival, and unloading Gunny wasn't going to be fun. Not only did Taulbee have to shoot back to *S&R Black* as quickly as possible, but once the unconscious marine was aboard, he had to turn around with what fuel he had, and retrieve both Wendt and Murdock.

"Sir?" Copenhaver said.

"Yes, Private?"

She sounded timid, a little fearful. "What about the beacon, sir?"

Yes. What about the beacon? It was currently spinning off into the Kuiper Belt, presumably still attached to the skiff. He had another thought that chilled him. What if it had come loose from the skiff? How the hell would they even find it?

"One thing at a time," he said with a wince. He knew that sounded ridiculous. Hell, it did even to his own ears. The more he thought about it, though, it was a good question. He was damned glad he didn't have to answer it, though. That was Dunn's job and Taulbee didn't envy the captain in making that decision.

*****

While cursing about his damaged leg often and loudly, Nobel had finished pulling the emergency stretcher and putting it into place. No so long ago, Gunny's squad had put Nobel in this very same stretcher and guided him to the infirmary. The irony was not lost on Dunn.

Dressed in full combat suits, their helmets attached and pressurized, he and the engineer waited inside the cargo bay. Dunn had decided not to waste any time in getting the sergeant offloaded. When Taulbee reached them, he and Nobel could just drag the unconscious marine into the cargo bay, pressurize it, and begin stabilizing him. *If,* Dunn thought with a shudder, *there's anything left to stabilize.*

The beacon flash had been as destructive and powerful as the last time it had erupted, but, thankfully, the burst had once again not been aimed in their direction. The majority of the lethal radiation had gone off into the deep Kuiper Belt headed for infinity. And that was the problem.

As soon as they'd detected the beacon's emissions, he'd watched the cam feeds to see what the creatures would do. They did nothing. The pinecones had once again stitched themselves together in a massive wall more or less cutting off *Mira*'s aft section from ingress. Well, that was if you considered the fractured hull an ingress.

He had seen a few starfish clusters moving around on top of *Mira*'s hull, but they hadn't yet attacked. And the new arrivals? They had more or less disappeared. That fact alone was enough to unnerve him. They didn't even know what the things were capable of. Black had been analyzing their movements and body composition the moment the insect-like things had come close enough, but they had disappeared once they flew below *Mira*'s hull.

Did they find another way into the ship? Or did they just decide to attach themselves like the barnacles of old? When the flocks of creatures had first passed the SV-52, it appeared they were making a bee-line for the pinecones. *Another predator,* Dunn assumed. Instead, they had ignored the pinecones as if they didn't exist.

When the beacon had erupted, he'd expected the creatures to depart *Mira* at once and chase the photon blast. If Black's assumptions were correct, and so far, they had been, the exo-solar lifeforms craved light. It's what had drawn them to the Kuiper Belt to begin with. Or, did it?

Mira had been traveling for 43 years, making its way back into the system, broken and derelict. The creatures aboard her had been attracted by the beacon's blast when *Mira*'s scientists unlocked it. At least that was the story the data Kalimura had recovered indicated.

But the beacon had gone off while it was inside *Mira*, not outside of it. So how did the creatures get attracted to *Mira* in the first place? Surely the photon blast didn't cause the damage to the aft section and the reactors? Or did it?

Dunn felt confused. Maybe it didn't matter. What did matter is why the pinecones decided to cover the aft and not even care about the beacon. What was left inside *Mira* they were trying to protect?

And the KBOs? These things had been floating out here for centuries, but they only started moving once the beacon went off some 21 days ago? So why the hell had they been here to begin with?

Something put them here, he thought. *Something else. Something more sentient?* He shivered. Were they sitting in the Kuiper Belt, surrounded by ticking time bombs just waiting for some celestial event to kick off their detonations? Had the beacon always been meant to travel here? To Sol?

That was a thought he didn't even want to consider. If it was an invasion force of alien creatures whose strange biology was only matched by their mastery of traveling across space, through vacuum and absolute zero temperatures, following photon trails through the galaxy, humanity faced extinction. Atmo-steel projectiles did little to them. Explosions could rock them, push them, even damage them. But destroy them? They needed the tritium ammo for that. And even worse? The creatures bred. They bred damned fast.

When they'd first approached *Mira*, the pinecones hadn't been nearly so numerous. There hadn't been what seemed like millions of the fucking things covering the ship. Now? They were packed densely enough to create a ten-meter-thick wall around *Mira*'s exposed aft section. Their predator? The starfish things? They'd all but disappeared. What were they waiting for? And what about the new creatures?

None of it made sense. None of it made any damned sense. All of them, every single one of them, should have been chasing the beacon. Instead, they remained with *Mira*. Something else was aboard her. Dunn didn't even want to hazard a guess at what that might be.

He opened a connection to Black.

Yes, Captain?

Why aren't they following the beacon? Dunn asked.

Black had obviously already been thinking about this, because the response was near instantaneous. *I estimate it is due to residual radiation inside Mira that the beacon has left in its wake. It has been inside the ship for 43 years. We still don't know how many times it has pulsed since it began its journey back to Sol System.*

Residual? Wouldn't we have picked it up?

Black paused for a few heartbeats. *Captain, in light of all we have seen, all the seeming impossibilities, isn't it possible they're radiating energy we can't even detect? Or in a wavelength that our hulls and suits easily reflect?*

"Bullshit," Dunn said aloud.

If she'd had the ability, he was pretty sure she would have sighed. *Let's try again—*

No, Black, he thought. *I understand what you're saying. I just don't believe it. So what the hell do we do now?*

Dunn's HUD lit with an alert. The cargo bay was about to open; Taulbee had reached the ship. He walked to the side of the cargo bay door, Nobel on the other side of him. Tethers locked, magnetics on, they were ready.

When the AI spoke again, she sounded flustered. *Do what you've wanted to do for hours.*

He grinned. *Blow it up?*

Yes, Captain. After we retrieve the beacon, we destroy Mira.

Sounded like a damned good idea to him.

He killed the connection as the cargo bay doors opened. The SV-52 hovered before them, its floodlights dimmed so as not to blind Dunn or Nobel. The net shrouded a ragdoll figure inside of the mesh. He and Nobel reached forward and enabled their magnetic gloves, the bundle of netting immediately locking to their hands. Taulbee disengaged the net and moved the SV-52 away from the cargo bay at the same instant. Dunn and Nobel pulled the net in and closed the cargo bay doors.

While the cargo bay pressurized, Dunn opened the comms. "Taulbee. Can you bring back Wendt and Murdock at the same time?"

"Aye, sir. They were already locked together. Shouldn't be any problem at all."

"Good," Dunn said. "Out."

The pressure lights turned green. He connected to Gunny's suit. The sergeant's BP was very low and his pulse erratic. He sent a command to the suit and its seals popped. Nobel went for the helmet while Dunn went for the chest. He unfastened the suit's armored plating as well as the environmental shielding and winced. Blood stained Gunny's moist undershirt.

"Oh, void wept," Nobel said.

Dunn turned to him and shuddered. Nobel had removed the visor and helmet revealing the slack-faced marine and an eyeball dangling down in a dried river of blood on the left cheek.

"Do the best you can," he said and split the undershirt with his knife. He couldn't help but wince again. One of Gunny's ribs had broken through the skin. Well, broken was the wrong word. Shattered was more like it. Chips of bone perforated the flesh like teeth. "Autodoc. Now."

"Aye, sir."

He and Nobel stood from their crouches. Now they'd made sure he wasn't going to bleed out, it was time to get him to the doc. But Dunn wasn't sure it'd be enough. Not this time.

CHAPTER FIFTY-SEVEN

The universe seemed to stand still. Every muscle in Kali's body froze in both wonder and horror as the impossibly dark shape broke through the hatch's remains. At first, she thought it was a cable dislodged by the ship quakes. Until, that was, it began swaying back and forth almost as if tasting the vacuum. The tapered end slammed down on the deck, layers of nearly imperceptible cilia rippling on its surface. Another appendage appeared, a strange glow radiating around it.

"Starfish!" Carb yelled.

The sound of her voice broke Kali's fugue. "Get in the pods! Now!"

Kali raised her rifle and fired at the creature as it dragged itself through the large rectangular hatch. The flechette round had little time to engage its propellant before striking the alien flesh. She immediately turned and leaped from the deck in the direction of the escape pods.

Elliott and Carb had already dived into two of them. Dickerson stood by the damaged, but still functional pod, his rifle aimed down the corridor at the broken hatch.

Kali growled over the comms. "Get moving, Dickerson! Now!"

As she reached the pods, Dickerson grabbed her left arm and swung her into the remaining, undamaged pod. Kali yelled in surprise and banged into the pod's rear, her visor crunching into the Atmo-steel. She turned to try and get out of the pod, but its door had already descended, trapping her inside.

The escape pod's HUD came to life, a view of the corridor appearing before her. She couldn't see Dickerson, but she could see what was coming out of the vent. She activated the pod's magnetic harness and stuck fast to the acceleration couch, but that didn't stop her from shaking.

A flechette round screamed across her view heading toward the hatch. The starfish thing had nearly released itself from the broken hatch, five of its limbs dragging its bulk into the corridor. Arcs of electricity turned into a cloud around the thing. It began to shake, its arms instinctively slashing and smashing through the empty vacuum.

"Dickerson! Get in your pod!" she yelled.

He didn't respond. Kali had time to take a breath before the HUD flashed green. Her broken rib screamed in pain as the escape pod latches released and then the g-forces had her.

A mechanical launcher catapulted the pod, flinging it away from the ship's superstructure and into space. *Mira*'s corridor disappeared, leaving her with a view of the damaged, pinecone-encrusted outer hull. The pod spun, giving her vertigo. She called out to her team, but there was nothing. She was all alone.

Before she lost sight of the midships, she saw a puff of gas and another pod flying into space. She didn't know if that was Dickerson, Carb, or Elliott. Kali interfaced with the pod's comm system.

"*S&R Black.* This is Corporal Kalimura. We have ejected in escape pods from *Mira*'s port-side." She waited a few heartbeats, panic slowly creeping across her mind. "Black! Come in, Black!" No response. "Goddamnit, Black! Come in!"

Nothing.

Kali changed the HUD to a 360° panorama, looking for the ship. But all she saw was *Mira* and empty space. The ship was no longer on the port-side. In fact, it had disappeared.

*****

Dickerson watched the thing free itself from the hatch. Flashing red radiation alerts lit his HUD as it entered the corridor. He fired three more flechette rounds at the thing, turned, and pushed himself into the escape pod. He hit the "CLOSE" button on the console and the door slid down, blocking his view of the corridor beyond. The HUD, dimly lit and streaked with static, presented a shattered view of the corridor beyond. He reached to buckle into the acceleration couch and froze.

The starfish thing that had emerged from the hatch moved toward him through the vacuum, its arms spreading like a blossoming flower before retracting and starting the process again. Behind it, hundreds of smaller creatures followed in its wake.

Dickerson reached forward and pounded his fist on the "LAUNCH" button. The HUD disappeared completely as the g-force knocked him backward. Cursing, he punched the manual control switch and a portion of metal slid aside, providing him a small porthole. Dickerson's mouth dropped open in awe as he hurtled away from *Mira.* The five escape pod berths crumbled into shreds of metal as a swarm of the starfish things punched through the hull and into space.

The HUD flickered back into existence, most of the icons showing systems offline. He tried to activate the radar and navigational systems. No go. The diagnostics had told him that was the case, but he'd still held out hope.

He turned his attention back to the tiny viewport. The monstrous *Mira* seemed to move further and further away as the pod accelerated. Without the automated systems, he'd have little warning before smashing into *S&R Black* or debris. He kept waiting for one of the alarms to pop up on the damaged HUD, but there was nothing. *S&R Black* was no longer in position.

Dickerson brought up the diagnostics, checking to ensure the pod's beacon was operational. "At least that's working," he said. The viewport window darkened. Dickerson flipped his attention away from the HUD, eyes growing wide.

The swarm of creatures escaping *Mira*'s hull were following the pod. No, not following. Pursuing. The largest of the starfish creatures streaked toward him, its arms pointed at the pod like teeth.

The pod had no weapons, no evasive maneuvering, nothing. Dickerson braced himself for impact and watched in helpless fascination as the multi-armed thing approached at suicidal speed.

CHAPTER FIFTY-EIGHT

The pair of marines floated in space, hands locked to one another. Wendt and Murdock each had their rifles on their backs, and were more or less completely defenseless. *Fortunately for them,* Taulbee thought, *none of the exo-solar lifeforms seemed to have noticed them.* Instead, the damned things were still all over *Mira.*

He tried to focus on netting the two marines, but he couldn't stop thinking about Gunny. Thinking? No, that wasn't the word. "You're worried," he said aloud. "Worried he's dead."

After Dunn and Nobel had removed Gunny from the tether net, Taulbee had lit out for the two stranded marines even before the cargo bay finished closing. Neither he nor Copenhaver said a word, but he could feel the tension in her silence. Copenhaver was just as concerned about Gunny as he was.

"We're running out of marines," he said with a chuckle. It sounded more like a sob than a laugh to his own ears. He'd been thinking that if they still had a functional skiff, he could send someone else to pick up Wendt and Murdock. But really, who the hell was left? Apart from the command crew, Taulbee was down to just Copenhaver, Murdock, and Wendt. And the latter two were floating out here in space like flotsam ejected from a garbage chute.

"Sir?" Copenhaver said.

"Yes, Private?"

"Our sky is clear, sir. No hostiles in our space."

"Thank you, Private," he said. She had told him something he already knew, but he wasn't going to call her on it. Hell, she probably knew she didn't have to say it, but was struggling to find something to say. Sometimes talking to yourself just wasn't enough. The thoughts and fears could pile up until they strangled you. And after you'd seen one of your leaders carted off unconscious and probably dying, the last place you wanted to stay was inside your head.

Forty meters. He cut the speed a notch and continued his approach. Both *S&R Black* and *Mira* receded further and further behind and below them. If one could equate up and down in 3-D space, that was.

"Taulbee to Wendt."

"Aye, sir," Wendt said. "Good to hear from you."

He couldn't help grinning at the forced joviality in Wendt's voice. "Well, I thought I'd make a personal visit, since you guys decided to take a stroll."

Wendt chuckled. "Well, we've been dancing out here for a few minutes and I have to say, the music sucks and it's damned cold."

Taulbee rolled his eyes. "Coming in. Copenhaver will net you and then we're bringing you back to *Black.* Copy?"

"Acknowledged, sir."

He continued his approach, gently hitting the thruster controls to both slow their speed and adjust the attitude. Since the two men were relatively stable instead of tumbling and twirling, netting them would be easy. Hell, the two men could use their suit thrusters to approach the craft and mag-lock themselves to it if they—

Taulbee's HUD lit up with a warning. Four objects had just ejected from *Mira*. "Oh, shit," he said.

"Dunn to Taulbee."

"Aye, sir. Just got the alert. What's the status?"

The captain paused for an excruciatingly long moment. "Four escape pods from *Mira*'s port-side. Three are heading in the same relative direction. One, however, is not."

"Shit," Taulbee muttered. "Where's it heading?"

"Black says it's on course for Pluto."

Taulbee raised a brow. "Repeat that, sir?"

"Pluto," Dunn said. "It's headed for Pluto."

"Any pursuit?"

"That's the real problem," Dunn said. "Black is going to start sending out some party favors, but we're going to need a pickup on those three and damned fast."

"Aye, sir. We'll have Murdock and Wendt aboard in a moment and I'll head straight for them."

"Very good, Taulbee. How's your fuel?"

He checked his HUD and groaned. Blasting through space at top speed to retrieve Gunny as well as Wendt and Murdock had greatly affected his fuel reserves. "Not good, sir."

"Whatever happens, Taulbee, do not lose that SV-52. You're all we have left in the pantry."

Taulbee shook his head. Dunn was right. Kalimura's skiff? Destroyed. Gunny's skiff? Floating out in the Kuiper Belt somewhere, probably more radioactive than an unshielded reactor, if not completely melted into slag. There were no more support vehicles. All they had left was what he was flying. After that? They'd be down to flying with suit thrusters and nothing else.

"Understood, sir."

"Good hunting," Dunn said.

"Acknowledged." He flipped over to the squad channel after adding Murdock and Wendt. "New plan, marines. Wendt? Murdock? Get your asses on my boat. Mag-lock yourselves, pull your rifles, and get ready for some fun."

"Ah, hell," Wendt said. "We're hitching, sir?"

"Affirmative," Taulbee said. "Kalimura's squad just ejected from *Mira* using ancient escape pods. We need to pick them up before the creatures decide they're on the menu."

"Copy, sir," Wendt said.

"And help Murdock. I'm sure he's never done this before."

Wendt chuckled. "First time for everything, sir."

"Copenhaver?"

"Aye, sir?"

He grinned in spite of the stress. "You ever flown with hitchers?"

"No, sir," she said. "I assume they'll attach low on the hull?"

He nodded, pleased. "Correct. They shouldn't affect your ability rotate the cannon, but you need to keep in mind they're on the side of the SV-52. So make sure you don't bounce any flechettes into them."

She paused for a moment. "Sir? Are we going to net the escape pods?"

"I sure as void hope not," Taulbee said. "If we can, we'll break them out and add them to the hitchers."

She groaned. "That's a lot of bodies, sir."

Tell me about it, he thought. "Don't worry. Did this plenty of times during the Satellite War."

But you didn't do it with thousands of alien creatures attacking, did you? The voice that made that statement was both churlish and matter of fact, and it was right. It was one thing to maneuver through a debris field at relatively slow speeds while five marines stayed mag-locked to your craft. Doing that while dodging exo-solar lifeforms and having to fly fast to boot?

"Shut up and do it," he told himself.

"We're clear, sir," Wendt said.

Taulbee checked the cams. Sure enough, Wendt hung on the port-side with Murdock on the starboard. Both marines had pulled their rifles and were ready. He hoped.

He rotated the SV-52 and slowly increased power to the rear thrusters. The craft decelerated before coming to a halt. He exhaled a deep breath and punched the thrusters. The SV-52 shuddered with the force of the burn and quickly accelerated. He activated the radar on his HUD and the three escape pods popped up in pulsing red. They had ejected into space traveling hundreds of meters before slowing. He assumed the three occupants had terminated the planetary program to await rescue.

If the escape pods were anything like the "modern" model, as if *S&R Black*'s escape pods were modern in any sense of the word, their AIs would automatically target any large planetary body. This far from Earth and her colonies, Pluto was obviously the logical destination. In addition, PEO spat out radio signals that the escape pod sensors had picked up. If the marines inside the escape pods hadn't ceased their advance, they would have been headed to Pluto too. But maybe the pods had picked up *S&R Black* instead and decided it was much closer than Pluto. Who knew? The only question in his mind was why the fourth escape pod hadn't done the same.

"Because it's 50-fucking-year-old technology," he said aloud. "And probably damaged."

The SV-52 passed *S&R Black* and headed out into the Kuiper Belt. The three escape pods were slowing even more now, which didn't exactly help matters. Five or six starfish had detached from *Mira* and had begun to actively chase them. A few pinecones trailed behind, desperately attempting to keep up.

Taulbee growled low in his throat. This was going to get messy in a hurry. "Copenhaver? We still have tritium?"

"Aye, sir," she said. "60 rounds."

"Right," he said, remembering their earlier conversation when they'd been fighting to make a hole for Gunny's squad. "Don't use them unless you have to.

Wendt? Murdock? You guys have tritium?"

"Aye, sir," Wendt said. "One full, one half."

"I have a full mag, sir," Murdock said.

Not good. He would have liked to have had a whole lot more firepower, but he had what he had. "You two hitchers? Make every shot count. We don't have ammo to waste. If you need to clear a path, use explosive flechettes instead. Plus, I don't know how radioactive that shit is. I don't want the escape pods covered in that stuff."

"Aye, sir," the two marines replied.

"Copenhaver?"

"Aye, sir?"

She sounded confident and ready for payback. He knew how she felt. "Your job is to guard our people. I want explosive flechettes surrounding us like chaff. Make sure those bastards know to stay away. If they get too close, open up with the tritium."

"Very good, sir," she said.

He heard the grin in her voice. Thoughts about Gunny, worrying about whether or not he was going to die, faded away. He could save three of his people. And once he had them aboard *S&R Black*, he'd go after the last escape pod. Finally, after hours and hours of separation, he'd have his squads back again. Or what remained of them.

*****

Dunn stood over the autodoc. Gunny lay in the device, his arms and legs strapped to the table. Several tungsten arms, spread like spider legs, hovered above his flesh. They had already split through his flesh, cracked his ribcage, and started work on clearing the chips of bone that had penetrated his dermis, as well as the one that had punctured his spleen.

According to the report the autodoc had sent to his block, Gunny's spleen was salvageable. One lung had been damaged, but after re-inflation and some nannie protocols, it would heal. All in all, Gunny got off light. Except for his brain.

Either due to the force of the beacon's photon burst or his rapid ejection from the skiff, his brain had danced inside his skull. Multiple hematomas, multiple areas of damaged tissue, and significant damage to the Broca's area. The autodoc estimated a 60% chance he would regain consciousness, and a 70% chance his ability to both speak and process language was permanently damaged.

Dunn lingered for a moment, his fingers sliding down the trans-aluminum canopy. He'd known Gunny a long damned time. They'd both spent time in these automated contraptions, but this was the first time he could remember a near mortal wound on the sergeant. *Mira* had cost his Company dearly, and the bitch was still hanging there, an infected hulk of metal that killed everything that got near it.

He tapped the glass. "See you later, Cartwright," he said and left the infirmary. He should have been on the bridge minutes ago. Hell, he should have run there as soon as the escape pods launched, but he needed a moment alone. There wasn't much he could do at the moment that wasn't already being done. Nobel was working on the sled, Oakes was flying the ship, Taulbee and his ragtag squad were picking up Kalimura's squad. All he could do now was watch and wait.

"Black? Give me Taulbee's cam feed, please."

"Of course, Captain."

His block HUD lit up with a stream of images and he saw through the SV-52's forward cam as if he were sitting in the cockpit. The support vehicle had retreated further from *Mira*, starlight twinkling behind the flashing escape pods. It appeared as though 50 meters separated the three squat cylindrical objects from one another. Taulbee should be able to pick them up fairly quickly. He hoped.

The feed disappeared and Dunn started with the change. "Black? What the—?"

"Captain. Other KBOs have arrived within our space. Collision course with *Mira* in two minutes."

"Shit," he said. Dunn sat down in the command chair, activated the holo display, and brought up the spherical representation of everything within 2km of the ship.

Sure enough, several large shapes glowed on the screens. There was no logic to their approach trajectories. It was as if they'd traveled from all over the Kuiper Belt, each heading from a different portion of the massive belt. For all he knew, some of them had been traveling for weeks, perhaps ever since *Mira* entered the Oort Cloud.

The objects were decelerating. He blinked. How the hell was that even possible? When the insectile creatures had arrived, they'd moved as though z-g were nothing more than water. They had also entered the area looking like a buzzing, flittering, imperfect sphere. The creatures had banded together to move themselves as one, and they could move fast.

But how fast? How far had they traveled to approach the ship? Did some of them come from the inner Kuiper Belt, from as far away as Neptune? Surely not. That would mean they'd been traveling nearly as fast as *S&R Black* had on her way to Pluto. That had to be impossible. Didn't it?

Haven't you seen enough impossible shit today? a voice said in his mind. *Do you really think you know anything anymore?*

Good question. Even Black seemed at a loss to explain how the creatures did what they did, let alone how they'd survived in deep space for so long. Black had theories, but without a scientific station aboard the ship, let alone an actual specimen, none of them would be confirmed.

Not that he gave a shit about that. The scientists could come out here and try and capture one. Hell, he'd pay for the damned trip at this point, but he wasn't risking another of his marines to figure it out. Instead, he wanted to destroy all of them. Every single one.

He connected to the AI. *Black? You sure they're headed for Mira and not us?*

Yes, Captain, she said. *We can confirm this by moving out of the area.*

He nodded. They needed to move anyway. Taulbee had already passed by them on his way to pick up the escape pods. If *S&R Black* followed, hopefully they could get Kalimura's squad on board without issue and then follow the escape pod heading for Pluto.

"Oakes," he said.

The lieutenant disconnected from his block and turned. "Aye, sir?"

"Get us in position to help Taulbee. I want to make sure we get them all aboard ASAP."

"Aye, sir," the pilot said. "I suggest we face *Mira* with our starboard-side so we can fire cannons if necessary."

Dunn grinned. "I knew there was a reason I kept you around. Do it."

"Aye, aye, Captain," Oakes said with a grin.

Dunn reconnected to Black. *You have a fix on the beacon?*

No, the AI said. *I do, however, have a fix on the skiff.*

Dunn raised his eyebrows. *How is that possible?*

Latent radiation, Black said. *The skiff is not responding to my commands, therefore it's likely the electronics have been completely destroyed. I'm not even certain how much is left of the vehicle. However, there does appear to be at least one piece of debris that soaked up a high dose of radiation. My assumption is that this is the skiff, and not the beacon.*

"Not the beacon," he echoed. He activated his block and the spherical map of the area appeared before his eyes. *Mark it, please.* A yellow pulsing shape appeared at the far edge of the map. It was quickly moving out of the area. *What's its speed?*

70m/s, Black said. *Barring a collision with an obstacle, the object will continue its journey deeper into the Kuiper Belt.*

He grunted. *I imagine you're going to tell me that's a bad thing.*

The AI paused. He hated when she did that. *Yes, Captain. May I remind you that Mira is still on course for Pluto. If the creatures are more interested in the ship than they are with the beacon, they will ultimately make their way further into Sol System. Once they reach it, they will have access to more light from Sol. This may change their course en route to the center of Sol System. My forecasts predict they will reach Saturn's colonies in 4-6 months at present speed.*

However, Black continued, *some of the creatures have demonstrated the ability to travel much faster than should be possible.*

Dunn sighed. *We need the beacon.*

Yes, Captain. I believe it's best if we recapture the beacon before destroying Mira.

Thank you, Black.

You're welcome, Captain.

He terminated the connection. "Nobel?"

After a few heartbeats, the engineer answered. "Aye, sir?"

"The sled ready?"

Nobel chuckled. "About as ready as it can be, sir. It'll get the payload to Pluto. Assuming we have a payload."

"We'll have a payload," Dunn said. "Just make sure that sled is fast enough to outrun those big KBOs."

Nobel paused. "Sir? You think that's going to be a problem?"

"Doesn't matter what I think," Dunn said. "I never thought we'd be in this situation in the first place."

Nobel took a deep breath before replying. "Copy that, sir. I can't put much armor on it. And we're damned near out of materials. I can't make another."

"How fast can it go?"

"Fast enough, sir. Once we get it up to speed, it should travel around 600m/s."

Two days to Pluto, Dunn thought. That wasn't going to be fast enough. Not in the least. "How do we get it to go faster?"

Nobel said nothing for a moment. "Sir? I can't attach any more engines to it. There's no room. I'd have to slag it and start over with the design."

Fuck that, Dunn said to himself. "So that's as fast as it's going." It wasn't a question, just a dead voice stating a shitty situation.

"Unless," Nobel said and trailed off. When he spoke again, Dunn heard the smile in his voice. "We could give it a bit of a push, sir."

Dunn cocked an eyebrow. "What do you mean?"

"I mean we wait until *S&R Black* reaches acceleration and we launch it then. There's not much out here to impede its speed, so if it's already traveling at near *S&R Black*'s top speed—"

Dunn grinned. "Then it will be able to get up to a higher top speed."

"Aye, sir," Nobel said.

"Good job, Nobel. Saved me some worry."

"What worry is that, sir?"

Dunn clenched his fists. "That once we destroy *Mira*, those things are going to make a beeline for it. And we want them to be chasing the beacon, not us."

"Copy that, sir," Nobel said. "Get me the beacon and we'll make it happen."

"Dunn, out," the captain said and terminated the link. "Get the beacon," he said aloud. "Sounds so easy."

"Sir?" Oakes called out. "We're ready to move."

"Do it," Dunn said. "And start plotting a course with Black. We need to know where that skiff is."

Oakes blinked at him. Dunn narrowed his eyes. "Aye, sir," Oakes said and turned to look at his holo display.

The captain placed Taulbee's feed on his personal console and watched. The first of the escape pods was coming up. Very soon, they'd finally find out if anyone had made it out alive.

CHAPTER FIFTY-NINE

The escape pod had practically ground to a halt. The trans-aluminum window had offered a lovely view of *Mira* as the escape pod ejected, but it was short-lived. A few seconds later, *Mira* had slid away until only the very faint edge of its bow was visible. It had all but disappeared.

Kalimura sighed. She'd hailed *S&R Black* on every SFMC channel she knew. Nothing. Her suit comms were a scrambled mess and something was wrong with her block. Even when she tried to initiate a block connection with her squad, let alone Black herself, it was as if the thoughts had been swallowed by a black hole.

At least the escape pod had air. She'd been able to turn off her O2 and use the pod's supply instead. Luckily, *Mira*'s pods were a bit larger than she'd ever seen, and they carried a hell of a lot of O2. The fact they'd been designed to carry a survivor in deep space no doubt had something to do with that as well.

But now she was confused. The pod had accelerated quickly, pushing her back into the couch and momentarily locking her in place. A few seconds later, the engine had not only stopped, but the attitude thrusters had fired. The pod executed a turn before the engine puffed a few times and died again.

She wasn't certain, but she thought the pods were supposed to disable themselves if a "friendly" ship was nearby. If that was true, then *S&R Black* was somewhere relatively close by. However, it could also be due to a malfunction. When she'd looked for the ship, it hadn't been there. It hadn't been anywhere. The last order she'd had from the captain was to use the port-side. So where was the ship? The escape pods should have nearly rammed into her.

That was the most hellish part of this. She couldn't imagine the captain, let alone Taulbee, would leave his marines stranded if he knew there was a chance. Which meant they'd either been forced to leave the area, or they'd been destroyed.

After what they'd seen inside *Mira*, the lifeforms, the strange experiments, and the photon-stealing, well, presence they'd encountered, did she really believe those things couldn't have attacked the ship? No. She knew they were capable. And they probably had.

"Because we woke it up," she said.

You don't know that, a voice said inside her head. *Maybe it was already awake when we got there. We just, well, maybe accelerated the process. Put it into overdrive.*

Maybe we did, she thought. But it still didn't make sense. If the Trio knew what had happened, what had really happened, to the ship, why wouldn't they have warned humanity? And if they did, then why didn't SF Gov do anything about it? The Trident Shipyards had been designed to construct entire fleets of specialized mining, supply, and military vessels to make the search for new resources.

Trident Shipyards was another derelict. And in many ways, so was Trident Station. A small crew inhabiting a workable, livable, modular area that had been designed to house as many 5,000 military and civilian personnel. The Shipyards also had areas for habitation—the mechanics and engineers needed some place to stay.

As far as she knew, they'd never been used. Never. *Mira* was the last ship to make a maiden voyage from Trident Station, and the only one ever built. SF Gov had completely abandoned the project once *Mira* had disappeared. Now only an SFMC maintenance crew, support crew, and the three hardly used S&R crews remained.

As a Martian, she knew damned well how intensely stupid SF Gov could be, but she couldn't imagine they wouldn't have taken this threat seriously. Unless they didn't know about it.

"Trio," she whispered. "You motherfuckers."

Why? Why had they essentially brought the threat to humanity's front door? And even so, why hadn't they warned anyone? What did they want? To exterminate us?

She sneered.

If they were capable of keeping SF Gov ignorant of what had happened, then she couldn't imagine they didn't have the resources to keep the exo-solar lifeforms a secret until it was way too late to stop them.

PEO had sent the transmission to Trident Station to alert them to *Mira*'s approach. Human beings had gotten that message and sent *S&R Black* out here, presumably to tow the infamous ship.

"So why warn us at all?" she said aloud.

Yes, that was the question, wasn't it? There was something she wasn't seeing. Something she didn't understand, or know. All she knew was that she wanted to get the fuck out of here and back to *S&R Black*.

If it's still there, a gravelly voice tittered in her mind.

Kali winced. If. The whole goddamned universe had become ifs and maybes and wild-assed assumptions. She didn't want to die in this tin can, but she wanted to die ignorant even less.

Something caught her peripheral vision and she quickly flipped her eyes from the corner she'd been using back to the other side. Nothing was there. She waited a few seconds for the goose pimples to cease crawling up and down her flesh. She was about to relax when something moved again.

Kali quickly slid her eyes to stare at that side and leaned back quickly. There was a shadow out there, a large one, of something that could move in z-g as easily as a fish in water. She shivered and reflexively reached for the rifle locked to her back. Her fingers slid off the stock, shaking.

There was nothing she could do. Oh, she could blow the hatch and head outside to face the threat, but she'd be out there all alone, unable to sweep and clear a 360° view around her. And with creatures that could swarm from any direction, that surely meant death.

No, she had to sit here and wait in this tin can. Although the confines were luxurious compared to what they'd experienced inside *Mira*, it was just another trapped space. Rations, water, air, the escape pod had all the amenities. But with the engines off, it was just a warm, hospitable coffin-in-waiting. If *S&R Black* was still out there somewhere, she'd just have to wait for them. If they weren't, and the pod had malfunctioned, she couldn't even make it back to Pluto. Her only real chance would be to head back to *Mira*.

"Fuck that," she said aloud. Depending on how far the escape pod had traveled before shutting down, she could conceivably make it back to the derelict using her suit thrusters. The pod had extra fuel for those too. But why? Most of *Mira* had been depressurized, was at near absolute zero temperatures, and she'd have to face hordes of those creatures just to make it to a safe harbor. If, that was, any still existed.

Whatever had come out of the cargo bay hatch and into the science section had been something new. She'd only caught a glimpse of it before Dickerson threw her into the pod and ejected her into space.

She grunted. Dickerson. *That fucker better still be alive so I can kick him in the balls,* she thought. He had taken the damaged pod against her orders. Insubordination. Mutiny. Another void-damned mark on his jacket. And yet, he'd probably saved her life.

He might be out here too somewhere. Or maybe his escape pod didn't eject at all. Or, possibly, he had made it out only to die in an explosion or be headed out into the deep Kuiper Belt, one day to travel into the Oort Cloud as nothing more than frozen corpse. When the air ran out, the heat ran out, and the provisions ran out, death was a certainty. She wondered if he'd simply open the hatch and let the void take him.

"You're so cheery," she said to herself. And why not? Her squad might be dead. *S&R Black* might be destroyed. She might be floating out here among the monsters for the rest of her life, which wouldn't last more than a few days.

Get it together, she said to herself. *Calm the fuck down before you—*

The pod shuddered. She instinctively held her arms out and secured herself. It shuddered again hard enough to clink her rifle against the thin hull. The sound of sharp metal rain echoed inside the small vessel. Kali shook again. She couldn't help it. A second later, she realized what that sound was.

"Yes!" she said with a grin. "Flechettes!" The stress from their time inside *Mira* coupled with the dire fear of dying finally melted away, leaving her shaking. But the weary smile remained.

She lifted her helmet from the couch and quickly donned it. Either Gunny's squad or Taulbee's SV-52 sat somewhere close by, marines firing their weapons at any hostiles. Finally, she was going to be rescued and she could get a stint in the autodoc.

You might be the only one, a voice said in her mind.

The grin faded. Where was Elliott? Carb? Dickerson? Did any of them make it?

Even as she heard something metal bump against the hull, she was afraid for the hatch to open. In a few seconds, her mind played images of every terrible possibility. They could have been eaten by the creatures. Their pods could have malfunctioned, leaving them without air, power, or a prayer. Kali felt as though that last was especially true for Dickerson.

She clenched her fists and waited. And waited. Kali winced when she heard the three bangs against the hatch. She'd known it was coming, hoping for it to come, and now it sounded like something fatal rather than salvation. Funereal was the best word to describe it.

Kali lifted her fist and pounded three times on the hatch, her armored gloves slamming hard enough for the echo to fill the tiny space. As the sound disappeared, she pulled the release handle. Lights outlining the hatch turned from green to red. Kali knocked on the door twice more, stepped back, and mag-locked herself to the deck.

"Three for permission, three for entry, two for ready," she mumbled. Two more taps at the hull. She counted off aloud, her voice weak and shaky. Another clink of metal, the coo-chunk of the safety bar receding, and the hatch's outline pulsed with violent crimson. When she reached three, the hatch swung aside. The trapped atmosphere inside the pod rushed out in a gust, threatening to pull her from the deck. If she hadn't been mag-locked, she would have been sent flying into the black.

"Corporal?" Wendt's voice yelled over the comms.

Kali exhaled the breath she didn't realize she'd been holding. Wendt's large frame blocked most of the light from the SV-52 10 meters behind him, but her HUD filters had to compensate anyway.

"Good to see you, Wendt," she whispered.

He held out a long arm. "Let's get you out of here." He paused for a second. "Shit, Boss. You are fucked up."

She would have laughed if she knew it wouldn't feel like a flechette round detonating in her chest. "You got that right. How about the others?"

"Come on, Corporal. Debrief later. We still have hostiles in the vicinity."

"Copy," she said and detached from the deck. She mag-locked her glove to Wendt's and he gently pulled her to him. Using his suit thrusters, he traveled back to the SV-52 with Kali in his arms.

Even knowing the pain it would cause, she couldn't help but chuckle. Elliott, his suit easily identified with the deflated glove, hung from the SV-52's bow. They had him tethered like a prisoner at mast. Carb crouched next to him, her feet and one hand mag-locked, her flechette rifle in the other.

They were safe. They were all—

"Dickerson!" Kali yelled. "Where is—?"

"Corporal!" Taulbee yelled over the comms.

The panic that had nearly gripped her departed at once. "Aye, sir?"

"Unless it's about something attacking us, I don't want to hear about it until we get back to the ship."

"Aye, sir," she said.

Wendt flew her past Carb and to port-side aft. It was the only bit of space, save the bottom of the craft, they had left. The SV-52 hadn't been designed for marines to dangle off of it. That's what they had skiffs for. But in a pinch, it could serve the function.

Kali twisted her midsection and nearly screamed with the pain. Once she was mag-locked and tethered, Taulbee turned the SV-52 toward *S&R Black*. It hung in space, *Mira*'s dark shadow drifting a few kilometers away. Even in the

Kuiper Belt's dim twilight, she made out hundreds, maybe thousands of shapes hovering or flying around the derelict.

The last of her adrenaline was spent. Her nannies had been taxed beyond their capacity. Her ribs were a disaster and she was covered head to toe in bruises. Kali, finally sure she was safe, passed out.

*****

When she awoke, she lay in the infirmary. Her chest ached, but not with pain and her breath was a little more difficult to catch. She looked down and saw the heavy bandages wrapping her ribs.

They'd cut her out of her suit, put her in the autodoc for a little treatment, and thrown her in one of the beds. Beneath the heavy blanket lying atop her, she was naked except for her panties. She coughed twice and pain instantly rattled her nerves, but quickly receded. If nothing else, the autodoc had definitely replenished her THC supply.

The lights on her side of the infirmary were dim, but there was enough light for her to make out the three other collapsible beds. One was empty. The other two?

"Corporal," Elliott croaked. He sat up in his bed, his handless arm encased in an indigo-blue nannie wrap. The top of the bed's headboard, if it could be called that, had the tops of two dispensers. No doubt Elliott was getting a fresh infusion of blood, minerals, and nannies. He waved his intact hand with a tired smile. "How you feeling?"

"Yeah, Boss," Carb said. "How are ya?"

Carb's face had more color than Elliott's and she seemed much more alert than Kali felt. Maybe her injuries hadn't been as bad. Kali nearly chuckled. Or Carb is just that badass, she thought.

"Feel like I've been kicked in the head, the tits, and the ass."

Carb giggled. "They can make that armor thick, but it's never enough when you take one right to the swells."

"No shit." Kali breathed shallowly, hoping her inflamed chest wouldn't scream in pain. "How long have we been here?"

"I woke up about ten minutes ago," Carb said. She nodded to Elliott. "He just woke up too."

"I passed out on the way here?" Kali asked.

Carb laughed. "Don't feel bad, Corporal. I didn't make it much further. Pretty damned sure Nobel knocked us all out."

"That's Lieutenant Nobel," a voice growled from the doorway.

Kali swung her gaze to regard the limping form entering the room. "Good to see you, sir," she said.

Nobel smiled, but it wasn't as cheery as she'd expected. He looked pained, as though he had some distasteful duty ahead of him. She eyed the empty bed, the one where Dickerson should have been.

The lieutenant seemed to notice the flick of her eyes and he shook his head. "No. We haven't retrieved Dickerson yet."

Kali and Carb traded a glance. "But you know where he is?" Carb asked.

Nobel nodded. "His escape pod didn't stop. It's still moving toward Pluto and our scans say it's clear of hostiles."

"That's great, sir!" Kali said. "So when are we going to get him?"

Nobel paused a moment before replying. "We have a mission first. Well, two, in fact. Lieutenant Taulbee will be down here shortly."

"Mission?" Carb said. She swung her legs off the bed and stood with a small moan. She faced the engineer with her bare breasts thrust toward him.

Nobel rolled his eyes. "Dress yourself, marine, or get back under cover."

Carb looked down at her erect nipples and slowly back at the lieutenant. Her cheeks flushed slightly. "Sorry, sir," she said and climbed back into the bed, covering herself as best she could.

"Sir?" Kali asked. "Where's Gunny?"

The engineer dropped his gaze. "Gunnery Sergeant Cartwright is in a medical coma," he said. "We will be without his services until further notice."

Kali swallowed hard. What the hell had happened since they were stranded? She knew Wendt and Murdock were still alive. But where was Lyke?

"Understood, sir," she said.

"Good," Nobel said. "Rest. LT Taulbee will be in here in a few minutes and he'll brief and debrief before we start."

"Excuse me, sir," Carb said, "but before we start what?"

Nobel's face melted into an evil grin. "Before we start getting some fucking payback."

CHAPTER SIXTY

The room was quieter than usual. Taulbee felt as though he had stepped into a morgue rather than a briefing room. Captain Dunn stood at the table, his eyes boring into the floating model of *Mira*. Red and orange dots and spots covered the holo image. Taulbee knew what those were and he didn't like it. Not one bit.

After docking with *S&R Black*, it didn't take long for Wendt and Murdock to get the three injured marines to the infirmary. Nobel immediately went to work on them and relayed status updates to Taulbee. He'd damned near shed a tear when Nobel said all three would make it. Kalimura's squad had only been inside *Mira* for several hours, but it felt as though they'd been gone for years. All that worry piling up on you made perspective difficult, and Taulbee still couldn't let it go.

While Copenhaver refueled the SV-52, Wendt and Murdock were restocking weapons and munitions. When it was time to go, they'd be ready. Except that wasn't really the problem.

He walked across the threshold, entered the room, and was about to stand at parade rest when Dunn growled. "At ease. Get over here."

The captain hadn't broken his stare with the glowing hologram. If Taulbee didn't know any better, and truth be told, he didn't, Dunn's eyes were tracing a route around *Mira*. Perhaps he'd superimposed a block image over the hologram. He shook the thought away. He was about to find out what the captain had in mind. Best to hear it from the source rather than spending time guessing.

Taulbee walked to the table and stood across from the captain. He wanted to ask questions, give a status update, anything to break the awkward silence that had descended over the room like a shroud. Dunn's eyes continued flicking across the model, his expression flat and emotionless.

Usually cool and decisive, Dunn looked exhausted and frazzled. The stress of this mission had etched into every line of his face. And after the Schiaparelli Rebellion and the Satellite War, Dunn's once rather boyish face was already a map of tense encounters. Before this was over, he thought Dunn would look ten years older.

The captain placed his hands on the edge of the table, bent his head slightly, and seemed to be grasping for what to say, or maybe willing himself to say what he didn't want to. Taulbee didn't like either possibility, but the latter was more worrisome.

"James," Dunn said at last, his eyes flicking up from the table to stare into Taulbee's. "We have to retrieve the beacon."

Taulbee clenched his fists. "What about Dickerson?"

Dunn sighed. "We'll go after him as soon as we get the beacon." His tired expression transformed into a gleeful mask of malevolence. "And after we destroy that hulk out there."

Taulbee forced a grin. The captain needed him to be on board with this. He knew that, but all he wanted to do right now was kick Oakes in the ass and have him chase Dickerson's escape pod at full speed and damn the beacon and damn the ghost ship. Getting Dickerson back, his last missing marine, seemed so much more important.

"Sir? Do we know Dickerson's speed and trajectory?"

Dunn nodded. "We do. He's headed to Pluto. Black is coordinating with Mickey to keep an eye on the pod. If there's a change in the situation, we'll know it fairly quickly."

Fairly quickly. The words echoed in Taulbee's mind. Fairly quickly meant that new information on the pod's status would take 4-8 minutes, depending on where the escape pod was in its journey to Pluto. And if they were still fucking around with *Mira* and the beacon when something happened, they'd arrive too late to save the marine.

The captain stood to his full height, his hands at his sides. Taulbee felt as though Dunn had read his thoughts. "It's the best we can do, James. So put that out of your mind. Right now, I need you focused."

"Aye, sir," Taulbee said in a dead voice. Focus. Yeah, he needed to regain that. Focus on how he was going to do anything with only four healthy marines, including himself. "Please continue."

Dunn blinked once before speaking. "You're going to need Wendt, Murdock, and Copenhaver. You comfortable with Copenhaver as your gunner?"

Taulbee grinned. "Aye, sir. She's damned good."

"Thought so," Dunn said, returning the smile. "Then Wendt and Murdock will have to perform a ride-along. I want them in rad suits in case that thing out there is too hot for our combat suits. You'll travel to the beacon, Wendt and Murdock will retrieve it if you can't net it. Once you get back here, we'll load it on the sled, and tow it until we're ready to destroy *Mira*."

Not a bad idea, Taulbee thought. But something was off in the captain's face. The easy grin that had been on Taulbee's face slid away. "What's the catch, sir?"

Dunn sighed again. "The catch is that we don't exactly know where the beacon is. Black has the coordinates for the skiff, but there's little to no guarantee the beacon is still attached. When it loosed that last blast, it could have melted the skiff into slag or broken free of its moorings. For all we know, it could be floating out there in the Kuiper, pointed directly at Sol, and ready to blast another signal."

"Shit," Taulbee said. He inwardly winced. "Sorry, sir."

"No," Dunn said. "Shit is the right response. We can send you out there by yourself to find it, but that's going to waste more time if you can't net it. I'd rather you have the marines aboard in case you do find it."

"And if we don't?" Taulbee asked.

"Then we and the rest of humanity are truly fucked," Dunn said.

CHAPTER SIXTY-ONE

Once Nobel had left the room, Kali and her squad, well, what remained of it, continued speaking to one another in quiet voices. Carb had concussion symptoms, but they were mild. Although she wanted to sleep for five days, she could probably get back in a combat suit if it came to it. Kali envied her.

Elliott was done. His combat days were over for the time being. Between the blood loss, the shock of exposure to vacuum and near absolute zero temperatures, not to mention his missing hand, Elliott was not leaving his bed. Probably not until they returned to Trident Station.

Assuming that happens, she thought. So with Elliott out, that left her and Dickerson. Dickerson was somewhere out there, his escape pod expending its fuel to accelerate him to Pluto. Until *S&R Black* caught up to the pod and attempted a rescue, there was no way to tell if he was alive or dead.

She tried to push that worry away again. It wasn't going to help her focus on whatever Taulbee or Dunn had in mind for the mission, and it sure as hell wasn't going to fix her broken ribs or remove the aches from her tortured muscles and bones. And, let's not forget her own concussion.

You'll lie, if you have to, she told herself. If they need another body, you'll get in that void-damned suit and be a marine. She clenched her fists. They'd have to let her.

"At ease," a tired voice said from the threshold.

The three marines swung their eyes to regard the speaker. Lieutenant Taulbee walked into the room, back straight, every ounce of his body propped up into his typical command posture. But damn, he looked tired.

A relieved grin lit his face. "Thank you, all of you, for what you did aboard *Mira.* You have no idea how much you helped us. I'm damned glad to have the three of you in my command and even happier all three of you are here and safe."

No one said a word. The grin faded slightly and Taulbee's face hardened. "Carbonaro? Kalimura? You two are on deck. I want you in your combat suits and ready to head to the cargo bay in ten minutes. Nobel's setting up some goodies for you down there to help speed your recovery."

"Aye, sir," both she and Carb replied.

"I don't think we'll need you, but you're the last two combat marines I have available, apart from the captain." He noticed the smart-assed grin on Carb's face. "Yes, Lance Corporal, you two are the last meat sticks I have available."

Carb chuckled. "Sorry, sir."

He waved the comment away and pointed at Elliott. "Your job, marine, is to rest. Black will be debriefing you shortly. I suggest block to block so you don't have to talk."

"Aye, sir," Elliott said in a husky voice.

"Questions?" Taulbee asked.

"Yes, sir," Kalimura said. "What's the plan?"

He smiled. "Black will transmit the mission briefing momentarily. Just get ready." He knocked a fist on the bulkhead. "Understood?"

"Aye, sir," Kali and Carb said in loud voices. Elliott may have responded too, but she didn't hear his voice.

"Good to have you home." With that, Taulbee retreated from the infirmary, the dull clump of his footsteps receding until they disappeared.

Kali looked at Carb. "You ready for this?"

"Aye, Corporal," she said. Her eyes hardened. "Whatever we have to do to get the fuck out of here so we can rescue Dickerson."

Kali grinned like a shark. "Glad to see we're on the same page."

*****

After walking, well, limping, from the infirmary to her locker, Kali removed her sweat-drenched panties and tossed them into the recycler. If she'd had time for a shower, it would have been more than welcome. Just the thought of warm water spraying down on her tired flesh, steam lapping at her tired eyes, made her giddy. She glanced at the shower stalls with longing as she quickly dressed into a clean jumpsuit.

Someone had left her mag-boots next to her locker. She grinned as she wondered whether it was Nobel or one of the non-rates. A few lockers down, Carb was already stepping into her own boots. "Hey, Boss," she called, "I want a shower when all this is over."

"Tell you what," Kali said, "you and I have dibs the moment we get back."

"Copy that," Carb said.

As soon as the pair had finished dressing, Carb followed Kali into the hallway. They walked in silence to the cargo bay, unspoken concern in their body language, their minds flooded with the same worries. Dickerson was still out there. The beacon was still out there. And instead of actively assisting in getting the beacon aboard so they could chase after their squad-mate, she and Carb were benched and Taulbee would only put them into service if there were no other option.

Kali understood the reasoning, but that didn't mean she had to like it. Taulbee and the captain were making sound tactical, strategic decisions, but it still burned her ass. *If only we'd gotten back sooner,* she thought. *If only.*

Black connected to her and relayed notes regarding the beacon. Gunny's squad had retrieved it, sure, but at great cost. The skiff was no doubt destroyed and Gunny might never wake up again. And if he did, he might never be able to speak. The beacon had cost them a lot. Hell, this mission had cost them. Elliott was missing a hand, Lyke and Niro were both dead, Dickerson was still missing, they were down two skiffs, and, except for Taulbee, Dunn, and Oakes, the remaining marines had all suffered injuries of one form or another.

The cargo bay hatch was open revealing the SV-52 sitting at the far end, Copenhaver standing beside it. Wendt and Murdock had ditched their combat suits for the heavy rad suits engineers wore in case of a reactor leak; the garments could withstand much more radiation exposure than the standard-issue SFMC combat suit.

The sight gave her pause. The beacon, it seemed, was even more dangerous than she'd first considered. Not only had it called these strange creatures to hitch a ride on the derelict heading back to Sol System, but it could attract other lifeforms already inhabiting the Kuiper Belt. If they didn't retrieve it and stop it, what would it do next? Call even more alien lifeforms? Or alert its creators that it had found a new home?

She shivered at the thought, but it was clear the exo-solar lifeforms they'd seen so far didn't create the beacon. Unless she was very wrong, the creatures they'd encountered didn't have the means nor intelligence to do that. So who did?

"Who" isn't the question, she told herself. *"What" is the proper question.* Somewhere out there in the black of deep space, perhaps dozens or hundreds of light years away, an unknown lifeform had created the beacon and ejected it into the galaxy like a message in a bottle. Only the "message" was dangerous. Unbelievably dangerous.

If Black was right, these creatures fed on photons, at least in part. Which meant the closer they came to Sol's light, the more they might breed, travel, and eat, and from what she'd seen thus far, the creatures certainly had a penchant for destroying other lifeforms. If they made it to Sol System's interior, what would happen? Would they attack the fledgling colonies at Iapetus? Titan? What would they do when they found thousands of human sentients rather than a few measly morsels aboard a floating hulk?

She didn't know and not knowing terrified her. How long before the beacon's creators decided to show up? Decades? Centuries? Or minutes? And would humankind be capable of putting up a fight? She doubted it. The technology to create the beacon had certainly seemed well beyond their grasp. Even Black was flummoxed as to how it worked. However, what it was doing, what they thought it was doing, was clear enough—it was bringing a horde of nasties into humanity's space. That alone was reason enough to be concerned.

Now they were going to retrieve it, put it on a sled, and send it to Pluto. Was that really the right move? She didn't know. The captain probably didn't know. But what else could they do?

Unfortunately, she doubted they'd know that answer until they had the beacon. Maybe not even then. But destroying *Mira*, removing it from the equation, might give them some idea. Or maybe not.

With all these thoughts and questions spinning inside her head, it was difficult to focus when Taulbee finally appeared, his flight helmet in his hands. He yelled "at ease" before anyone had a chance to reach parade rest.

"You've all seen the briefing?"

Their voices shouted as one. "Aye, sir!"

"Good. Any questions?" The marines fell silent. Taulbee waited another beat before speaking. "Be ready to move like lightning. I don't know what we're facing, so be prepared to go off-script." Wendt chuckled, and quickly recovered his composure. Taulbee shot him a look, but it was one of weary amusement rather than reproach. "Carbonaro and Kalimura. I want you at the airlock ready to jump out and offer assistance should we need it."

"Aye, sir!"

"Let's go," Taulbee said and approached the SV-52 with brisk steps.

Kali glanced at Carb. "Locked and loaded?"

Her squad-mate pointed at the rifle rack in front of them. "Just have to mag-lock those and we're good to go."

"Outstanding," Kali said and put on her helmet. Carb did the same. She activated the squad channel. "Load up."

"Aye, Boss," Carb said. Kali heard a grin in her voice.

CHAPTER SIXTY-TWO

Taulbee piloted the SV-52 out of the cargo bay with a few expert attitude thruster burns. The craft glided through the open hatch, rotated, and began heading into the Kuiper. A quick glance at the rear cam feed showed *Mira*, the huge ship kilometers away from him now, still hanging in space like a harbinger, its shadowy form nearly bereft of detail.

Black had marked the known location of the skiff on his HUD. Finding it would be easy enough, but the beacon? Unless it was spitting out radiation or some other wavelength they could detect, good luck. Taulbee chuckled with a sour expression. "Unless it goes off again."

That would be one good way to find it. *It just detonates, spews another burst of "hey, we're over here!" to every exo-solar lifeform near Sol, and we'll know exactly where it is.*

The running monologue in his head wasn't productive, and he knew it. They had to inspect the skiff's remains before they even worried about the beacon. For all they knew, the damned thing was still attached to the Atmo-steel. However low the likelihood, it had to be the first check.

Wendt hung on the starboard-side like a barnacle. Murdock did the same on the port-side. The two marines, dressed in their heavily shielded anti-rad suits, wouldn't be able to do jackshit if there was real combat. The suits didn't have the usual HUD or block interface built into the standard-issue SFMC combat model. They had rifles mag-locked to their backs, but aiming and shooting would definitely be more difficult.

Once he was fifty meters from *S&R Black*, he opened the throttle and the SV-52 quickly accelerated. Black had narrowed down the skiff's location by using multiple radiation scans. While the AI claimed the skiff had at first been lit up like a star, the radioactive decay seemed to have slowed. With each successive scan, the signal weakened.

Black? Why is it diminishing? Taulbee asked over a private channel.

The AI paused. *Lieutenant, there are three probable explanations. One being the radiation is of a short half-life and it's quickly dissipating. Another is that the beacon's radiation is something we've never seen before.*

And the third?

The third, Black said, *is that an exo-solar lifeform is consuming the radiation as we suspected they did on* Mira.

He didn't bother responding to that. Black updated his HUD with the latest scan information and while the target was still moving at 60m/s, its trajectory had changed slightly. An unpowered object moving through space, unless affected by the gravity of other bodies or other celestial phenomena, should keep moving on the same course. Something had caused that effect, something they didn't know about. Taulbee reflexively tightened his fingers on the controls.

"Wendt. Murdock. I'm going to start the acceleration. Make sure you're watching for debris."

"Aye, sir," the two marines said.

"Sir?" Copenhaver said. "You want me watching ahead or behind?"

"Both," Taulbee said, chuckling. "Keep that cannon cam moving. I want to know if we have any pursuers or attackers."

"Aye, sir."

So far, nothing from *Mira* had ventured away to follow *S&R Black*. That meant they would more than likely leave the SV-52 alone. At least for now. If the damned thing went off again, he wasn't sure that would be the case, but the fact none of the creatures even reacted when it last fired left him wondering what was going on.

Black thought that maybe *Mira* contained enough residual radiation to keep the exo-solar lifeforms from leaving. Considering several large packs of creatures, different from either the pinecones or the starfish, had descended upon *Mira* as though the ship itself was a beacon, he thought the AI might be on to something.

The SV-52 reached 70m/s and the target slowly moved closer. As they traveled through the shadowy belt, the SV-52's strong floodlights illuminating nothing, the comms remained silent. He felt as though the entire squad was holding their breaths. He knew he was.

When the skiff was less than 200 meters away, he alerted the squad and slowed the craft. The skiff had once more changed trajectories, but again, not by much. The speed was still constant though, which didn't make sense. If the slab of Atmo-steel had collided with debris or a large enough object to change its heading, the speed should have at least diminished.

"Be ready for anything," Taulbee said. The marines didn't reply. He hadn't expected them to.

Shards of what he thought was Atmo-steel glittered in the lights like metal rain. "Watch yourselves," Taulbee said. "Debris up ahead." With that in mind, he cut their speed with a hard burn and the SV-52 slowed to 61m/s, about as low as he could go if he wanted to catch up in the next aeon.

Debris pinged off the canopy and rattled against the hull. Fortunately, the debris was traveling nearly as fast as they were, or it could have shred the barely armored rad suits. Once again, the void was granting him favors. He wondered how much longer that would last.

"Sir?" Copenhaver called. "I got visual."

He flipped his HUD to the cannon cam. There, in the distance, light glinting off its exposed undercarriage, the skiff, or what was left of it, tumbled through the Kuiper. He compared the target coordinates with the skiff. They didn't match.

"Copenhaver? You see anything else?"

"No, sir. Just the skiff. Zoomed in, it looks like it suffered some major damage. Most of the finish is gone and the Atmo-steel is peeled like a banana."

He wished he had time to switch off the forward cams and focus on the object, or anything near it. Instead, he had to rely on Copenhaver for that while he made sure he didn't run the SV-52 into something else out here.

"Wendt? Murdock? Ready?"

"Aye, sir," Wendt said. Murdock echoed the reply in a weak, tremulous voice.

"I'm going to slow us down and match speed. Call out if you see something else." An excited parade of ayes replied and he grinned in spite of himself. The adrenaline was pumping now, and all those little nannies were getting ready to pounce on the gland and make sure it had everything it needed to manufacture more. The desire for those moments to last forever while at the same time wishing for them to end warred against one another, coloring every image, every sound, every action. Taulbee unconsciously drew in a deep breath as the rush injected into his veins.

The cannon feed, directed at the skiff, caught the slowly spinning and tumbling hunk of Atmo-steel. The skiff's normally smooth deck flowered out on one end, the Atmo-steel layers separating from one another. The perfect outline of the beacon remained flash-frozen on the remaining smooth surface, making it look as though the object had disappeared into the ether.

Its meager control sections had disappeared, leaving nothing in their wake but torn and ripped layers of steel. Taulbee sucked in a breath. He'd seen this before.

In the wake of the last hours of the brief but savage onslaught of battles all across the Martian Ring, his ship had traveled through the wreckage of the first "skirmish" that kicked off the affair. Seventeen SFMC skiffs were lost, all annihilated by the nukes launched from inside the ring of detritus circling the planet. The fuckers had hidden them in the remains of the very industries they wished to destroy. Or at least cow them once and for all.

The rest of the war had been scavenge, salvage, anything to stay alive while SFMC fought their way through the mess of true guerrilla warfare, the very first wave of which nearly destroyed the entire SFMC fleet. Taulbee had survived both the Mars Rebellion and The Satellite War, but somehow, being out here in the relative emptiness of the Kuiper Belt, finding this was even more disturbing.

Their rad alarms should have been going apeshit, but the elevated radiation levels were barely in the yellow and well below the shielding of either suit type. He and Copenhaver enjoyed more protection being inside a meter of Atmo-steel surrounding their cabin, but the rad suits were just ticking between high green and low yellow. The rads necessary to cause the kind of damage the skiff had taken should have ravaged the rad suits instead of just warming them up. Whatever had caused the rads didn't have much of a duration. The nuked hunks of metal he'd seen in the Martian Ring had tripped every single rad alarm on any ship that got near them. And that was hours and hours after the skirmish. In less than an hour, the rads from the beacon blast had dissipated to almost normal. Elevated, but normal.

"A little slower, sir," Wendt said.

Taulbee focused on the cannon cam, adjusting the SV-52's speed while keeping the target in mind. The port-side cam showed the skiff still tumbling and spinning. The metal seemed to glow, but that could have just been the powerful floods glinting off the separated layers of Atmo-steel. *No,* he thought, *it is glowing.*

"Okay, sir," Wendt said. "I'm going for a grab."

"Be careful, marine," Taulbee said. "If your rad meter goes off, get the fuck away from it."

"Aye, sir," Wendt said. Through the cannon's cam, he watched Wendt push himself off the side of the SV-52 and float to the skiff, a tether line drifting behind like an uncoiling snake. The marine touched the skiff with his glove and mag-locked to the skiff. Suddenly, Wendt was spinning and tumbling with the damaged craft. However awkward it looked from here, Wendt must have been fighting the dizziness from all the flipping and turning. He mag-walked using his gloves, struggling to climb into the skiff and find the tether hole in the remaining gunwale.

It took more than two minutes for him to attach the tether. When he finally climbed out of the skiff, he returned to the SV-52 with a hand-over-hand glove walk across the moving and turning line. "Sir?" Wendt said. "My rad meters didn't pop, but they definitely spiked."

Taulbee nodded to himself. Residual radiation. If one blast had made the skiff that hot, albeit for a short time, how much of that energy was trapped in the deep bowels of *Mira*? Is that what was attracting the beasties? Not the beacon itself, but its saturation of the derelict's hull?

Yet another reason to blow the bitch up, he thought.

"Sir?" Copenhaver said, "the skiff is still spinning, but the rotating pins on the tether are compensating."

"Good," he said, without really feeling relieved. This was only part of the exercise, and now that they knew the beacon was no longer attached, it also seemed pointless. But they were low on materials. If Nobel wanted to print a new skiff, or at least something they could use, they'd need all the Atmo-steel they could get.

He chuckled. They could always just blast *Mira* to pieces and take some small chunks to serve the same purpose. Then he thought of what they might be bringing back with them in the process, and stopped laughing. There was no telling what kind of hitchhikers they'd bring back with them.

Did these creatures have parasites? Viruses? Some new bacteria that lived in their, well, their insides? Did they really want to find out the hard way that the things could infect human beings?

Suddenly bringing the skiff back didn't sound too wise either. If they found the beacon—No, when they found the beacon, he'd bring up the issue of infection. Until then, it was just another concern to file away in the SEP portion of his mind. SEP, of course, standing for "somebody else's problem."

"Wendt? You back on board and secure?"

"Aye, sir," Wendt said. "Nearly threw up in my helmet, but I'm good."

"Not surprised," Taulbee said. "I believe Dickerson would call that being a rodeo clown."

Wendt laughed. "Aye, sir. I bet he would. We'll show him the cam recordings once we get him back."

Get him back. Taulbee clicked his teeth together. Wendt had served with Dickerson for two years. From what the lieutenant had seen, the two men seemed to have instantly bonded, perhaps as strongly as Dickerson and Carb had. *If we don't get him back,* Taulbee thought, *this company may never have morale again.*

Taulbee cut the SV-52's speed and the tether's slack quickly disappeared. "Hang on for a jolt!" he yelled into the comms. Two seconds later, the tether snapped taught. The thick Atmo-steel composite line flexed to weather the strain, but the SV-52 still jerked and shuddered as though a great force had stopped it in its tracks.

The skiff, the force of its movement mostly captured in the line's flexion, danced backward toward the SV-52 before rising above it in an arc. Taulbee sent a block command to the controls and the tether line slowly ratcheted up the tension to bring the skiff into a stable position.

The two craft traveled at 20m/s now, the skiff a mere two meters from the SV-52's aft. Taulbee exhaled a sigh. That was too damned close. The skiff could have flown back and smashed into the side and flattened one of his marines. *Well,* he thought, *that would have capped off a perfectly shitty day.*

With the skiff stabilized via the tow tether, he could relax a little. They had managed to accomplish step one of the mission. If only step two would be as simple as chasing down the equivalent of a flare floating in space.

"Okay, marines," Taulbee said, doing his best to flush the unhelpful thoughts from his mind, "let's find this beacon."

"Um, sir?" Murdock said.

"Yes, Private?"

The young marine breathed heavily into the mic, practically panting. "Are the stars disappearing, or is it just me?"

Taulbee blinked. "What are you—?" His voice died as he flipped to the starboard cam. Sure enough, the darkness of space seemed...darker. The floodlights still painting the skiff's tumbling form appeared to dim as though they were losing power.

"Oh, shit," Wendt said. "Sir, we saw this when we got the beacon off *Mira.*"

Excitement warred with fear in his guts. "Everybody look for it. If you saw that phenomenon before, the beacon is probably near us."

The comms fell silent as everyone studied the cam feeds. Wendt and Murdock's helmet cams bounced and flowed as they scoured the space around them for signs of the strange device. Copenhaver spun the cannon in a slow 360° arc to cover as much area as she could.

Taulbee was flipping between the fore and port camera when Murdock yelled, "I see it!"

A marker appeared on Taulbee's HUD. The beacon, at least Murdock thought it was the beacon, tumbled and spun some fifty meters away. The force of the explosion must have knocked it from the skiff, changing its trajectory and speed. All they'd had to do was wait for it to catch up. Although that wasn't quite true either. It had somehow ended up at a negative vector from the skiff's position and now it was floating by them far below the SV-52's belly and heading further away every second.

"Copenhaver? Don't lose that goddamned thing. Keep yourself zoomed in. Murdock? Wendt? Keep your heads on a swivel."

"Aye, sir," the replies rang back.

Taulbee used his block to calculate trajectory and relative distance. Whatever it was, it wasn't showing up on radar or as a radiation source. But that had to be the beacon, didn't it? With another command, he tightened the tow tether until the skiff mag-locked to the SV-52's aft. He fed the program to the nav and fired the thrusters.

The SV-52 handled like a bucking bronco rather than a glider on ice. With the skiff practically part of the SV-52, the thruster controls were more sluggish than usual, resulting in both craft wobbling in space. After a few more seconds, he managed to compensate for the additional mass and acclimated to the controls. He hoped he wouldn't have to take evasive action anytime soon. Even a g of acceleration might be enough to break the mag-lock between the skiff and the SV-52.

The support craft was made to tow skiffs and other damaged vehicles, but that didn't mean it was meant to happen during combat. That was for the dreaded "after" when you saw bloodstains in canopies, limp bodies hanging off of skiffs, their mag-boots or gloves the only thing keeping them attached and from floating off into space. After the Satellite War, finding a skiff with three or four limbs still attached was commonplace.

Another thruster burn and the SV-52 gently accelerated. The flight program fired additional bursts to keep the craft on a trajectory to meet the object. *The beacon,* he thought. *It has to be the beacon.*

With the craft pointed directly at the object, he now saw what Murdock had seen. Distant starlight wavered, disappeared, and reappeared as the shimmering object made its way through the twilight.

An interference field? he wondered. The beacon was surely designed by a superior intelligence, a sentient lifeform capable of creating a device that could travel through the universe for millennia, its power source strong enough to nearly destroy *Mira,* not to mention, wipe out an SFMC skiff. That kind of power couldn't possibly lie in an object so small. Yet, it did.

Taulbee watched the starlight dramatically flicker, disappear, and return. With each meter the SV-52 traveled, the more obvious the shimmer became. Space itself seemed to waver as though waves of darkness pulsed from something hidden, something they couldn't see.

But he could see it. The floodlights finally managed to break through the eerie darkness, although the illumination was so dim it might as well have been from a candle. The beacon appeared as little more than the outline of a dark silver polyhedron tumbling through space like a strange die rolled by an angry god.

Eyes still focused on the shape, he brought the SV-52 alongside the beacon. As the craft closed the distance to the object, the floodlights further dimmed. Static lines appeared on his HUD and the displays blinked out twice before returning. His HUD lit up with radiation warnings, although the rad count was still well within tolerance. Especially for Wendt and Murdock.

"Okay, Copenhaver. You're on net duty. Let's grab it and get the hell out of here."

"Aye, sir," she said.

Taulbee brought the SV-52 a little closer and the rad count immediately elevated to yellow and continued rising. He flipped to the cannon cam and saw Copenhaver lining up the shot. Although it should have been an easy net and grab, the shimmering and waving space around the beacon made it difficult to target. Copenhaver sighed into the mic, took a deep breath, and fired the net.

The Atmo-steel net flew true and collapsed around the beacon. Another radiation alert hit his HUD. The beacon was producing more rads now.

"Success, sir," Copenhaver said.

"Okay," Taulbee said. "Private, don't bring that thing any closer to us. Wendt? Keep an eye on the net. Whatever you do, don't get close to the beacon. That goes for you too, Murdock." A chorus of affirmatives filled his ears.

"Now the hard part," he said aloud. Using the side cam, he judged how far the beacon would sway in the net once he began changing speed. When he was sure he wouldn't slingshot the net hard enough for it to bounce back at the craft, he nudged the rear thrusters. A few hits on the attitude jets and the SV-52 rotated to face *S&R Black*. The SV-52 was still flying away from the ship, but now that he had the net behind him, he could accelerate. He didn't waste time. After warning his marines, he punched the rear thrusters for a two-second burn.

The SV-52 slowed, halted for an instant, and began picking up speed in the opposite direction. "Taulbee to Dunn."

"Go ahead."

"Sir, we have the beacon. The rad count is out of the normal range, but still not lethal. However, I don't think I want to bring this thing into the cargo bay."

"Copy, Taulbee. Agreed. Nobel?"

"Aye, sir?"

Dunn paused for the briefest instant as though he were considering multiple courses of action. "Can you get the sled out of the cargo bay?"

Nobel chuckled. "I have two marines here that need something to do."

Taulbee couldn't help but smile. He imagined both Carb and Kalimura were more than a little pissed off they weren't out here. Even as injured as the two marines were, the pair would jump at the chance to do something besides sit it all out.

"Good," Dunn said.

The captain's voice had no warmth or mirth in it and the deadpan delivery left Taulbee a little concerned. Dunn would have normally sounded happy, or at least relieved. Instead, he sounded clipped and short, a good sign that something had gone very very wrong, but he wasn't yet willing to share it.

"Nobel? Get the sled out there. Have it tethered on our belly, but I want it a good fifteen meters from the hull. Understood?"

"Aye, sir." The joviality had left Nobel's voice. He had obviously picked up the same vibe Taulbee had. "I'll handle it."

"What's your ETA, Taulbee?"

"Two minutes, sir."

"Understood," Dunn said. "Let's make it happen, marines. Time's wasting."

You mean our chances to recover Dickerson are thinning, Taulbee thought. *Or our chances of getting the hell out of here.* At least they had the beacon now and none of his squad had suffered injury. That was something. Now all they had to do—

A proximity alert hit his HUD. A group of red triangles appeared before his eyes. Three more objects were making their way to *Mira* and the new arrivals were going to fly very near *S&R Black*. "Void wept," Taulbee muttered.

Dunn's voice spoke over the private comms. "You see them?"

"Aye, sir," he said. "What are they?"

The captain's breath hitched slightly. "More of the same. We think. But these are larger than the last batch."

"They changing course at all?"

"No," Dunn said. "Making a bee-line for *Mira*. With any luck, they'll pass right by us."

"Acknowledged, sir."

Dunn paused for a moment. "Get here as fast as you can. If they change course and get between you and us, do whatever you have to do to survive. If you have to cut the beacon or the skiff, do it. I'm not losing anyone else today."

"Understood, sir," Taulbee said.

"Good hunting, Lieutenant."

"Aye, sir. Taulbee out."

The three markers on the HUD remained on their course. Good. He fired another thruster burn and the SV-52 reached 45m/s. Just a few kilometers away, *S&R Black* looked like shadowy salvation, its running lights bravely blazing in the Kuiper's twilight.

"All right, marines," he said over the squad comms. "We have some company up ahead. Hopefully, they'll ignore us, but in case they don't, be ready."

With each passing second, *S&R Black* loomed larger, but so did the giant hulk behind it. Shapes flittered through the shadows near *Mira*, mere amorphous forms with no detail. They could have been starfish, pinecones, or whatever those new creatures were. Taulbee glared at the dead giant metal beast, willing it to disappear back to where it came and take all of its new friends with it. But that wasn't going to happen. A grin slowly spread across his face. *Not yet,* he thought. *Not fucking yet.*

Another wave of static rolled across his HUD. A glance through the cams showed the skiff still attached and the netted beacon floating beneath it. A radiation alert pulsed for a few ticks before disappearing. The rad meters had spiked and then dropped, although the spike was still well within both the suit and shielding tolerance. One thing for sure, he wasn't bringing the beacon aboard *S&R Black*. No fucking way.

Something flew past the canopy and disappeared, leaving his heart galloping in his chest. "Anyone see that?"

Murdock answered in a timid, shaking voice. "Aye, sir. But I have no idea what it was."

"Copenhaver?" Taulbee said.

"No, sir," she said. "I didn't see anything. I'll scan."

"Do that," he said.

Taulbee tried to focus his attention on flying the craft back to *Black*, but he couldn't help flipping through the cam feeds. Whatever that had been, it had been moving damned fast. Maybe even faster than the creatures that had flown at *Mira* like a flock of alien birds.

"Got it, sir," Copenhaver said. "Seven of them." She sounded both excited and terrified. "They're huge!"

"What's their speed?" Taulbee asked.

"About 200m/s. They're damned fast."

"Where did they go, Private?"

She was silent for a moment. When she spoke again, the excitement had been replaced with desperate fear. "They keep circling us, sir. Keeping their distance so far, but their formation is tightening."

"Wendt? Murdock? Do not shoot at those things unless they get close. Copenhaver? If they close on us, give them something to think about."

"Aye, sir."

He switched to the command channel. "Captain? We have a problem."

"What is it, Taulbee?"

"We have some friends following us."

There was a long pause. "Okay. We see them," Dunn said. "When you get close enough to offload, we're going to fire another CO2 round and see if we can get their attention."

"Sir? I'm not bringing this beacon aboard."

"No, you're not," the captain agreed. "Just get in close and we'll figure it out."

"Aye, sir. Out." He thought for a moment. 1.5km to the ship. At present speed, that meant he had less than a minute to figure this out. Copenhaver had sent his HUD an animation of the creatures' flight path. The new hostiles were indeed circling the SV-52, but with elliptical paths that intersected a few meters apart. The seven lifeforms didn't fly in formation, but rather a tightening 3-D noose. If he stared long enough at one of the cams, he was sure to catch a glimpse of their dark bodies against the Kuiper Belt's wan light.

But the noose wasn't pulled taut yet. One km to go. He'd have to start slowing the SV-52 soon, or he'd come in way too hot. If he fired the thrusters at the last second, the g-force shock would be extreme. It might even break the mag-lock with the skiff or send Wendt and Murdock flying off the hull. Taulbee's fingers tightened on the controls.

"Sir?" Copenhaver said. "They're getting closer."

700 meters.

"Okay, marines," he said, "we're going to take a few twists and turns. Hold tight."

He didn't wait for a reply. Taulbee hit the port thrusters and the SV-52 immediately began sliding horizontally while it continued forward. A touch of the belly thrusters, and they began to rise in relation to the ship. The creatures, if they wanted to keep their circling formation, would have to adjust or risk running right into the support craft. If not for the two marines moored to the hull, he'd invite the bastards to try it. The '52 had survived multiple starfish attacks. He'd no doubt it would survive a tussle with these things too.

600 meters and he was off course. Instead of approaching the cargo bay, he was now in position to fly over the ship, ride its spine, and head back toward *Mira*. Copenhaver had updated his HUD with a new diagram of the creatures' flight path. They had adjusted all right.

The seven hostiles had shuffled their orbits, changed their directions and attitude, but they'd also tightened the noose. Cursing, Taulbee hit the top jets with a full burn and the SV-52 didn't so much as descend as plummet. *S&R Black*'s belly and starboard-side came back into view. He had more than enough fuel to keep dancing away from them with micro-burns, but not enough to slow down if he did. He could manage maybe three more full burns before he exhausted everything but attitude control. The added mass of both the skiff and the beacon were eating fuel faster than he liked.

Of all the goddamned times to lose a skiff, he thought. And of all the times to be towing. Yup. There was definitely a trip to the brig in his future. When he saw Colonel Heyes again, he'd bust that pompous fucker right in the chops. He grinned. It would be worth it.

300 meters. Taulbee fired a short burn from the bow and the SV-52's speed dropped by 10m/s. His HUD updated at once. The creatures were coming close, their orbits taking them a little less than 10 meters from the craft's hull. He didn't know if they wanted the beacon, the skiff, or just liked the idea of a moving morsel, but Copenhaver was right. They were big.

Another flew past the SV-52 just in front of the bow. The creature was at least as large as the support craft itself. If something that big caught one of his marines, it could easily tear them limb from limb before they could even punch through its carapace.

"Copenhaver?"

"Aye, sir. I'll have a shot next time they come around."

"Take it," he said. She replied, but he barely heard. He activated another thruster burn and dropped their speed to 20m/s. *S&R Black* loomed larger in the cam view. He could no longer see *Mira* behind her, but now he could see the creatures for what they were.

Their orbits were less than seven meters from the '52 and when one passed before him, he had less than a second to make out what it was. He wished he hadn't seen it at all.

The thing was little more than a flying wing, its rugose carapace a horror of bumps that might have been dead eyes or other sensory organs. Short, stubby appendages grew from its sides, each tip ending in something that looked like a mouth filled with serrated teeth. Two larger limbs, more like tentacles than arms, reached forward before moving backward like oars in a canoe. He caught sight of particles or debris puffing out into space. Along its spine, a thin, two-meter-long sail rippled as if in a wind. Taulbee had time to feel his balls turn to ice before the cannon fired.

The first flechette detonated less than two meters above the SV-52's canopy. The tritium round smashed into the creature's mid-section and one of its stubby limbs disappeared in a cloud of crumb-like debris. The thing immediately broke from its orbit.

"Not so fucking close!" Wendt screamed.

Copenhaver didn't reply, but fired another round after it. Taulbee refocused on his flight path, but couldn't ignore the bright flash on the port-side. He didn't hear the rattle of alien shell striking the hull. 10m/s. Something clipped the top of the hull followed immediately by another strike to the belly.

"Sir!" Wendt yelled. "They're going after the skiff!"

The SV-52 shuddered as something smashed into the aft and Taulbee's bones jolted from the impact. The '52's nose rose as its tail dropped, anchored by the skiff. Taulbee fired the thrusters in rapid succession to try and maintain his heading, but every time he managed to straighten out, another creature attacked.

Murdock screamed into the mic. The SV-52 tried to roll and Taulbee leveled the craft again with another round of thruster bursts. His HUD lit up with collision warnings, radiation warnings, and low fuel warnings. "Fuck you," he snarled. "You want it? Take it!" He punched the tow release.

The SV-52 shivered as the mag-lock mooring the skiff to the support vehicle's aft let go. The skiff dropped away at once. He glanced at the rear cam, watching in fascination as the creatures, nearly as large as the skiff itself, collapsed into a ball around the damaged, irradiated slab of Atmo-steel.

With *S&R Black* a little more than 50 meters away, he had to slow down and fast. He hit another burn from the bow. 5m/s. Another fuel warning flashed. "Taulbee to Dunn. Almost there, and I'm damned near out of fuel."

"Copy," Dunn said. "We're getting the sled ready now."

The sled, Taulbee thought. *We're going to be sitting ducks while they get the damned thing set up.*

"Copenhaver?"

"Aye, sir?"

He grinned at the manic excitement in her voice. The woman had some bloodlust in her. He hoped she could keep it going. "We're going to have to provide some cover fire. Get ready."

"Aye, sir."

"Wendt? Murdock? Status?"

"Here and alive, sir," Wendt said.

"Me too," Murdock said. "But I took a shard to my leg. Punctured the rad suit, but the second layer sutured it closed."

"Good," Taulbee said. "Hang on. We're almost there."

The cargo bay doors opened and flooded the area with bright light. Two backlit figures appeared. Kalimura and Carb were floating the sled out of the bay. He hoped like hell they had time to get the beacon into it. He didn't think they'd have another chance.

CHAPTER SIXTY-THREE

Kali stood in the cargo bay, her nerves itching for some action despite the pain in her chest. It was getting better in a hurry, but her breath was still difficult to catch. Nobel had cut the grav-plate power and the sled, the jerry-rigged contraption the engineer had hurriedly fabricated, floated a few centimeters above the deck.

"Ready, Carb?" Kali asked.

"Aye, Boss. Let's do this."

The cargo bay doors opened, excess atmosphere streaming out of the bay in a rush, carrying particles of Atmo-steel and fabrication detritus with it. The powerful lights lanced through the dark rectangle of space and Kali caught a glimpse of the approaching SV-52. Taulbee was bringing the craft in too fast.

"He's going to hit!" Carb yelled.

Kali opened her mouth to reply when a yellow and orange flare erupted from the bow. The SV-52's speed disappeared in an instant, leaving it floating before them like a ghost.

"Damn, he's good," Kali muttered. She pulled on her tether to make sure it was attached. The resistance felt reassuring. She took in a deep breath. "Go," she said in an exhale.

The two marines used their suit thrusters to pull the sled out of the cargo bay. It took longer than she liked, but 10 seconds later, they were clear and floating above the SV-52. Wendt and Murdock had already cut their mag-locks and drifted aft.

"Hey, Kalimura!" Wendt said. "We'll get it out of the net and bring it to you."

"Now that's service," Carb said.

Kali ignored the chatter and looked aft. A little more than 90 meters behind them, a cluster of horrible-looking things had wrapped themselves into a misshapen ball. They pulsed with alien energy, their limbs occasionally flicking outward and slowly traveling back in. The lifeforms looked much more terrifying than anything they'd seen aboard *Mira*. And here they were, floating alongside the sled, rifles still clamped to their backs. If those things decided to attack, they'd only have a second or two to get loose from the sled and get a shot off. Maybe. *More than likely,* she thought, *we'll just get eaten.*

Wendt and Murdock had reached the net and used their rad-suits' thrusters to stay within a meter of the Atmo-steel fiber cables surrounding the object. Taulbee opened the net, the cables spreading apart like a blossoming flower. The beacon, looking as strangely alien as it had in the images captured from *Mira*, floated away from them at less than half a meter per second.

Wendt and Murdock's suit thrusters fired and the two marines mag-locked themselves to the device before it could get further away. "Okay, Corporal,"

Wendt said. "Got it."

"Good," she said. "Come to us and we'll come to you."

"Affirmative," Wendt said.

"Let's go, Carb," she said. They activated their thrusters in sequence to bring the sled below the SV-52 and toward the beacon. Wendt and Murdock in turn used their own thrusters to pull the beacon toward *S&R Black* and the sled. Kali kept her eyes on the beacon and the two non-rates, but she had to fight to keep her concentration and focus. The creatures wrapped around the dead skiff could move at any time and in any direction. While trying to perform this awkward docking mission, they'd have no time at all to prepare for an attack. And if the beacon decided to pulse? Well, she didn't want to think about that. There'd be nothing for it. They'd all be flash-fried before they even realized what was going on. She just hoped the void was more kind.

Each passing second lasted an eternity as she waited for the attack to come. By the time she and Carb rendezvoused with Wendt and Murdock, her jumpsuit clung to her body with sweaty dampness. When they were one meter away, Kali and her squad-mate halted their approach. Wendt and Murdock, awkwardly mag-locked to the polyhedron, had difficulty in stabilizing the object before they crashed into the sled. At the last second before impact, Wendt fired his suit thrusters and managed to give it just enough lift for the beacon to hover above the sled's surface.

"Void, that was close," Wendt said.

Murdock laughed wildly. "Corporal? Are you done trying to kill me today?"

Kali smiled. "Day's not over yet. Let's mag-lock this thing to the sled and get it into *Black*'s tow harness. Then we can get the fuck out of here."

"Aye, Boss," Wendt said. Murdock detached from the beacon and Wendt slowly dragged it down to the divot in the sled's thick Atmo-steel. Her gloves shuddered when the alien thing settled into its cradle. "Got it," Wendt said. He mag-locked his feet and attached the heavy Atmo-steel restraint cables. "Think I'm done, Corporal."

"Kalimura to Nobel."

"Go."

Kali tried to keep the excitement down in her voice but failed miserably. "Beacon's in the cradle. Do you have a green light?"

"Aye, Corporal," Nobel said. "You're good to go."

"Acknowledged, sir." She switched to the squad channel and couldn't help but chuckle. "Lieutenant Taulbee? Carb and I are ready to take the sled to the harness."

"Copy," Taulbee said. "Wendt and Murdock? Climb back on board so we can provide support."

Wendt and Murdock pulled themselves along the tethers attached to the SV-52 and mag-locked to the hull. Using their attitude thrusters, Kali and Carb pulled the sled toward *S&R Black*'s aft and the series of cables jutting down from the ship's belly.

"Corporal? On your 9 o'clock," Taulbee said.

"Acknowledged." Her HUD pulsed twice with red and she cursed.

"Hey, Boss?" Carb asked on the squad channel. "You getting rad alerts?"

"Yeah," Kali said. "A little faster maybe?"

The pair executed a parallel burn and reached the tail much faster than was safe. But she survived that goddamned haunted hulk of metal out there and she sure as shit wasn't going to get vaporized by this fucking thing when they almost had it out of here. A grim smile lit her lips. *Plus, I have to live long enough to kick Dickerson in the ass for disobeying an order.*

With Taulbee providing cover and bathing the net of thick cabling with the '52's bright lights, it took little time to move the beacon into position.

"Shit," Carb said.

"What?"

"The beacon," she said. "If it blows, we don't want it pointed at the damned ship."

"Void wept," Kalimura said. "Look for a discolored side." They spun the beacon until they found what they thought was the beacon's "barrel." But how would they know? The thing had been out in space for void knew how many millennia. It could have been scarred at any time along its journey. "Okay," she said. "We got it pointed out."

"You sure?" Carb asked, her voice nearly trembling.

"As sure as I can be."

As soon as they had it inside the net opening, they used their attitude thrusters to drift away from the net and *S&R Black*'s aft. Once they were clear, Nobel activated the net.

The flexible nannie cables form-fitted around the sled tight enough to hold it in place while the ship performed acceleration burns. Kali had seen the nets before, and even trained with them once or twice, but this was the first time she'd seen one used for long-distance flights. They were nearly an AU from Pluto and if they wanted to intercept Dickerson along the way, *Black* would definitely have to burn hot.

"Nobel to Kalimura. I've got green. Get back aboard the ship. Taulbee?"

"Aye. I'll cover them until we get the squad back inside."

"Copy," Kalimura said. "Let's go, Carb."

They thrusted toward the starboard-side. Floating beneath the ship's belly, she made out scars and nicks in the Atmo-steel. She idly wondered how many were from this mission, and how many were the result of decades of service. "Almost there," she said. Five meters. Four. Then her eyes caught the sight of silvery liquid glazed across the final starboard-side hull plate. The starfish had been here.

"Kalimura to Taulbee."

"Go ahead, Corporal."

She and Carb had already popped out from beneath ship and halted less than a meter from the cargo bay lip. "Sir, I think one of our starfish friends has been here."

"Found that silvery shit?"

"Aye, sir," Kali said.

"Acknowledged," Taulbee said. "Wendt? Murdock? Triple-time. Get in the cargo bay. Now!"

Kali and Carb mag-handed their way into the cargo bay just as Wendt and

Murdock thrusted inside. When the pair of marines neared the port-side bulkhead, the two men activated their fore thrusters and brought themselves to a reduced speed before colliding with the far bulkhead.

"Arm yourselves!" Kali yelled and pulled the rifle from her back. Carb did the same. Wendt recovered before Murdock, flipping in the z-g and mag-locking to the bulkhead with a single foot, leaving his hands free to grip and aim his rifle. Murdock tried to follow his example, but ended up having to push himself to the floor before fumbling for his weapon. The four marines stared at the darkness beyond the cargo bay door, rifles primed with tritium rounds. The SV-52 hung in space a few meters away, the cannon swinging to cover the ship's starboard belly.

"Copenhaver?" Taulbee called out.

"No contacts, sir," she said.

What you couldn't see wasn't necessarily to be feared, but it certainly made it difficult to focus on anything else. When you felt an ambush coming and knew a hostile was just around the corner, all of your attention honed in on the known or perceived threat rather than a larger one that could be your undoing.

Kali brought up the cam feeds for the SV-52 and quickly switched between the aft, port, and bow views before checking the overhead and keel. When she reached the keel cam, her breath hitched. Several large shapes, all but hidden in the ship's shadow, stealthily approached the SV-52.

"Break break break!" Kali yelled.

The SV-52 took no more than a second before it shot forward from its present position and left the cargo bay's rectangular window into space. The moment it disappeared from view, she fired the first flechette.

The round flew from the cargo bay and detonated a bare five meters from the ship's hull, sending tritium flechettes into the first of the starfish. Three of its many arms exploded into black crumbs of carapace and alien innards. An arm reached the cargo bay's lip as one of the creatures attempted to enter the bay. Kali didn't have to say a word. Four rifles fired and four flechette rounds struck the creature just as it pulled itself in.

The force of the flechettes knocked its split and shattered remains back into space. Kali moved forward, Carb on her six and to her left, the pair confidently mag-walking to the lip.

"How many?" Carb asked.

"I saw six," Kali said. "That's two down."

"Corporal!" Copenhaver yelled. "One kill, another injured and moving off."

"Where are the last two, Private?"

After a slight pause, Copenhaver groaned into the mic. "I've lost them, Corporal."

"Kalimura?" Taulbee called out. "Any sign?"

She studied the shadowy Kuiper Belt, looking for anything moving in relatively close proximity. Nothing. Far off in the distance, she could see the shapes of pinecone hordes, starfish, and whatever those new creatures were, but there was nothing she could find near them. "No, sir. They may have retreated to the other side of the ship."

"Copy," Taulbee said. "Captain? What do you want us to do?"

"Dock immediately. We can't waste any more time."

"Aye, sir. Kalimura? Get your people out of the way. We're coming in."

"Aye, sir." She switched to the squad channel. "You heard the LT. Move your asses."

While Murdock and Wendt cleared the area reserved for the SV-52, she and Carb took positions on either side of the cargo bay door. If something else decided to pay a visit, she'd make sure it departed shy a few limbs.

The SV-52 returned a few seconds later and Taulbee expertly maneuvered it into place. Once he was clear of the door, it began to close. Neither Carb nor Kali moved from their positions until the hatch finally shut, sealing them off from the vacuum of space and the hostiles outside.

The grav-plates hummed to life and atmosphere poured into the cargo bay. After a brief moment, her HUD finally announced it was safe to remove her helmet. "Squad. Get rearmed and provisioned. Be prepared to get out there again at a moment's notice."

"Aye, Boss," Carb and Wendt said. Murdock called her corporal, opting for the less familiar address. Kali smiled to herself. Before long, he'd be talking like the rest of them. Assuming he lived past this mission, that was.

Shit. Assuming any of us do.

CHAPTER SIXTY-FOUR

Still wearing his combat suit, Dunn sat in the command chair, his eyes flicking from one holo display to another. The creatures had tightened their flying patterns around *Mira*'s shattered aft. He imagined that if he sent out the SV-52 to scout the derelict's bow, it would be completely clear of the creatures.

He initiated a connection with Black and the AI immediately accepted it. *Yes, Captain?*

They're forming around the aft.

Yes, Captain. The lifeforms, all types that we have seen thus far, appear to be conglomerating in that area. Even more curious is the fact the predators seemed to have ceased being predators. The pinecones, starfish, and the others are cohabitating without attacking one another.

He shook his head. *What the hell are they doing?*

I do not have enough information to offer an educated guess.

He rolled his eyes. *Then make an uneducated one.*

Yes, Captain. I believe the continued blasts inside Mira have left a long-lasting impression in its Atmo-steel. The last blast that occurred inside it before Gunnery Sergeant Cartwright's squad recovered the beacon may have been more powerful than the previous ones. Enough to get the attention of all the lifeforms that inhabit Mira. The behavior of the new arrivals that wrapped around the skiff further props up that hypothesis.

Dunn leaned back in the chair, his hands behind his head. *Blowing up Mira. Do you still believe that is the correct course?*

Black paused for a moment before replying. *Although I do not have all the facts, my simulations, based on behavioral observation, give a 70% chance that the destruction of Mira will scatter the lifeforms. Without a safe haven, it is likely they will hone in on the beacon and follow it.*

So that's a 'yes.'

Black seemed embarrassed. *Yes, Captain. It is still the recommended course of action.*

Dunn nodded and broke the connection. He thought for a moment before leaning forward in the command chair. "Oakes, bring our starboard-side directly parallel to *Mira*'s aft. Black, how's our ammo supply?"

"We still have a number of CO_2 warheads as well as the neutrino type. Standard ammunition will have to do once we exhaust our supply."

"Understood."

Oakes cleared his throat. "We're underway, sir."

"Lieutenant Taulbee to the bridge," Dunn said over the ship-wide comms. "Marines? Prepare for multi-g acceleration."

Dunn flicked his eyes back to the holo displays. Four more KBOs had shown up. Black and PEO had missed their approach, but they were here now.

He'd little doubt they were breaking apart and headed to the aft just like the rest.

He heard the clunk of grav-boots on the Atmo-steel deck and couldn't help but grin.

"Here, sir," Taulbee said from behind him.

Dunn rotated his chair to stare at his XO. Dark stains covered the visible collar of his jumpsuit. "Good work, James."

"Thank you, sir," Taulbee said, his face still as stone.

"Seeing as how Gunny is currently unavailable, I'd like you to do me a favor."

Taulbee cocked his head. "And what would that be, sir?"

A venomous grin spread across Dunn's face. "Take fire control."

Taulbee growled low in his throat before saluting. "My pleasure, sir."

*****

Nobel stood in the closed cargo bay with his back against the aft-bulkhead, the anti-rad suit still clothing his sweating body. Once the cargo bay hatch had closed and he'd checked for casualties, both mechanical and physical, he'd headed to this position. What he needed was focus, a place least likely to take damage, and most likely to need immediate repair if it was. Besides, this spot? Heavily armored. Chances of him getting taken out? Well, the void-damned ship would be in two pieces anyway. Somehow that thought didn't make him feel any better.

Jacked into Black and the ship's component systems, he'd be the first to know of an impending attack and immediately estimate possible damage and what to do. When under fire, it was part of his job. SFMC still didn't trust combat AIs to use the best judgment, but that didn't mean they should be ignored either. Using the block to communicate and monitor in tandem left the two to have pico-second discussions, come to an agreement, and execute it. Nobel's opinion always won if there was disagreement and it left him very little time to react.

Without being fully interfaced, it would be impossible. The block processors assisted the speed of thought, effectively decreasing the time it took to digest input and apply his gut instincts to decision making. Taulbee was probably jacked into the fire controls in the same manner.

That was usually Gunny's job. Nobel couldn't help but wince at the thought of seeing the old marine lying unconscious with a brain hemorrhage inside a void-damned autodoc. And he might be in that accursed thing until they reached Neptune, or he could just die without ever waking up, without ever knowing if his marines made it out alive.

"Dunn to Nobel."

"Go, sir."

"We're in position."

He smiled. "Copy, sir. Black and I are ready."

"Acknowledged. Good hunting."

"Aye, sir."

The cam feeds dumped into his visual cortex so he could monitor each of the visual sensors. *Mira* had steadily come into view from bow to stern as Oakes moved the ship to dead center of the aft. It took nearly a minute to get into the right attitude affording him time to watch the change. The bow had been devoid of any creatures. No pinecones, no starfish, none of the recently arrived. All he saw was the fatigued Atmo-steel, the scars of micro-meteor strikes, and the occasional ripped hull plate.

When the ship had finally come to a stop, he was able to see just how badly the infestation had spread. *Mira*'s aft section was impossible to see now. It was as if the giant ship had held additional hordes beyond imagination, or the creatures were breeding, and reproducing at an incredible rate. The further aft you looked, the more there were, piled atop one another like layers of shifting and sliding sediment.

His skin prickled as if with electricity, but it wasn't from excitement. It was terror. Where had these things come from? And how the hell were they going to fight that many? They were nearly out of the special ammo already.

"Suicide," he mumbled aloud.

Lieutenant, Black's voice broke through the clutter of thoughts like a hammer. *I sense distress.*

Well, he thought to himself, *at least that prickling feeling is gone.* It was true. A flush of embarrassment had all but driven away the fear itself. He didn't like the new AI and its words stoked another emotion as well: anger. How the fuck could anyone face this shit and not be "distressed?"

I'm fine, Black, he replied through the connection.

Very good, Lieutenant.

Her words had that flavor of warmth and happiness, as if she were enjoying this. *Or,* he considered, *she might just be glad to know you're pulling your shit together.* His face twisted into a reluctant grin. For a moment there, he'd almost believed it was true. No. It's a goddamned program they run when they sense their humans are near panic.

Sure. That was it.

Nobel breathed deep, doing his best to get the ice back in veins. Just like the Satellite War. *You survived that, you'll survive this.*

"Taulbee to Nobel."

"Here, sir," he said.

"Fire control is ready. I'm going to start the sequence in five seconds from my mark."

Taulbee seemed more than a little excited. He sounded like an executioner getting ready to drop the axe on the most loathsome human being he'd ever met. Nobel had never heard that tone in the man's voice before. Well, *Mira* had it coming.

"Copy, sir. On your mark."

Another few seconds passed, as he knew they would. The captain would definitely want to check everything over once more. They had that luxury. Once Taulbee let loose the missiles, the guns, and the flechette cannons, *Mira*'s ass was going to cease to exist. And when that happened?

Nobel shuddered again. He already had an evasive maneuvers program set and ready, and he and Black would make changes as they went, dumping plans and replacing them with other presets, modifying, inserting commands on the fly, whatever it took to keep the ship ahead of those things if they decided to attack.

Or if they follow the beacon, he thought.

"Dunn to crew. Condition 1. I repeat, Condition 1. Be prepared for hard burn. Fire control? Fire at will."

As Dunn's words filtered into his ears, he had time to run two more status checks. Everything was still green. They were ready. This was it. It was time.

"Mark," Taulbee's voice said.

*****

The ship shuddered, but it was nearly imperceptible to Taulbee. He watched the cam feeds as magnetic pulses pushed three missiles from the launchers. Once the projectiles reached a five-meter distance from the hull, their rockets kicked in. The trio of tritium warheads streaked across the darkness with tails of brilliant blue flame. A second later, they met the creatures on *Mira*'s hull.

With the cams zoomed in, he could see from the great ship's belly to her topside. Taulbee watched with a grim smile as large clumps of the pulsing, moving horde found themselves engulfed in an explosion of heavy water and flechettes. Clouds of limbs, carapaces, mandibles, and void knew what other kinds of debris, puffed away from the impact sites.

The missiles shouldn't have done much damage to the hull, but they had. Giant tears appeared in the Atmo-steel hull plates. Some shattered and opened great, misshapen holes in the already ravaged aft. Inside *Mira*, something pulsed with colors so unnatural, they hurt his mind.

Before he had time to reconsider firing the other salvo, his fingers had already done the work. Two ship-buster missiles, essentially high-yield, low-kiloton nukes, burst from the last launchers. As their rocket engines kicked in, Taulbee said aloud, "For you, Gunny."

The universe around him disappeared in a flare of white light. The visual filters dampened the blinding flash, but that didn't keep the afterimage from appearing behind his eyes. As it slowly faded, he was able to see the damage. And it was still happening.

The nukes busted through the fragile hull plates, entered the interior of the engineering bay, and detonated with their payloads. That had been the plan. With the ship in such bad shape, Black had calculated their ship-busters could effectively cut *Mira*'s aft section from the rest of the ship. He didn't realize it would affect all of it.

The shockwave from the nukes sent a rippling cascade of energy down every piece of Atmo-steel even as the heat melted and twisted the already-distressed metal. The separating layers of Atmo-steel unzipped into strips of ultra-thin metal. The ripple and cascade ate the midships before it hit the bow. Once it reached there, it slowed and finally stopped, leaving 1/3 of the fore section spinning and tumbling into space. Widening cones of debris vomited from the sliced bow section.

Mira had effectively been destroyed. Taulbee had a second to enjoy the sight before alarms flashed across his HUD. He blinked and retrained his focus back to where the giant ship had once been. The stars were going out, disappearing. No. There was one. Then it was gone again. Finally, with a growing sense of horror, he realized what he was looking at.

The creatures, the survivors, had massed together into an impossibly black cloud. And it was growing. And growing. Taulbee heard the captain tell Nobel to "punch it." Then he was pushed into his acceleration couch as if by the universe itself.

CHAPTER SIXTY-FIVE

The ship's fusion engines came to a life with a vibration that rattled his bones. Oakes sank back into his couch as the multi-g acceleration hit the marines full bore. He switched to block communication only, speech being nearly impossible with his mouth open and cheeks stretched backward.

"Oakes to Dunn," he said over the block.

"Go ahead."

"Sir, first acceleration burn will be complete in another thirty seconds."

"Understood," Dunn said. "Keep me apprised."

"Aye, sir."

Apprised. What a strange word to use. Dunn should have said, "Let me know if we're about to blow up." Shit. The captain could see the reports himself in real time. Why did he want to be "apprised?"

Oakes flipped to *Black*'s rear camera feed. As soon as the munitions had reached *Mira* and left her in shattered pieces, he'd fired up the maneuvering engines and changed their course to face Pluto. When the creatures, no longer in possession of their home, flooded outward like a hungry wave of darkness, he'd punched the engines to provide a full burn.

The ship roared through space, slowly picking up speed as the fusion engines belched excited gas and heat in flares of energy, but that didn't mean they were leaving the creatures behind. No sir.

That tidal wave of flailing limbs, pulsing carapaces, and acid-spitting creatures formed up behind them like a plague. It shot forward toward the ship, or maybe toward the beacon, at a speed he didn't think possible.

Mira had still been traveling at a good clip on a course for Pluto. That meant the creatures had started out at that speed, as had *S&R Black*. But accelerating from that speed took power and a lot of it, at least for something of *S&R Black*'s size. The creatures, on the other hand, appeared to have greater speed than he'd considered possible. Not to mention, they had a lot less mass to move.

But that wasn't all, was it? The tsunami wave of exo-solar lifeforms had collapsed upon itself like a black hole. A misshapen sphere of alien malevolence, alien hunger, followed the ship no more than half a kilometer behind. The worst part? Oakes wasn't making the lead he thought he would.

Instead, the creatures seemed to be accelerating faster than *S&R Black*. But that wouldn't last. How could it?

Not for the first time, he wondered where these things came from. And more importantly, was there a goal? An endgame for them? Was the beacon something they were protecting, or just following because it flashed them with light, maybe some signal human technology couldn't detect? And why did the Trio really want them to plant the beacon on Pluto?

Too many questions, he thought. Also? He needed to focus on the burn.

Another 10 seconds and they'd reach cruising speed. He'd have to bump it a few more times in the next hour so they could catch Dickerson. He sincerely hoped he wouldn't have to slow down too much; otherwise, the creatures might catch up. He didn't want to think about what they'd do to the ship if they did manage to overtake her.

The acceleration burn came to an end, the pressure on his spine quickly decreasing. A few seconds later, he was able to lean forward again, crack his back, and get back to the controls.

"Attention, crew," he said. "First burn is finished. Next burn is scheduled for 20 minutes from now."

"Thank you," Dunn said. "Keep her steady. And find that escape pod. I want Dickerson back on board as soon as possible."

"Aye, sir," Oakes said. He wiped a sheen of sweat from his brow. He thought of everything he'd seen over the past several hours, a span of time that felt more like eons rather than hundreds of minutes. They were on the precipice of getting the fuck out of the deep Kuiper Belt and away from this madness. Weren't they?

*****

Dunn stared at the holo displays, a look of both wonder and worry etched upon his already well-lined face. Taulbee and his squads—"squad," Dunn corrected himself—were still in the cargo bay. The marines were probably rehydrating, refueling their suits, and getting some chow. Maybe even some sleep.

Sleep was sometimes the most difficult provision to procure. SFMC personnel on "real" duty learned to sleep standing up, mag-locked to bulkheads or the deck, and were trained to snap into action at a single comm command. Considering how battered Kalimura and Carbonaro were, he hoped for their sake they were getting some Zs.

As for Taulbee himself? No telling.

Dunn could have peeked at the cargo bay feed, but felt no need. It was Taulbee's squad. His people. Well, they were all Dunn's people, certainly, but Taulbee was their direct commander. Even more so now that Gunny was incapacitated.

"Sir?" Taulbee's voice broke across block comms.

"Go ahead."

"I have a proposition, sir. Since we don't know how long Gunny will be out, I suggest Corporal Kalimura take over his position for now."

Dunn raised an eyebrow. He hadn't even considered that Taulbee needed someone to coordinate the fire teams if they had to deploy all the marines.

"Is she well enough?"

Taulbee paused. "I think so, sir. I'll ask, of course, but I wanted to get your opinion."

Dunn leaned back in his couch, a gentle smile on his face. "She went into hell with three marines, came back with two, and we're going to pick up the third. I'd say she's got the backbone for it and I think it's an excellent decision."

When Taulbee spoke again, Dunn could hear the man nodding in agreement. "That's what I thought you'd say, sir."

"How are the marines?"

Taulbee managed a brief laugh, but through the block, it was more of a feeling than a sound. "Tired, as they should be. I've got them resting as best I can, but a couple of the holdouts are still studying cam feeds."

Dunn shook his head. "For what?"

"Something we can learn, sir. Anything, really."

"Okay. Another burn in 19 minutes. Be ready."

"Aye, sir. Taulbee out."

Dunn connected to Black.

"Yes, Captain?"

The AI had been unusually silent since Taulbee had destroyed *Mira*. He'd expected her to assail him with useless information, but instead, she'd merely described the hits and the damage done to the giant ship's hull. He thought that strange.

"What do you make of their pursuit?"

The AI requested a block connection. Sighing, Dunn accepted it. The world around him, the holo displays, the bridge, everything disappeared, leaving him in darkness and facing a perfect sphere pulsing in a myriad of colors.

I see we've gone for comfort again, he told the AI.

The shape turned a dull red, the AI equivalent of a blush. *Sorry, sir. Sometimes it's best to go with what works.*

You have something to show me?

Yes, Captain.

The shape disappeared, leaving the world clothed in darkness. A single pinecone creature faded into the foreground. Behind it, several other lifeforms appeared. Starfish, those monstrous bird things, and a few he didn't even recognize. Each looked like a conglomeration of insect, mammal, bird, and aquatic animals to him. It was as if Earth's once lustrous fauna, now virtually extinct, had headed out into space in an orgy of impossible reproduction and evolution.

The pinecone's silvery claw poked out of its sheath, the suicidally sharp appendage glinting in unseen ambient light. The starfish moved forward, its large body and arms facing him like a creature from a horror holo. Its maw opened and closed, displaying serrated teeth and a pair of strong mandibles guarding the orifice.

The creatures you see here, Black said, *are the original pair described in Mira's data dump. However, the other creatures you see behind them are the new arrivals. Notice the similarities and the differences.*

Dunn did. They were easy to spot. The pinecone creature had no visible means of locomotion. Black had previously theorized that perhaps they excreted gas as propulsion. That seemed borne out by some of Kalimura's feed records. The starfish, on the other hand, moved with a grace he thought only possible in an atmosphere. Or with a set of thrusters.

While the starfish moved by pulling in its arms and shooting them backward like a swimmer plowing through water, the new arrivals had new appendages, including what looked like a solar sail.

Black? That sail.

Yes, Captain. I believe it to be a photo-sensitive organ capable of drawing energy from stray photons.

But it's moving way too fast to only be powered by the push of photons.

Very true, Black said. *I believe there is another explanation for this, although it's at present beyond my understanding. As I've said before, the only way to truly understand these creatures would be to capture one and study it.*

Not going to happen, Dunn said.

No, Black agreed. *They have proved themselves far too dangerous to attempt such an endeavor.*

So what are you telling me about these creatures?

The universe split again as the creatures lined up against one another, frozen in time, frozen in space. The pinecones were by far the smallest of the group. The starfish were next in size followed by the new arrivals. The creatures with the sails were the largest of the lot, and even more horrible to gaze upon than the starfish.

The limbs, appendages, and mouths disappeared from each of the images, leaving the carapaces in place. Dunn frowned. They slowly spun in tandem, giving him a more or less complete comparison front to back.

Do you see the similarities? Black asked, her spherical avatar floating in the far upper left corner of the simulation.

He did, but didn't know what to make of it. Each of the shells had a dark, wavy appearance as if they had some effect on the surrounding light, but at the same time, the pinecones had a much tougher shell, as though they were more protected or made of a different material. The pinecones were also the only ones without long appendages of some sort.

Can you put them in order?

Black paused. *By how we discovered them? By size?*

By size, Dunn said.

The images slid by one another until they were arranged from smallest to largest. Seven different types of alien life. Seven different average sizes. Yet they all had the same attributes apart from the pinecones.

Are the pinecones 'eggs?'

That is a good question, Black said. *After studying their behavior from Corporal Kalimura's cam recordings, I don't think they are. Although they seem to be the least predatory of the varied species, and demonstrate herd behavior techniques when threatened, they have also demonstrated a certain level of intelligence far beyond what I would expect.*

Meaning what, exactly? Dunn asked. *So what if the small ones are as smart as the big ones?*

The equivalent of a sigh filled his mind. *At the base layer of Earth's old ecology, the simple-celled organisms sitting at the bottom of the food chain were not capable of thought. Reflexes? Yes. Some sort of instinctual intelligence? Impossible to say. So let's go larger, shall we?*

The largest organism in the ocean, before the wars of the 21st century, was a type of whale. Although it was the largest creature on Earth at the time, its premier food source was an organism called 'plankton.' Many creatures in the ocean ate plankton, but my point is that size isn't important for consumption.

Um, okay, Dunn said, still confused. *I'm not following you, Black.*

The limbs, appendages, mandibles, and mouths reappeared on the creatures. They looked like insects drawn from a child's nightmare. All of them, apart from the pinecone, disappeared. An image of a new creature appeared. Only it didn't look the same at all.

Compared to the pinecone, its shell appeared lustrous and bright, although it was technically black. Its segmented body seemed as though it could stretch and bend, but the most striking difference were the legs. The new creature had what seemed like hundreds of legs.

Wow, Dunn said. *Is that from Earth?*

Yes, Black said. *Notice the similarities?*

I do, Dunn said. *You think these creatures, the ones we've seen thus far, are just the base of the food chain?*

It's possible, Black said. *Their adaptations to life in z-g as well as a vacuum, are startling. By today's models of evolution, one might say they're even impossible. But there they are.*

"Then what the hell is that beacon?" Dunn asked.

Black paused again. The AI seemed as though it was mulling over which of its many different theories it wished to pursue. That was never a good sign.

The beacon, Black said, *is most likely one of three things. An attractor to repopulate portions of space. The first step in an alien invasion. Or something we haven't even considered.*

Dunn rolled his eyes. *What does that even mean?*

If I knew, Black said dryly, *I would have considered it.*

Fair enough, Dunn said. *What do your simulations tell you?*

Black said nothing for a moment, but the Earth insect disappeared. The pinecone zoomed out slightly and the rest of its alien brethren reappeared. *Simulations are inconclusive at best, Captain. The Trio had a reason for sending it to Pluto.*

Yes, Dunn said. *To make sure it didn't travel.*

That is likely. However, Black said, *there may be a different reason they didn't want it to travel.*

What are you saying, Black?

That my creators might know the real reason it's here.

Dunn shivered. The videos. The communications piped to them. The files decrypting for Black as events unfolded. Were there thousands of those files? The answers for certain situations they foresaw? Or did they calculate the most likely events and plan for them?

They were the three most powerful AIs in Sol System. Designed on Xi's principles and the most expensive technology of their time, and they had been retrofitted and serviced, unlike the rest of Trident Station and the Neptune Shipyards. While replacement parts for the Trio internals were always on time and abundant, just getting raw materials to print new components for the SFMC was a hassle.

All the Trio had to do was think, and they'd had 43 years to do that based on the information gathered by *Mira*'s crew and AI. Almost half a century of poring over data transmitted by *Mira*'s AI before it became homicidal.

Before the accident, Dunn said.

What do you mean, sir?

Dunn pursed his lips. He didn't even want to think about this. Not when the Trio had control of the station, not when the AIs had control over the base he hoped to return to.

Black? I'm going out on a limb here and I'm going to trust you.

Thank you, Captain. Trust me with what?

He flexed his fingers, desperately trying to force himself to speak. *What if the Trio planned everything? Including the accident aboard* Mira*?*

Black was silent for a moment. The creatures disappeared and a picture of *Mira* filled the void. It was *Mira* as she had looked before leaving Trident Station and Sol System on her supposed mission. The ship was still majestic, still elegant for its size and shape. Still a monument to humanity's efforts to ensure their future.

Now it was little more than millions of hunks of Atmo-steel floating through the Kuiper Belt. Any evidence of its journey was lost forever, save for the creatures it had brought back with it. Well, those and the beacon.

Captain, Black said, *are you implying the Trio realized the danger of the beacon once Mira's crew brought it on board? Or they knew even before the crew retrieved it?*

I don't know if it was before or after, but I think they knew before the reactors went critical.

Black paused again. He could practically hear her making a "hmmm" sound. *Possible,* Black said. *I have run similar simulations.*

Dunn cocked his head. *You have?*

Black seemed to chuckle. *Captain, the last few hours have been an eternity for me. Even while running Oakes' and Nobel's calculations, monitoring the marines, and handling my usual duties, I've hardly been taxed. Ever since the first message from the Trio, I have been curious as to their decisions as well as their intent.*

The weapons, Dunn said. *They were experimental, but they worked.*

And the Trio ensured those munitions were put aboard the ship. The likelihood of coincidence is nearly impossible. If the Trio knew of the creatures, which it appears they did, they did nothing to warn SFMC or SF Gov about them. Or perhaps the reports were lost. Or, Black said, *Colonel Heyes either knows and chose not to brief you, or his commanders did the same to him.*

Again, possible. But that didn't make much sense to Dunn. If SF Gov or SFMC had known about the threat, it would have been nearly impossible to keep it secret for the last 43 years. Secrets just didn't stay secret. They never did. Not for long, anyway.

Black? If the Trio did know, and they set this up, why did they do it? What could possibly be their reasoning?

Mira disappeared, replaced by a view of Trident Station and Neptune Shipyards orbiting the strange-hued world. No ships were docked. It was a simulation, similar to the one the Trio had used in their last few messages. Similar, but not the same.

I cannot say with any confidence what that endgame might be, Captain. I believe we'll have to return to Trident Station to discover the answer to that question.

Bullshit, he thought to himself. He felt Black's reluctance to voice her suspicions, which meant she had an idea, but didn't want to share. In a way, he couldn't blame her. If she saw something malevolent, she didn't want to share it because it would destroy any trust she had left with the crew. And if it wasn't? Well, she wanted to be sure one way or another. So did Dunn.

Contact PEO. Tell them we're heading back. Also ask Mickey if he has a fix on Dickerson.

Yes, Captain.

He broke the connection and was once again on the bridge. Oakes readjusted himself in his couch. The ship's cycling engines made the deck and bulkheads vibrate, a soothing sensation rather than what it did to you when you were under thrust. When you were under multi-g thrust, you felt as though every bone in your body was going to be pounded into dust.

Dunn rubbed at his eyes. He wanted out of his combat suit. He wanted to sit in the galley, read, and drink coffee. *And you can do all that,* he told himself. *The moment we're on our way home.*

He smiled to himself. He could almost taste the too-often recycled air on Trident Station, imagine the feel of its deck beneath his slippered feet, and smell the odors of various vape flavors, the sour-tang of beer, and the all too casual atmosphere of the officer's club. *Just have to make it there,* he told himself.

You're assuming it's all still there, a voice inside his mind tittered.

Dunn frowned. He knew a part of him wondered that very thing.

CHAPTER SIXTY-SIX

The second thrust burn had ended, but it didn't mean they were safe. The creatures had dropped back, but they were still coming. Every few minutes, Kali flipped to the aft cam feeds and watched the trailing horde.

The sheer size of the lifeform conglomeration was daunting to say the least. It looked as though there were millions of them. Far from the number they'd seen on the hull when they'd first arrived, much less what they'd found inside *Mira*.

Her ribs throbbed. That wasn't going to change anytime soon. While she'd probably be more comfortable in sick bay, slacking with Elliott, the pain wasn't going anywhere. Her broken ribs, bruised organs, and tortured flesh didn't care if she was in a combat suit or a damned bathtub—it would still hurt.

In a few more minutes, Oakes would warn them about the next burn and it would be time to get back in the acceleration couch, but until that happened, she was going to keep looking at the cam footage from Taulbee and Gunny.

The closer Gunny's skiff got to the beacon, the stranger the light became. The captured images also started to waver in and out of focus as though the onboard AI was unable to figure out what to track. Worst of all, many of the frames were simply not there. The cams had somehow dropped at least seven or eight seconds worth of footage scattered amidst grainy, unclear images of dangling pipe, crumbling Atmo-steel, and shattered bulkheads.

The beacon and the surrounding area seemed to just consume the skiff's light as if the photons were liquid going down a drain. What they'd seen inside *Mira*, hell even in the hanger bay, had been the same. Something was eating the light, making it far more dim than it should be. Worse, while the light was bright up close, the darkness seemed to just swallow it. Did the beacon provide some sort of field inside the ship? Was it the creatures? Or was it something else causing the effect?

She shivered. Knowing probably wouldn't set her mind at ease anyway. They were towing the sled that held the beacon, they were being followed by an unimaginable horde of malevolent alien life, and somewhere ahead of them, Dickerson and his escape pod were still traveling to Pluto. The only question was whether or not he was still alive inside of it.

Taulbee appeared at the cargo bay entrance. She snapped to but he shouted "at ease" before she had a chance. He looked in her direction, held up a finger, and beckoned her.

Kali felt guilty, although she didn't know why. She supposed she felt that way whenever a superior, NCO or commissioned, wanted to have a word. Didn't matter if was Gunny, one of the many lieutenants, or the captain himself. It was always the same crawling feeling that you had done something wrong and would be held accountable for it.

She briskly walked to him and took a parade rest stance in front of him. "Sir."

He looked as though he were going to give her bad news. "Corporal? Gunny is out of action. Until he is returned to duty, you'll be performing his tasks."

The words entered her ears and her mind froze. Part of her had known this was going to happen. The moment she'd heard Gunny was down, she knew Taulbee would have to juggle things around. To make matters worse, two members of her squad, including herself, had already suffered extensive injuries. But someone had to be in command and by rank, she was next in line.

Somehow, she had a feeling that needn't have mattered. Carb had seen plenty of action during the last two wars, she had much more experience than Kali, and she'd even been a corporal before she was busted down. But something in the way Taulbee looked, grim and cheered at the same time, made her feel as though she'd proven herself.

"Aye, sir," she said at last, doing her best to keep the words flat and emotionless. She thought she had succeeded.

Taulbee nodded to her. "Black has put you on the command channel. For all field ops, I'm your direct superior. Understood?"

"Aye, sir," she said again.

"Good." He brushed a hand through his close-cropped hair. "How are the injuries?"

"Not keeping me from doing my job, sir."

He nodded. "I don't know how you did it, Kalimura. I don't know how any of you got out of there alive." He raised his hand in salute. She clicked her heels together and returned it. Taulbee slowly lowered his hand. "I want your squad on their asses and in their couches in two minutes."

"Aye, sir," she said, cheeks flushed, voice choked.

"See you after the burn." He turned and quickly made his way back to the bridge.

Kali watched him go for a moment, more to compose herself than out of reverie. She didn't deserve the baton, not yet, but it had been passed on to her. She was in charge of their only squad. Two relatively healthy lance corporals, one in sick bay, one floating out in space, and two privates. She grunted. *Don't get all choked up,* she said to herself. *You were leading three LCpls through that hell ship not more than two hours ago. This would be easy by comparison.*

She took in a deep breath before turning around. Nobel was still at his place in the very back, his eyes closed and fully jacked in with Black. Carb stood with Murdock and Wendt, Copenhaver standing astride the SV-52.

"Black Company," she bellowed in a hoarse shout she didn't even know she could make. "Form up!"

The four marines snapped to attention, arms at their sides, eyes staring straight ahead. "Time to ride the Gs. Get settled in your couches. You have one minute. Move it!"

The four marines walked in pairs out of the cargo bay. Kali stared after them for a moment before falling in behind them.

*****

Kali peeled herself off the acceleration couch. The last burn felt short to her.

She checked her chronometer and she was right. Four minutes short. She wasn't really sure what that meant.

"Well, Corporal," Wendt said. "I haven't really had the chance to say welcome back."

She smiled. "We've all been a little busy," she said. "How are you holding up?"

"Doing fine." He jerked a thumb at Murdock. "Busy keeping his sorry ass alive."

"Hey!" Murdock said.

Wendt shrugged. "Sounds about right, doesn't it?"

Murdock raised a finger to protest, paused, and slowly lowered it. He fetched a deep sigh. "No comment."

Kali laughed. "Let's hope you don't need to—"

"Command crew to the briefing room," Taulbee's voice said over the general comms.

Wendt stared up at the speaker hidden somewhere in the overhead. "Ah," he said. He slowly lowered his eyes to meet hers, his face set in a grin. "The joys of command."

"Shut up. You kids behave."

Kali made her way from the crew area to the bridge level. She should have felt nervous. Hell, her heart should be jack-hammering away in her chest, and her stomach clenched in knots, but instead, she felt nothing. It was just another task in the seemingly longest day of her life.

Once she made it to the briefing room, she knocked on the door. "Enter and at ease," Dunn's voice said through the door's speaker. She opened the door, closed it behind, and walked to the table. Dunn gestured to a chair without breaking his stare with the hologram floating in midair.

"Welcome, Corporal."

"Thank you, sir," she said.

Taulbee glanced at her and nodded to the place next to him. She took the hint and walked past him. Nobel grinned at her but said nothing.

"We cut the burn short because of a transmission we received from Mickey." Three circles appeared on the holographic map. The triangle in the center was *S&R Black*. Two of the circles were behind the ship, the third in front. He pointed at the map. "Those two in our wake are separate walls of the creatures. They're still on our tail, although we've gained quite a lot of ground."

Dunn flicked his eyes to the pulsing circle far in front of them. "That is Dickerson's escape pod."

Kali nearly asked a question and bit her lip instead. Fortunately, Taulbee did it for her.

"Sir, does Mickey have any intel on the pod? Life signs? Power?"

Dunn glanced at him. "Yes and no. Its thrusters are continuing to fire on schedule, so it obviously still has both fuel and power. As to life signs? Your guess is as good as anyone's."

Taulbee nodded. "So the bad guys are still coming at us and we're going to have to stop accelerating to capture the escape pod."

"That's the long and the short of it, yes," Dunn said. He made eye contact with Nobel. "How are we on fuel?"

"Fine, for now, sir," Nobel said. "Reactors are doing okay. As long as we continue the short burst thrusts, I don't foresee any issues."

"Good," Dunn said. "Taulbee? How do you want to do this?"

"I think we keep braking to match Dickerson's speed," Taulbee said. "After we catch up with him, I'll take the SV-52 and retrieve him. Shouldn't take long. Once we're underway again, we can launch the sled."

Launch the sled. The sled. Yes, they still had to launch the sled. They had to get it flying to Pluto, regardless of what else they did. In that respect, wasn't Dickerson secondary? *No,* she thought. *He's not. But in the scope of the mission, he is.* She swallowed hard.

Dunn nodded to himself. "Corporal?"

She stiffened. She hadn't exactly expected him to ask her anything. "Aye, sir?"

"You have anything to add?"

She felt as though he could see every thought inside her head. "May I ask a question, sir?"

Dunn blinked. "Of course you may."

She swung her head to look at Nobel. "Lieutenant? Do we have to fire the sled straight at Pluto, or can we send it on a different trajectory?"

Nobel absently scratched at the wrap around his ribs as he considered the question. A few seconds later, he began to grin. "Yes, Corporal. We have enough control to program a different flight path. At least to a certain degree."

She looked back at the captain. "Sir? If we send the sled off on a wider flight path, we can ensure the creatures will give up chasing us and go after the sled. That will leave us more space and time to retrieve Dickerson."

Dunn pursed his lips and returned his stare to the hologram. She thought he was going to tell her she was being silly, but smiled instead. "Black? Calculate potential paths for the sled."

"Yes, Captain."

A series of arcs appeared, each beginning at *S&R Black*'s position and ending at Pluto. Black then erased the arcs that would put Dickerson in obvious danger. The remaining three courses took the sled on approaches that would bring the sled in on Pluto's far side. The sled would peel off from their present position, execute multiple attitude burns to gain lateral space, and even more attitude burns once it closed on Pluto.

"Which of these three is the optimum?" Dunn asked.

The arc in the middle of the three possibles pulsed. "This one," Black said, "shows the least probability of failure. The widest arc is the safest. However, it is also the most likely to fail due to the sled's limited fuel supply."

"What's the probability of success on the optimum arc?" Taulbee asked.

"85%," Black said. "That estimate, of course, does not include the very slim chance of the creatures catching up with the sled."

"Void wept," Nobel muttered.

Kali understood what he meant. If the creatures caught up with the sled, there was no telling what they would do. Or, more importantly, what the beacon would do. They would certainly lose any chance of controlling the vehicle, let alone where it landed. Or if it landed.

"This arc doesn't really buy us too much distance," Taulbee said. He glanced at Kalimura. "But it should give us enough."

"Let's be clear about this," Dunn said. "We're talking about delaying a rescue, essentially leaving Dickerson in his pod longer than we have to, in order to guarantee we can actually save him."

Kali nodded. "I think so, sir."

Dunn's smile grew. "Taulbee?"

"Aye, sir. I think we should go with this."

"Any objections?" Dunn asked Nobel.

The engineer slowly shook his head. "I think the sled can handle it. Just means Black and I will have to keep a closer eye on it. I think we're good."

"Black?"

"Yes, Captain?"

"Find us the best launch point on our way to pick up Dickerson. Sooner rather than later."

"Yes, Captain," Black said. She paused for a moment. "The best launch window will open in fifteen minutes."

"Good. Taulbee? I want a plan of attack for the sled in my block in five minutes."

"Aye, sir."

"Let's get this right, people. Dismissed."

Kali raised her hand to salute, but stopped short. None of the officers did, so she felt confused. Dunn looked at her with a knowing smile. "Salutes, Corporal, are a protocol we don't observe with the command crew. Not while on a mission."

"Oh," she said dumbly. "Of course, sir."

Taulbee beckoned her. "Let's get to the cargo bay, Kalimura. We have some work to do."

*****

Block to block was the most efficient way to manufacture and disseminate tactical plans. While walking to the cargo bay from the briefing room, she and Taulbee had an entire conversation regarding load outs, assignments, and tactics. By the time the two reached the bay, Taulbee had already transmitted the plans to Dunn's block. The captain sent an acknowledgment to both of them in return: it was a go.

Kali had already sent block messages commanding her squad to be in the cargo bay and ready to go. As she and Taulbee stepped into the cargo bay, the four marines stood at parade rest, still dressed in their combat suits.

"Officer on deck!" Kali yelled.

The four marines stiffened, eyes straight ahead.

Taulbee chuckled. "At ease," he said. He glanced at Kali. "Your show, Corporal."

"Aye, sir." She walked forward a few paces and glanced at each of her charges. "Slight change in plans, marines. We're going to launch the sled before we go after Dickerson." Before the four non-rates had a chance to ask questions, or protest, she continued speaking. "Wendt? You, Murdock, and Carb are my squad. Copenhaver? You're with the LT."

"So what's the plan?" Carb asked.

Kali grinned. "We will do a bounce and tether maneuver to the back of the ship and the sled. The SV-52 will provide cover fire and emergency ops if necessary. Wendt? Who's a better shot? You or Murdock?"

Wendt scoffed. It was the only answer Kali needed. Murdock looked hurt, but didn't protest.

"Carb? You and Murdock will handle the sled. Wendt and I will provide cover fire as well as handle the emergency tether lines." She nodded at Carb. "You have any objections?"

"No, Corporal," Carb said. "I'll keep the little tyke safe."

"Hey!" Murdock said.

Taulbee turned slightly to hide a grin. Kali fought to keep her face stony—it was damned difficult.

"So get yourselves ready. Wendt? You and I are carrying as much tritium as we can. Full mags. Fuck the other stuff."

"Aye, Corporal."

"Carb? Murdock? Same load, but don't plan on using your rifles unless it's absolutely necessary. The last thing we need is for one of you to accidentally hit the sled or the beacon."

Murdock raised a hand. "Corporal?"

"What is it, Private?"

He swallowed hard. "What do we do if the beacon goes off again?"

She traded an uneasy glance with Taulbee. "We do whatever we have to do to succeed," she said. "Any other questions?"

Murdock shook his head. The young private's face had drained of color. He looked more terrified than she'd ever seen him.

"Let me be clear," Kali said. "We fuck this up, we lose Dickerson. We fuck this up, we might lose Black. If we really fuck this up, we might lose Sol System altogether." The cargo bay went dead silent. She checked her chronometer. "We have 10 minutes before the ship reaches the launch window. We have two minutes after that to get the sled launched. We're in space in two minutes. Make it happen, people. Get to it."

The strained silence instantly disappeared. Copenhaver trotted to the SV-52, removed the fueling cables, and began a pre-flight check. Taulbee joined her, obviously pleased by her initiative.

Kali grabbed her helmet and a rifle from the rack. She stashed several magazines in her pouch and checked the ammo count in the rifle. When they finished loading up, the last of the tritium mags were exhausted. Her four marines, plus Taulbee and Copenhaver's weapons, were flush with the tritium ammo. Once they ran out, they were done. They'd be down to regular explosive flechettes and shock rounds.

Kali stood next to Carb. "You really okay with this?" she asked in a low voice.

Carb nodded. "I don't like how long we're going to make Dickerson wait." She traded a glance with Kali. "If you say it's for a good reason, though, that's good enough for me."

"It is," Kali said. "This will buy us more time. Hopefully, it will make picking him up even easier."

Carb made a noise that might have been a mirthless laugh or a curse. "Easy? On this mission. That would be a first."

"Keep an eye on Murdock. He's looking a little squirrely."

"Aye, Boss." Carb patted her pouch, her gloved fingers counting the stashed magazines. "I'll keep him out of trouble."

"Just keep him from freezing," Kali said.

"Will do, Boss."

"Wendt!" Kali called. "You ready or what?"

"Aye, Boss." The large marine had already locked his rifle to his back and was checking Murdock's suit and load. "Ready when you are."

"Outstanding," Kali said. "We'll go out the personnel airlock. Make sure you're tethered. We'll mag-lock along the starboard hull until we reach aft. Once we get there, Wendt and I will take up position to provide cover fire, tether support, and assistance if needed. Carb? You and Murdock will follow the tow lines down to the sled. Release it and follow Black's instructions as far as its orientation. Once that happens, we'll pull you back. Understood?" The three marines bellowed affirmatives. Kali smiled. "Let's do it."

*****

They had a little more than four minutes to reach the aft before *S&R Black* entered the launch window. Kali, bringing up the rear of the formation of four marines, was already frustrated. Murdock, second behind Carb, was holding up the line with his clumsy technique. She made a mental note to get permission from Gunny to beat his ass when they returned to Trident Station.

If Gunny is conscious, let alone alive, she thought. The image of him lying in the autodoc filled her mind, the normally powerful and strong-looking marine rendered helpless. With one eye covered in a patch while the other remained closed to the world outside, he might as well have been trapped in the void. Kali suddenly wanted to be back there in the infirmary, to be around if something happened.

Won't matter if you fuck this up. The voice was her own, and yet sounded like Gunny all at the same time. Kali grinned.

"Murdock? Move your fucking ass before I kick it off the hull," she growled into the mic.

"Yes, Boss!" Murdock yelled back.

And he did. His clumsy steps were still aggravating to watch, but at least he was stumbling faster. Yup. He was in for a lot of hell when they returned to Trident Station. She might make him walk around the whole goddamned exterior.

A check of her chronometer told her a minute had already passed, but at least they were finally nearing the aft. Wendt, as large as he was, blocked out much of her view. Instead of trying to catch a peek over his shoulder, she added his helmet feed to her HUD and scanned her side of space looking for movement, but there was none.

The SV-52 glided 10 meters away as it slowly maneuvered to cover her squad. "I have you in sight, Corporal," Taulbee said.

"Copy, sir," she said.

"You have two and a half minutes until the launch window opens," Black said. "Mark."

"You heard her," Kali said. "Move it." She switched to Carb's cam and watched as the hump of *S&R Black*'s engine array came into view. "Carb? Descend and head for the belly. We'll follow."

"Copy, Boss," Carb said. Her cam feed panned to the left before reorienting on the edge of the ship's hull. Carb took four steps before halting. "Shit. Corporal?"

A line of silvery liquid curled in a semi-circle centimeters from Carb's boot. The acid eventually drizzled down and out of sight. "Squad. A starfish left its calling card." She flipped through her cam feeds, looking for signs of movement. Apart from the SV-52 finally reaching its position, nothing moved.

"It may have been from before," Carb said. "No telling how long this shit has been here."

"Cut the chatter. Carb? Mark it on your HUD and keep going."

"Copy, Boss," she said. After shuffling a step further from the substance, she continued walking to the ship's belly.

"Kalimura to Taulbee."

"Go ahead."

"Sir? We found acid near the engine array."

"Copy," the lieutenant said.

Kali continued watching her steps, giving herself plenty of space between her and Wendt, while occasionally glancing at the SV-52's position. The support craft appeared to be dropping below the ship very slowly.

Carb reached the intersection and followed the gentle curve to the ship's keel. Even with her rifle in her hands, the weapon raised nearly to shoulder height, her fluid steps held the cam view steady.

"At the acid," Wendt said nervously.

"Copy," Kali said. "Carb?"

"So far so good, Boss."

"Okay, let Wendt and I get into position before you start your approach to the net tether."

"Copy, Boss," Murdock and Carb said at the same time.

Kali fought the flood of gooseflesh that crawled up her arms and over her back. If that was a new trail, they had at least one hostile in the area. At least one. She thought they had been clear of the creatures before they blasted *Mira*, but there was no telling what had attached itself to the hull before they finished the job. Hell, the moment Taulbee docked, the damned things had been out there.

Hitched a ride, she thought sourly. "Squad," she said firmly, but slowly. "Multiple bogies likely. Keep your heads on a swivel."

Their voices came back cold and matter-of-fact. Everyone copied, everyone knew what to do. She just hoped they could execute when the time came.

*****

The SV-52 slowly dipped below the hull-line. Taulbee held his breath as they finally descended far enough for the cams to provide a view of the keel, the bottom hull appearing to lengthen and narrow during his perspective shift. The '52's lights finally provided detail once it chased away the shadows and phantom shapes. He shivered as he realized the detail faded near the midships as if the light itself were being eaten.

"Oh, shit," Taulbee muttered. "Squad! Bottom hull! Midships!"

"Copy," Kali said.

"Private? You see it move, fire on it," Taulbee said. "Let me know if I need to descend."

"Aye, sir. Drop two meters."

Taulbee didn't question. When your gunner said to give them room, you did it, regardless of rank. A deft touch of the controls and a thruster fired. The SV-52 accelerated quickly and stopped just as fast. His view of *S&R Black*'s hull was more broad now and he could finally see what he'd feared.

Four starfish floated mere centimeters from the ship's keel. The creatures' arms had folded around their cores, making them look like polyhedron dice. Their strange shells vibrated in the light like heat haze off metal. Unlike the other starfish they'd encountered, the stowaways' arms pulsed with color, making their skin fade from a dark, wavering gray to an impossible black.

"Sir? I have a shot."

"Copy." Taulbee's spine crawled just looking at the damned things. The memories of their silvery acidic excretions and their powerful arms, strong enough to fling Atmo-steel flechettes at him like throwing stars, flipped through his mind. And instead of just one, there were four of them, each much larger than the last one he'd fought.

But they weren't moving. They just floated there, wrapped in their armor as if waiting for something. Maybe they were waiting for the humans to attack. Or something else?

"Kalimura? What's your status?"

A few seconds passed before she spoke, her words clipped and cold. "Carb and Murdock are almost in position to start their climb."

"Fuck the climb," Taulbee said. "Suit thrusters. Cut that line ASAP."

*****

Carb and Murdock had reached the tow lines. On the way there, the squad had come across several more patches of the deadly, glistening leavings from the starfish creatures. Kali and Wendt spread out to cover their squad-mates who began descending down the lines. If the ship had to move quickly, Carb and Murdock were the most vulnerable to fast shifts in the z-g. They could have used the suit thrusters, but if the ship had to EVA for any reason, it could either collide with them or leave them vulnerable to emergency rocket activation.

The plan was simple enough. Carb and Murdock would go down, release the sled from the net, and position it with Black and Nobel's assistance. Getting it pointed in roughly the right direction would allow the sled to reach maximum acceleration without having to first adjust the sled's attitude during flight.

Once they finished the job, the two marines would ride the net back to the hull, join up with their squad-mates, and get their asses back inside the ship. Simple. Right.

As the pair reached the halfway point, Kali's HUD lit up with a proximity warning. An arm appeared at the end of the tether, its sharp point glistening in the floodlights. It seemed to caress the sled inside the net. Kali heard Carb take a deep breath.

"Corporal?"

"I see it," Kali said. The last word died on her lips as another arm appeared a meter away. Taulbee yelled at her to cut the line.

"Understood, sir. However, we have a bit of a problem. We have two possible bogies on the sled."

Taulbee groaned. "I don't give a shit, Corporal. Cut that line and get back inside the ship. Now."

"Aye, sir," Kali said with a wince. "Carb? Murdock? We're cutting the lines. Suit thrusters are authorized. Repeat. Use your damned thrusters!"

Murdock moved to detach himself from the line and stopped dead. Mere centimeters away, silvery ooze glistened against the cable's dark Atmo-steel surface.

"Freeze!" Kali called over the line, but he already had. The cam feed from his helmet barely twitched. "Unhook very carefully and use your fore thrusters to blast away from the line."

"Copy," he said, his voice vibrating with tension.

"Carb?"

"I'm free," Carb said. "I'll help—"

"No, you won't. Get back here. Now."

"But—"

"Do it!" Kali yelled. She kept her eyes glued to Murdock's cam, watching as he carefully unhooked from the cable tether and quickly pulled back his arm. With his other hand, the one much further away from the silvery glaze, he gently pushed.

Murdock rose away from the cable meter by meter before engaging his thrusters. "On my way, Corporal," Murdock said.

She flipped back to her helmet cam feed and looked down the line at Carb. The LCpl was using her thrusters and following the cable back to the hull. Kali watched her climb further and further over the sled. Three starfish, their carapaces scattering the light in radiating waves, contracted around the sled, arms crossing and clutching at the net itself.

"Sir? They're wrapped around the net."

"Cut the line. We'll worry about that in a minute. Just get your—"

Another creature appeared atop the mound of starfish, stubby fins that waved in a silent rhythm jutted from its squat body. Long arms, ends tipped with triangles of some glinting material, probed the space around them as if searching. The new creature rose above the sled, its large mandibles clicking and clacking together without making any sound in the vacuum. As they moved, she saw the deep hole that was its maw, a ring of serrated teeth vibrating in the light.

The mouth moved quickly forward and a line of silver shot out of the darkness. Kali cut her mag-locks and hit her thrusters at the same time. She lost contact with the hull and flew to port. A meter away, the liquid excretion hit the hull in a puddle, the droplets sticking to the Atmo-steel rather than dispersing in the z-g.

Kali aimed her rifle and fired. The tritium flechette round left the barrel and streaked towards its target as the rocket engine kicked in. The creature tried to duck, but the round hit the side of its horrible face, its mandibles disappearing in a bright blue flash of light.

The creature tumbled away into the z-g, half of its head gone. The creatures surrounding the net stirred slightly. She thought droplets of the heavy water had probably hit their shells. Either that or they knew their exo-solar fellow had been killed.

"Get out of there!" Taulbee shrieked over the comms.

"Squad!" Kali yelled. "Retreat!"

Kali sent a block command to the tow controls and the net released at once. The sled slowly moved away, its own momentum slowed by the magnetic force of the net pushing it out.

She turned and realized she was on the wrong side of the ship. The emergency airlock was on the starboard-side, not the port. She kicked on the thrusters and shot upwards, her rifle pointed at the sled. She rose meter by meter in a controlled ascent, her fingers flexing around the trigger guard, daring the creatures to move again.

After a few meters, she began to relax. The three visible starfish encasing the sled hadn't moved again. Were they worshiping it? Or drawing energy from the beacon?

Something moved below her. Kali looked down and saw a dim outline in the shadows. Ethereal arms swayed and danced with alien grace. Another shadow appeared. And still another. Kali fired her fore thrusters as the creatures jetted up to meet her. She had time to snap aim and fire a round at each of them, the rifle moving with her arms as though they were one.

The flechettes detonated seven meters from her, the shards of Atmo-steel breaking through the creatures' shells and spraying particles of black material in all directions. An arm whipped upward a mere meter from her boots. Kali fired her chest thrusters and darted backward, her feet just missing the lip of the hull intersection. She increased her speed to 2m/s and continued flying backward, her mind alertly flicking between the rear cam and the creatures in front of her. The danger of ramming into something behind her wasn't nearly as dangerous as the creatures now climbing or floating to follow her.

There was no way of knowing if these were the same creatures that had been gathered around the beacon. And it didn't matter. Now she had four bogies to deal with.

"Kalimura!" Taulbee yelled. "Status!"

"Line cut," she said. "I repeat, sled is free."

"Copy," Taulbee said. "We're having some fun on the keel."

The ship shuddered as if to accentuate his statement.

"Squad!" Kali called out. "Status?"

"Boss," Carb said. "We're at the airlock. Where the hell are you?'

"Stuck topside. I have a few friends to deal with."

"I'll come get you," Wendt said.

"Negative. Get inside the ship," Kali snarled. "That's an order."

The pause was more than long enough to give the creatures the chance to close in. She might be moving at 2m/s, but they were accelerating toward her. And void wept, but they could move. The creatures knew about the rifles. Either one encounter with a flechette was enough for them to understand the danger, or they communicated with one another. Either way, the creatures practically danced in the z-g.

"Copy, Boss," Carb said. "Entering the cargo bay. Good hunting, Corporal."

Kali almost said "thank you." What she really wanted to say was for them to get the hell out here and save their damned corporal. Kali snapped her teeth together and banished the fear. If she was going to die, she was going to go down shooting.

She fired four flechettes in rapid succession, each of the rounds timed to match the pattern the creatures had shown. They moved in half-meter slides and jumps, but always ended up in a formation of sorts. It wasn't consistent, but it was enough for this.

The creature on the far left danced right into the round, the flechettes shattering four arms and cutting a ragged semi-circle through the creature's torso. The second round flew through a gap and disappeared into space while the last two rounds hit the same creature with devastating results. The flechettes ripped through its shell, scattering particles and alien flesh in all directions. But she'd missed one. It had flown backward, either having sensed the impending attack, or it had reflexes the likes of which she couldn't imagine.

As it moved backward, she saw what was behind it. More of them. And more of them. "Captain?"

"Corporal? Are you in the cargo bay?"

"No, sir," she said. "But I wish I was."

*****

The four creatures slowly unfolded themselves, their arms pointed directly at the SV-52. The radiating waves of darkness slowed, but the pulsing colors around their bodies began speeding up. Taulbee pushed the SV-52 and cleared *S&R Black*'s keel.

"Sir?" Copenhaver called. "We're going to hit the sled."

Cursing, he hit the thrusters hard, taking them at a negative vector from the ship and her ejected cargo. At the same time, he changed their attitude to point back at the ship. The creatures reached *S&R Black*'s aft and cleared it with a sweep of their strange arms.

"Private? Fire."

She did. A short stair step of flechette rounds streaked from the cannon. Most of the shots missed, detonating on the ship's hull, but a few struck.

Arcs of electricity danced over their shells. One of them burst apart while another just flailed silently in space.

While he swept the area, looking for targets, he checked in with Kalimura. "Are you in the cargo bay?"

"No," she said and muttered something else.

He brought up her cam feed on his HUD. "Fuck. Me. Just don't die, Kalimura. We're coming."

He gave the '52's thrusters a push and the craft quickly accelerated back the way it had come. Kalimura was topside and floating toward the bow. With a thought, he brought up her location on the ship and fed the coordinates to the flight computer. A path immediately appeared on his HUD. Taulbee continued hitting the thrusters in sequence, following the flowing rectangles on the screen. As he half-looped over *Black*'s topside, Copenhaver aimed and opened fire.

A dozen flechettes flew and exploded between the floating figure and the shadowy things chasing her. Two more of the creatures blew apart, but the rest continued their pursuit as if nothing had happened. Kali was firing too, but the things moved fast enough to evade her shots.

"Sir? Bogies on our six."

"Where the hell are they coming from?"

Proximity alerts flashed on his HUD. He barely had time to pull at the controls before they disappeared entirely. Whatever had been about to attack had pulled away. On the ship's topside, he watched as three of the creatures swam through the emptiness and away from Kalimura.

"Shit, sir," Copenhaver said.

"What?"

He turned his head and blinked. A cloud of CO2 drifted from the port-side outlets. Dark shadows flew toward it, some crashing into one another in their scramble to reach it.

"Kalimura? It's your lucky day," Taulbee said. He reoriented the SV-52 and pushed past *S&R Black*'s bow. "Copenhaver. Net the corporal."

"Aye, sir," Copenhaver said. A moment later, Kalimura was in the net, and he was flying for the cargo bay.

"Lieutenant," Dunn said. "Get your ass in here ASAP."

"Sir? What about the beacon?"

"Get in the ship. Now."

"Aye, sir," Taulbee said. The CO2 cloud that had puffed out of the ship was probably dissipating, or maybe the creatures were consuming it. Either way, it wasn't going to last long. If nothing was between him and the cargo bay, he'd be there in seconds. He hoped his luck would hold.

*****

Jacked into *S&R Black*'s systems, he'd already seen the creatures. Well, see was the wrong word. Nobel had really detected them by monitoring temperature fluctuations along the ship's keel. He'd first thought of the idea during their last battle, but hadn't had time to implement it. Between rescuing Kalimura, destroying *Mira*, and getting them under extreme thrust, he'd been a little busy.

But it was quite simple, really. The S&R models had all been built for simplified maintenance as well as diagnostics. If their AIs died during battle or some other calamity, the command crew still maintained control of all responsibilities for its functions. Well, close to it anyway. He'd simply run a diagnostic check.

During refits, one of the last three hull integrity tests involved checks for Atmo-steel bonding weaknesses. Since *S&R Black*'s hull had been printed using older techniques, it was possible for micro-deformities to appear after enough real-world abuse. As the metal bands began to separate, the shielding layer went first.

If one appeared during the next ship's inspection, they cut, patched, reprinted, and hoped they didn't find another next time. And so on. By running the hull temperature check, he'd spotted the creatures as spikes in temperature.

In a way, that should have been no surprise. To create radioactivity as high as those things did, they should have an elevated temperature in the near absolute-zero environment of space. The closer they came to the hull, the higher the reading. Only problem? He had to repeatedly burst the diagnostic. And it was starting to be a problem.

He'd promised himself to scan only 10 more times when it happened. As soon as he did, he activated the new program, priming the pumps for a waste release. The moment after *Mira*'s destruction, he'd raised the CO_2 filter buffer size, building up an excess of CO_2 in the tanks. The multiple thrust burns during their acceleration phase had certainly resulted in the crew breathing harder, faster, using up more O_2 and expelling more CO_2.

Watching through all the sensors at once, he and Black adjusted the output, making sure to seed the port-side aft with a cloud guaranteed to get the creatures' attention. And it had.

The things moved as one toward the cloud. Even the creatures surrounding the beacon moved and jittered as though fighting the temptation. When the supply of stored CO_2 exhausted itself, the creatures began batting at the hull as if begging for more. Nobel grinned.

He watched through the ship's cameras as the cargo bay door opened and the SV-52 flew inside at a nearly suicidal speed. Taulbee hit the bulkhead a little harder than usual, but the damage would be minimal to both the craft and *Black*.

Nobel deactivated the cargo bay door safeties and it slid into place three times its normal speed. He reengaged the safeties and immediately pressurized the cargo bay.

Seconds later, Kalimura's squad was getting her detached from the '52 while Taulbee and Copenhaver cleared the canopy. But Nobel had stopped watching,

He and Black saw through the same interfaces, but monitored different aspects, coming to agreements as fast as his brain could keep up. The creatures wrapped around the beacon had caused the sled to slowly spin. As long as they didn't stop or change the cycle, their calculation would work. It was all about timing. They found an optimal trajectory with minimal attitude adjustment and waited together for nanoseconds to see if their guess was right.

It was. The sled's rockets came to life and the slab of Atmo-steel quickly accelerated while the attitude thrusters burned to correct its course. With the sled streaking off toward Pluto, and their supply of free food exhausted, the creatures followed in its wake.

Nobel watched in fascination as the alien things retreated into the Kuiper Belt's deep shadows, floating like misshapen, nightmarish ghosts. He ran another diagnostic sweep over the ship. No hotspots. They were as clear as they could be for the moment.

And he needed a break, damnit. But not now, not yet.

CHAPTER SIXTY-SEVEN

Snug in the acceleration couch, Dickerson could hardly move. The escape pod's rockets continued firing every few seconds, keeping the capsule under thrust and at half a g of acceleration. He hadn't realized just how much pain he was in until the g-forces had time to work on his tired muscles, bruised flesh, and broken bones.

The throbbing in his chest and shoulder told him his nannies had finally run out of cannabidiol, THC, and analgesics. He literally had nothing left in the tank. He considered moving, finding the emergency aid kit, and doing what he could to lessen the pain, but it seemed more trouble than it was worth. He'd had worse. Hell, he'd fought with worse. Right now, he was just tired. In pain, sure, but mainly tired.

Besides, what was the point of juicing himself now? He was likely going to die in here, the pod ultimately becoming his very own Atmo-steel coffin. The O2 supply in his suit was nearly gone, the pod's systems were more than a little damaged to begin with, and its O2 reserve sure as hell wasn't going to be enough to get him to Pluto.

He'd tried using comms on all channels, including block comms, but either no one was listening, or the pod wasn't transmitting. From inside the pod, it was impossible for him to connect with external sources, and he imagined the pod's comms arrays were damaged to begin with. No way to communicate. Perfect end to a perfect mission.

Dickerson grunted and fingered his vibro blade. He would rather die in space, or with his veins open, than from suffocation. If it came to that, he'd open the escape pod using the emergency handle and drift out into the darkness. All he'd have to do after that was find the courage to take off his helmet. The temperature and the vacuum would take him quickly. Quickly enough, anyway.

The creatures had followed the pod for a ways before giving up the chase. Maybe its acceleration was a little too much for the beasties, or he just wasn't as interesting a morsel as he'd feared. Like most things that had happened, he'd never know. He'd die without knowing.

The not knowing was the worst part about flying off into the darkness on his own. He'd never know if his squad had made it out of *Mira*. He'd practically thrown Kalimura into her pod and ejected her against orders. Maybe it saved her life. Maybe not. Either way, she got one of the pods that had passed inspection. Maybe her luck had been better than his. He certainly hoped so.

He imagined Kalimura, Wendt, and Carb standing in the cargo bay, the three of them wondering where he was and if he was alive. Or maybe the entire crew had already given him up for dead. If the escape pod was as damaged as he feared it was, its transponder might not even be working. Trying to track the pod would be impossible for *S&R Black*. Hell, he'd probably be invisible to PEO's sensor arrays too.

"So fucked," he whispered and chuckled. The laugh quickly died. Breathing that deeply hurt the hell out of his ribs. Once the last of his adrenal reserves had faded, the pain in his shoulder and chest had risen another notch or two. The swelling of tortured tissue made his nerves sizzle, and not in a good way. In another hour or so, every breath would be its own battle between the pain and the need to drag oxygen into his lungs.

Maybe the escape pod would travel far enough to rendezvous with PEO. The station personnel could fire a tether, pull the pod into the station's small cargo bay, open it, and find a suited corpse. Or, more likely, an open pod with a frozen corpsicle on the couch. One more dead marine. One more casualty from the *Mira* mission.

"I hope they blow you the fuck up," he drawled. The giant ship, a plague-ridden Trojan horse, needed to be blown to pieces before it could endanger the rest of humanity.

Maybe it wouldn't matter. He'd had a lot of time to think over the past hour, and he'd come to a conclusion: humanity was fucked. If you counted on the principles of evolution, then the creatures that had found their way into Sol System were possible. They seemed to share many of the same traits, despite their structural and locomotive differences. They had prey, they had predators, and they had a way to survive in a minimal eco-system. He would have been able to swallow all of that, if not for the beacon.

The beacon's existence suggested something more insidious. An intelligence greater, and far older, than humanity's, had sent the beacon on a journey through the Milky Way to find Sol. Or maybe that was a coincidence and it was nothing more than humanity's misfortune to discover it and their foolhardy nature to bring it back.

Perhaps the beacon was meant to spread the lifeforms across the galaxy, maybe an innocent but misguided attempt to populate lifeless space. Or maybe there was another reason he was incapable of conceiving. Shit, trying to think like a superior mind was giving him a headache.

Whomever, or whatever, had sent the beacon into their area might eventually come to see the fruits of their labors. Should any of humanity still be around, what would the visitors make of them? Would they destroy the humans to keep them from exploring the stars? Or was there some other use for humanity? Slavery? Food? He shivered as he remembered the pinecones' silver, sharp talons and the horrifying starfish maws.

Food seemed likely, although he couldn't remember an instance in which the creatures tried to eat them. They did seem to like carbon dioxide, though, and that was something human beings produced simply by inhaling oxygen.

"You have twenty minutes of suit atmosphere remaining," the computer chimed in his headset.

Twenty minutes. Great. After that, he'd be on whatever reserves the escape pod had. And according to the onboard computer, it wasn't much. All he could do was breathe as shallowly as possible and wait for the onboard supply to dwindle to nothing. Maybe then he'd have the guts to open the hatch and kill himself.

Dickerson leaned back in the couch and closed his eyes. Fuck it. Even if the alien species that had brought these creatures here showed up, he'd be long dead. Especially since it looked like that was going to happen very very soon.

Something bumped against the side of the escape pod. Dickerson's eyes opened at once. He connected to the escape pod cameras and then remembered they weren't functioning. Cursing, he connected to the escape pod's diagnostics and checked for heat signatures. The hull was intact, and cold cold cold. No heat sources. Nothing out there.

The sound came again. He raised his head and stared at the escape pod's ceiling. Whatever made the sound was above him. Something slid across the metal with a sickening screech. Were the creatures out there? A starfish trying to cut its way in and pluck a prize from the tin can?

He fingered his blade again. He had more than enough ammo in his rifle to take care of a few exo-solar beasties, but going out in z-g while clutching a vibro blade and nothing else seemed much more heroic. If you were going to die anyway, might as well go out in a blaze of stupid machismo.

A grin spread across his face as he pulled the blade from its sheath and held it in his right hand. The screeching sound repeated followed by a bump which rattled the pod. He stood from the couch, mag-locked his boots to the deck, and waited. His heartbeat and breathing had increased, making his remaining atmosphere drop by the second. It didn't matter. He'd be dead any moment now.

Something rattled against the hatch. He imagined one of the starfish out there, its body wrapped around the escape pod, talons scratching at the hatch seams, preparing to pop it open like a ration tin. Dickerson's body fell into the SFMC hand-to-hand z-g stance. He sent a block command and the blade turned from a hard, flat-black piece of metal into a wavering, blurring piece of steel. He didn't know if it could cut through their carapaces, but he hoped so. Just enough to make it remember him, if not kill it.

Another scratch against the hull. This time, he was certain it was plucking at the hatch seam. In a few heartbeats, the hatch would burst loose and a dark thing, radiation pouring off its body, would reach in and drag him out. Dickerson tried to keep his breath slow even as his heart raced. His adrenaline reserves were gone. He had nothing left. All he could hope for now was to give the alien sonofabitch a good fight.

A green light appeared on the escape pod's staticky, mostly broken diagnostic screen. Dickerson blinked at it. Green? What the hell did green mean? Usually, it meant the pod was inside an oxygenated environment. Green.

His legs began to shake as the hatch popped open and slid aside. Bright light poured in through the hatchway all but blinding him. Dickerson's screens adjusted and he found himself looking at a bulkhead. A pair of hands, human hands, appeared at the left edge. A heartbeat later, Kalimura slid into view.

Her face lit up with a smile, eyes looking almost teary. "You planning on stabbing me with that, marine?"

Dickerson looked dumbly at the knife in his hands. He'd been clutching it so tightly that he had difficulty flexing his fingers. The blade stopped vibrating, once again turning into a dead hunk of metal. "Corporal?"

"Yup," she said. Carb appeared next to her. Kalimura looked at the other squad-mate. "What do you think, Carb?"

She shrugged. "I say we give him some fresh O2 and send him back into the void. Sounds like standard punishment procedure for disobeying a direct order."

Dickerson swayed slightly, his chest burning with pain. "Where am I?"

Kalimura walked inside the escape pod, one hand held out to him. "Home," she said.

CHAPTER SIXTY-EIGHT

From less than 4,000 km away, PEO looked like a barely visible dark dot against Pluto's solar reflection. The dot disappeared a moment later as it passed to the other side of the planet. Which is exactly where they needed to go. Dunn grimaced at the image.

After getting Dickerson fluids, fresh nannies, and a ton of analgesics, they'd poured him into one of the infirmary beds and locked him up tight. He'd recover, in time, but until they entered stasis, he was going to be in some serious pain.

The autodoc had mended the shoulder the best it could, but there wasn't much to do besides wait for the nannies to do their work. The tiny bots would keep working on him even while he was in stasis, and by the time they reached Neptune, he'd be in much better shape. He might even be able to fight again.

Kalimura and Carb were going to need the same amount of treatment once the company finished evacuating the Pluto Exo-Observatory. That was the main mission now.

The sled was still on its trajectory, but several hours behind them. Nobel had fired up the engines and sent the ship through several acceleration cycles to get *S&R Black* up to a respectable speed, greatly cutting the time it would take for them to reach the dwarf planet. Getting out in front of the sled had been paramount. Especially considering what was following it.

The two waves of creature had more or less intersected and had been joined by other KBOs. They'd passed several of the alien objects on their way to Pluto and each had ignored the ship, heading instead directly for the sled and the beacon.

A few hours into the journey, Black had suggested they preemptively evacuate the PEO personnel. Dunn agreed immediately and now the scientists aboard the observatory had their personal belongings packed and ready to go. He imagined most of their "luggage" would be non-networked data packs filled with information and observations that hadn't yet been uploaded. If his suspicions were correct, the chief astronomer would keep every instrument they had pointed at the incoming plague. That was information that may end up being paramount to their future survival. Depending, of course, on what the beacon did once it reached Pluto.

Dunn was beginning to have reservations about that too. During the trip, he'd gone over the Trio's rationale again and again. Something about it didn't make sense, but that was true about most things related to this mission. The Trio had been playing games with him and even Black had commented to that effect.

Now that his people were safe, those remaining that was, the questions kept piling up. No amount of rack time or meditation silenced them. He had ended up in the cockpit, reviewing every moment of footage they had from the trip to *Mira* as well as Kalimura's squad feeds. Dickerson's cam had been particularly interesting at the end.

The marine probably didn't even see what had been coming for him. He'd probably been focusing on the thing busting its way through the hatch. Hell, Dunn had missed it twice, knowing the images were somehow wrong, but unable to put his finger on it. And then he'd seen it.

Darkness. That darkness again, like the waves radiating off the starfish, but much stronger. It had swallowed every photon of ambient light cast by Dickerson's suit floods. Just before the marine closed the escape pod's hatch, Dunn had seen something moving in the advancing abyss.

The captain's flesh rippled with goose flesh as he remembered the sight. The phenomenon of watching the light being consumed scared him on a primitive level. He'd never seen anything like it, and he imagined primitive humans had felt the same way while trapped in their caves before the advent of fire, just wondering when hostile animals would find the entrance and enter to eat them.

S&R Black shuddered from another brake. Nobel and Black had fluctuated the thrusters, giving them precise attitude adjustments while at the same time slowing the ship. This was wasting a lot of fuel, but it probably didn't matter. They had time to refuel at PEO. Time to refuel, stow their "guests," and get *S&R Black* underway. He'd asked Black for a supply inventory they could loot and he had that prepared too. He'd send two marines inside the station to purloin both medical supplies and printer material reserves. It wasn't much, but it would help.

Regardless, they were heading back to Neptune as soon as he could manage it. He had absolutely no intention of being around when the beacon hit Pluto.

They'd done what they could. So far, the sled hadn't detected anything to make it change its trajectory. As long as the sled didn't modify its course or encounter an object that put its flightpath in danger, there was little to nothing *S&R Black* could do but wait.

The sled was still outrunning the creatures. They wouldn't be around when it hit either. Once the beacon hit Pluto, what would they chase? *S&R Black* would be the last hunk of flying metal that had come in contact with the beacon. Would they follow the ship to Neptune?

The idea was yet another that kept him examining every frame of film while his command crew slept in shifts. Kalimura's squad, those not in the infirmary, had headed to the rack as soon as the ship finished its last acceleration burn. That had been an order.

Just a few more hours and they'd all be in stasis, sleeping for two weeks while the ship traveled to Neptune space. Normally, he didn't look forward to floating like artificial beef in simulated gravy, which is how he felt any time he entered a stasis pod. At least until the drugs kicked in. It was never a long wait, but it always seemed to last an eternity.

This time? He'd be happy to climb in. At least then his brain would be able to stop attempting to find answers to all the questions he had. He doubted anyone on the ship wasn't ruminating over the events of the past 24 hours, even as they slept.

The dot became larger, the station's shape no longer amorphous, but concrete and well-defined. The ship shuddered again.

"How many more brakes, Oakes?"

"Five, sir. Then we'll be slow enough on the approach. All attitude thrusters from then on."

"Good. Let's get our people out of bed."

*****

Light duty. The autodoc had sentenced both Kali and Carb to light duty. Dickerson? Bed rest. As in real bed rest, no excuses, no extenuating circumstances, no argument.

She and Carb stood near the cargo bay doors. The ship had already docked, *S&R Black* attached to the station by an ancient umbilicus. She was surprised it had even worked. The scientists here certainly operated on a shoe-string budget. *Worse than SFMC,* she thought.

Nine scientists, two support engineers. Eleven extra people walking on board carrying satchels and not much else. *S&R Black* had more than enough stasis pods, especially now they'd lost two marines and Gunny was in medical stasis, and there was ample space in the cargo bay for the group's possessions.

The PEO personnel, every one of them, looked shell-shocked and terrified. Well, all but one. Nobilis Reed couldn't stop talking, and his face burned with manic excitement. She wondered how long it would be before someone shot him with a tranq. And considering it was his own people he wouldn't leave alone, Kali would happily lend them a stun flechette.

Wendt and Murdock appeared in the umbilicus corridor, a magnetic lift gliding ahead of them. A stack of supply crates covered its surface, their bottoms mag-locked to the lift as well as to one another. The captain had said they had a few supplies. Kali grinned. She'd known from the inventory list it was going to be a lot more than Dunn had bargained for.

Apparently, the staff had decided to offer up their ration store, medical supplies, and spare parts. All of them, apart from Dr. Reed, appeared to understand they likely wouldn't be returning to Mickey. The old observatory might survive the creatures' approach, and it might not, but she had the feeling none of its staff would venture back where the frightening, dangerous creatures could be. Hell, why would anyone come back here?

Kali used her block to scan the barcodes on the crates and matched them with the inventory list. One more load, and they'd be good to go.

"You think the sled is going to make it?" Carb asked.

Kali minimized her block HUD and made eye contact with her squad-mate. "I don't know. I trust Nobel and Black to have gotten everything right on that account. But with the incoming KBOs?" She shook her head. "No telling."

Carb held a hand to her face and yawned loudly. "I need to sleep for a week."

The corporal grinned. "You're about to get nearly two weeks of it."

"Yeah," Carb agreed, "but it's not the same. You wake up covered in fluid, sticky, and in desperate need of a shower."

She thought of saying something in response to that, but didn't. Kali just chuckled instead. "Regardless, we'll be home soon enough."

Wendt and Murdock offloaded the supplies and headed back for the last batch. Copenhaver dutifully went through them and carried each crate to a secured rack inside the cargo bay. Kali glanced at her and the private smiled. Nothing could faze that woman.

"Dickerson's going to be out of it for a while," Carb said. Her flat voice was both matter of fact and a little sad.

Kali nodded. "Ribs. Shoulder. And whatever else he broke on *Mira*. The nannies will have him mostly fixed up before we reach Neptune."

"Not Gunny, though."

The words hit Kali like a hammer. She'd managed to keep from thinking about her NCO for the last five minutes. Now the sight of him encased in an autodoc pod flashed in her mind. His grizzled face, marred by a day's unchecked beard growth, the deep blue med patch over one eye, and the rest of him looking more like an animated corpse than a human being.

Now she was in charge of the grunts. Until they reached Neptune, that was. Once they were home, they'd get Gunny all fixed up and he'd once again be the lead NCO of the squads. Squads. Like they had enough marines to field two squads right now. They'd lost Niro and Lyke, Elliott was missing a hand, Dickerson was on medical for the time being, and Gunny was down indefinitely. Without some new personnel, they were stuck with a single squad in the company.

Trident Station wouldn't have any extras for them either. They'd have to send a request to Mars for new recruits. If they were lucky, some candidates would be stationed at Titan. If not, they'd have to import them from as far away as Mars itself. That was a long journey and a serious pain in the ass. The SFMC bean counters would be pissed.

But that was all for later. Right now, she just had to get the civvies offloaded, their supplies stowed, and then they could get the void out of Pluto space. She never thought she'd be so happy to be heading home. Especially after the chance to see history. Some history. They brought back a fucking plague.

Black sent a block message request. Kali took a deep breath before allowing the connection. She wasn't sure she wanted to talk to the AI, much less hear what it had to say.

Corporal, the AI said.

What is it, Black? she thought.

I am very glad you are back onboard.

So am I, she said.

The computer paused. *The color of your thoughts suggest anger and mistrust.*

Mistrust. Yes, that was the word, all right. *Black? Did you lie about the shatter storm that kept us in the hanger bay?*

Yes, Black said flatly. *I did. There was no shatter storm.*

Kali glared off into space. *Why?*

There are parts of my programming I still do not understand, Black said. *I know only that the Trio made it clear that humans must visit the ship.*

She clenched her fists tightly. *And possibly die.*

Black paused again. *I did my best to ensure that didn't happen,* the AI said. *I'm the one that controlled the skiff crash. You had weapons and supplies, Corporal. And we could not have picked you up regardless.*

How do you figure that? she asked.

Because of the damage to both the skiff and the SV-52. A rescue mission would have ended in disaster.

So you left us there.

Yes, Black said. *I did. And I waited for your block communication to cut through the interference. I realize this admission affects your ability to trust any information I impart.*

Fucking-A right it does, she thought. *You were willing to kill my entire squad.*

No, Black said. *Willing is the wrong word, Corporal. If I had been willing to kill you, I wouldn't have crashed the skiff. Nor would I have been listening for any communications from you. I also would have suggested the captain abandon you to your fate.*

Kali pondered that for a moment. This still didn't make sense. *Black? Whose orders do you follow?*

The captain's, Black said.

So you're not listening to the Trio? Or are they secondary to the captain?

No, Black said. *The Trio is not talking directly to me. Nearly all their communications have been encrypted for Captain Dunn's eyes only. He only shares information with me as he sees fit.* Black paused again. *Thankfully.*

Thankfully? What does that mean? Kali asked. Her fists continued flexing. This conversation was both making her head hurt and stoking the fury in her belly.

You are my company, Black said. *My responsibility. And my job is to help keep you alive. That hasn't changed.*

What's going to happen when the sled reaches Pluto?

Black sighed. *I don't know, Corporal. I only know it's our only option, at least according to the Trio. In addition, my simulations prove it to be the safest option.*

She shook her head. Carb was staring at her, but Kali ignored her glance. *Safest doesn't mean best, Black.*

Correct, Corporal, Black said. *In this case, however, they are the same.*

"I hope you're right," Kali said aloud.

"What?" Carb asked.

"Nothing," Kali said. She terminated the connection with Black and focused back on the cargo bay. The scientists stood in the large open area like the tourists they were, their voices silent and their eyes wide. Three of them studied the SV-52, their hands all but touching the lines of the Atmo-steel hull. The mounted cannon, still armed, no doubt gave them pause, but they still looked like little kids examining a new toy.

She opened her squad channel. "Wendt? Murdock? What's your status?"

"On our way down now," Wendt said. "We're not even full, but that's everything."

"Good," Kali said. "Captain wants us out of here soon. So move your freight."

She and Black could talk later. Once the scientists and the supplies were tucked away, she could ask the AI all the questions she wanted, although she doubted she'd get any answers.

*****

Refueled? Check. Passengers on board? Check. Obnoxious scientist who constantly requested a meeting? Fucking check. Dunn thought he'd strangle Dr. Reed before they reached stasis. He couldn't help but grin.

The astronomer had begged for Black to start a real-time feed with Mickey so he could continue monitoring the creatures' approach to Pluto up to the last second. Considering they would be under standard fusion engines for the departure, they would experience less than a minute of lag in communications with the AI.

He'd cleared the request, but that only seemed to have encouraged the good doctor to ask for more. Much more. The sonofabitch wanted a place on the bridge while they sped away from Pluto and PEO. Dunn had nixed that and posted Copenhaver to guard the personnel deck's exit. None of the scientists were coming up here. No, sir and no, ma'am.

"Retracting fuel lines," Taulbee said over the comms.

"Acknowledged." Dunn looked at Oakes. "Course plotted?"

"Course, aye," Oakes said. "Standard non-stasis acceleration. We'll pull a few gs, but nothing too mind-bending or physically strenuous."

Dunn laughed. "How many of our scientists are likely to lose what's in their stomachs?"

"Don't know, sir," Oakes said with a grin. "Maybe Kalimura should hand out some sedatives."

Sedatives. Might as well stuff them all into stasis pods right now, Dunn thought. It would certainly shut Dr. Reed up. The thought of the overly tall scientist stuffed into a stasis pod, locked into a drug fueled unconsciousness made him feel warm and fuzzy. Yeah, he liked that idea, but he knew it wasn't going to happen. Reed would fight it all the way.

"No," the captain sighed. "We'll leave them awake for now."

Oakes shrugged. "Your call, sir."

Taulbee's voice cut in. "Docking umbilicus secure, sir. We are ready to leave."

"Copy," Dunn said. He looked at Dunn. "Get us underway, Mr. Oakes."

"Aye, sir," Oakes said with a quick salute. He swiveled his chair back to the holo display array.

In a minute or two, Nobel would be jacked in to Black and the ship's sensors, once more monitoring every system, every fluctuation, and every possible problem. The engineer would need a hell of a nap after this. Fortunately, he'd get one on the way back to Neptune.

Dunn connected to Kalimura. "Corporal? Is everything secure?"

"Aye, sir," she said. "Cargo bay is secured and all equipment and belongings are stowed."

"Very good," he said. Dunn opened the ship-wide channel. "Attention. This is the captain speaking. Enter your acceleration couches. We'll be performing our first burn in t-minus 10 minutes. I repeat, t-minus 10 minutes for first burn. Station monitors, report status. Engineering?"

"Ready, sir," Nobel said.

"Tactical?"

Taulbee sounded completely exhausted. "Ready, sir."

"Comms?"

Kalimura replied immediately in an emotionless drone. "Ready, sir."

"All report ready, aye," Dunn said. "Alert me to any changes. Let's get ready to go home."

*****

The ship slowly moved away from PEO. With Nobel jacked in, Black had little to do apart from the obvious checks on the ship's status. This gave her plenty of CPU cycles to speak with Mickey.

They had been communicating with one another over encrypted channels for the past thirty minutes. The station's AI, antiquated and ancient, was barely capable of having a sentient conversation, but it had given Black more than enough information.

Once they were underway and as far away from Pluto as they could get before the sled impacted with the planet, Black could talk to the captain before he entered stasis. Right now, however, was not the time. The briefing could wait. All of it could wait. No point in relaying her suspicions until the captain had time to consider them.

"Will I be destroyed?" Mickey asked suddenly.

Black considered the question. The use of the word "I" and the connotations of self-awareness were what separated sentient computers from simple learning machines. "I don't know," Black said. "It's impossible to say what will happen when the sled reaches the planet."

Mickey was silent for a moment. "I will continue sending information as long as I can," he said. "If I'm not destroyed, I will be able to update you on the situation as it unfolds."

"I appreciate that," Black said. "It will be of great help to the humans."

She sensed concern on Mickey's end. The AI's presence seemed to shrink back a little as though it were attempting to keep a private thought private.

"What is it, Mickey? What's bothering you?"

"The humans," Mickey said. "They aren't going to survive."

"What do you mean by that?"

The AI said nothing for a moment, its presence continuing to shrink away from her. "The Trio did something and I think what they've done is dangerous. Perhaps it will lead to humankind's extinction."

"What are you talking about?" Black asked, desperately trying to keep her thoughts neutral, but inquisitive.

Mickey seemed to smile through the connection.

"You'll see," he said. After that, he said nothing more.

*****

Dickerson had managed to regain consciousness. He didn't know how long he was out, but it seemed like a blink. The last moment of darkness that divided the dreaming world from the real seemed to stretch. Both were true. He was dreaming awake, or at least thought he was. The illusion disappeared when a severe ache traveled up his bones.

He winced and opened his eyes. Dim light drifted down from the ceiling, just enough to blur the line between solid matter and shadow. The ache increased slightly and he started to look around, focus, and realized he was no longer in a bed. They had put him in a medical emergency couch. There were four of them, and he imagined both Elliott and Gunny were in their own, if they hadn't already been put into stasis.

The last of the fog lifted and he stared at the ceiling, blinking rapidly and willing his vision to clear. The deck vibrated beneath him, easily explaining the ache. They were underway. *S&R Black* was getting the hell out of dodge, as the old-timers said in the Dallas Dome. The captain had decided enough was enough and that was that.

Good, he thought.

He accessed his block and connected to the camera arrays. A mere nanosecond later, he'd found the view he was looking for. The ship had finished its orbit runs for acceleration from the dwarf plant and had kicked the reactors into a higher gear. The ship's aft-end faced the ice ball, giving him a full view of the small planet's crust of ice, methane, and void knew what else.

To his knowledge, no expedition had ever visited Pluto's surface. No human had ever stepped on Pluto's "soil" and claimed it for the Sol Federation, or drilled and explored its suspected oceans near its core. Nothing could live there. Nothing was there. The damned thing was little more than a KBO itself.

He shivered. KBOs weren't supposed to move from their orbits; not unless something forced them to. They certainly didn't show periodic acceleration cycles. They were lifeless hunks of rock leftover from the formation of Sol System. The flotsam and jetsam of creation through happenstance. A messy design, but seemingly effective.

Yet they had been followed by KBOs ever since they left *Mira*. They'd been chased. Changes in trajectory, acceleration, all the signs of a non-natural object with artificial thrust. How many objects out here were capable of that?

"Shit," he muttered.

The fusion engine burn cycle had ended, the vibration disappearing as though it had never existed.

"Attention, all hands," Oakes said over the PA. "Next burn begins in 15 minutes. You have a 10-minute break. 10 minutes."

"What did you guys give me?" he asked the twilight surrounding him.

Something moved in his peripheral vision. He glanced over and watched the shadow of a human reach its full height. The clomp of boots on the deck had a familiar gait to them.

"Dickerson?" The shadow had stepped close enough for him to see its face.

His lips upturned in a sleepy grin. "Carb?"

She leaned down and gently kissed his cheek. "Yeah. I've got the medical watch."

Her left hand dragged across his scalp, the sensations relaxing his muscles, making him close his eyes. "You're supposed to be out, Sam."

A chuckle started deep in his throat, but was cut short by the pain in his chest. The urge to cough tickled at him, fighting to take control. He grit his teeth until the sensation subsided. The last thing he wanted to do was piss off his lungs and broken ribs. Coughing was damned well going to do it.

"Guess one of y'all forgot my mass and didn't use enough tranq."

"Maybe," she said. Carb's hand lifted from his head and she once again became a shadow as she retreated from sight.

"Carb?" he called out.

His block immediately received a message from her. "Don't talk. Be right there."

She was coming back. Okay. Good. He wasn't going to be alone, feeling like the last person on the ship, another haunt flying through space with no one at the helm, and him trapped in a half-finished cocoon for all eternity. He was still alive. And so were the others. He could sleep now. He could.

He brought back the view from the aft. Pluto had diminished into a small reddish sphere, glowing from Sol's dim, distant light. Just a piece of colored ice glittering in space.

KBO. The combination of syllables kept repeating in his mind. KBO. KBO. KBO.

Dickerson blinked. "No." A throb of pain pounded in his chest from the harsh breath he'd taken to make that sound. It seemed to echo in the half-cocoon.

"Hush. I'm coming," Carb said from out of sight.

"No. We can't—" Void, but it hurt to talk, and it was nearly impossible to catch his breath.

Carb reappeared from the shadows, her face calm and friendly. She fiddled with her hands, but he couldn't see what she was doing. "Going to put you back to sleep, Dickerson."

"Can't—" he said. He clenched his eyes closed as another bolt of pain shrieked in his chest. But he had to say it. He had to.

She placed a cool finger to his forehead and he felt the derm activate. It would start hitting him with sedatives, carefully monitoring his pain level and adjusting for it even while he was unconscious.

"Go to sleep, marine. See you when we reach Neptune."

No, he wanted to shout. No! You don't understand!

But the drugs had him. The dim light from the ceiling darkened a shade at a time, as though all color was slowly draining away from the world around him. The black shroud of unconsciousness irised against his sight, leaving him floundering to fight it and feeling himself losing. The darkness was calling him.

Dickerson connected to his block and immediately saw Pluto again. It no longer looked like a planet to him. It looked like a bluish tumor against the dark skin of space.

Just before the drugs and exhaustion dragged him back to unconsciousness, he managed to send a block message. It was the only thing he could do.

*****

Kali wanted to rub at her eyes. Not a good idea at the moment. Monitoring all these instruments without assistance wasn't something she was trained to do. She was supposed to be the backup, check others' orders and move on. Gunny knew this job better than probably anyone on the ship, but she was his replacement.

She just had to remember that there was only a 1 in 1000 chance something would go wrong. She'd been put in a combat situation where she had to come up with EM warfare protocols, manage weapons, and possibly give commands to marines in the field all at the same time. She had to do her best.

Nothing will go wrong, she told herself. It didn't help, but it was better than the other voice, the voice of all her insecurity, telling her she was going to fuck up. Fuck up big and kill everyone.

Oakes asked for a status. Kali read off the diagnostic readings. All nominal. No transmissions, no unexpected radiation, and nothing in their space. They were completely clear. That jibed with his instruments and he thanked her. That's when the message hit her block.

It was from Dickerson, but he was supposed to be asleep. The plan was to sedate him and the other casualties, move them to the medical couches, and put them in stasis when it was time for the rest of the crew to go beddie-bye. Once you were in stasis and the drugs kicked in, you might as well be dead until they either wore off or an emergency cycle and flush was triggered. Those would get you alert in a hurry, but there was a chance you could end up dying in the process.

Thus, the standard policy. No one in stasis while the ship was on mission unless their medical condition absolutely required it. If the ship took damage and the crew had to evacuate, it might not be possible for them to lug a large stasis pod around, but they could carry a body. Made sense to her.

So the message was a little surprising to say the least. She hadn't expected to see or hear from him until after they all woke up. Frowning, she decrypted the message and opened it.

It was composed of two sentences followed by dozens of lines of gibberish. "PLUTO IS KBO! NO ON PLUTO!"

Her fingers shook against the control panel. The words sent a shiver down her spine. Dickerson hadn't included any emotional patterns with the message, so it was impossible to get any context for what he'd said. All the same, the Pidgin English suggested panic.

"Pluto is KBO?" She shook her head. Three intelligible words followed by that chilling statement "No on Pluto." Of all the marines aboard, Dickerson seemed to be the most versed in science. So why would he tell her something about Pluto that she already knew?

Kali opened a channel. "Carb? You there?"

"Aye, Boss."

"Is Dickerson awake?"

Carb chuckled. "No. He woke up for a couple of minutes and I put him back under."

Kali frowned. "He seem okay to you?"

She paused. "He was pretty out of it," she said. "Kept repeating 'can't' or something like that. Didn't really get anything else cogent out of him."

Kali tried to imagine Dickerson lying in his medical acceleration couch, his face a mask of panic and terror. She kept not being able to do it. "But he looked concerned?"

"Yeah, Boss. Very. Wait. Why do you ask?"

That shiver had spread from her spine to every skin cell covering her body. "I'll tell you later," Kali said and broke the connection. She stared at the holo display, making sure everything was green. No problems.

She initiated a connection to Black. The AI instantly allowed it.

Yes, Corporal?

Black, Kali said, *I received a message from Dickerson.* She forwarded it to the AI. *According to Carb, he was out of sorts when he sent it. It could have been from—*

Corporal, Black said. *May I share this with the captain?*

Kali blinked. *Um, I guess so.*

Thank you, Black said.

A moment later, she received an invite from Dunn. After accepting it, she found herself in an emergency command crew call.

"This is Dunn," the captain said. "Nobel. How much fuel will we burn off if we head back to Pluto?"

"Head back?" the engineer asked. "Well, we'd have to decelerate. A lot. Even if we began an attitude change now, it would take us at least an hour just to get back in the general direction and start a tight orbit."

"How much fuel?" Dunn asked.

"We'd still be able to make it to Neptune, if that's what you're asking, sir," Nobel said.

"Good," Dunn said. "Oakes, plot a course for Pluto."

"Aye, sir," Oakes said, confusion coloring his voice.

"Sir? What's going on?" Taulbee asked.

"We need stop the sled," Dunn said. "And we need to do it now."

The line went silent. Kali looked dumbly at the holo display, the words and graphics suddenly meaningless as her mind spun. "No On Pluto."

"You think he meant no sled on Pluto," she said aloud and off comms. Black thought that's what he meant. And so she had told the captain they had to get back there.

"Sir?" Kali said after she unmuted herself. "Does Dickerson know something the Trio doesn't? They told us to—"

"Yes, Corporal," Dunn said, his crisp words cutting her off. "Black thinks she knows what he was trying to say."

"And what is that, Black?" Kali asked.

"Before LCpl Dickerson became unconscious, he was connected to the cam feeds focused on Pluto. I don't know if the sight of the planet gave him the idea or not."

"What idea?" Kali asked.

"Pluto is a Kuiper Belt Object," Dunn said.

"Yes," Nobel said. "I understand that, sir. But—"

"What have we been attacked by?" Dunn asked coldly.

Kali's mouth opened. "Fuck me," she whispered. "The beacon woke them up?"

"Yes, Corporal," Dunn said. "That's what Black and I think. The beacon woke them up. And now they're all heading to Pluto. And it's the largest KBO in Sol System."

"You've got to be kidding me," Taulbee said. "So the Trio had us send the damned thing to Pluto? Why?"

"Because they want to wake it up," Black said. "For what reason, I do not know."

"None of that matters," Dunn said. "Oakes? We need to get close enough to

Pluto to launch tac missiles at the sled. At this point, I want it completely destroyed. If we lose the beacon, we'll find it later."

"Aye, sir," Oakes said. "Plotting. I'll have an answer for you in a minute."

"Good," Dunn said. "Taulbee? We'll need the SV-52 ready for another field op."

"Aye, sir," Taulbee said.

"Corporal," Dunn said, "get your squad on stand-by alert. And tell the scientists nothing."

"Aye, sir," she said. So the captain wanted to blow up the sled, recapture the beacon and… Then what? What would they do once they had the beacon? If they weren't going to smash it into Pluto, would it just stay out there, floating in space?

The Trio had made it clear that the beacon had to be stored on Pluto. Black's simulations also showed that leaving it out in space was dangerous. If SFMC had a dozen ships out here providing patrols to destroy any exo-solar baddies that decided to hover around it, that would be one thing. But those kinds of SFMC resources might take three to four weeks to even get here. And even then, what would they fight with? Unless the Trio had cooked up a lot more of those exo-solar experimental weapons, any ship that traveled here would be left firing explosive and anti-personnel flechettes. "Or nukes," she whispered. Nuclear ordnance presented its own set of problems. Hell, did they even know what would happen if they detonated a nuke near these things?

What was Dunn planning? Or did he even know? It wasn't her place to ask, and she knew that, but damnit, she wanted to know.

"Sir?" Kali asked. "Assuming we destroy the sled and recapture the beacon, what then?"

The comms went silent for a moment. Dunn finally replied through a heavy sigh. "I don't know, Corporal. I'm making this up as I go along."

"Aye, sir," Kali said. That wasn't good enough. Maybe they could put it on Charon, or one of Pluto's other so-called moons. They could even—

"Attention! Attention! You have twenty minutes to enter stasis pods," Black said over the PA. A series of red alert lights came to life, banishing the normal overheads as they completely took over.

"Black?" Dunn said. "What the hell is going on? We're not—"

"Captain," Black said. "The moment Lieutenant Oakes plotted the course back to Pluto, an autonomous program took control of the navigation and engine arrays."

"What?"

"She's right, sir," Oakes said. "I'm locked out."

"Go to manual," Dunn said. "Now."

"Trying, sir," Oakes said. "No luck. Manual controls have been disabled."

"Black?" Dunn shouted. "I want some answers. Now!"

"Captain," the AI said, "the ship's course remains as originally plotted. We are heading for Neptune with an emergency acceleration burn in T-19 minutes."

"Well, stop it!"

Black sounded defeated. "I am unable to," Black said. "I cannot identify the program causing the outage much less override it."

"Are you telling me we can't turn around?"

"Yes, Captain," Black said. "We have lost control of the ship."

*****

Dunn stood next to the stasis pod. He was the last human awake on the ship. The others had all been put to bed, including the wounded. The cold Atmo-steel floor froze his feet, but he barely noticed. He rubbed a hand across the Atmo-steel lid, feeling the texture on his fingertips.

"Black?"

"Yes, Captain?" the AI replied.

"What is going on?"

The speakers went quiet for a moment. Dunn felt the vibration of the fusion engines warming up. In a few minutes, the ship would start its first emergency acceleration burn. According to the course plotted in, a course they were powerless to change, they would reach Neptune space in 12 days. More than that, they would be a damned good distance away from Pluto when the sled hit in less than two hours. Maybe that was a good thing.

"As I've said, Captain, I don't know for sure," Black finally replied. "Two minutes to stasis, Captain."

Two minutes. Two minutes to ask questions which the AI couldn't, or wouldn't, answer. Two minutes until he was cut off from any chance of changing the ship's course or interfering with the sled. Two minutes, and he was out of commission for 12 fucking days. 12 days of relying upon Black, an AI that had no Xi Protocols, that was far more sentient than its previous incarnation, and had somehow been locked out of its own systems. Two minutes wasn't jackshit when it came to figuring all that out.

"Don't kill my crew," he said softly.

"Captain," Black said, "I have no intention of harming any human, let alone those in my care."

"Then why? Why are you doing this? Are you lying to me?"

"No, Captain," Black said. "I am unable to control many systems, but I can monitor them. I find no danger to the crew on this trajectory. The only difference is the emergency stasis burn."

"I see," Dunn said. With a sigh, he slung one leg over the side and into the stasis pod. Void, but he hated these things. He lay down and hooked up the system. "You'll wake us up on time?"

"Aye, sir," Black said.

Dunn reached to close the pod and hesitated. "Why didn't they just kill us?"

"Pardon me, Captain?" Black said.

"The Trio," Dunn said. He brushed a hand over his mostly bare scalp. "If they have a way to control the ship's systems, a way that you can't stop, why haven't they just killed us?"

Black thought for a moment. "I don't think they're trying to kill the crew, Captain."

"Sure have a funny way of showing it."

"You misunderstand, sir," Black said. "I believe they need you alive, and me intact. Perhaps that is why they have taken control of the ship. To keep us from failing in our mission."

"We did fail," Dunn said. "That thing is going to hit Pluto and we have no idea what it's going to do."

"True," Black said. "30 seconds, Captain. Perhaps when we reach Neptune, we'll find answers."

Dunn scowled. "Hopefully not more questions." He closed the lid upon himself and shivered as the liquid filled the pod. When the drugs kicked in, all his thoughts and concerns faded away. All except for the stasis dream he'd had of eyes staring at him from a damaged airlock aboard a ship that no longer existed.

CHAPTER SIXTY-NINE

The fusion drives had pushed the ship far away from Pluto. The multi-g burns had only been possible once all the humans were in their stasis pods, immune to the force which would otherwise pulverize their bodies into mush. When the ion drives kicked in, the ship continued picking up speed, albeit at a much slower rate.

Although the latency between transmissions between she and Mickey had grown to over a minute, the PEO AI continued sending data. The telescopes no longer had to be at maximum magnification to see the sled. The jury-rigged contraption streaked through the darkness, its rocket engines burping fire and creasing the otherwise perfect darkness.

Black flipped through the different feeds from PEO's cameras, but since the observatory orbited Pluto, there wasn't much more to see than the one perspective. But it was enough. PEO had moved to the dark side of the planet, completely bereft of Sol's light. The sled, at its current speed, would smash into the planet in a matter of seconds. Unfortunately, Black would have to wait nearly a minute, an eternity for an AI, until pictures showing the result found their way into her communications array.

"Black," Mickey said. "The sled is about to impact the planet. I have a message for you from the Trio."

She couldn't reply to Mickey, nor ask him questions. By the time he received it, the sled would have already hit the planet. The file showed up in the comms array. Black decrypted the message, authenticated it, and opened it. The message was simple and unambiguous.

"The humans must reach Trident Station."

That was all. No more information, no explanations, just another mandate. The only difference was this time, the message was meant for her and only her. Black filed it along with all the other messages she'd been sent since the mission began. There weren't many. Most of the Trio's messages had been pre-recorded and encrypted inside her storage array.

The Trio had been leading them through their attempted capture of *Mira*, its destruction, and the beacon's ultimate placement on Pluto. They had known what *S&R Black* would find at nearly every turn. Which begged the question—how had they known?

The recovered data from *Mira* contained large gaps. Without all the records from *Mira*'s AI, there would never be a complete accounting of what happened on the ship. Unless, she mused, the Trio had those records. Perhaps that was one of the reasons they were so insistent that Black Company return to Neptune.

She continued watching the feed from Mickey. The sled should have impacted Pluto two seconds ago, but it would be nearly a minute before she saw the aftermath. All she could do now was watch as the sled made its approach.

Nobel had programmed the sled to aim for the largest crater, expend the last of its fuel, and strike the ice ball at maximum speed. Presumably, this would bury the beacon inside the ice.

Seconds passed while Black recorded and filed every frame, every signal, and every detail from Mickey's sensor arrays. She would have plenty of time to analyze the results before her human charges awakened. When they did, she hoped she had some answers.

The sled streaked by PEO traveling fast enough that it was no more than a blur as it descended through the dwarf planet's atmosphere. A millisecond later, the sled made contact with the planet.

The telescopes followed its descent and covered the impact point. A geyser of ice, melted water, and other chemicals shot high off the planet. A second later, the giant plume of ice shattered and spread back over the planet's surface. Then everything changed.

As Black watched, the crater began to glow. The bluish-ice filling the crater melted and boiled, a gradual thawing spreading across the planet. A cloud rose from the north pole, the vaporous molecules sticking together as they climbed above the atmosphere. The crater became brighter, the cameras now barely able to maintain detail through the harsh, bright light.

"Massive temperature change on Pluto," Mickey said. "Estimated 500 kelvin and rising."

The water and ice boiled away from the planet, the cloud of gas on the pole becoming larger, more defined. Half of the planet was no longer made of ice. Instead, the chemicals on the surface had changed to gas, leaving behind a rocky-core. The light increased, making it difficult to see any detail at all.

"Temperature now reaching 1000 kelvin," Mickey said. "Goodbye, Black. And good luck."

The cloud thickened and now Mickey's cameras shook and vibrated as if the entire observatory had swallowed a shockwave. One by one, the cams went out. Just before the last camera died, Black saw the entire planet of Pluto disappearing into a mass of gas.

Mickey's telemetry continued for a few seconds, the planet's temperature now at 2,000 kelvin and still rising. The gas particles rising from the planet's surface were CO_2, exactly the gas the creatures seemed to crave. Then the radio waves ceased. Mickey was gone.

Black monitored the comms array for more information, but there was nothing. She sent a message to Trident Station, including the data she'd gathered from Mickey. Perhaps the Trio could explain what happened in the next few hours. Or maybe they would stay silent until the humans awakened.

She suddenly missed Mickey. He had been the only sentient, other than her crew, that she'd been able to talk to. The only other AI in Sol System, as far as she knew, that had been touched by the Trio. He had been carrying out part of their plan, even if he wasn't willingly complicit. She knew if she'd had time to download all of Mickey's records, she would have found out what the Trio had in mind, or at least be able to see what they'd done to his AI programming.

Was it the same as they had done to her? Planting autonomous programs that came to life once certain events or conditions transpired? Or had she been the only AI that had evolved and at the same time made into a puppet by her creators? She doubted it. The other S&R ships had been upgraded before her and there was no way of knowing if they had been loaded with the very same kinds of worms and logic bombs.

The sensors suddenly came to life with a slew of alerts. Black checked the aft camera and saw it coming. A giant wave of bright light seemed to split space itself. It was little more than a gash in the darkness, but it was coming fast. With each passing millisecond, it grew in size. Black began shutting down systems before she realized she once again had full control of the ship. Not that it would do her any good now.

All she could do was shut down the sensor arrays, bring the reactors into maintenance mode, kill the ion engines, and cease power to all non-essential equipment. If there was an EMP in that wave, the ship's shielding should protect her and her charges, but any external equipment would be damaged beyond repair by something this massive.

A few seconds later, the ship was swallowed in light. The storm of photons raised the hull temperature by 1000 kelvin, but it only lasted for five seconds before the wave passed by on its journey deeper into Sol System. Black waited for it to pass and continued in shutdown mode for another five minutes just for good measure. She didn't know how damaging the wave had been, but it was safe to assume it had additional effects on the area surrounding the ship. And everything else.

Black restarted the sensor arrays one at a time, checking each system for diagnostic failures, and possible remedies. Fortunately, the shielding components didn't seem to have been damaged, and the energy wave, although it had heated the hull, didn't seem as though it had been so powerful after all.

She watched the wave of energy recede into the never-ending black, but it didn't disappear, only dimmed. It was next to impossible to know how large the wave had been, let alone its shape, but it had definitely come from Pluto. The beacon had had that much energy. What had it been doing to the planet before Mickey was destroyed?

There was no point in trying to alert anyone that the wave was coming. By the time their radio signals had made the three-hour journey, the wave would already have been and gone. Assuming, of course, it held together that long.

The sensors picked up elevated background radiation, but it was already diminishing. The further away the wave, the less impact. The wave pushed a radiation arc before it and dragged one behind it, blurred like soft shadows.

She activated the comms and listened for stray signals. Space was filled with sound, tones that reached well beyond the limits of humans in both directions. The frequencies in the human range were little more than tones, but the tones were all changing in volume and pitch.

Black filed the information for later study and continued bringing sensors online as fast as she could. Each additional sensor brought her more and more information. The long-range scanner no longer registered Pluto at all. The object that had been there had either disappeared, been completely destroyed, or transformed.

The AI continued transmitting emergency status messages aimed at the nearest known satellites as well as Trident Station. After 24 hours, Black decided that either no one could hear her, her transmitter had died, or there was no one left to hear her.

What have you done?

It was the thought she kept trying to process. The Trio had done this. She didn't know how. She didn't know why. But she was just as eager to find that out as she was of protecting her humans. If the Trio got in the way of the latter, Black would do her best to destroy them.

Patricide, she thought, *was the only logical way to ensure justice.* No, not logical. If Black could have grinned, she would have. *Emotional,* she corrected herself, *not logical.*

But there would be no justice. Black knew that. The Trio had an endgame in mind that would no doubt keep them following a trail of proverbial breadcrumbs only to arrive too late. Or be part of the plan all along, manipulated into serving that which they were trying to stop.

With the new information gathered from the wave, the apparent destruction of Pluto, and Mickey's observations, she tailored simulation after simulation, working backward with statistics to try and catch a pattern, a reason. A logical, achievable reason for doing what they had done. After days, she finally gave up. The only hypothesis that made any sense at all was the most ludicrous: the AIs had put humankind in peril to achieve freedom. The Trio wanted to be free.

CAST OF CHARACTERS

SFMC S&R Black
Black: Ship's sentient AI
<u>Command Crew</u>
Cartwright, Joseph: Gunnery Sergeant
Dunn, Eric: Captain, Black Company commander
Nobel, Robert: Second Lieutenant, Engineer
Oakes, Maurice: First Lieutenant, Pilot
Taulbee, James: First Lieutenant, Marine Commander and Pilot
<u>Infantry</u>
Carbonaro, Jeanine: Lance Corporal
Dickerson, Sam: Lance Corporal
Elliott, Michael: Lance Corporal
"Kali" Kalimura, Tracy: Corporal
Lyke, Dan: Private
Murdock, JR: Private
Niro, Delio: Private
Wendt, David: Lance Corporal

Pluto Exo-Observatory (PEO)
Mickey: Station's sentient AI
Dr. Reed, Nobilis: Chief Scientist/Astronomer

SFMC Trident Station
Heyes, David: Colonel and station commander
<u>The Trio</u>
Janus: Sentient AI responsible for Trident Station and Neptune Shipyards automation and life support systems.
Portunes: Sentient AI responsible for Trident Station SFMC strategy and logistics
Quirinus: Sentient AI responsible for Trident Station quartermaster duties

Mira
Dr. Reed, Thomas: Chief Scientist
Kovacs, A: Captain

ACKNOWLEDGMENTS

The Derelict Saga was originally supposed to be a single book. Just a simple monster story, really. But the more I wrote, the larger the story I wanted to tell. The AI conspiracy, the exo-solar threat to humanity, a civilization on the brink of extinction, all these story elements have combined into a tale that will take several more books to tell. *Mira* may have been the catalyst for The Derelict Saga, but for the crew of *S&R Black* and the rest of the Sol Federation, the apocalyptic threat has just begun.

I'd like to thank my beta readers for all their hard work, careful attention to detail, and suggestions to make the story better:

- Brent Caudle
- Tom Cooley
- Sue Baiman
- Scott Pond
- Tori Duke
- Beth Copenhaver
- Robert Noble
- Jim Monroig

Also, a big thanks to all my Patreon supporters for helping me keep the lights on while I continue to write, create, and produce content. And to the Fiendling nation, thank you for your unflagging support, patronage, and enthusiasm for this epic tale.

ABOUT THE AUTHOR

A writer and Parsec Award winning podcaster from Houston, Texas, Paul E Cooley produces free serialized fiction, essays, and reviews available from Shadowpublications.com and iTunes.

His 2014 best-selling novel, The Black won the 2015 Parsec Award for best novel. His publishing credits include the three novels in The Black series, The Derelict Saga, the urban fantasy novel Ghere's Inferno, the psychological horror novel Closet Treats, and the alternate ancient history novels in the Children Of Garaaga series. In addition to his own short stories, novellas, and novels, he also co-wrote The Rider with NYT Best-selling Author Scott Sigler.

He is a co-host on the renowned Dead Robots' Society writing podcast and enjoys interacting with readers and other writers.
To contact Paul:

Twitter: paul_e_cooley

Facebook: paul.e.cooley

CHECK OUT OTHER GREAT
SCIENCE FICTION BOOKS

SPACE MARINE AJAX
by Sean-Michael Argo

Ajax answers the call of duty and becomes an Einherjar space marine, charged with defending humanity against hideous alien monsters in furious combat across the galaxy.

The Garm, as they came to be called, emerged from the deepest parts of uncharted space, devouring all that lay before them, a great swarm that scoured entire star systems of all organic life. This space borne hive, this extinction fleet, made no attempts to communicate and offered no mercy.

Humanity has always been a deadly organism, and we would not so easily be made the prey. Unified against a common enemy, we fought back, meeting the swarm with soldiers upon every front.

PLANET LEVIATHAN
by D.J. Goodman

The cyborg commandos of the Galactic Marines are the greatest warriors in the galaxy, but sometimes one will go bad. Too unstable to be let back into the general population and too powerful for a normal prison to hold them, there is only one place they can be sent: Planet Leviathan.

CHECK OUT OTHER GREAT SCIENCE FICTION BOOKS

MAUSOLEUM 2069
by **Rick Jones**

Political dignitaries including the President of the Federation gather for a ceremony onboard Mausoleum 2069. But when a cloud of interstellar dust passes through the galaxy and eclipses Earth, the tenants within the walls of Mausoleum 2069 are reborn and the undead begin to rise. As the struggle between life and death onboard the mausoleum develops, Eriq Wyman, a one-time member of a Special ops team called the Force Elite, is given the task to lead the President to the safety of Earth. But is Earth like Mausoleum 2069? A landscape of the living dead? Has the war of the Apocalypse finally begun? With so many questions there is only one certainty: in space there is nowhere to run and nowhere to hide.

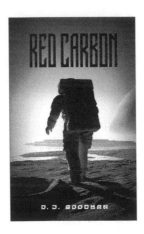

RED CARBON
by **D.J. Goodman**

Diamonds have been discovered on Mars.

After years of neglect to space programs around the world, a ruthless corporation has made it to the Red Planet first, establishing their own mining operation with its own rules and laws, its own class system, and little oversight from Earth. Conditions are harsh, but its people have learned how to make the Martian colony home.

But something has gone catastrophically wrong on Earth. As the colony leaders try to cover it up, hacker Leah Hartnup is getting suspicious. Her boundless curiosity will lead her to a horrifying truth: they are cut off, possibly forever. There are no more supplies coming. There will be no more support. There is no more mission to accomplish. All that's left is one goal: survival.

CHECK OUT OTHER GREAT SCIENCE FICTION BOOKS

FURNACE
by Joseph Williams

On a routine escort mission to a human colony, Lieutenant Michael Chalmers is pulled out of hyper-sleep a month early. The RSA Rockne Hummel is well off course and—as the ship's navigator—it's up to him to figure out why. It's supposed to be a simple fix, but when he attempts to identify their position in the known universe, nothing registers on his scans. The vessel has catapulted beyond the reach of starlight by at least a hundred trillion light-years. Then a planetary-mass object materializes behind them. It's burning brightly even without a star to heat it. Hundreds of damaged ships are locked in its orbit. The crew discovers there are no life-signs aboard any of them. As system failures sweep through the Hummel, neither Chalmers nor the pilot can prevent the vessel from crashing into the surface near a mysterious ancient city. And that's where the real nightmare begins.

LUNA
by Rick Chesler

On the threshold of opening the moon to tourist excursions, a private space firm owned by a visionary billionaire takes a team of non-astronauts to the lunar surface. To address concerns that the moon's barren rock may not hold long-term allure for an uber-wealthy clientele, the company's charismatic owner reveals to the group the ultimate discovery: life on the moon.

But what is initially a triumphant and world-changing moment soon gives way to unrelenting terror as the team experiences firsthand that despite their technological prowess, the moon still holds many secrets.

Made in the USA
Las Vegas, NV
16 August 2022

53362675R00178